Ten to the 405

by

Kevin R. Andrade

Ten to the 405

Cover Art by *Tina Lynn Stout*

The Wild Rose Press, Inc.
PO Box 708
Adams Basin, NY 14410-0708
Visit us at www.thewildrosepress.com

Publishing History
First Edition, 2025
Trade Paperback ISBN 978-1-5092-6217-5
Digital ISBN 978-1-5092-6218-2

Published in the United States of America

Dedication

To my hero, my idol, my best friend and my dad,
Rolando

Prologue

A dried twig snapped outside her apartment window, and Mckenna's eyes sprung open. Her paranoia had revved hot the past week, and her meth use charged that paranoia to level red. Still, drugs or not, she knew she was being followed and she was terrified. They were coming for her.

The mysterious death of her mentor, Joseph Smith, injected a shiver of terror down her spine. He'd confided in her a secret, luring her into his investigation, and the secrets they uncovered were juicy. At first, she'd been excited to make her hero happy, but the second she learned of his death, she regretted her efforts.

Joseph Smith wrecked a car on a lonely road with a hint of alcohol. But Joseph hadn't driven in twenty years, and he didn't drink. Ever. She knew she was next.

She'd crashed at Scarlet's tiny apartment, the week after Joseph's death, until she felt more at ease. Then Mckenna saw that tall man. Maybe Latino, but darker. Perhaps Asian? Indian National? He was tall but narrow build. She'd seen him at her coffee spot. She saw him at the taco stand. And then the co-op, but when she saw him waiting for her bus, she knew. She was being followed.

Sitting up in the bed of her pitch-dark room, Mckenna glanced to her left and saw her precious portfolio on the nightstand. Page after page of her drawings and sketches lived in that portfolio. If she were to make a run for it, that would be her lone possession. She'd also take her camera, but only until a safe spot for that item could be found; the camera held secrets.

Zane, she mused to herself. She needed to trust someone, and she thought she could rely on Zane Adkins. Zane was prettier than he was smart, but he was always decent enough when they were hanging out. Jake Hansen crossed her mind, but she wasn't sure about Jake after he'd ghosted her. Jake was certainly smarter than Zane, but she wasn't one hundred percent sure she could count on him.

Quietly, Mckenna slipped from under her covers and lightly tip-toed to her bedroom door. Hanging on the door was her slinky, black cocktail dress. After placing her long black hair into a messy bun, she slid into the skimpy dress and fumbled on the floor for her heels. Finding them, she held them in her hand.

She checked her cell phone for the time. One twenty-four a.m. Scarlet would still be at Lucky's, cage dancing. She could meet with Scarlet at her after-hours job, and she prayed Scarlet would let her crash with her until she skipped town. Mckenna would make a run for Lucky's.

The front door of her place creaked open, and Mckenna's heart stalled.

They, indeed, had come for her.

Stepping silently in her room, she slung her portfolio over her left shoulder and her expensive camera with strap over her right shoulder. She glanced around her room and sighed. Time to run.

Looking to her left, Mckenna peeked out of the window and saw the scaffolding, from the previous week, still erected outside of her window. Rushing to the long horizontal window, she pulled it open as far as it would go. She leaned out, momentarily grateful that her shitty place didn't have screens. She tossed her heels down two stories, landing with a louder than hoped for clatter; Mckenna grimaced at the sound.

Crawling out of the window, she grabbed onto the scaffolding. Her landlord had begun to paint the west side of the building and left the scaffolding up for a few days. She initially complained about it, but now it could save her life. She stealthily climbed down the rungs until she reached the ground. Finding her heels, she quickly picked them up.

Crouching to the ground, she snuck over to the edge of the building. A fierce looking Latino man was guarding the front door of the complex, waiting for her. Mckenna scurred over to the wood fence protecting the back of the complex. Tossing her shoes over the fence, she plied her fingers into a wood notch in the middle of the wood fence. She climbed and propelled herself, along with her portfolio and camera, over the fence.

"*No esta aqui,*" a thick, accented male voice carried from her bedroom.

Mckenna did not look back. She corralled her prized belongings and ran off into the darkness of Los Angeles.

Chapter One

Jake Hansen usually went on a three-day bender following a harrowing bad beat. Or beats. That's not to say he didn't go on benders when he wasn't losing. He was just always gambling, so he was almost always on some sort of bender. Jake could be described as a functioning alcoholic, although when one's career had derailed as his, what exactly defined functioning? The functioning of the dysfunctional is only as successful as optimism allows.

And he had suffered a bad beat.

The Vegas weekend had started out innocently enough. A little craps at the Venetian, some Texas Hold 'em at Caeser's, a few hands of blackjack at New York, New York, but as he made his way down to Fremont Street and Downtown, his old sports gambling demons emerged to haunt his waking hours. A few scotches at the bar in the Golden Nugget initiated the tingling sensation in his belly. He needed to place a bet. Or bets.

Jake owed Tony Tahoe, his bookie, a lot of money. A lot. And, to his mind, the only way to crawl from under the withering debt he owed was to win and win big. So, on Friday night, as he prepared for a night with the ladies of his favorite strip club, he placed a five-game parlay with the *coup de grace* being USC's first game of the season as the Trojans took on the PAC-12 neophyte, Utah Utes.

It didn't go well. Yes, Jake won his first four bets, but the fifth bet went sideways and flipped over, crashed, burned and went sideways again. He couldn't really remember much after USC didn't cover but he knew that a poor officiating decision played into his loss. He'd watched the game in the Golden Nugget sportsbook with fellow gambling degenerates, Li'l Jimmy Shit for Brains, Ten after Six (named after the crook in his neck), Jerry Dingleberry and the Chairman of the Bad Beats Board, the diabetic, Wheels Appleton—named Wheels after the wheelchair he scooted around in, lugging his oxygen tank. They all had money on the same game with the same bet: USC with the points. Eight and a half.

In disgust, following the loss, Jake tossed his ticket to the ground, littering the sports book with another tale of woe. Then, hours after the game ended, while nursing a drink at The Double Down Saloon, Jake saw on the TV a rule reversal worked in Jake's favor, providing the USC winning margin he required to win his five-game parlay. However, Jake had thrown his ticket to the ground on the floor of the sports book.

Jake rushed from The Double Down Saloon back to the sports book at The Golden Nugget where he witnessed Wheels Appleton collecting Jake's winnings after retrieving Jake's tossed ticket. Demanding his winnings, Jake confronted a stubborn Wheels, claiming possession was some tenths of the law or something or other. An insult here and a punch there and an oxygen tank to the temple rendered Jake unconscious and he awoke on a plane back to Los Angeles next to one of his two best friends and business partner, Pete Mills.

Jake couldn't completely piece together everything that occurred after Wheels stole his winnings. He remembered a few hours in the drunk tank at the Las Vegas Sheriff's headquarters. He knew Pete must have been called to come get him, but he couldn't remember anything else. He'd looked in the mirror and saw two black eyes and the remnants of a smashed nose. He just didn't remember how he got them. Finally, Pete informed him that he, former Detective Pete Mills, had blackened his face with a punch.

That began the bender. Sunday merged into Monday and another day and now he couldn't remember exactly where he was.

Jake groaned at the damning whirr whipping above his head. The sound reminded him of the thump of helicopter wings from a Vietnam documentary. Jake felt huddled like a baby. He rested upon something smooth and cold and as he reached for more covers, he realized there were no covers. As his mind slowly started to come into itself, he heard the noise of a television behind him. That, mixed with the unmistakable sound of clanking glasses, gave Jake the hints he needed to remember where he was.

I'm at my bar.

He briefly opened his left eye to see that he had passed out on the long high-top near the back bar of the tavern. The whirr sound was the metallic fan spinning above his head with exacting precision. Jake closed his left eye quickly as he recounted how his night had ended. Or tried to recount. Nothing came to him. He must have closed the place down with Lamar working. Lamar probably just left him be as he closed shop like Lamar had done for Jake a hundred times before.

The television broke Jake from his thought process. He knew the sound of the voice: Alex Vila, Mayor of Los

Angeles.

"I wish I could answer that question, Rick, but I really cannot." The mayor spoke in his baritone.

Now, Jake moaned. The mayor was Jake's own private Sisyphean millstone. Jake opened his eyes slightly and looked toward the television. Alex Vila, a strapping, Mexican- American man wearing a sharp gray Armani suit, stood at a podium in front of City Hall. Fifteen or so reporters, surrounded by cameras, hung on Alex Vila's word. Jake barely looked at Vila, staring rather, at the beautiful black-haired woman to the right of him. She wore a shimmering green dress with pearls around her neck. He focused on her long, caramel colored neck that Jake had kissed so often. She smiled her radiant smile and Jake briefly smiled back, as if she were smiling for no one else in the world but Jake Hansen. He saw flashes of Lily's smile. Lily in Santa Barbara on a chilly morning by the cove, as she sat astride him and looked down with passion in her eyes.

"Lily," Jake barely whispered, so as not to be audible to the outside world.

A reporter interrupted Jake's momentary glimpse of happiness with a question.

"So, you are not announcing your re-election campaign today, Mayor," the reporter shouted out.

"Apologies, I can't comment on that question at this time," the mayor replied.

Suddenly the television was turned off. Jake quickly shut his eyes and acted as if he were asleep. The unmistakable heavy footsteps of Lamar approached the high top and stopped. Jake knew Lamar was standing over him.

Probably with that stupid grin.

"You awake, boss?" the deep, happy voice asked.

Lamar. Fuck, he's gonna make me get up. Thank God it ain't Pete.

"I'm awake, Lamar."

"Your eyes are closed, Jake."

"Well, you're gonna have to take my word for it." Jake sighed, knowing full well Lamar was indeed smiling at him.

Jake gathered the necessary amount of energy and lifted his left eyelid. Sure enough, the massive Lamar, his Black friend for years and tears, stood over him with a shit-eating grin. Lamar always seemed to radiate positive energy and was a tightly wound ball of that energy. Jake, annoyed by the positivity, inwardly rolled his eyes.

"What the fuck are you smiling at?" Jake growled.

"Jus' you. I know your bender is over when you pass out on top of the bar."

Jake sat up and looked around him. Lamar was right. He did pass out on top of the bar at the end of his benders. Bender over.

Pete had smoked Jake in the face with a right cross and dragged Jake from the sheriff's office. Pete then fed Jake a shot of whiskey before the flight and after a brief haggle with the flight attendant—a Franklin may have exchanged hands—Jake passed out on Flight 281 from Vegas to the City of Angels. Despite Pete's assault, Jake was grateful that Pete hadn't used his claw or else he would've shattered his orbital bone. Jake was halfway surprised Wheels' oxygen tank hadn't taken care of that.

Jake grimaced as he shook his head and rubbed his battered and bruised face. He ran his fingers through his dark hair and sighed. He remembered looking in the mirror and seeing heavy black, purple, and blue tones circling his sharp nose (remnants of his Mexican mother) and blue eyes (gifts from his Danish father) with a deep concentration of black surrounding his left eye. This wasn't the first time Jake had left Sin City with a black eye, but it certainly was the worst beating he'd received. Jake laid back down onto the bar and closed his eyes.

"Jake, you gotta wake and shake, brother." Lamar called out.

Jake opened his eyes again. "What time is it?" Jake asked, delaying his movement by a few seconds.

"Nine bells."

"Jesus, Lamar, nine o'clock? We don't even open for another couple hours."

"Besides the point. You supposed to open today but I'll handle that. Still beside the point; you got someone here to see you."

This piqued Jake's interest, and he immediately sat up on the bar. Jake was a man who owed a large debt. Debts. Jake owed money on top of the money he owed and some of that money would never be paid but, Tony Tahoe, one way or another, was gonna get paid.

Jake leapt up from his position and stood. He saw his worn gray jacket on the bar stool, grabbed it and started to make his prison break. Jake got two feet from the bar when Lamar with all of his five-foot eleven, two hundred eighty-pound might, grabbed Jake's arm.

"It ain't Tony Tahoe."

Lamar let go, which gave Jake ease. The look on his brow put another smile onto Lamar's face.

"Thank God," Jake blurted.

"C'mon, Jake, you know Pete and I won't let that gorilla lay a hand on ya."

Jake chuckled and pointed to his left eye. "You saw what Pete did to my eye, right?"

"You deserved it and he didn't even use his claw, so, whatcha bitchin' about?"

"Touché," Jake responded, as Sophie Jones, Trotter's server, hostess, secretary, slash Swiss Army knife, stepped into view.

Sophie quietly entered the bar area. Tall and slender, she walked with a delicate gait and the look in her green eyes detailed the difficulties of the first nineteen years of her life.

"Mr. Hansen." Sophie quietly spoke.

"It's Jake, Sophie."

"I'm sorry…Jake, there's a man to see you." Sophie bowed her head, and Jake's heart cried for her as he knew her life prior to her arrival at Trotter's had been difficult. Sophie's mother, a constantly recovering substance abuser, begged Jake to hire Sophie and bring her to Los Angeles, away from the small, meth infested town of Hemet, and the nightmare of her uncle. Begging was unnecessary; Jake was more than happy to wrest Sophie away from that awful family.

"Thanks. Lamar was just telling me," Jake said to Sophie as she began cleaning.

Jake crept away from the bar toward the partition that separated the bar side of Trotter's Tavern from the front room. The sun shined brightly through the front window of the front room and silhouetted in the doorway stood a large man. The silhouette created the shadow of a mystery wrapped in the shadow of an unknown force. The sun stared into Trotter's, blinding the hungover Jake. Jake leaned slightly toward Lamar.

"Did he tell you…who he is? His business?

Anything?" Jake whispered.

"He said he was an old friend of yours from Palm Springs."

"Palm Springs." Jake pondered. "You might wanna grab Pete and have him sit in on this."

Lamar walked off in search of Pete.

Jake, indeed, was from Palm Springs. Born and raised, his family was of a modest enterprise up until both his parents' death in a car wreck when Jake was sixteen. Taken in by his aunt and uncle on his mother's side, Jake tried to find his place in Palm Springs. Mexican-American meant he lived in between two tribes. Not full Mexican, the brown side of the social chaste system in Palm Springs shunned him. Not fully white, he never fit in with that crowd either. His father had been a Danish Christian missionary and met his mother in Aguascalientes, Mexico. Jake found his way through his critical thinking.

He made his way to USC by befriending and tutoring the soon to be Hall of Fame Running Back, Billy Dixon. Jake graduated with honors in Journalism and married his high school sweetheart, Lily. He took his yellow dogged prowess to New York City where he made a name for himself as an undercover journalist in the South Bronx at the height of 1990's New York. He ensconced himself into the South Bronx and lived the chilling truth of the Jackson Avenue Drug Brawls of the late nineties. He witnessed and wrote about it all, landing a great gig back home in Los Angeles.

Cocky, full of pride, head full of dark hair, trim and fit, with the perfect complexion of a *Mestizo*, Jake returned to Southern California with his wife and a box full of commendations. Jake broke story after story, digging where others refused to dig. And then he broke a huge story. He uncovered police and local political corruption with ties to a Mexican drug cartel. It was to be his Pulitzer. And what happened? His story was killed by the editor, his police informant friend disappeared and another police officer at the center of the scandal, promoted. In a hasty and dramatic mistake, Jake released his killed article on-line and opened up a bottle of bourbon. By the morning, the bourbon was gone replaced by a hangover, his job was suspended for two years and his wife left him for an up-and-coming Public Defender, Alex Vila. It was quite a hangover. The two-year suspension eventually became permanent, and the divorce was settled with Lily Hansen marrying Alex Vila. Jake received enough in the divorce to purchase Trotter's Tavern on Washington Place with Pete Mills and Lamar Wagner.

And now, hung-over, Jake stood, staring at a silhouette of a man with the sun blasting him in the face. Jake attempted to hand comb his receding hairline and tucked in his shirt. Jake stepped toward the man. The man stood tall and erect; the silhouette slowly revealed.

"Mr. Tall Mountain." Jake contorted his face, confused.

Ed Tall Mountain smiled widely, displaying a set of white, even teeth. He cocked his head to one side and stared at Jake's face. "Jesus Jake, what the hell happened to you?" He extended his hand and Jake shook it.

"I fell down a flight of stairs."

Ed Tall Mountain stood over six feet tall and despite his sixtyish age, seemed fit and in good health. The dark tan of a Native American, who'd lived a life in the desert, offset a full head of white hair. They stood staring at each other for a few seconds.

Jake looked around and saw that the five bar tables' chairs had been set. "Please... have a seat." Jake motioned to the table nearest Tall Mountain.

"Thank you." Tall Mountain took a seat. "It really is good to see you."

Ed Tall Mountain stood out as the epitome of regal. He not only sat on the Board of an Indian council and the Gaming Commission in Palm Springs, but he was also one of the three or four most powerful men in the tribe and with that, one of the most powerful men in the Palm Springs universe. As Jake sat across from Tall Mountain, Lamar entered the room and sat at another table.

"I can't tell you how surprised I am... that you're here, Mr. Tall Mountain," Jake offered.

"Ed, please. We do go way back, Jake." Jake had worked for the Tall Mountain family for three summers, but Jake didn't recall that Ed had any fondness for him. In fact, Jake believed that Tall Mountain couldn't stand the sight of him.

"I did work for you that's true."

Pete entered the room, uncoiling his six foot three, three hundred twenty-pound frame and sat next to Lamar. Ed Tall Mountain gave Pete a full once-over. Tall Mountain's gaze momentarily stopped to eye Pete's gloved left hand. The hand, at least double the size of the right, was unavoidable to the eye. Tall Mountain looked away from Pete's disability.

"It was more than that. You didn't just merely work for me; you were an extended member of the family."

"The Mexican son you never wanted." Jake smirked.

"Ah, to be sure. Maybe extended is the improper

term. Moro always thought of you as a brother."

"And I, him. That is, until he hung himself."

Tall Mountain's smile became a hardened stare. Awkward. Jake chastised himself for his candor as a pall of silence crossed over the room. Jake knew the truth and the truth was that Ed Tall Mountain had hired Jake, years prior, to keep an eye on the effeminate Moro Tall Mountain and push him into more masculine activities. Ed Tall Mountain demanded his son to not be gay and to lead a straight life. Jake inwardly smiled at the ridiculousness of such a thought. Straight, Moro had not been and the inability of Ed to come to terms, or even acknowledge this fact, eventually led to Moro's isolation from the family and ultimately, his death. The regal Ed Tall Mountain, sitting in a dive bar in Culver City miles and decades away from his failure as a father, pulled a handkerchief from his lapel and wiped his brow.

"Yes," Tall Mountain began, "Yes, Moro…died. I always appreciated how you dealt with him."

"Why are you here?"

"I want to hire you."

"Ed—" Jake closed his eyes, opened them, and looked at the ceiling. "You have casinos full of restaurants for catering and in case you didn't notice… we don't even serve food here."

Tall Mountain chuckled, returning his handkerchief to its pocket.

"No, no, no, I don't require your…hospitality or entertainment services. I wish you to find someone."

"Find," Jake replied with a quizzical lilt, "find? Like, actually go look and find someone? I'm not a P.I."

Tall Mountain cocked his head and motioned toward Pete and Lamar.

Jake spun around and after a second, realized exactly what Tall Mountain was motioning toward. Lamar and Pete followed Jake's gaze and saw the intention. Above Pete and Lamar's heads hung three framed certificates that were legal Private Investigator certifications for Jacob Hansen, Peter Mills and Lamar Wagner. Chagrined, Jake looked back toward Mr. Tall Mountain.

"Yes, I do have a private investigator license but that was only for a bet," Jake offered.

"A bet?"

Pete spoke for the first time, breaking his silence. "Jake bet Lamar and I that he could beat us on the P.I. test."

"And did he?"

"No, I got third in a three-horse race," Jake answered as Lamar barely held in a chuckle.

Pete gently elbowed Lamar in the ribs and Lamar's laughter slowed to his normal smile.

"I've never practiced or used the license. If you want or need Pete or Lamar?" Jake pointed to his amused cohorts.

"I'm sure either one would suffice. But it is my intention to hire all three of you. Jake, you're a digger. You know how to find info. You did it in high school when you found the gardener padding his pockets. You did it in the South Bronx and you did it here. You find stuff people don't want found. I want you to find my daughter, Mckenna."

At the change of the timbre in Tall Mountain's voice, both Pete and Lamar stood and, grabbing chairs, sat on either side of Jake. Ed Tall Mountain had their full attention.

"Mckenna's missing?" Jake frowned, sitting forward in his chair. "I just saw her--"

"Five weeks ago," Tall Mountain interrupted.

"Wait, what?" Jake sputtered.

"If she's missing, go to the police," Pete advised.

"Not advisable. Mckenna and I … Mckenna and I haven't spoken in quite some time. For years, the only contact I've had with her is when she works the golf charity outing my casino throws every year. I've been trying to reach her, but she won't return phone calls."

"You know Jake saw her five weeks ago, so—" Lamar interrupted Pete and Jake interrupting.

"My position in the council is important to the tribe, in our dealings."

"You have a tail on your daughter." Pete spoke what Jake and Lamar already deduced.

"That is irrelevant," a voice boomed from behind Ed Tall Mountain. A tall, white man with a ruddy complexion entered Trotter's Tavern, as if he'd been skulking in the shadows waiting for his cue. He was dressed in a white linen suit with a white shirt and bright red tie. He entered and walked until he stood behind Tall Mountain. He placed an attaché case on the table and folded his arms.

"Wow." Jake clapped his hands with a sarcastic, slow clap. "Who brought the creepy guy?"

"My apologies. Gentlemen, this is S. Newman, CFO of our Tribal council," Tall Mountain explained.

"And why is the CFO of your Tribal council creeping into my bar?" Pete asked standing up with an air of intimidation.

"It's important you all know who you are dealing with," S. Newman spoke with a fey arrogance.

"I know who we're dealing with," Jake replied.

"Oh, you do, do you." S. Newman sneered. "Against my advice, Mr. Tall Mountain is launching this investigation."

"And why is it any of the CFO's concern that Mr. Tall Mountain wants to conduct an investigation into Mckenna?" Jake shook his head.

"Because it's being paid with Tribal funds," S. Newman answered. Newman opened his attaché case and removed three dossiers. Walking around the bar table he handed the dossiers to Pete, Jake and Lamar. Pete and Lamar opened their folders while Jake ignored his.

"To be honest," Jake began. "This is all irrelevant. I'm not a Brother Shamus and due to some level of relationship I've had previously, you think that—"

"What the fuck is this?" Pete asked. Pete and Lamar gave Tall Mountain and S. Newman severe glares.

Newman cleared his throat. "Detective First Grade Peter Mills, born in the Bronx August 14th, 1961. You ably served the New York Police Department from 1981 until forced retirement in 1998 following an injury caused by an off-duty act. You started your own security firm until you moved to Los Angeles in 2001 to work for Jacob Hansen." Newman paused and looked at Pete.

"Work with, not for." Pete's glare seared into the quiet Tall Mountain.

"Lamar Wagner, born in the South Bronx, October 20th, 1968. You have a quiet record until arrested in New York City for Armed Robbery. Pete Mills was arresting officer. A model inmate, Detective Mills visited you twice a month until your release in 1998. Upon which you were hired by Mills' firm. You worked there until you moved out here to work here."

Jake stood, irate. "That's it, Tall Mountain. Time for you to leave and take your flunky and dangle. We're not taking this case." He motioned to the door.

Newman started again. "Jacob Hansen. Born in Palm Springs, December 5th, 1975. You graduated USC with honors and made a name for yourself as an Investigative Journalist in the South Bronx in 1998, where you met Detective Mills. You moved to Los Angeles and became a top Investigator until an ill-advised decision led to your firing. Your wife left you and married present Mayor Alex Vila—"

"Enough." Jake slammed his fist on the bar table. "What is the point of this? You know who we are, so what? We are not taking your case."

"Jake." Pete softly spoke.

Jake looked at Pete and Lamar.

"Hear the man out." Lamar shrugged.

Jake, flustered, sighed and sat back down into his seat. He motioned with his hands for the meeting to carry on. Newman patted Mr. Tall Mountain on the shoulder.

"The floor is yours," Newman said to Tall Mountain. Tall Mountain stood and paced a moment.

"Five weeks ago, Mckenna worked the golf outing. She takes photographs for the outing and frames the pictures for clients. We never got the framed ones back from her and my tail hasn't seen her in three weeks."

"And you haven't contacted the police?" Pete asked.

"No. I haven't." Tall Mountain exhaled.

"So, she just don't want to see you, she ain't lost," Lamar inferred, and Tall Mountain waved off the suggestion.

"Be that as it may, her brother's death… she blamed

me."

"No kidding." Jake shook his head.

"I had to be strong for the family."

"For the family?" asked Jake, "or for your ego?"

Tall Mountain paused and started again. "Just find her. Make sure she's all right. Please."

Jake stood and extended his hand toward Tall Mountain. "I don't think we can help you."

"We know you owe Tony Tahoe fifty thousand." Newman smiled a devilish grin at Jake.

Jake looked foolish as he stared at his hand, unshaken. He glanced back at Pete and Lamar. Pete's head dropped to his chest and Lamar closed his eyes. The look of disappointment on both of their faces shook Jake to his center.

Tall Mountain lifted his hand to Newman in a stop motion and proceeded to speak. "I've taken the liberty of paying off the first twenty-five thousand of your debt. The remainder will be paid when you find Mckenna."

Pete's head snapped up and Lamar opened his eyes as a look of shock crossed Jake's face. Pete chimed in.

"And his associates?"

"Yeah, we're a team." Lamar barely got out.

"Another twenty G's for Jake's team. Plus, a line of credit for expenses and what not." Tall Mountain reached into his pocket, pulled out a wallet and removed a black AMEX card. He walked over and handed the card to Pete.

"I'll give the line of credit to you, Detective Mills. With Jake's gambling difficulties, I'd feel more at ease if you managed the funds."

With men like Tall Mountain, thought Jake, it always seemed so easy. He had no education to speak of yet was universally perceived as a man of substance, style and intelligence. He was rich, powerful and smug. Jake hated smug.

"That's terrific... so you think you can just buy us off?" Anger swelled inside Jake.

"I really don't see your alternative," Tall Mountain mused. "Tony Tahoe does like you, but he will break your legs and then your neck. Find my daughter and your slate is clean."

"Is she in danger? Why do you want *us* to find her?" Jake stalled, feeling the ebb of his resolve dissolve.

"Joseph Smith died tragically in an automobile accident two months ago."

"Joseph Smith?" Lamar asked.

"Joseph Smith was the head of the tribal council." Jake's mind started to wrap around the burgeoning case, and he could feel the old butterflies stir in his belly. "I read about his passing. Why was he driving, he had epilepsy?"

"Clever boy." Tall Mountain smiled. "Joseph was a stubborn old man. More as to the point, his death leaves a void at the head of the council. The election for the new lead is November eleven."

"And you're running," Pete chimed in.

"Yes, I am running for the head. This isn't just the head of a council. It's the Chieftain. The head of a family."

"And you want to be big chief," Jake cracked wise.

"The head of the council," Tall Mountain continued, "is the head of a heritage. The head of a legacy. When Moro passed away, Mckenna became the last of my progeny. My wife died many, many years ago and Mckenna was the result of an ill-conceived affair with a

20

woman named Sherry Murphy, I'd had some years after my wife's passing. Moro was seventeen when she was born. She was one when he took his life. She is the last of a legacy."

Tall Mountain faced the group. "She is the last of my legacy. This position is about familial obligation. I need you to find her and I want to bring her back to the tribe."

Jake spoke with a disgusted tone. "You need her to garnish votes. Pity you didn't shower Moro with this kind of affection."

Tall Mountain stepped up to Jake and placed a hand on Jake's shoulder.

"Jake. I know you blame me for Moro's death."

"Did you ever cry for him? I saw you at the funeral. Always the glad hander."

"We all grieve in our own ways." Tall Mountain patted Jake on the shoulder and looked past Jake toward Pete and Lamar. "Gentlemen, I am offering you a large sum of money to find my daughter. Not bring her to me but find her. I will do the rest."

The room stood in a hushed silence for a few beats.

Lamar broke the silence. "And if we refuse?"

Ed Tall Mountain straightened his suit, but it was S. Newman who spoke.

"I have given Tony Tahoe the means to put a lien on your liquor license."

Jake closed his eyes and lolled his head back.

The SOB has us.

Jake opened his eyes and looked toward Pete and Lamar. They both shrugged in defeat.

"Sophie! Could you please bring us a standard written contract?"

Sophie ran into the front room from the back bar. "The Banquet contract?" Sophie asked.

"Yeah, I guess that'll do. Thanks Sophie." As Sophie ran off, Jake approached Ed Tall Mountain, his new client.

"Well, you can't threaten us, and you can't bribe us. But when you do both, I guess we're your guys." Jake extended his hand to his first P.I. client.

Chapter Two

By nine a.m., she'd walked for hours along the streets of Los Angeles and her feet were a shade of hot pink and blistered. Her once expensive and sexy, now sad and rundown, heels were not built for extensive hiking through the concrete jungle of the Southland. A wave of revulsion overcame her as she attempted to shove away the memory of the greasy middle-aged lothario she'd serviced and bedded the night previous. That memory would live in the quadrant of her mind marked repression. Ted did have a nice place in the Hollywood Hills, and he had been polite in a creepy, 'I own you,' sort of way.

She walked away from that encounter carrying her art portfolio, the expensive watch she'd swiped from his dresser and her shame. After she snuck out of the home, she'd just walked. First, straight down, off that damn hill but once off the hill, she'd just walked. South and then south by southwest. It wasn't until she reached Fairfax that she understood her feet were taking her to Jake Hansen in Culver City. She'd wanted to confide in Jake five weeks prior but after a night of carnality and cocaine, honesty didn't seem to be in the cards. Her drug use had begun her unraveling and her extracurricular activities were beginning to put her in dangerous spot after dangerous spot. She'd left a decently crappy job for a really crappy job and had started to spiral.

And then, Joseph Smith died mysteriously. Joseph had always been more of a father figure for her than her dad ever was. She didn't even carry her father's last name, Tall Mountain. After the way she learned he disowned her brother, Moro, and how he'd behaved following Moro's suicide, she'd almost completely severed ties. Yes, she took pictures at the annual golf outings and yes, she knew her father had her followed, but she wanted away from him.

Joseph was different. Fatherly, as a concerned parent should be, she found herself asking him for advice as her relationship with Ed Tall Mountain disintegrated. And Joseph reciprocated because it was Mckenna he confided in. Him, Joseph Smith, CEO of the tribal council, confided his suspicions to the strung-out daughter of his chief rival.

"There's something amiss," he told her, unfolding a tale of deceit, thievery and potential disaster in the finances of his people's council. He attempted to be as cryptic as possible but became more transparent as he continued to speak.

"The golf outing. Every year, finances are funneled the day after the annual golf outing." Joseph had gone on to explain that key members of the conspiracy would be at this year's outing and he would ferret them out.

"Take pictures of everyone. Everyone and focus on the people you're not familiar with and their familiarity with people you do know. That's how we'll find the villain. But be careful," he warned, "these are very dangerous men."

Joseph had hugged her and spoke no more of his intent and plans. And then he was dead; a car accident in a BMW driven by him.

"Bullshit," Mckenna said aloud, continuing her walk south.

Joseph had never driven a day in his life. He had a severe form of epilepsy, and his constant seizures disallowed him from attaining a proper driver's license. The idea that this great man at the age of seventy-one, would commit the one act he'd never committed and drive, crashing and burning the vehicle to the ground, was ridiculous. And yet, no one pursued the case, and his death drifted into the past.

Then she noticed she was being followed. Not by her father's normal idiots, but a new man. A professional who followed her everywhere she went. She'd taken precautions, even as she fell further into her own personal rabbit hole of drugs and horrible life decisions. She'd crashed at Scarlet's home, which was both fortuitous and disastrous. She loved Scarlet, but her lifestyle of proclivities mixed with Mckenna was a toxic cocktail.

Mckenna held tightly to her portfolio, hugging it to her chest. She may not have used her college degree to success, but her art was her world, and she knew that one day, she would return to it.

"Come work for me," her father had asked her, in a half-hearted attempt at parenting. "I paid for OTIS Art School and the degree isn't worth the paper it's written on. Or scribbled on."

"Thanks for the support, asshole," she said to herself.

She would never forgive her father for what she'd learned about Moro. She had been too young to know him, but everyone said he was sweet, honest, troubled and hopelessly lost.

As Mckenna approached her destination, she began to take the alleys, as a precaution. She was positive no one had followed her to Ted Lechstein's Hollywood Hills home, but her paranoia wouldn't let her believe she was safe. After she'd come home to find her home ransacked, she was grateful she'd given Rosemary, her neighbor from across the hall, the framed sketch. She'd taken the pictures at the golf outing and as practice, sketched them. It was just groups of men and women, enjoying a golf outing. It was when sketching, she replayed the words Joseph told her and she realized who the offenders must be. Two photos stood out and from those photos she drew two sketches. She placed the one sketch that had been her epiphany into a frame and gifted it to Rosemary.

Perhaps all the coincidences of the photos and the spotting of the strange man following her, was the meth paranoia but when she came home and her house was trashed, she knew. She had crawled out of the side window and repelled herself down to the adjoining alley. She hadn't returned.

Now, she'd walked all the way to Culver City and fuck, did her feet hurt. Mckenna crouched in the alley across the street from Trotter's Tavern, Jake's bar. Or at least, partly Jake's bar. He owned it with Pete and Lamar. She looked across the way and saw a pretty, young female, sweeping the sidewalk in front of Trotter's. After a momentary pang of jealousy, Mckenna realized that this was the girl Jake brought in from Hemet. She had been abused by her uncle and Jake took her in, giving her a job and a place to stay. Yes, Jake was a scoundrel and rogue, but he had a big heart and loyalty to those he loved.

She gazed past the tavern and spotted Jake's two-bedroom apartment slash bachelor pad, adjacent to Trotter's. She smiled, in spite of herself. It had been a wild night and day, between them. One night at his and one night at hers. A corroboration of desperation and a childhood crush, exploding into a ribaldrous moment of sexual dynamic.

Mckenna steeled herself, preparing to seek Jake's help, on many fronts. This was a step.

But as Mckenna walked, a long Black Lexus pulled up in front of Trotter's Tavern. She knew that Lexus. And as the distinguished looking man emerged from the passenger side, her father, she knew her time would have to wait. Mckenna back pedaled on her heels and stepped into a different direction.

Chapter Three

Detective Danielle Burkle looked down at the nearly headless corpse, and her gag reflex didn't activate. Well, not at first. The almond flavored acid in the back of her throat pushed what seemed like a quart of saliva into her mouth and her armpits sweat, but she didn't projectile anything. The contents of her stomach desperately wished to empty but Danny held fast.

"Detective," a low, gravelly voice spoke behind her.

It's a vurp, she thought to herself of the vomit/burp burning in her throat. As she forced her eyes to stare at the corpse, she continued to motivate herself.

Must be tough, must be strong.

She couldn't let the eyes of the Forensic team, the uniforms or her partner catch her unprepared for the vision of this mangled mess of a body in front of her.

"Detective."

This was her second week at Robbery-Homicide and Chambers had placed her with the well-oiled and well-heeled Detective Allison. The senior-most member of the elite squad had run through ten partners in the past seven years, since the Benitez hearings. He was a veteran, a good cop and a difficult man, by reputation. Danny was a good cop in her thirties, younger and a female which meant she had to be twice as good. She wanted respect, but now all she wanted was to not puke on her new shoes.

"Danny!" Detective Frank Allison called out from behind her, exasperated.

She'd heard 'Detective' twice, but it hadn't registered that it was for her. Detective Burkle eyed the crime scene. Johnson, from Forensics, was snapping pics of the corpse, Hudson and Choo, uniforms, applying crime tape to the front door and Allison, arms folded, shaking his head. Frank Allison was annoyed.

"What do you think, Detective?" Frank asked with a lilt of frustration.

Danny looked to Frank as he unfolded his arms and wrote in a notepad he pulled from his jacket. She was still holding in a puke but kneeled, eyeing the position of the deceased, Rasual Dominguez. She took a deep breath, inhaled her vomit into her lungs and nearly asphyxiated herself.

"Burkle," Allison growled.

"He committed suicide."

Rasual's body lay prone on his back atop his bed, a shotgun sprawled on the floor at the head of the bed. He had situated the rifle so that he could pull the trigger with his toe, blow his face off and end whatever pain was his existence.

"Yep." Frank closed his tiny notepad and placed it back into his jacket. "He blew his fucking face off. Johnson, take those pictures to Somoza. This is his case. Thanks."

Allison stepped carefully aside as a surprised Danny stared, silently. Detective Allison motioned to her with his hands.

"Detective Burkle. Shall we?"

Danny stepped away from Rasual Dominguez and walked past the detective, who followed her out of the

Venice flophouse. Danny quickly raced down the steps from the second floor to the first, rushing past the coming paramedics who averted their eyes. Frank slowly ambled down the stairs, five feet behind the shorter Danny. She closed her hands and packed them into fists three quick times. She did this to calm herself when she wanted to let loose anger.

As she exited the rundown complex, the breeze struck her face, and a blink of tears threatened to fall. Like her fortitude in holding back the puke, she held in her tears. She was pissed. She stopped walking to keep from hyper-ventilating.

The stout Allison nearly ran over the parked, stationary Burkle. Burkle placed her index finger right into Allison's chest. Her fist flexing had barely helped.

"What the fuck was that?" Danny's face contorted into a mask of rage, embarrassment, and more rage.

"Calm down." Allison placed up his hands.

"Are you trying to embarrass me in front of the unit?"

"Detective Burkle, you are new to Robbery-Homicide, and I have taken you on as my partner. In the future if you have questions—" Allison placed a playful smile onto his face and pushed his hands into his pockets.

"Cut the crap," Danny interrupted, "I may be new to the unit, but I've spent a decade moving up. I've earned my stripes and worked my way up and you will afford me the respect I've earned."

"Fair enough. We were the secondary unit on the 187 on Cesar Chavez two days ago. Remember?"

Danny had experienced a similar reaction to the corpses of the mother-daughter victims. She hoped her green in the gills look avoided detection; apparently the veteran had seen her squeamishness.

"Listen, Burkle, this is a tough gig. The toughest. And I've been through a few partners lately."

"I'd heard," Danny responded. "It felt like you were trying to embarrass me in there."

"I got a call about a suspicious death. Romero told me more than likely suicide and it was a mess. Practice makes perfect. I'm trying to see what you're made of."

"I walked a beat. I worked Metro and GND. I can do the job."

"Then do the job. And toughen up." Allison walked past her toward his gray Lexus, parked on the street.

He smiled a little smile. Frank had no problems working with a woman and he didn't mind a younger partner. In fact, he'd asked for it. Since the Benitez hearings, and he'd been removed from his longtime partner, Martin Cruz, he'd run through many partners. He liked Danny Burkle. She was tough, smart and honest. He endured the ribbing from his fellow vets about the attractiveness of Burkle, and she was a looker for sure.

"Annie ain't gonna like you out on stakeouts with that hottie." Marty the desk sarge had given him grief. He'd laughed because he was happily married and anyway, he didn't shit where he ate.

"Let's hit up Tito's Tacos off Washington. Just down the way."

"It's breakfast time," she replied.

"I know Oscar. He'll set us up with some breakfast tacos."

Danny strapped herself in on the passenger side as Frank got on his side and fastened in. "Why did Romero call you on this one?" Danny asked.

"I wasn't in to work yet. It's early in the day. It's like being stiff in the joints when you wake. Need to get movin' to get them knees oiled up. For me, detective work is the same way. I like to get the scent first thing in the morning. Chambers usually calls me for the early ones."

"But it would be Daniels' or Martinez's case?"

"Yep. I like to get the sense of the day. I have a feeling we got a big one coming."

Chapter Four

As Tall Mountain exited Trotter's, S. Newman took a brief second to speak with the trio.

"She was last spotted at her Hollywood apartment," Newman spoke from the side of his mouth. Newman gave a sideways smirk and slippery wink, as he walked away.

Jake leaned over, grabbed his knees and closed his eyes for a second.

"Holy fuck, I've screwed up. Holy fuck, holy fuck." Jake whispered below his breath. "Where's Mckenna?"

As the front door of Trotter's closed with a thud, Pete and Lamar approached Jake and stood around the high top. A silent shroud spread its gray matter over the bar and Pete crinkled his face, momentarily unable to form his thoughts with words. He unknowingly scratched his gloved hand.

"Well… that was unexpected," Pete spoke.

"Not how I pictured my day rolling," replied Lamar.

Jake moved his eyes nervously until they rested on Pete whose eyes bore into Jake's.

"Guys," Jake began, "I don't know what to say. I fucked up. Again. I'm sorry."

"You owe… Tony Tahoe… fifty Thousand!!! Fifty!!!" Pete screamed so a vein popped in his neck.

Jake dropped his head in shame.

"Damn, Jake," Lamar whispered.

"I know, I know. I just… I won a parlay and…then there was a bad beat. A series of bad beats and I just… couldn't catch up."

"Shut up! Shut up, just shut the fuck up," Pete yelled, his voice filled with anger.

Jake rubbed his head and then his jaw. The bruised areas of his face no longer hurt so much from the physical pain but more from the pain projected from a different injury; the injury he had inflicted on his friends. His peeps, his die-hard most trusted friends. Fifteen minutes prior, his only concern was his massive hangover and his battered face but now the realities of his life laid claim. Every aspect of his life stood in disarray, and it all swelled on him. The shit of his life was overwhelming and circling the drain, dragging Pete and Lamar with him.

Pete slowly walked up and stood right in Jake's face. The anger rose in red umber from Pete's neck to his forehead. His lips began to tremble.

When Pete was a detective at Fort Apache, The Bronx, he had been the man who spoke in the box. He interrogated because his temper never consumed. He flowed his anger into serenity, until time came for serenity to become fury. Pete now stood, nearly consumed with fury. Jake looked up at Pete with woeful, sad, knowing eyes. A son disappointing his father. Pete knew the sadness. He knew the look. He'd seen it before and knew of it. The look of ire shading Pete's face crossed over and morphed into a type of sadness. And then calmly Pete placed his good hand on Jake's shoulder.

"Pete," Jake murmured.

"Shut up, stupid," Pete muttered. Pete's face

transformed from an angry grimace to a thin smile. He knew Jake, he'd known Jake. Pete looked back at Lamar. Pete knew these two men more than anyone he'd ever known. They were his family.

"Your old friend, Tall Mountain, has given us the means to get out from under your debt."

"And make a little scratch," Lamar added from behind.

Jake looked up, acknowledging his two best friends in the world.

"I'm not a P.I." Jake shook his head.

"You're a digger. Let's go digging."

****

Pete sat upright behind the steering wheel, in his sedan, as Jake looked silently out the window. Jake tapped his index fingernail on his teeth, deep in concentration.

Mckenna. Where is Mckenna?

Jake had last seen her five weeks prior. He'd left her passed out and naked atop her bed, covers kicked to the floor. They'd spent a very sultry, sexy few hours together after he'd joined her at Tiki-Ti. She'd sent him a drunken text and he, as any man of worth, responded. He chewed a nail, wondering why he hadn't done a follow up with her. She wasn't a two-night stand but a longtime friend.

Pete briefly caught a glimpse of Jake from the corner of his eye. Pete and Jake had been through battles between each other and against all others. Pete had known Jake as a cub reporter and Pete had taken on a mentor role with Pete as the detective in the neighborhoods Jake covered. Pete now saw Jake falling apart. How many bets would Jake lose, how many drinks would he consume, days and years would he squander before the bottom hit?

Pete drove east on Venice, bisecting through mid-morning traffic. The sedan sat in the left lane, preparing to turn onto La Cienega. Mckenna's place was on Saturn Avenue just off La Cienega in a neighborhood bordering respectability.

Following the departure of Tall Mountain and his flunky, Pete took immediate control of the situation. Pete knew there was little time to ruminate and point fingers. Point A, they were going to be paid well to find Mckenna Murphy. Point B, Tall Mountain had them by the short hairs and this rested at the feet of Jake and his gambling addiction.

After a brief *mea culpa* from Jake, the three quickly devised a plan. Pete, as the former detective, took the lead in plotting the plan. It was agreed that a visit to Mckenna's apartment in Hollywood should be the first step.

"You know where she lives." Pete pointed to Jake.

Pete and Jake would handle investigating Mckenna's home as Lamar opened Trotter's Tavern. They did, after all, have a business to run.

As Pete drove in silence amidst the insane jungle of traffic, Jake thought on Mckenna. She had been a baby when Moro took his own life. Jake remembered as she remained calm as the adults howled with sorrow and panic. Mckenna sat in the doorway, her Bugs Bunny stuffed animal in her hand. Just sat there amidst the commotion. A slice of earnest heaven in the middle of the worst chaos and loss a family can absorb.

Pete finally broke the silence. "You've known the family a long time?"

"Eh, too long. I was an assistant to the family, but

my real job was Moro. Until…"

"Suicide?" Pete asked.

"Awful. I knew it was coming. But Ed Tall Mountain was … is, a powerful presence. As powerful as I've ever known, and I've dealt with—"

"The worst of the worst," Pete finished for Jake.

"Moro was gay," Jake continued. "We all knew it from a young age. It's Palm Springs so being of that bent didn't, shouldn't, have mattered. It was other pressures that drove him to suicide."

"His father."

"Yea. Mr. Tall Mountain was never okay with Moro's lifestyle. In high school, Moro and I took different paths. I ran around with Lily and Billy, Moro got in with some other people and hard drugs. I remember the last Christmas party. Tall Mountain laid into Moro. Called him a degenerate, drug addict…fag. It was direct and awful. Later that night, a drunk and drugged Moro, told me he was hearing voices telling him to kill himself. New Year's Eve… he listened to the voices." Pete shook his head sadly.

"Seems there's no love lost on Mckenna's end. Toward Tall Mountain," Pete offered.

"Sherry Murphy was an Interior Designer in Palm Desert, having an affair with Tall Mountain. When Mckenna was born, the Tall Mountain clan pretty much shunned Sherry and her daughter. Tall Mountain paid for Mckenna to go to art school. Other than that, not much interaction between the two of them." Jake looked out of the window as the sedan drove onto La Cienega.

"So why now? Why pursue his estranged daughter?"

"You heard him. He wants that chief gig. Legacy and blah, blah, blah."

"The man is loaded. It's that important to him?"

"It's a money tree and yes, he would kill for it." Jake briefly thought back to his time in the employ of Tall Mountain. "The money and privilege."

"Well," Pete started. "We need the money, but she could just be running away from Tall Mountain or hiding out with some fella."

Jake sadly agreed. "Maybe she is just hiding. But maybe she's in trouble. Listen Pete, we find Mckenna and pass the info on. That's it."

"Seventy K is not a finder's fee. It's desperation money." The sedan passed under the overpass.

"Yeah. Well, we're desperate," Jake replied, rubbing his head. "Mckenna never wanted anything to do with her father. He shunned her. She basically grew up without a Father. But—"

"Here we are finding her for him."

"I don't like it, Pete, I don't hate that man, but I have no love for him," Jake spoke, his head pounding.

"So why does he come to you?" Pete asked, confused. "Surely he knows—"

"Mckenna and I hooked up a few times. And if Tall Mountain was trailing her—"

"Then he knows." Pete interrupted. "He thinks you might know where she is."

"I don't. Listen, this is my fault. If I didn't owe Tony Tahoe—"

"But you do," Pete interjected. "You do owe Tony Tahoe. So, let's go find this girl."

****

Lamar took a bar rag to the brass bar top as Sophie placed table settings for the day on the bar tables. Trotter's didn't serve food, but patrons were encouraged to bring food from other establishments and eat. On this day, UEFA Soccer Championships would be playing on the television; Real Madrid was playing which always brought in a crowd.

"Mr. Wagner?" Sophie asked from across the room.

"Yes, sweetie. Please call me Lamar." Lamar beamed a smile at Sophie.

"Is Mr. Hansen in trouble?"

"Sophie, Jake's always in trouble." Lamar let out a low chuckle and continued to smile.

"I'm sorry, Mr. Wagner, I shouldn't be nosy."

Sophie had a way of retreating when she felt uncomfortable. She had a quietness about her and walked with the softness of someone who had always tip-toed, not only around her house, but around her life. Meek, almost to a fault, her relationships with her father and uncle had left her barely able to trust a male figure. In her brief time working and being around Lamar and Pete, she had gradually begun to thaw her feelings and reception to them. Jake, she had known for a long period of time, and trusted. When she hugged Jake, upon hearing that he would hire her and give her a place to live, it was the first time she'd initiated contact with a man that she could recall.

"Sweetie," Lamar began, "this is your home now. Be as nosy as you like."

"Mr. Hansen has been good to me. You all have. Taking me in, giving me a job."

"When Jake said you were family, that mean that you're our family." Lamar stepped from behind the bar so that he stood a few feet away from Sophie. She crossed her arms, awkwardly.

"I know Mr. Hansen drinks too much and gambles

too much but when I see him beat up…"

"Jake is like our little brother. We love him. He's our Jake but that boy needs to get his shit together."

"Mama always said Mr. Hansen was a big success."

"Jake was a swinging dick for a while…uh…Pardon my French… but he had some rough luck, some of it his own doing. He's been moping too long. Needs to find some of that old Jake Hansen swagger."

"I do appreciate how you and Mr. Mills have looked after me," Sophie spoke looking up to Lamar and making eye contact for the first time with him.

"It's okay, sweetie, please call me Lamar."

"Okay Lamar. It's Sophie." Sophie spoke with a not before heard, force.

"Sorry, Sophie." Lamar chuckled. "I call everyone sweetie."

"My uncle called me sweetie."

Lamar's face transformed from a smile to a dark scowl, and it suddenly was as if another face had been placed onto his own. Sophie could see the altering of his visage and wondered if this was the mask he wore on the inside of prison. The face that became Lamar's was shaved from a murky soul. Lamar had seen and lived in the most repugnant of places. He'd known a world of total darkness, having been kept in a hole for nearly two months. He'd witnessed the vulgarity of the world, complete evil. Knowing Sophie had seen the vile depravity, made Lamar's stomach turn cold and a rage he hadn't felt since being on the inside, awoke in him.

"Your uncle… uncle?" Lamar asked.

"I'm sorry, I shouldn't have…"

"Don't you ever apologize for setting me straight, Sophie. And I won't never call you that name again. And if that man ever tries to step foot in here or anywhere near where you are...I'll tear his motherfucking head clean off and do my stretch on the inside standing on my head with a goddamn smile on my face."

A tear dropped down Sophie's cheek as she quietly wiped it away. She stepped up to Lamar, leaned up and kissed Lamar gently on the cheek.

"C'mon now, Sophie, we gonna be busy today. Let's get this place up and running."

****

Jake recalled stumbling from the cab to Mckenna's place, half holding, half carrying Mckenna into her apartment. As Pete and Jake approached her apartment, the same question emerged from Pete that had crossed Jake's mind then.

"What is the daughter of a multi-millionaire doing living in a shit hole like this?" Pete blurted.

"Precisely," Jake agreed.

Jake and Pete climbed the steps to the complex. Pete looked up at the complex and a pitiful little sign read: Rosewood Apartments.

"And her answer?" Pete asked.

"She didn't really give one." Jake hit the number buzzer on the complex door to get buzzed in. A few seconds later, a buzz indicated they were allowed entrance.

Jake and Pete entered, stepping over a few boxes of old Chinese take-out left on the floor. The complex mailboxes were placed on the east side of the wall near the entrance. Pete stood in front of the boxes.

"What's her number?" Pete asked.

"Three fourteen." Pete ran his fingers across the boxes until he reached three fourteen. The box assigned to that number was slightly ajar.

"Someone's been picking up her mail," Pete thought out loud.

Jake tapped Pete on the shoulder and started to climb the steps of the complex. Pete followed as they ambled up the stairs. Reaching the third floor, they followed the numbers down the dingy, poorly lit hall.

"I barely remember this hallway," Jake said.

"I don't understand the desire to live in Hollywood. It sucks," Pete muttered.

"Here it is. Three fourteen."

As the two stood in front of three fourteen, Pete reached into his pocket and pulled out a small black sack. He unzipped the sack and pulled out two lock picks. With skill and precision, Pete fiddled with the picks and the doorknob. And Abracadabra, the door popped open.

"Great security system." Jake laughed.

As they entered Mckenna's apartment, Jake immediately tripped over a desk lamp.

"Fuck a duck," Jake cried out as he stumbled to the floor in embarrassing fashion.

The apartment had been trashed.

"I'd say we're not the only ones looking for her." Pete whistled, looking at the destruction.

"Jesus."

The place had been ransacked from neck to nuts. The living room couch flipped over with the backing ripped out with a knife as the serrated edges of the fabric dictated. Papers were scattered all across the floors and cabinets full of dishes emptied. As Jake stood, the pit in his stomach started to calcify. With this much attention given to Mckenna's apartment, it stood as obvious that she wasn't just playing hide and seek with daddy. She was in real trouble.

"This is a pretty thorough search." Pete bent down to look at some of the papers on the ground.

Jake stepped from the living room and entered the bedroom. The mattress had been taken from the bed frame and stood upright against the far wall. He looked out of the window and saw scaffolding just outside.

"Jake," Pete called from the living room, "come take a look at this!"

Jake stepped over a few torn pillows in the hall and entered the living room. Pete was holding onto a sketch.

"You said Mckenna went to art school?"

"Yea, she's really talented."

Pete revealed the sketch in his hand so Jake could see it. The sketch was of two men, dressed in full golf gear: slacks, polo shirts, wearing golf gloves. The man on the left was a white male with blonde hair and the man to the right was a very tanned white male with white hair.

"Why would … Tall Mountain said she'd take pictures of the golf tourney."

"She'd sketch the pictures she'd take. For practice, maybe?" Jake asked.

"Your guess is as good as mine." Pete looked at the floor and realized most of the paper on the ground was other sketches.

Jake kneeled and started to leaf through them. "Look at the sticker on the top left of the sketch," mentioned Jake and indeed, every sketch had a tiny circular sticker at the top left of the sketch and the stickers were numbered.

Jake started to place the sketches in order. Pete looked past Jake and saw an open file cabinet with all of the drawers opened. Pete stepped over Jake and walked over to the cabinet. Inside the cabinet were pictures of men at a golf tourney. At the top left of each picture, there was placed a small circular sticker with a corresponding number. Pete started to file the pictures in order.

"Hold that first sketch up, Jake."

Jake flipped through the sketches until he reached the first one. He held it up for Pete to see. The picture matched the sketch. Jake continued to sift through the sketches.

"Bingo," Jake called out. He lifted a sketch, and it was a likeness of S. Newman.

Pete moved his fingers through the pictures until he stopped at one. He lifted the picture to show Jake the photograph in his hand. It was a photo of S. Newman.

"Isn't that, that Newman creep?" Pete leaned over Jake and looked. "It's a match. This sketch with Newman has the number fifteen on it."

"See this?" questioned Jake. "Number's sixteen, and seventeen are missing."

"Could mean something, could mean nothing." Pete clapped Jake on the back. "Let's get the fuck out of here. This place is giving me the creeps."

Pete put his hand out and Jake grabbed it to help him up. Jake held onto the sketches.

"I'm taking these, Pete."

As Jake and Pete exited Mckenna's apartment, Pete grasped Jake by the shoulder. "This was a desperate, angry search for something."

They stepped into the hallway and as they did so, from across the hall, an older woman, tiny in stature and pale, poked her head out from her apartment.

"What do you think, Detective?" Jake asked Pete.

"Tall Mountain pays seventy G's to find his estranged daughter and our first step is a trashed apartment? This is no simple case of finding a girl."

"Are you Mckenna's friends?" the elderly woman, rasped out.

Jake and Pete looked at her.

"Yes, ma'am, we are. My name's Jake and this is Pete. Did she tell you we were coming?"

The woman stepped into the hallway. She wore a white robe and pink house slippers. She took a hard look at Jake's face. "My goodness. What happened to you?"

"I was attacked by a gorilla." Jake smiled.

"Oh my. My name's Rosemary. Would you like to come in for a cup of tea?" Rosemary motioned for them to come into her apartment.

"We would love a cup," Pete answered, as she took his arm and led him into her apartment.

After Rosemary walked them in, Pete and Jake looked around the apartment. Her apartment was sheltered, shuttered, claustrophobic and moth balled to the point of gagging. Framed sketches covered the walls. Seeing the sketches, Jake took a walk, looking at every sketch.

"Are these Mckenna's?" Jake pointed to the sketches.

"Oh yes. She's a wonderful artist," Rosemary said as she entered her kitchen. "Always drawing. She's always giving me a piece of her work. Would you boys like mint tea?"

"That would be lovely, miss." Jake caught Pete's eye and motioned to him. Pete stepped over to Jake.

"She said I'd know when her friends arrived," Rosemary called out. "The other gentlemen didn't seem like her friends."

At the mention of 'the other gentlemen' Pete's head whipped around and focused on Rosemary.

"Other gentlemen? Could you describe these other gentlemen?" Pete asked, as Rosemary placed the tea kettle beneath the water faucet.

"Two men. They appeared very sinister. They broke into her place. One man was bald with a tattoo on his head. The other... I didn't get a good look at him. And then a few hours later, another man came. He knocked politely and then left. He appeared as if he were... Pakistani maybe?"

Pete and Jake exchanged glances. This was a description they were not expecting. As Jake and Pete continued to search the sketches, Jake dug for more info.

"Did Mckenna say where she was going, or, or, or what she might be up to?" Jake asked.

"Mckenna did say she was going away for a time." Rosemary walked up to Jake, leaving the kitchen. "Didn't say where."

"Had she giving you any sketches lately?" Jake asked.

"Come to think of it, yes."

Rosemary grabbed Jake's hand and led him across the room to a framed sketch. Jake immediately recognized S. Newman with wire rimmed glasses talking with a man in the sketch. The drawing was in line with the other drawings from Mckenna's sketches. The other man's face was not visible.

"You are her friends, aren't you?" she asked.

"Rosemary, I've known Mckenna since she was born." Jake smiled at Rosemary.

Rosemary placed her hand on Jake's arm. "Such a

sweet girl. Bad choices in boyfriend's but always sweet with me. Also had terrible work choices. Some dive place in Hermosa Beach."

Mckenna had worked at Barnacles in Hermosa Beach. That would be stop number two. Pete made eyes at Jake which Jake recognized as being the move to start wrapping things up. Jake took a closer look at the sketch of S. Newman.

"Miss Rosemary, would you mind if I removed the sketch, just for a second, from the frame?"

After Jake asked his question, Rosemary gave him a quizzical glance.

"What an unusual request, but I don't see why not."

Jake pulled the sketch from the wall and carefully removed the sketch from the frame. As Jake lifted the picture from the frame, he lifted it to show the top left to Pete. The sketch had a sticker with the number sixteen on it.

"We appear to have a person of interest." Pete smiled. The flow was flowing.

Chapter Five

Pete raced his car onto the Ten toward the 405 as a jolt of excited energy revved through both he and Jake. It felt to Pete like he was back on the force in New York City; his first year in uniform. No, his first case as a detective. He and Detective Roger Schmelzle took the call for a body found at The Flaherty Fur Coat shop just off the Deegan Parkway. The body was the mistress of Mr. Flaherty, spread prone across the warehouse floor, blood trickling from her eyes and ears. Pete scratched his chin, in remembrance of the case.

"The wife, Roger knew it was the wife," Pete whispered, audibly mumbling.

"What?" Jake, pulled from his distracted trance, asked.

"Nothing…just remembering…nothing…" Pete trailed off. Mr. Flaherty's wife had taken a Ben Hogan Nine-Iron to the skull of the mistress, bludgeoning her to death.

Pete had felt the surge of energy from the clue at Mckenna's old apartment. He smiled, despite himself. Any clue beginning a case is bound to be swallowed whole by later clues, but Pete found that he always loved the tingling that came with the first big clue. And although the sketches seemed sketchy at best, any clue would do. It had been more than a decade since he'd carried a badge and despite finding a few older ladies' missing dogs for a price, this felt more like a case than anything he'd done since that long ago, sad retirement party at the Bronx Police precinct.

Pete flowed into traffic and the Ten opened before him as the mid-morning traffic subsided and the freeway blossomed into a wide free style mode. He shoved his sedan into the center lane and released the hounds, pushing the car to ninety and ninety- five miles per hour.

"You sure about this next move?" Pete was trying to temper his born-again enthusiasm.

"I'm sure," replied Jake, as he looked at the vehicles blurred by Pete's driving. "I'm sure, that I'm sure."

Pete's abundant excitement lasted only momentarily. Yes, they had found something that perhaps would lead to another something but more than anything else, they discovered that Mckenna was in distress. There was the temperature of panic in Mckenna's apartment as whomever had broken into her apartment, desperately searched for an item. If she was on the lam, they needed to find her first and they still had very few threads of the quilt to work with.

"All we got is two missing sketches," reminded Pete. "Why the bar job next?"

"I visited Mckenna there a few times. She'd, quote-unquote, dated Zane before our trysts and was still super close with him."

"Zane?"

"Yea, Zane is the bar manager there. He used to run numbers for Tony Tahoe," Jake murmured slowly.

"Terrific. Are we gonna have to deal with that gorilla?"

"Nah, Zane isn't a gorilla," Jake reassured. "Zane was strictly a take bets guy. You'll see. He doesn't have the stones to be hard with me. Or anyone else, for that matter. In fact, he's of a queasy countenance."

"Famous last words." Pete raced past the National exit.

"It'll be fine. Zane and I aren't friends, per se... but we did have Mckenna in common. She always mentioned that he would always have her back. Mckenna engendered loyalty like that."

Pete dared another sideways glance toward Jake and a different feeling swelled inside of him, an emotion of hope. He'd known Jake when Jake was a rising star, a comet across the sky. Jake was the man everyone wanted to write for them. Jake had been relentless, unstoppable. A thirst for the truth and a willingness to go to the grimiest places the truth inhabited to find it. Jake's insight, will and ambition were perfect partners, creating a writing juggernaut.

Pete remembered the first time he'd seen and met Jake. It had been in New York City in 1998. The South Bronx was a troubled war zone back then. He caught Jake in the aftermath of a shooting near the Jackson Avenue Triangle, on Eagle Avenue. Jake's friend, and one of many inside sources, Nery Polin (a real tough character and Jackson Avenue heavy) had taken the brunt of machine gun fire in the chest, a few feet away from a stunned, Jake. The spray of bullets that struck Nery led from his waist, zig zagging up toward his head, hitting the jugular. The cascade of blood that exited the jugular splashed Jake so that half of Jake's face and most of his clothes were covered in blood and viscera. Jake, having vomited onto himself, was a disheveled mess.

However, Jake regained his calm, despite looking like some blood splattered medic at a MASH unit. Pete had been impressed by that. As Pete would learn, Jake's need to discover answers, in a world bereft of them, shoved his fear and revulsion into a chasm in his soul, even with a torso-less Nery five feet away. Jake insisted to Detective Pete Mills that he needed an interview and would not be dismissed until this occurred. The Detective respected that and took an instant liking to Jake Hansen. He had a fierce determined look of a man who didn't know his limits or limitations.

As Pete roared down the Ten, he smiled because Jake had that fierce look again.

"You're just excited about going to a bar," Pete said.

Jake loved bars, absolutely loved them. But Jake also liked to dig. Dig for information, dig for knowledge. Digging into the discovery of what people had hidden. The breadcrumbs of a person's life and past, the hidden secret of shame and disdain, shoved under a floor mat or spare room futon, that is what Jake loved to unearth. It gnawed at his sleep and fed him in a way no vice could ever truly fulfill. He had to know, and he couldn't let it go. It's what made him a great investigative journalist. That desire to know what lay beneath the veneer of gild and pomp. And Jake now felt the surge running through his veins for the first time since Lily left him.

Jake could smell the salt air of the ocean as it began to reveal itself. Few sights are as majestic and magnificent in the world as the sight of the Pacific Ocean exploding into view as you reach the crest that brings the beautiful waters into sight. The inhabitants of the beach communities, Hermosa Beach especially, took for granted the view they beheld every day, and it is a view that millions in the country dream of as they shovel, rake, and mow their respective driveways, yards, and alley ways. Hermosa Beach is the home of the perpetual Peter Pan, a paradise of sun, ocean and a lifestyle that is as carefree as any in the country.

The beach communities were once thought of as the trash heap of Los Angeles. Venice Beach was a drug addled cesspool and every beach south of Santa Monica, until you reached La Jolla, consisted of Bikers, homeless bums and borderline indigent. Hermosa Beach endured a seedy history of Hells Angels and Mongols and Bikers bars, but a new frontier of social activity emerged in the nineties and early Aughts as Hermosa became a community on the rise. The bikers were shoved out by yuppies.

After parking in the structure south of the famous Hermosa Pier, Jake and Pete walked the few blocks south on Hermosa Avenue to the Taj Mahal known as Barnacles. The definition of 'watering hole', what Barnacles didn't have in aesthetic beauty or solid structure, it more than made up for with a mosaic of local riff and surfer raff. Barnacles was beautiful in its inert simplicity. Moldy and flimsy dry wall upheld shingles passing for a roof. As Jake and Pete approached, four surfer dudes emerged from the well-worn establishment.

Jake stopped at the front window of Barnacles to give himself lay of the land. Pete stood right behind Jake, literally breathing down his neck.

"Do you mind, Detective?" Jake chuckled back toward Pete. Pete backed up with mock sincerity. Jake returned his focus into the bar. He recognized the bartender.

Name, name, name.

"Molly," Jake said aloud. "Let's do it."

Jake and Pete entered the dimly lit bar as Molly

spoke to three barflies at the front of the long and windy bar. Barnacles stood as a marvel to the 1950's and 60's architecture, well not architecture, but the utter disdain for adherence to codes and standards. The walls of Barnacles were held together by rubber cement and best wishes. It always seemed as if it would only take one big, bad wolf to blow the whole house down.

The crowd consisted of one hundred percent men at this hour and Molly provided the entertainment. A beautiful leggy, blonde, she encompassed all that stood right and good with California girls. Songs about Cali girls may not have been written for Molly but they certainly had the fetching vision of Molly, or someone resembling Molly, in mind. Tall and shapely, she wore tight jeans with a gray t-shirt that read *I Break for Paramecium*, which indicated her time spent as a Biology grad assistant at UCLA. She may have looked like eye candy, but she outbid every male's IQ in the room by at least fifteen points. Regardless, she would keep the full bar of men entertained enough to drink for hours on end.

The crowd at noon in Barnacles may have seemed sparse but few bars at noon in the South Bay had more than a handful of patrons. Three tan, young surfers took possession of the right end of the bar, where the bartender could come and go. To the left of the three 'brahs', sat a man with an ochre complexion. The boys sipped margaritas, Molly's specialty, while the man of Middle Eastern or Indian descent sipped on a boring Soda water.

"What's a paramecium?" Pete asked.

"Single-cell organism." Jake chuckled.

"Hey, love bug," Molly cried out upon seeing Jake.

She raced around the bar and hugged Jake with a bone crunching hug as the bar full of men stared at the douche bag who'd stolen their girl. As Jake felt the heat of jealousy, his eyes cased the bar and saw Zane at the far end, behind the bar, weaving a tale to three older men. Jake kissed Molly on the cheek as Pete, uncomfortably, stood behind, his good hand in his pocket. Molly pulled back and looked at Jake's face.

"Muffin, what happened here?" Molly caressed Jake's mangled face.

"Ah, you should see the other guy."

"It's been a minute, Jakey," Molly cooed. "You stopped paying Mckenna attention and left us all in the cold."

Jake caught Zane's eye.

"Funny you should mention that," Jake spoke into Molly's ear, kissing her other cheek.

"Mckenna doesn't work here anymore," Molly offered.

"Well maybe I came here to see you, sweetie." Jake smiled his most winsome smile at Molly as she pulled away toward the bar.

"Uh huh," Molly replied, back in work mode as a customer waved to her from down the bar. She ignored that customer and maintained focus on Jake.

"Whatcha havin' today, mister?"

Jake's insides cheered and mouth watered at the question. He was hungover and he did want a little hair of the dog. He snuck a peek at Pete.

"Do what you gotta do," Pete replied.

"You know what a Prairie Chicken is, Molly?" Molly scrunched up her nose at the question.

"Uh no."

"Ya got tequila and ya got hot sauce. You got any eggs?"

"Yes?"

"Okay, pour two ounces of tequila in a bucket glass, drop three shakes of hot sauce and crack an egg in there." Jake beamed a smile at Molly.

Molly made a puke face after hearing the instructions. She slowly walked off in search of eggs. Jake felt the eyes of Pete on him and the hairs stood up on his neck.

"I'm hungover."

"You got problems." Pete shook his head.

When Molly returned with an egg, she proceeded to make the drink, measuring the tequila in the bucket glass. After the hot sauce, Molly had the rapt attention of the surfer dudes and the Indian National. She cracked the egg and dropped it into the drink.

"Oh brah, that's rancid," exclaimed the blondest of the surfers.

Molly nudged the Prairie Chicken toward Jake, who quickly snatched and downed the drink. The blondest surfer put his head down, barely able to withhold an upchuck.

"Well played," the Indian National spoke with a slight accent.

"Thanks." Jake smiled.

"That's on the house, love bug." Molly blew Jake a kiss as she walked toward the previously waving customer.

Jake motioned to Pete and Pete, rolling his eyes, pulled a twenty from his wallet and left it on the bar. Jake slowly walked toward the side of the bar where Zane held court. Jake's ears perked up at the sound of Zane's malarkey. Jake recalled that even though Mckenna maintained a close friendship with Zane, his philandering ways had been the unraveling of their coupling.

"Once a cheater, always a cheater," she said, as Jake unzipped her jeans and proceeded to work his way into her panties and heart. He'd agreed with her, as the mission at the time was to gain access to what laid beneath the G-string panties and enter forthwith. No answer would suffice other than to agree and agree he did, and he proceeded to enter her over and over. His trashing Zane and agreeing with Mckenna provided the result he sought.

A pang of guilt and sheepishness washed over him and held firm in his belly as he now knew he needed Zane to GPS him in the right direction. Zane spoke louder as Jake and Pete approached, Zane's ego plainly in view.

"Yea, I fucked her right on that pool table," Zane exclaimed.

"Bullshit," replied the aged, white man at the end of the bar. Jake recalled the older man's name was Dirt, obviously a *nom de plume*.

Zane waved Dirt off. "Hey. old timer, there's a security camera in that pool room. It all goes to a monitor and machine in the office two doors down if you need proof. I made doubly sure to save that tape just for you, Dirt."

"Now why wouldn't anyone believe an up-standing guy like you, Zane?" Jake spoke up, as everyone's eyes and heads rotated toward him.

"Well looky what asshole rolled in here. Jesus, Hansen, what the fuck happened to your face? Ya gotta pay your debts on time, mister. You got some kinda nerve showing your ass around here."

For standing only five foot nine, Zane held a presence. Good looking enough, with light olive skin and the prerequired douchey LA haircut, his stocky stature spoke to his prior days as a bookie.

"Molly didn't seem to mind my presence." Jake poked the cub.

Jake delivered Molly a wink. Zane caught the wink, and a nasty sneer took over his face and the look Zane gave Jake told him everything that he needed to know.

"Damn Zane, ya gotta stop shittin' where you eat, brother."

Pete nudged Jake in the shoulder. "We need his info," Pete spoke softly, "play nice."

Jake sighed slightly. "Zane…we need a word with you."

Zane looked at Dirt and a smirk crossed his mouth.

"The word should be sorry, or I'll kick your ass out after I kick your ass." Zane put his toughest hard ass look on his face.

A little slice of rage opened itself inside of Jake, but Pete placed his large mitt onto Jake's shoulder. Zane, briefly, put his eye on the gigantic hand that rested on Jake's shoulder. The look on his face transformed. Jake watched knowingly the change of Zane's demeanor. Not that it surprised him, but Jake was always impressed how Pete could intimidate with something as little as a small hand gesture. A small hand gesture from a massive and deformed hand.

"Please," Pete started, "just a minute of your time."

"I don't do numbers or any of that anymore. Whatever you owe Tahoe is not my problem."

"It's not that business," Jake got out, shrugging Pete's hand off of his shoulder.

"Really? I hear you owe Tony fifty large."

"Technically half that."

"You're not enlisting the help of loan sharks, are ya? Tony Tahoe might give you a love tap but those fuckers will break your legs."

"Gambling's not why we're here. We want to talk to you about Mckenna," Jake blurted, desperate to get to the point.

"She doesn't work here anymore, thanks to you, asshole." Zane started to walk away.

"She's missing."

Jake hadn't meant to divulge such information, for the rest of tarnation to hear, but that's how it happened. The only aspect more startling than the sudden silence on that side of Barnacles was how quickly Zane stopped in his footsteps. He stepped toward Jake.

"I just... what do you mean, missing? I just saw her. She came in...I thought it was last week."

A look of concern stretched over Zane's eyes and Jake knew the truth. Zane still loved Mckenna.

"Come on, Zane," Pete spoke, motioning with his right hand to Zane, "pool room."

Zane dropped his head and pulled the towel from his belt. He slowly walked around the bar, touching Molly lightly on her shoulder. He led Pete and Jake to the pool room.

As Pete and Jake followed Zane, Jake bumped into two gentlemen, sitting at a high top a few feet from the bar.

"Sorry fellas," Jake apologized. Saying his apology, Jake took a full look at the two men. Two Latino men of a disconcerting continence, the men didn't fit the beach vibe of Barnacles. The man on the left sported a shaved head with a spider tattoo covering his dome. A black mustache never wavered as he nodded his head to Jake's apology, his brown eyes betraying a menacing stare. The other man, with a thick head of black, spiky hair, didn't move, nor did he acknowledge Jake. He stared straight ahead. A severe scar slashed across his left cheek. It was a smooth scar in a crescent sliver. Jake stared a beat too long and as the tattooed headed man stood, Jake made haste in following Zane into the other room.

The pool room was a tiny slice of dive bar heaven. The regulation table covered nearly half of the room. For such a hole in the wall establishment, the table was quite nice. Correct size, well-crafted felt and since it was the home of Zane's prior bookie business, the room was always kept in quaint shape. Zane entered and placed his hands on his head.

"I knew it. I knew something was wrong." Zane paced the floor.

"Your psychic talents are wasted in this room, Zane, spill it," Pete growled.

"Mckenna's missing." Zane spoke with less of a question lilt and more matter of fact.

"Yes. We were hired by her father to find her."

"No way. Mckenna hated her father."

"We got that drift," Pete added.

"She put her notice in here a few weeks after you stopped stopping by. She and I… started to pick up where we'd left off, but something was different."

"How so?" Jake chewed on a fingernail.

"She'd gotten into a little more of the Hollywood scene. More drugs, more…something wasn't right. She started hanging with a new friend in Hollywood. She quit here and said she'd gotten a job at the Cat n' Fiddle."

"I know the place," Pete interjected.

"Okay so she got a job closer to home… and then she came in last week?"

"Yea, yea, she came in here… I think she came in a week from last Thursday. Molly was working and got a load of jealousy when she saw Mckenna in here."

Jake smiled at the small bar drama. "How did she seem?"

"Funny you should ask. Scared."

"Scared?" Pete asked.

"Yeah, something was wrong for sure."

"Did she say anything, allude to anything… ask anything?" Jake tried to pull all he could from Zane.

"No, she wasn't specific. She hung out for an hour or so. Kept scratching herself… her neck, tapping her foot and looking at her watch. I said, 'You late for a date,' but she didn't even respond. She was on something, but it was more than that. And then…" Zane trailed off before finishing his thought.

"Come on, Zane, out with it," Jake cajoled.

"I don't think I should say anymore." Zane folded his arms and sat on the edge of the pool table.

"Zane, and then what?" Pete stepped into the foreground.

"She made me promise not to say." Zane eyed Pete.

Jake blinked slowly and held his breath for a second or two. He had anticipated this but still paused. Yes, part of the magenta bruising of his mug was due to Pete, but along with Lamar, there was not a person on planet Earth Jake revered more than Detective Pete Mills and he didn't undertake an action that could be as shaming and humiliating as the act he pondered, lightly.

Jake briefly moved his eyes toward Pete with hesitation. Pete looked Jake in the eyes and Jake knew Pete understood the plan.

In many ways, it's why Pete and Jake were such close friends. For all Jake was and could be and for all he asked and required, Pete and Lamar loved Jake's loyalty and fealty to his friends. They also knew and trusted each other. Jake was beloved, not because of his rights, but because of his wrongs. But one of his rights was undying loyalty. And so, Jake knew Pete understood this was something that needed to be done, even though he didn't want to ask.

"Zane, do you see my partner's left hand? Do you know why he always wears a glove?"

"No. No I don't," Zane responded. Zane stared at Pete's hand, transfixed.

"To gift the world from it. Pete…" Jake motioned to Pete.

Pete slowly unbuttoned the snaps at the base of his left glove and started to unwrap the Velcro that wrapped around his massive wrist leading to his unusually large and gigantic left hand. As he pulled the rigged glove off, the purple discoloration slowly revealed itself.

No matter the intestinal fortitude of a man (or woman) the first sight of the diabolical always causes a pause of all functions from breath to bowels. The only organ that works is the Adrenal glands. Zane's adrenal glands were pumping at a high rate. The disfigured hand was everything nightmares are made of. A large, Titleist golf ball sized knot, the result of a massive infection, consumed the top center of the hand with gnarled tendrils shooting out as rivulets from the painful looking scar.

Picture a map of the mighty Mississippi River pouring into many younger tributaries. The tendrils from Pete's scar spread like the boundaries seen on a Richter scale following an earthquake. Angry lavender-streaked tendons intersected with bright, red, busted vessels, screaming with a vitriolic crimson; the tributaries on Pete's hand had long since healed improperly. Though perhaps exacerbated by its grotesque appearance, it appeared that the hand was twice its normal size. And in truth, it was three times larger than normal.

As painful as the hand could be to Pete, and the warm California winters removed much of the cold New York City pain, the look of shock and horror caused more pain, not just to those who bore witness but to himself. The years of knowing the heinous visage of his hand built a tolerance in the native New Yorker. He knew. He always knew. For decades he'd been the bigger or fatter officer but, still, he aced every fitness test and when the shit went down, and it always did, he was always first on the scene and first through the door. Pete Mills was a man of integrity, will and effort. And fuckin eh, he was Pete Mills.

Jake was always amazed at how his friend's disposition neither altered nor wavered, but he knew that every time the scar was revealed it took a little life from Pete and created a little death. He didn't undertake the task lightly, but he knew to at least give a tangential pass. Jake looked at Zane and saw that he was mesmerized by Pete's hand. Entranced.

"How much do you know about Pete?"

"I know he's scary, but not as scary as Lamar."

"Lamar's an ex-con, he's supposed to be scary. This man, Pete Mills, was detective first grade in New York

City. See that hand, Zane. Thirteen years ago, Detective Mills placed that paw over the muzzle of a perp's gun to break up a heist. Do you understand the will it takes to place your own hand over a gun knowing full well it will be shot off? Do you have that will to match? Do you have the will to place your hand over the muzzle of a gun? What makes you think you won't tell us everything we want to know?"

Zane gulped, swallowing his nervousness. "Okay, Mckenna was frightened. And she gave me something to hold on to."

Jake looked to Pete as Pete started to place the glove back over his hand. "She gave you something?"

"Yes. She gave me a camera." Zane answered as if the secret weighed five hundred pounds.

"What kind of camera?" Pete prodded.

"I dunno, digital." Zane placed his hands on the pool table.

"And?" Pete stepped toward Zane.

"And what?" Zane folded his hands under his arms.

"Did you take a look at the pictures?"

"Yeah, I took a glimpse. All the shots were of a golf scramble."

"The sketches," Pete murmured.

"Yeah, the sketches," Jake responded dumbly.

"Sketches?" asked a confused Zane.

"Never mind." Jake shook his head. "Where's the camera?"

"It's gone. She said if ten days passed without hearing from her that I was supposed to mail the camera to an address she gave me."

"She asked you to mail it? Why would—" Jake wondered but was interrupted by Zane.

"I don't know but I mailed it yesterday."

"Thanks Zane. Really, this really helps." Jake put his hand out and Zane shook it.

"I wasn't a good boyfriend to her. But she came to me when she was in trouble…I figured the least I could do was do as she wished." A look of sadness crossed Zane's face as he spoke.

Jake breathed deeply, knowing the sickening feeling Zane probably felt in his stomach.

"Zane, where did you mail the camera?"

Zane looked Pete in the eye.

"What happened to the perp, Detective Mills?"

"I shot and killed him."

Chapter Six

Jake tripped over the door-jam as he and Pete emerged from the dimly lit bar and into the sharp sunlight, as the sun escaped from the prison of the Hermosa marine layer.

"Son of a bitch," exclaimed Jake, as he shook his head at his clumsiness.

"Did that Prairie Chicken, or whatever that was, fuck you back up?"

"No, smart guy, I just… I just fucking tripped."

Jake dusted himself off and thought about the info they'd gleaned. Bizarre at best, Jake visualized the pieces of the scattered puzzle but didn't see how the information brought Mckenna any closer to the fold.

"That gives us something." Pete folded his arms.

"It gives us a location; 29 Palms Inn. But even that is—" Jake hesitated.

"Strange," Pete finished.

"Bizarre. Beyond Bizarre. I mean, she is from the desert but 29 Palms? That's one giant step way beyond the norm." Jake put his right fingers in the crease of his forehead.

"Beyond the mountain pass?"

"Beyond the mountain pass? That's forty-five minutes to an hour past."

"You know 29 Palms?"

"I'm from the desert, Pete. But 29 Palms is the

asshole of the world. Maybe not the asshole, but it's near the taint. Marine base is out there amidst all of that… shit."

"Sounds charming." Pete pulled his phone from his pocket.

"You think 29 Palms is bad? You should see beyond that toward Amboy. Talk about off the grid. There's this grocery store in 29 Palms; you see people waiting for the bus to take them beyond the marine base and you think, 'Man! Where the fuck does this bus go?' Toothless, teeth-less, eye-less people. Something right out of a 70's horror movie."

Pete laughed and started to hit some numbers on his phone.

"Who're you calling, first?"

"The 29 Palms tourism bureau."

"What? Why?"

"Nothing, kidding. Let's get to it. I'm gonna call the Inn. Maybe, just maybe she's there."

Pete stepped away from Jake. Jake removed his phone from his pocket, and thought of a long past trip to Vegas, driving the Amboy Road. He had heard that Amboy Road was some miracle elixir to the endless drive to Vegas, but a scary road and scarier terrain. A Two-lane, winding morass of road. Never again, he had said. He and his buddy Kurk decided on a quick road trip to Vegas and took the Amboy Road. The desert at night is as black as the ocean at night and he and Kurk had driven carefully, blasting their brights, just to see fifteen feet in front of the grill. Stopped at a train crossing near Amboy, the rain had started to fall, adding a hint of moisture to the already creepy atmosphere. As Kurk sat behind the wheel, Jake had glanced to his right, looking into the Valley below. Two hundred or so people dressed in dark robes carrying torches had congregated at the center of the valley, creating a flaming pentagram. At that point, Jake prayed for superpowers to physically leap over or run through the train.

"Never again," Jake spoke aloud. Jake pulled out his cell and dialed Trotter's Tavern.

"Trotter's Tavern," the optimistic dulcet voice of Lamar announced. "Happy Hour three to six, Monday through Friday and we got Johnny Rodriguez playing tonight, this is Lamar."

"Geez, Lamar, you say way, way more than I do." Jake laughed.

"What do you say?"

"Trotter's Tavern."

"Ya gotta sell the business, brother. Jesus, have some hospitality in ya, would ya. You boys making progress?"

"Yea, I guess. We might have a line on her. It's too confusing to explain on the phone but it might have to do with that golf scramble she took photos for."

"That does sound confusing. Did someone threaten her?"

"Good question." Jake wondered how Mckenna had gotten wind of the situation. If the sketch of a single person was the issue, how did she know?

Pete let out a loud sigh of disconsolation.

"That sounds like Pete's frustrated," Lamar remarked.

"Yep. Gotta go. Can you cover Trotter's til we get back?"

"I got it. I figure I get a split of Mckenna money even if I don't do shit."

"Touché."

"And I get all the tips," Lamar said. Jake could hear Lamar's smile from ten miles away.

"All right, I get it." Jake laughed. He shut off his cell. "Good old Lamar."

"Place is closed for renovations," Pete spoke from behind Jake.

"Really?"

"Yea, apparently, it's some kind of high priced get away. They open up in a few days."

"Poor timing."

"Maybe she knew as part of her plan?" Pete shrugged.

"That's just speculation."

"Everything about this is speculation, shithead," Pete said, clapping Jake on the arm.

"Ow! Too hard!"

"Shit," Pete exclaimed.

"What?"

"That means our next step is the Cat n' Fiddle." Pete closed his eyes.

"Right. Shit. We gotta drive back to Hollywood."

"AHHHH, goddammit!"

"Well, there's a bright side, Pete."

"What's that?"

"I'm not driving." Jake smiled.

"Come on, asshole."

****

"Freeways or side streets?" Jake asked, as Pete pulled from the parking garage.

"I'll decide when I get to that bridge."

"There's no bridge."

"There oughta be one big one."

Pete took Pacific Coast Highway weaving through traffic to Aviation Avenue through the less gilded regions of the South Bay. Pete mumbled for divine guidance to grant him the right decision. If you take the freeway and it's packed, a one-hour drive is three or if you take side streets and there's construction or a fender bender, you could be there all day and night.

A short little j'ete to the 405 North and briefly past LAX? Past the hidden ugly residentials off Slauson and Jefferson toward Stocker?

Pete shook his head knowing there was no easy way from Hermosa Beach to Hollywood.

Traffic in Los Angeles is always a nightmare. The phrase, 'Rush Hour,' doesn't apply to Los Angeles; it's just Rush, at every hour. There are so many cars on top of each other struggling to find any avenue, any side street, any glimmer of hope for a quicker trip that gridlock is inevitable. And that doesn't even add to the equation the melting pot of an entire continent of different styles of driving converging on the confluence of the Los Angeles highway system. You take a pinch of the Mass-hole driving style, mixed with the sensibility of the gentile Southern driver and a modest helping of the idiots who drive in from Michigan and add a dash of the South of the Border mentality that only what's in front of their car matters, to the already maniacal, home bred Southern Californian driver and that is a recipe for the worst driving meat loaf on the planet.

405 to the Ten to side streets? 405 to 105 to 110?

With the incessant parking lot traffic on the 105 toward the bottleneck of three freeways on the 110 near downtown, the North by Northeast route to Hollywood would be a colossal mess. Jake looked out his passenger window.

"How is it possible that a sprawling, and in every way, insanely sprawled, metropolis such as Los Angeles could only have so few roadways and outlets?" Jake wondered aloud.

"I don't know but the original city planners should be reanimated and shot."

Pete pursued the Stocker, La Cienega and Fairfax route, which is the last chance saloon effort to get quickly to Hollywood. As Pete and Jake passed Wilshire from La Cienega, they moved on toward Restaurant Row, eclipsing The Stinking Rose, named for the blossom of garlic that highlights every single dish. They passed legendary Lawry's, the famous Prime Rib Steakhouse, which hosts both participants of the Rose Bowl, every year. Fogo de Chao, STK, Morton's. As Pete's car slowed to a crawl, the silhouette of Cedar-Sinai Hospital became visible and the awful structure of the Beverly Center came into view.

Jake rolled down his window and stuck his head out. He caught the familiar glint of dayglo, representing the bulbs of a Caution sign. Road construction was ahead.

"Right onto Beverly," Jake told Pete.

"I hate taking Beverly."

"There's construction ahead. And so, what if you don't like Beverly? Take left onto Fairfax and right on Hollywood. It's a better route anyway."

Pete reluctantly took the next right onto Beverly. The traffic was no better.

"Jesus Christ." Pete slammed the wheel. "I told you I hate Beverly."

"What are you so upset about?" Jake smiled, "I'm the one who needs a drink."

****

The jaunty strains of new age rock streamed above the buzz of the eclectic crowd of the Cat n' Fiddle. The essential Los Angeles, British Pub, the Sunset Boulevard space originally was a Laurel Canyon joint. Since the British Invasion the Cat n' Fiddle was a gift to the music world. The spot had remained a hub for musicians and artists, perhaps not as much as The Rainbow Room, but a hub all the same.

From his time on the Felipe Ochoa Case, Jake had spent many nights in Hollywood and fondly remembered the bangers and mash of The Cat n' Fiddle. Pete had a thing for bangers and mash from his New York City days, so the cuisine was perfect for Pete. Pete tore into the bangers like a fat kid with chocolate cake and ordered a second order.

Pete wasn't necessarily fat, but he was big. Not husky either, he was just fucking big. Pete's stories about the situations in New York City where his mass affected certain outcomes were Jake's personal favorites. Pete told a story of how he ordered two Extra Large Pizzas to go from Frankie's on 28th street. As he left the pizzeria, holding the two pies, one in each hand, a couple of Puerto Rican guys standing by a phone booth jawed at him, one guy in particular.

"Hey fatty, ya gonna eat both of those by yourself, ya fat fuck," the kid mocked.

Pete deviated from his destination and walked toward the two punks. He politely asked the one kid, who didn't speak, to hold the pizza from his left hand and the kid acquiesced. Pete proceeded to remove the pizza pie, piping hot and right from the oven, from the box and wrap the entire pizza around the jibber jawer's face. The kid screamed, scrambling to get the pizza off his face as his face sizzled with boiling hot cheese. The thought of the boiling cheese on skin, always gave Jake the shivers.

Jake and Pete perched at the near end of the packed bar as Jake sipped on a lager and Pete nursed a scotch on the rocks. Pete flexed his left hand, rubbing it slightly with his right hand. Jake caught a glimpse of Pete massaging the scarred hand and a twinge of guilt coursed through him.

I didn't need to use his hand as a prop.

He looked up to Pete and Lamar, revered them both, in many ways. During the stretch Jake worked in New York (living, breathing, and writing the South Bronx) Pete had emerged as a mentor, a shoulder and a friend.

January 7th, 1998. Jake would never forget the date or the day. He flew into New York City January 3rd, after spending Christmas with Lily in Palm Springs. It had been a real family affair, missing her family, and including Ryan, his brother. The two weeks were glorious with Lily, especially watching the year become 1998. They spent New Year's Eve in Los Angeles at a downtown hotel, partaking of the downtown festivities held every year. At midnight, Jake mused about his notion to go to New York for a year and make a name for himself. He had been reading about the world of the South Bronx, the poorest congressional district in the United States, at that time. His reading had sparked the idea of a writing series. In the latter months of 1997, as graduation from USC was approaching, he'd wowed the New York editor with, not only his journalistic acumen but his ability to sniff out trouble and by doing so, discover an undiscovered story. Jake had the eye for mischief and always seemed to be in the right place at the right time. The editor saw this and offered him a one-year contract.

Shortly after arriving to New York, the first blizzard of 1998 struck, leaving him stuck in the community center where he arranged housing. The arrangement had been greased with the aid of a local Bronx minister named Donnie Chalk. Chalk ran a multitude of programs with the eye to the betterment of the neighborhood. New Saints had an After-School Program for teens that created a local Newspaper. As Chalk worked with kids, the center sponsored a Violence Prevention Program, Needle Exchange, Soup Kitchen, A Delivery Service for End Stage AIDS patients and featured two rooms in the upstairs of the Church that housed Jake.

The church's location gave Jake ideal position to be a frontline observer to the Jackson Avenue Triangle Drug War. The fact that he spoke Spanish fluently was also an aid. The blizzard jailed him to New Saint's but the timing couldn't have been better. In a coup for Hansen, a local tough, Nery Polin, also stayed at the Community Center. Nery took the room across the hall from Jake. Nery helped Jake with the local Spanish slang and a friendship was built. As Jake would discover, sadly through second-hand information, Nery had his trigger finger on the pulse of the South Bronx.

Over the course of three snowed in days, Nery Polin gave Jake a crash tutorial on the ins and outs of the Triangle War. Nery laid out the three drug Kings and their turf, right down to the street address. He explained how the product passed from Manhattan to the Bronx and how each street had a crew that distributed and the intricate rules, codes, hand and hat signals that each crew utilized. Jake had entered a hornet's nest at the ripest moment of explosion.

The drug turf initially had as many as twenty Kings fighting street for street and block for block for superiority. In January of 1998, the Kings had dwindled to a deadly three. Progress in the eyes of police and the mayor, but in terms of collateral damage, the worst period of the turf war was about to commence. There were three kings looking to wipe each other out with no concern as the cost.

On the 7th, around six p.m., Jake spoke, via a pay phone, with his editor and the deal was struck that would lay the groundwork for a series of articles that would make Jake's reputation. Finishing his phone call, in the freezing cold just outside of the corner Guatemalan bodega, Jake hung up, giddy with his impending gig. He entered the bodega and sat at the lunch counter next to Nery and Polito Marin. After enjoying a piping hot bowl of Ox-tail Soup, Jake, puffed with cockiness, picked up the trio's tab. The three exited the warm bodega and stepped into the frigid air of New York. Bundled up tightly in the sub-zero cold, the California boy in Jake shivered as the three walked up the hill of 163rd street toward Eagle Avenue. Jake recalled that he gave Nery shit about his Army surplus jacket and teased Polito about his newly in place, corn rows. It was at that exact moment Nery appeared to trip.

Still, to this day, late at night Jake would ponder the exact details of the moment (while also thinking on the finite inches that separated him from his own end). Jake could not recall hearing the shatteringly loud clang until after Nery had tripped, but he knew the clang must have come first. Nery appeared to trip and as Jake began to tease his new friend on his clumsiness, there was the loud clatter and shattering noise of metal on metal, perhaps the sound of an explosion. Jake, frozen, stared down at the fallen Nery, lying on his back in an awkward position.

"What a strange way to fall," Jake had murmured.

A fast stream of blood streaked from Nery's neck, splattering the parked Honda Nery fell next to. The splatter of blood reminded Jake of a Samurai's death he'd seen in a movie, year's prior. Jake, dumbly eyeballing Nery, saw that Nery's eyes were open with a sad look of shock. Jake didn't even realize that much of Nery's blood covered himself. Jake couldn't recall if he saw the blood splatter first or Nery's body first. It felt to him as if he were participating in a fluid movie and his eyes represented the camera. He still edited jump cuts of his film to help play the scene over and over in his mind.

"Nery," Jake spoke, barely a whisper, rasping out the name meekly. He couldn't even hear him say the name as the sudden screams of loud bangs overtook his voice.

"Get down," Polito screamed from behind Jake.

Confused, Jake continued to stare down at the bloody Nery.

Something had torn through the Army surplus jacket he had just made fun of and in the darkness, Jake couldn't make out the substance flowing from Nery's body. He was unable to comprehend that the blood that splattered the Honda was Nery's and that Nery had been shot.

Holy shit. That's blood.

He looked at the Honda and, in shock, saw unmistakably, suddenly and with deafening clarity, five holes appear in the side of the Honda. He heard metal on metal.

"What the fuck," Jake yelled out loud, finally realizing with mild hysteria, that Nery had been shot and whomever shot him, was still shooting.

Before Jake could say another word, or scream, he was tackled to the ground, by the slight Polito. The moments following the initial attack remained blurry and, for the rest of his life, Jake would argue that he fell into a coma-like state. He seemed positioned in a state of mental stasis. He remembered huddling beneath the wheels of the Honda, fearful with an equally scared Polito, next to him. Jake's hand touched his jacket. He was covered in blood. Jake moved to face Nery. Nery's chest quivered and he breathed for nearly a minute and stopped. Jake knew his friend was dead.

Panicked, Jake made eye contact with the fifteen-year-old Polito and saw a fear in the kid's eyes that must have matched his own.

The street fight continued as two factions fired, north and south for what seemed hours but in actuality was probably ten minutes. Jake was able to discern that one group had three guns and the other group four but as the fight persisted the numbers of guns seemed to dwindle. They were being killed off.

Jake couldn't remember how long he sat on the curb, in the aftermath, staring at the lifeless body of Nery Polin, now covered with a white sheet. Just prior, he'd glorified his assignment to his editor, extolling the words to emerge from the Jackson Triangle war. And now he sat, staring at the reality of that war; the senseless death of a seventeen-year-old kid.

Suddenly Jake stood up, his stomach in full revolt. As he frantically searched for a receptacle for his vomit, an enormous white male with a buzz haircut, wearing a gray trench coat, approached Jake.

"You the writer?"

Before Jake could answer, he emptied his stomach of every ounce of Ox-Tail soup he'd eaten. The puke didn't hit Detective Mills but left a vomit Maginot Line between Jake and Pete.

From that inauspicious meet developed a friendship that eventually grew into a business partnership. As Jake lived in the heart of one of the darkest, most violent moments in Bronx history, Pete showed Jake the ropes, giving him access to ride alongs and insight into the inner workings of one of the toughest police precincts in the United States, Fort Apache.

Jake shook his head at the memory of so many years past and snuck a glance at his friend, scanning the crowd of the Cat n' Fiddle, casually. Pete finished his quick scan and stared at his whiskey glass. Jake knew Pete appreciated the strong whiskey and scotch collection, but the Hollywood crowd didn't suit him. At times like this, Pete still stuck out like a cop because he still looked and mostly acted like a cop.

Pete took another shallow-eyed glance around the room and hesitated a second, as he caught a slight abnormality. He dropped his napkin to the floor, leaned down and picked it up, furtively darting his eyes across the floor of the room. Sitting up, he stirred his drink quickly and Jake, remembering the signal of years before, caught the hint. Jake knew it was time to look and think fast.

"At your three o'clock about twenty feet away," Pete softly spoke. He lifted his glass and took a sip as he finished his words.

Jake stood and feigned a stretch, a little too obvious, but acceptable. Gathering the lay of the land and measuring Pete's directions, he caught a side view of a familiar looking man.

"You recognize him?" Pete asked.

"The guy from Barnacles? Indian maybe?"

"Uh-huh. We're being followed."

Jake remained standing, nervously cracking his knuckles.

"Calm down, calm down. Have a seat."

"Tony Tahoe?"

"No. No. A, we just put twenty-five G's on your tab and B, too Svengali like for Tony. He'd send Bruckner or DJ to handle biz."

As Jake sat, Pete eyed the Indian National from a sideways glance. The man, in question, took a small sip of water and calmly remained sitting.

This guy's good. Nearly invisible.

"Funny, I thought it would be—"

"The Mexicans from Barnacles," Pete finished Jake's sentence. "The high top."

"You saw them?"

"I was a detective, remember. And a spider tattoo on a bald head? That's memorable."

Jake nodded, realizing he had profiled his own culture.

"Don't get all racially sensitive." Pete pushed. "In that bar, three people didn't fit the demographic. You just got the wrong stereotype."

"Sooo…?" Jake asked.

"How would this guy even know to come here. He must have been the guy at Mckenna's apartment?"

"So, he could be on to us, but—"

"Maybe, he too, is working for Tall Mountain?" Pete asked.

"Again, how would he know we were coming here?"

"Okay… Jake, when the bartender comes over, be direct about Mckenna."

"The place is too loud, and that guy is twenty feet away. He'll never hear me talking to the bartender."

"True, this place is perfect but you're out of practice and if this guy is following us… just be direct with the bartender. Ask me a question."

"What?" Jake shook his head, confused.

"Ask me a question."

Christ, I'm nervous. Seven years out of practice.

"Why'd you retire so early?" Jake asked.

"Excuse me?"

"Forget it. None of my business."

Pete sat in silence for roughly a minute, deep in thought. "I couldn't take it anymore," Pete finally responded.

"Take what anymore?"

"All of it. The desk assignment…the whispers…the sly stares. That's not true, I actually didn't mind the whispers or stares. Fuck 'em. I was born to be on the street. And they wouldn't let me do it." Pete took a long look at his hand. "All I ever wanted was to be a detective. The best. Get the cases, start the Murder book, follow the clues, interrogate. I got to live my dream. And then, it was over."

"Do you think he'd have killed you?"

"Li'l Jimmy Montoya, fuck yea. One hundred percent. Half cracked out of his gourd. I remember seeing his mom afterward. You know she apologized to me? I killed her kid but she, she kissed my cheek and apologized. That fucked me up. But you know, same situation, same cards dealt... I'd have done the same thing. I'd shoot him again but Mrs. Montoya apologizing to me... still gets me."

Pete nudged Jake with his foot and, with his head, motioned toward the male bartender approaching the two of them. A young white guy, late twenties with an unfinished sleeve of a series of tattoos on his right arm that looked like the hollow Color by Numbers set of the late seventies and early eighties. Jake thought he made out what appeared to be an eagle, but it may very well have been a dragon. Or a robin.

The bartender stood in front of Jake and Pete, wiping his hands with the bar towel hanging from his belt. Pete had grabbed a sketch from Mckenna's apartment that was a self-portrait pencil drawing. Pete removed the drawing from his back pocket.

"How is everything?" the bartender asked with a hint of an Irish accent.

"Super." Pete placed the drawn sketch of Mckenna onto the bar top. "You know this girl?"

"Mckenna? Of course. Good likeness of her."

"She drew it," Jake replied.

"No shit?!? She came in quite a bit about a month or so ago. She'd come in with Scarlet."

"Scarlet?" Jake asked.

"Yea Scarlet worked here about a year ago. She's something else, that Scarlet. Mckenna's a hottie but Scarlet is a next level smoke show. And next level nuts."

"Seems to go hand and hand." Jake smiled.

"Do you know where Scarlet works now?" Pete asked.

The kid thought a minute. "You know, I hear she was working a couple nights a week at Trocadero on Sunset."

"I know Trocadero," Jake chimed in, "new ownership I hear."

"Nah, same owners but they've kinda gone in for that hipster thing. Perfect for you guys. All the girls who work there are working some kind of Bettie Page thing. When you go there, ask for Jenny Girl. Tell her Jimmy sent you."

"Jenny Girl? Nice, thanks, Jimmy."

"On to Trocadero." Pete pulled a fifty from his wallet. He set it on the bar for the bartender.

"Thanks, old man." The bartender smiled.

Pete didn't return the smile but did pull the fifty back and replaced it with a ten.

"What the…" Jimmy began to inquire.

"That's for the old man comment," Pete interrupted.

"Pete…" Jake scolded.

Pete rolled his eyes and put the fifty back onto the bar.

"Thanks for the info, kid. Hope that fifty helps to finish that stupid tattoo." Pete scowled walking away.

Jake and Pete walked away from the bar and out of the loud and happy Cat n' Fiddle. The two walked through the courtyard toward Sunset. Jake poked Pete on the shoulder.

"Would you have preferred he called you 'Pops'?"

"Fuck you, Jake. 'Old Man'… what a douche. Figure out your tattoo, ya fuckin' hipster."

Jake couldn't help but let out a full belly laugh. Pete looked at his feet and started to laugh, a bit, as well.

Pete and Jake drove through the heart of Hollywood

racing onto Sunset Boulevard, driving past the Chateau Marmont, The Laugh Factory and some of the newer spots on the strip. When Pete saw the strip club the block prior to Trocadero, he pulled over, parking on the side of the street.

"This is the place, I probably should do all the talking," Jake offered.

"It kills me to say this, but this is Lamar's territory." Pete spoke gravely.

Jake understood Pete's inference. They were going to be headed toward territory where a cop wouldn't be able to gain trust enough for answers. Pete would stick out like a father working as a chaperone at his daughter's prom.

"You wanna head back and have him meet me?" Jake attempted to look and appear sympathetic; Jake just wasn't very good at it and it made Pete feel worse.

"Yeah. Fucking convict. I'll call him."

"Tell him to meet me at the Frolic Room." Jake pulled his phone from his pocket and Pete did likewise.

"Frolic Room? How long you gonna be here?"

"Just long enough to get some info from Jenny Girl. I've got Lamar on speed dial. If Scarlet is indeed there, I'll text him. But tell him to meet me at the Frolic Room. I got someone I'd like to see." Jake exited from the passenger side and leaned in the window. "It's gonna take a village to find Mckenna. You did good work today." Jake smiled and extended a fist bump.

"Shut the fuck up." Pete ignored the fist bump and Jake exited, laughing.

As Jake entered Trocadero, he stopped and watched Pete drive off. It was the correct decision to send in a relief pitcher. Pete could be scary, and these places would require a modicum of finesse. Jake stepped up toward the small bar where a gorgeous Black bartender, who'd spent a little too much money on her boob job, tended bar. She eyed him casually and he saw that her nametag read: JENNY GIRL.

"What can I get for you, handsome?" Jenny Girl asked Jake.

"Manhattan, I require no cherry juice."

"I didn't think you would."

"I'm Jake."

"Jenny Girl."

"Is that your Christian name?"

"No, that's my Trocadero name. We got four Jen's who work here. Tall Jen over there." She pointed behind Jake to a brunette, six-foot Goddess. "Mean Jen is cocktailing." She gestured with her chin to a petite, blonde and attractive female with a tight haircut.

"She don't look so mean." Jake winked.

"Wait for it, it'll happen. And the other bartender is Tattoo Jen." Behind Jenny Girl, Tattoo Jen made her entrance, and her nickname was befitting her appearance. She was sleeved with a unique Boa Constrictor that wrapped around her right arm and neck and led to a serpent, down her left arm. Jake struggled to shift his eyes away from the mesmerizing tattoo.

"Wonder why they call her that," Jake facetiously spoke. He looked to Jenny Girl who gave him a blown kiss. "Jenny Girl?"

"It's what my daddy used to call me." Jenny Girl topped Jake's Manhattan with a cherry and handed him his beverage. "Nineteen dollars."

Jake choked on his drink. He pulled his money clip out and found a twenty but knowing a one-dollar tip wouldn't get answers, gave her two twenties. "Keep it."

Jenny Girl accepted the twenty, held it to her chest and batted her eyes. Jake was in love. Jake took a quick look around the room and stepped into the front room, scanning the room for Scarlet, as described by Jimmy. He saw no one resembling her. Spotting the space at the bar still open in front of Jenny Girl, he decided to make conversation. As he sat down, Jenny Girl spoke first.

"Didn't find who you were looking for?" Jenny Girl asked, making another cocktail.

"I thought I might see an old friend."

"Oh yea."

"Scarlet?"

"Scarlet? You lookin' for Scarlet?"

"Ah yea…Jimmy from Cat n' Fiddle sent me down here." Jake tried to backtrack as Jenny Girl's voice spoke to issues with her and Scarlet.

"Why that fool Jimmy would send you down here asking about that bitch?"

"He said she was working here a couple nights a week."

"She did work here a couple nights a week. She runs with some people I'm not a fan of."

"Did she ever come in with a Mckenna?"

"Mckenna Murphy? I loved that girl. She and I were in art school at OTIS together. Such a sweetheart." Jenny Girl's demeanor changed.

"You know, Mckenna?"

"I did. She's so talented. Lost track of her after school but she came in one night a few weeks back to see Scarlet. I guess she and Scarlet were tight."

All right, all right. This is good.

"You said Scarlet, ran with some …bad people?"

Jake pushed.

Jenny Girl looked around her with a sudden angst in her eyes. "Listen, Jake? I don't know you and …"

"Mckenna is my friend and I'm looking for her, Jenny Girl. On the up and up." Jake bore his eyes into Jenny Girl's and she returned the look.

"I haven't seen Mckenna around for a few weeks. But Scarlet works at Lucky's."

"Lucky's? A strip joint?"

"No, No, it's a club. But Scarlet and Mckenna were dancing over there. Cage dance stuff."

Jake casually put his hand over his mouth and thought about Mckenna as a dancer. He wondered, quickly, if he was going to have to leave that information out of his tale to Tall Mountain. No father wants to hear his daughter is on the pole.

"Jenny Girl, thank you." Jake blew a kiss to Jenny Girl and guzzled his drink. "I gotta go. I'd love to stay and find out more about you and the other Jen's."

"We're here every week, handsome. Come back and give me a few hours with those blue eyes of yours."

Jake ran out of Trocadero, pulling his cell phone from his pocket. Jenny Girl placed her attention to a middle-aged white man entering Trocadero.

"Hey there, handsome," Jenny Girl said.

Jake looked up and down Sunset attempting to track a taxi. He typed into his phone, sending a text into the dark Hollywood night.

I'm gonna be at Frolic Room. I assume you're at Musso and Frank's. Meet me.

Jake hit send.

Chapter Seven

Lamar stepped up into his high Durango, shifted himself behind the wheel and revved the engine. After adjusting his mirror (Lamar had allowed Sophie to borrow his prized possession for a bar supply run) he pulled from his spot in front of Trotter's. He gunned his vehicle down Washington, making a quick right onto Sepulveda.

After Lamar hung up with Pete, he tossed the Trotter's keys to Sophie, giving her the conn until Pete's return. It wouldn't be an issue; Sophie was imminently competent and there was only a couple playing huggy bear-kissy face at table six and Old Man Ginger nursing a beer at the end of the bar. Johnny Rodriguez's set didn't start for another hour or so and by that time, Pete would be back.

Lamar had a quick decision to make; side streets to Hollywood or the 405. Lamar jerked the Durango onto the Freeway entrance lane and immediately regretted his decision. He saw a two-car fender bender had closed up the right two lanes with the Ten interchange just ahead.

"God damn LA traffic," Lamar lamented to himself.

He willed his Durango two lanes west, believing the constriction would relent and he'd get a go at the 405 til he reached Santa Monica Boulevard. As he drove, he smiled to himself, thinking on the phone talk with Pete.

"Now don't be thinking too much on this," Pete

cautioned, as he explained to Lamar the world they were entering, case wise.

Pete alluded to the fact that Lamar was a better fit in partnering with Jake, at this juncture of the case. Lamar had chuckled at the circuitous, round-about, back-handed compliment.

"Well, get your ass back here. Sophie gonna need your help," Lamar had responded with a giant grin on his face.

"You can't tell me what to do, convict," Pete growled.

Pete had been correct. Lamar certainly knew the texture and terrain of the world they were entering more than the former detective.

"Former detective." Lamar thought aloud. "Always gonna be 5-O."

Lamar had never been a Hollywood club guy, but he knew the shades of the spectrum more than Pete ever would. To help pay the bills, when he first moved to Los Angeles with the boys, Lamar had done some security work. His record aside, it was perfect work for him and he for it. Always smiling with a delicate hint of menace, Lamar could be gracious and scary all at once; affable yet frightening.

He'd worked the door for a number of hot spots in Santa Monica and Hollywood, and he was still a recognizable face. His day job had been as an aide to Jake when Jake worked his stories. Jake's stories often took him into the mouth of madness and Lamar and Pete always had his back. He'd never failed, but he wished he'd been more insistent of his position during the Benitez fiasco. Lamar knew the dark places of the world that swallowed people whole. And he'd known *that* story was going to end badly.

For as long as he could remember, Lamar had been the biggest kid on the block, and the classroom, and, ultimately, the cell block. He always laughed at the words that rang true to his life. "If you call your mom, sister, and your grandma, Mom… you going to jail."

For the most part, that had been true. Lamar did call his mom, Pam, but it was his Aunt Clem he called Mom. Mama Clem, he called her, Clem being shy of Clementine. Lamar never knew his real father, but he knew he musta been one big son of a bitch.

"No need to speak of your daddy," Mama Clem would tell Lamar as he stood next to his cousin Peanut.

Peanut was Mama Clem's only progeny and whatever DNA Lamar used from the Wagner DNA pool none was saved for poor Peanut. A runt from the birthing doctor's slap, Peanut followed and idolized Lamar. Lamar was a gentle, kind-hearted hulk of a human and he didn't like to fight none. But Peanut had the Loki in him with a chip on his shoulder the size of his Napoleon complex. Whatever check's Peanut's mouth bounced, Lamar covered, and Lamar covered a lot of bad checks. Lamar ended up fighting plenty and he was sure good at it.

Lamar was raised in the South Bronx, not too far from where Jake had spent his harrowing year in 1998. He, Mama Clem and Peanut lived in a Forest Housing projects bonded by Trinity and Tinton Avenues on a stretch near 163rd street. He grew up and was raised there eventually attending South Bronx High School with Peanut until they both dropped out after the sophomore year of school. Well, one dropped out. The apartment was not a big place and was even smaller during the brief stretch that Pam lived there.

It would have been Lamar's fifth grade year. Pam had always been a solitary, lonely figure to Lamar. A shimmering wraith that once had been a swan, Pamela Wagner had been a beauty of the Bronx, at a young age. Lamar never investigated much into the past of his mother, but he did recall once seeing a picture of an eighteen-year-old Pam with a twenty-some old Clementine.

"She was beautiful." Lamar remembered.

Dazzling blue eyes in sharp contrast with the ebony darkness of her skin. Lamar had the same eyes but not the sadness. Even in the picture, Pam's eyes held sadness.

What was your sadness, Mama?

Lamar often felt her sadness and never truly felt any love from her. Only once could he remember her even giving him a gift. He'd returned from school one day to find a tiny Gnome doll sitting on the table with the name Lamar written on the back, in pen. It wasn't much of anything to look at, just a Gnome. It had that wretched face with purple hair with silver streaks. Mama Clem told Lamar his mother had seen it at a corner store and bought it for Lamar. It was Lamar's pride and joy.

Pam either was never home or slept always in her room with the door shut. Mama Clem did the cooking, the cleaning, worked two jobs and did all the mothering for Lamar. It was not until years later that Lamar came to understand that his mother was a heroin addict, and her sanctuary was behind her closed door.

Lamar recalled one distant memory when he was age ten. Lamar sat at the tiny, rickety card table Clem utilized as a kitchen table.

"Oatmeal," Lamar spoke out loud as he merged onto Santa Monica Boulevard. "I was eating oatmeal."

Pam entered the kitchen, silent, gliding into the midst. As Lamar ate, she gently touched the back of his head, putting her hands through his hair, ever so sweetly. Lamar couldn't recall ever receiving a hug, a kiss or even a touch but here she was, caressing his head.

"You've got your daddy's hair," she spoke barely above a whisper. And just like that, she disappeared, back to her sanctuary and her medicine.

A few weeks later, she disappeared for good. No explanation given and none asked for, from Lamar. But she'd taken his Gnome, the one she'd bought for him. At first, Lamar was angry, believing she'd selfishly taken the only gift she'd ever bought for him. But he came to realize, she took it to remind her of him.

****

After Lamar's freshman year at South Bronx High, Peanut's trouble making ways took a turn to the severe. Lamar barely recognized his little cousin; the sweet, mischievous Loki had turned a nasty corner. Following a harrowing assault on the vice principal, Peanut was expelled from school. After his expulsion, Peanut would stay out later and later until some nights, he didn't come home at all.

Lamar began to work at a corner, family-owned, little grocery store up Third Avenue owned by Mr. Wilson. Mr. Wilson was a life-long resident of the Bronx, and he had owned the store for forty years. He treated Lamar very well and often added some groceries for Lamar or an extra fifty on his paycheck. Lamar would come home around nine or ten and would often beat Peanut home. One Wednesday in February, Mr. Wilson asked Lamar to deliver some groceries to an elderly customer who struggled to leave home during the winter. It was following this delivery, that Lamar spied Peanut with Quincé, a member of the Dominican gang, 42's.

Quincé's reputation had traveled to Jackson Avenue and all Lamar knew was that Quincé was not only a drug dealer but a sociopath. Rumor had it that Quincé sold dirty needles to desperate junkies, making a quick buck. Lamar wondered how many AIDS victims had acquired HIV from an infected Quincé needle. As Peanut and Quincé milled around the corner, Lamar hid around the corner and despite his size, hid quite well. As Peanut and his friend stood on the corner, a pair of junkies approached and as Quincé stood silent, Peanut brokered the drug deal. Lamar closed his eyes and slammed his fist into his thigh. Lamar understood Peanut's late hours; he was now a Clocker, a corner drug dealer.

When Peanut returned home, Lamar put him into a serious chokehold.

"Are you fucking serious?" Lamar whisper slash yelled, so as not to wake Mama Clem. "A drug dealer?!? That's how you pay mama back for all she done?"

Peanut struggled and yanked a Butterfly knife from his winter jacket, slashing Lamar's forearm. It was the first act of violence the two had ever committed against each other. Clutching his torn arm, Lamar stood face to face, with the scared Peanut.

"Lamar," Peanut gasped, holding the bloody knife in front of him.

"Get out of here, cousin." Lamar's normal cheery voice was cold as the sharp wind outside of the apartment.

"Lamar, I'm sorry..." Peanut set the knife on the

table. Lamar grabbed it.

"Don't come back. Don't come back until you back to being Peanut."

Peanut slowly snuck toward the door with a heartbreaking sadness in his eyes. He stole at glance at Lamar and Lamar turned away. Peanut opened the door and ran away. Lamar grabbed a tea towel from near the sink and wrapped it around his arm.

Peanut had escaped from Lamar's clutch and run from home, not to return. As Mama Clem worried, Lamar searched, hoping to see if he could instill some of the old Peanut into his cousin. After a month or so, Lamar had found him holed up with the 42's. Peanut was one of them now. It was just Mama Clem and Lamar now.

****

As Lamar continued to drive toward Hollywood, he played back some memories in his mind. As Lamar worked for Mr. Wilson, his interest in school completely disappeared. He went less and less and finally just stopped going. Mama Clem was getting older and working two jobs was taking a toll. He began to take more hours at the store but still had plenty of idle time.

"Don't you be thinking you gonna hang around the house, all day long, Lamar," Mama Clem chastened Lamar. "Go get a job with that new minister at New Saints."

Reverend Donnie Chalk came to the South Bronx from Philadelphia and began to put a stamp on the neighborhood. Lamar went to visit him and soon enough, he was working for him. It wasn't a paying job, but it did provide meals for Lamar and Mama Clem. Lamar didn't have any interest in the New Saints newspaper or the

Anti-Violence programs', in fact, he had no interest in the politics of anything.

But he did enjoy helping with the Soup Kitchen and found, his most rewarding job, delivering food to the end stage AIDS patients of the neighborhood. It was rewarding, but humbling and sad. Three days a week, he'd deliver food to people whom he realized may be dead by the end of the week, if not the day. When he first worked the delivery route, he focused on being friendly with the patients but as patient after patient died, he hardened.

It was the dead cold of winter in January; Lamar couldn't recall the year. As he delivered on his route, he noticed a new address, which meant a new drop and AIDS patient. No name was attached to the address, merely an order of Minestrone soup and a grilled cheese sandwich, one of the staples of the delivery service. The address was on Tinton in a housing project reserved for the most indigent of people. Lamar usually reserved a new address for the last stop of the day and this day would be no different.

As he arrived at the tenement, he climbed the steps of the stoop and hit the buzzer of Room 343C. After a few minutes without response, he struck the buzzer again.

Perhaps the poor soul has already passed.

Lamar's thoughts were interrupted by the return buzzer sounding off, indicating the gate was open. Lamar pulled open the gate and entered.

The structure smelled of old urine and decay and as he entered the front foyer, a homeless man lay asleep in the corner by the elevator. The elevator displayed a sign, made from the back of a Budweiser Box, and written in crayon, which read: NOT ACESIBLE. As Lamar stood in front of the poorly spelled sign, he heard a door creak behind him. It was the door to 4A. An elderly black woman peeked her head out from her apartment and quickly shut the door at the sight of the massive Lamar.

"Old people and AIDS patients," Lamar whispered aloud to himself.

As he passed from the second floor to the third, he nearly stepped on a young junkie, napping on the steps with the tourniquet still wrapped around his bicep and the spike still in his hand. Above the sleeping junkie, on the wall, was a poster with Nancy Reagan saying, HUGS NOT DRUGS. Written in day-glo marker next to the picture of Nancy were the words: 'FUK U OLD BITCH'. The sickly boy sat serenely, his head resting on the concrete wall, eyes closed; Lamar continued on.

Reaching the third floor, he walked the twists of the maze of the building until he reached Room 343.

"New Saints," Lamar called out, knocking on the door. He touched the door handle, and the door opened.

Lamar hesitated at the door to the apartment as it opened before him. He could already sense the scent of impending death. It was an acrid, sweaty smell that stung the eyes. Lamar took a deep breath and entered the apartment.

Stepping inside, the stench really struck him. The windows, obviously closed in the heart of winter, left no draft and lights were all off. It felt like walking into a coffin to Lamar. With the curtains nearly pulled all the way closed, a sliver of light from the grayness of the New York sky snuck in. Lamar made his way to the pitiful little kitchenette area and placed the brown bag of food on the counter.

"Uh…your food is on the counter." Lamar couldn't wait to leave that hole of death. He quickly turned to leave the apartment.

As he stepped past the window, he briefly followed a streak of light, catching a shelf on the left side of the apartment. He wasn't quite sure what exactly caught his eye, but he stopped. He stepped back into the light, such as it was, and looked at the shelf on the far wall. He recognized a shape of familiarity. He cautiously stepped toward the shape and reaching the shelf wall, with astonishment, saw the Gnome Pam had given him so many years before. The Gnome sat upright on the shelf, staring at Lamar as if unsure of its long, lost friend.

Horrified, Lamar reached forward and gently grabbed the tiny doll. He flipped the doll over and saw a faded LAMAR, written on its back. It was his Gnome. The hair was the same and the face hadn't changed.

"Mama," Lamar barely rasped.

Holding onto the toy, he stepped farther into the apartment. He walked back toward the back room. He tiptoed or approximated a tip toe for a man his size and crept toward the room. The door to the bedroom wasn't closed and Lamar, looking into the room, could see that a window showed light to the tiny bed in the corner of the room. A cocoon of clothes huddled in the corner, opposite the bed.

Lamar could barely make out a skeletal figure, asleep under a solitary bed spread on the bed. Lamar snuck slowly toward the bed. He knelt next to the figure and saw the face of his mother, Pam.

"Mama." Lamar whispered. Pam's eyes fluttered ever so slightly, and she opened, a tiny bit, her magnificent blue eyes. She looked up at the giant that had become her son, standing over her and a brief smile crossed her lips.

"Lamar…be a good boy and close the curtains, please." And with those words, she closed her eyes to sleep.

Lamar knelt next to his sleeping mother for an hour or so until the light of the descending day crawled into darkness. He silently wept, as tears of sadness, anger, torment and despair raced down his cheeks until the tears struck the woeful bedspread.

Lamar didn't return to deliver food for a week to Pam's place as the horror of seeing the dying remnants of his mother struck a mighty blow to his soul.

But he pulled himself together on the last day of February and took the walk to Tinton to deliver. Stepping onto Tinton, he approached the tenement and spotted an ambulance in front of the project with two white, EMS men, loading a gurney with a covered body. Lamar knew.

In his own mind, a coward, he hid himself from view until the men finished loading Pam and drove the ambulance away. He waited outside of the complex until an inhabitant exited the building and Lamar was able to sneak in. He made his way to 343C and entered the open last resting place of Pamela Wagner.

He stood in her shabby little room, staring at the bed that had held her last breaths. He didn't cry. He didn't speak. Before leaving the apartment, he saw the Gnome on the shelf, nearly laughing at him. Lamar grabbed the Gnome and tossed his childhood toy to the floor, beating the inanimate object with his massive bare fists until only tiny bits of plastic were surrounded by purple and silver hair. He never told Mama Clem of her sister's fate and he had never told another soul of the events of those days.

And life carried on. Mama Clem got older and moved from two jobs to one. Lamar became a more active member of New Saint's and worked more and more hours with Mr. Wilson. Mr. Wilson trusted Lamar and their mentorship became more of a friendship with Mr. Wilson taking on the role of a father figure. A few years passed and though the world seemed small, Lamar had a niche. 'Big Lamar', as he was called, was a respected face and person.

And then one day, Lamar came home to find Peanut sitting on the stoop of their building. As Lamar walked closer toward Peanut, he could make out the black and blue markings on Peanut's face. Someone had tuned him up pretty well.

Peanut stood up and made as if embrace Lamar. Lamar placed his enormous hand on Peanut's chest.

"Nah man," Lamar forcefully told Peanut.

Peanut backed up and placed his hands in his pockets. Peanut eyeballed the long scar on Lamar's forearm, a reminder of the knife slash from a few years prior.

"Looks like it healed, all right." Peanut pointed toward the scar.

"Whatchu doin' here, Peanut?"

"Just in the 'hood."

"Seeking sympathy? Looks like someone had a disagreement with your face."

"Just a misunderstanding."

"Nah man, punching you in the arm." Lamar smacked Peanut in the bicep with his right paw, hard. "That hit is a reaction to a misunderstanding. That,"

Lamar said, pointing toward Peanut's face," means you fucked up."

Peanut rubbed the spot on his arm where Lamar smacked him. He sat down on the stoop.

"I fucked up. I really fucked up." Peanut held his chest.

"And you came here. You thinking…time has passed…."

"You're my family, Lamar. Mama…. Ask about me?"

"Not no more. She think on you, though. That I know."

"Well, I think about her all the time. And you." Peanut sniffled. Lamar sat down next to Peanut and a tear fell down Peanut's right cheek.

"I'm sorry."

"What you sorry for?"

"Everything. The way I treated Mama, the… the dealing. What I did to you."

"Uh-huh," Lamar stood again. "Now here comes the part where you ask for that favor."

Peanut stood up, walked past Lamar, and began to pace.

"I fucked up a drop."

"Whatchu mean?"

"I fucked up a drop. One of the *42's* got killed and I lost some money."

Here it is.

"How much?"

"T-twenty," Peanut stammered.

"Twenty G's?!?"

Peanut hung his head and nodded.

"Dammit, Peanut."

For a second, as Lamar drove down Santa Monica, he chuckled thinking that his cousin had started a shit storm by losing twenty thousand to the *42's* and here, all these years later, Jake and his fifty G debt might have started a new shit storm.

"Song remains the same," Lamar spoke aloud as his Durango passed through West LA.

He went back to thinking on the past.

"I know, I know. And now I'm in the hole with Quincé." Peanut started to cry. Lamar grabbed him by the shoulders and shook him.

"You gotta keep it together, brother. Why …. There's more isn't there."

"Yes. There's more."

As Lamar sat and listened, Peanut went into detail on how now he would have to run a string of jobs to pay back what was lost but nothing could pay back the loss of the *42's* member. Lamar knew that no matter what Peanut did, they would kill him.

"You need to get out of town, Peanut. Tonight."

"Nah man. That can't happen."

"Why not?" but a thought started to form in Lamar's mind.

"Quince´… knows where you and Mama live."

And so there it was. Peanut's recklessness had put a marker on Lamar and Mama Clem. Peanut begged forgiveness, while at the same time explaining that Quince´ wanted, nay demanded, Lamar's help in the next set of jobs. After nearly an hour of begging and pleading, Lamar got to the gist of it all.

"You need to meet Quince´ tomorrow. Or he's gonna kill me, you and Mama."

That night, Lamar rested in bed, wide awake and

staring at the ceiling. He ran scenario after scenario through his mind and every scenario ended with the death of him and his family.

He would meet with Quince´ but in the end, he knew, nothing would ever be totally right.

And meet with Quince´ he did. The next afternoon, Peanut walked Lamar into the *42's* den on 144th and Third.

For such a thug, Quince´ was uncommonly short. Maybe five foot three, but the menace dripped off him and his disreputable reputation was warranted. He sported a blue basketball sweat suit with Knicks moniker on the back that hung off him so much that only his reputation kept Lamar from calling him a kid. Quince´ surrounded by two, much taller gang members, was verbally and physically admonishing a third gang member.

On his knees in front of Quince´, the bloody nosed, black eyed Dominican kid was actively crying as Peanut and Lamar entered the back room of the *42's* hang-out. The kid wore only a white undershirt, soaked in sweat and blood with bloodied and muddied jeans and a pair of Jordan high tops. Posters were plastered on the walls of the room; the film posters were of mob and gang movies. Quince´, upon seeing the much larger Lamar enter the room, bitch slapped the quivering victim at his feet. Quince´ shoved the kid to the ground and kicked him in the ribs.

"Take this shit outta here," Quince´ ordered his two henchmen. The henchmen obeyed and dragged the poor little *42's* member from the room. Quince´ lifted a small towel from the couch in the corner of the room and cleaned his bloody knuckles.

"You want something done right, you do it yourself. Wouldn't you agree, Lamar?" Quince´ asked Lamar.

"I got no argument with that."

Quince´ chuckled and stepped up into Lamar's face. Peanut stood behind Lamar's left shoulder.

"Has this little *pendejo* explained the situation?"

"He told me enough."

Quince´ looked past Lamar to Peanut. "So, you know he's my bitch. I own his ass. But I can be gracious."

"That's good to know," Lamar replied.

"All I need is three to four jobs handled and he's free. Once again in my good graces." Quince´ put his finger into Lamar's gigantic chest, cocking his head to the side.

"And until those jobs are done… you're mine as well."

"Just fucking tell me the job."

"All business. I like that. We got one preliminary job before we get to the meat of the jobs." Lamar looked to Peanut.

"One preliminary job?"

"Yes, Lamar. To prove your loyalty." Quince´ walked to the closet by the couch and opened the closet door.

He pulled three handguns from the closet. He handed the guns to Peanut and Lamar. Lamar felt the weight of his gun and knew it wasn't loaded.

"You ever handle a gun?" Quince´ asked Lamar.

"Yes."

"No matter, you won't be using yours. Only mine is loaded."

"You're going on the job?" Peanut asked.

"You want something done right." Quince´ loaded a clip.

Lamar closed his eyes a second. He knew the probability of him moving beyond these sad days' activities were limited. Peanut had condemned him to a life he never would have pursued. But he was doing this to protect Mama Clem and to a lesser degree, Peanut.

"What's the job?" Lamar asked.

"We're going to hold up Mr. Wilson's store on Third."

****

Quince´ provided them with ski masks and explained that the store would be empty from two to three, which Lamar already knew. They would enter, guns drawn, pull Mr. Wilson from the cage and Quince´ would take the money from the drawer. It wouldn't be a bad haul, but the money was secondary. This was all about seeing if Lamar had the stones and if he could be loyal to Quince´.

The drive to the job was surreal. As Quince´ drove through Lamar's home neighborhood, he tried to focus on the job ahead and the scenarios. Technically, he would be masked so Mr. Wilson may not know Lamar but with Lamar's size and gait, it seemed likely Mr. Wilson would.

Lamar knew that, somehow, he needed to get Quince´s gun. But if he did get it, what would be his plan of attack? Lamar did everything he could to remove the thought of committing armed robbery against Mr. Wilson. He'd come to look at the man as the father he'd never known and now he would be committing the ultimate betrayal. He briefly hoped that Mr. Wilson wouldn't be working but he quickly remembered the only other staff was him.

True to form, the store was empty and suddenly they were there. Quince´ ran into the store and fired a gun shot toward the back fridge reserved for sodas and a can of Seven-Up shot out all over the door of the fridge. Peanut guarded the door and Lamar stood guard over the middle of the store. Alarmed and frightened, Mr. Wilson stood behind the caged counter with his arms extended up. Quince´ pointed the gun through the screen, right into Mr. Wilson's face.

"Open the cage, motherfucker, or I'll blow your fucking head off," screamed Quince´.

Mr. Wilson froze. Controlled by terror, Mr. Wilson did nothing. Whatever occurred inside Mr. Wilson's mind came crashing down. He went into an almost catatonic state and was laid siege by fear. He didn't move.

"Motherfucker." Quince´ fired the gun into the ceiling so that large chunks came down in clumps.

Lamar stepped closer to Quince´, who was losing his patience.

"Fucker, I'm gonna count to three and that fuckin' cage better be open or we gonna see brains sprayed!!!"

Lamar panicked and made a decision. It wasn't even a bad decision. It was the only decision to be made.

"Mr. Wilson! Open the god damn cage!" Lamar yelled at Mr. Wilson. Mr. Wilson seemed to snap from his daze.

"Lamar?" Mr. Wilson asked hesitantly, lowering his arms.

With a mention of his name, Mr. Wilson had transformed a bad situation into a nightmare. Though his face was hidden behind the mask, Mr. Wilson knew who was behind the mask.

An ocean of disgrace struck Lamar in his solar plexus and he knew immediately that eviscerating that guilt would take a lifetime. A look of fear crossed Mr. Wilson's face. He knew he'd made a mistake.

Quince´ laughed at Lamar. "Motherfucker. Motherfucker recognizes you."

"I won't say anything," Mr. Wilson offered, opening the cage and stepping out.

Quince´ struck Mr. Wilson with the butt of his gun. Mr. Wilson fell to the floor. Blood poured from his nose. Lamar, incensed, took a step toward Quince´ but Quince´ whirled and pointed the gun at Lamar.

"What the fuck you gonna do? You got no motherfucking bullets in that motherfucker."

"Quince´… don't do this," Lamar pleaded.

"Don't do what? I ain't done a damn thing. You done this." Quince´ kicked Mr. Wilson in the ribs and the older man cried out.

"Please," Mr. Wilson pleaded, "Please don't kill me."

Lamar took another step toward Quince´. Quince´ wasn't having it.

"Don't take another step, Lamar. I'll blow your fucking head off."

"Leave 'em be, Quince´. The cage is open. Get the money and let's go." Peanut spoke up.

"Nah, it ain't that simple. Lamar been spotted." Quince´ pointed the gun at Lamar.

"So, here's what it is, Mr. Good Guy. I could shoot this old fucker in the face and we split. Or. I can kill your dumb ass but if I kill you, Ima kills Peanut as well. It's your decision, Lamar. Who dies, who lives."

The rage built in Lamar. It seared inside of him with every millimeter of stomach acid burrowing a hole in his stomach. But he controlled it. It was that one decision time for Lamar. His stomach calmed and he took a deep breath. He knew who he was, and he knew who he wasn't.

Lamar pulled off his ski mask and stared right into the camera in the center of the cage. He waved at the camera.

"What the fuck, Lamar," Peanut screamed.

"Dumb motherfucker," laughed Quince´. "You dumb motherfucker. Now I gots to kill you. Then Peanut and probably this old man."

"Leave him be, Quince´," Lamar spoke with a suddenly deeper voice.

"Leave him be? Man, how dumb are you? Runs in the family. Just like your mama." The rage that had built in Lamar's gut appeared on his face. From a distance, he could hear police sirens.

"Don't talk about my mama."

"Not Mama Clem, asshole. She's a righteous bitch. I'm talking about your real moms. Look at you. So, pissed but can't do nuthin. You know I knew your mama. She had a nasty habit and I fed her. She'd do anything and I mean anything."

Peanut walked up behind Lamar and touched his shoulder.

"Don't Lamar," Peanut whispered.

"She did my whole crew. I mean the whole motherfucking crew. But man, eventually, that horse takes a toll. I couldn't even get it up for her. So, I sold her some of my real cheap special needles. You know which ones I'm talking about."

Lamar looked down at the floor as the sirens, still a few blocks away, were clearer.

Quince´ laughed.

"That's right…. I sold your mama her death needle."

Lamar rushed toward Quince´; no thought, nor worry nor care about the loaded handgun aimed at him. It would take more than a handgun to bring him down.

And then, the first miracle happened. Quince´s gun jammed. As Quince´ attempted to fire, the gun clinched up and wouldn't fire.

Lamar reached Quince´ and knocked the gun from his hand. Using the gun Quince´ had given him, Lamar pistol whipped Quince´ across the face, striking him on the bridge of his nose, which exploded with cartilage and blood. Lamar's open palmed smashed Quince´ in the face and he fell where he stood, splayed next to the bloody Mr. Wilson. And Lamar struck him in the head with the pistol again and over and over and over. Lamar beat him with bare fists and knuckles until Peanut grabbed him screaming.

"We got to get out of here," Peanut screamed.

Mr. Wilson struggled to his feet and stood next to Lamar. "Lamar," Mr. Wilson spoke gently and placed a hand on Lamar's shoulder. Lamar dropped the gun. "You better get going."

Lamar looked up at Peanut who was waiting for Lamar. Lamar shook his head. "Nah. I'm ready for the consequences," Lamar matter of fact intoned.

The sirens were one hundred feet from the store.

Lamar sat down next to the unconscious and badly beaten Quince´. Peanut sat down in the aisle of the store and held his head, sobbing. Mr. Wilson sat across from Lamar and looked at Lamar, not with disappointment but with the love of a father to a son.

"I'm sorry, Mr. Wilson." Lamar mournfully spoke.

"My name is Ira, Lamar." And there they sat as the cops entered. And then the second miracle occurred. The arresting officer was Detective Pete Mills.

****

Lamar and his Durango stopped at the stop light at the intersection of Wilshire and Santa Monica. To his left sat the famous Trader Vic's. Lamar stared aimlessly at the Los Angeles institution and put aside his memories. He smiled.

"Let's go help Jake."

Chapter Eight

Frolic Room. Musso and Frank's. The Formosa Café. Chez Jay. Tiki Ti. Dear John's. The Mermaid, Joe Jost and The Harbor Room. These were old school legendary spots, where the ring-a-ding crowd of the 50's slugged down bourbon and bad gin while dancing to music of sock hops and swing. The history was sunk into the cracks of the floors by the likes of the Rat Pack and molded into the walls by the men and women who made these spots timeless. One could almost see Johnny Stompanato goosing Lana Turner in the corner of The Frolic Room.

Jake stared at the imaginary scene from his bar stool at The Frolic Room. The legends were gone now; all that remained were memories, stories and pictures of dead people on the wall. Jake stirred his drink aimlessly, listening to the mindless conversation near him. He'd made a career eavesdropping. Secrets had been something people yearned to share with Jake since he was a boy. He knew more about his mom than Father did in certain areas and vice versa. People just wanted to offer tidbits of info to him, but not only that, his keen sense of hearing and eerie ability to listen and glean at just the right time, paid dividend time and time again.

Jake could remember the night of a Policeman's Formal Ball, where he caught pieces of a conversation between Assistant District Attorney Art Simcox and a comely opposing counsel. Simcox was making a concerted effort to get in the pants of this opposing counsel and dropped info that discrepancies in daily reports coming from LA's Robbery-Homicide had led to the creation of a joint Task Force of LAPD, ATF, San Diego PD, DEA and potentially FBI. Alphabet soup. The project was being pieced together to ferret out the guilty parties and it was believed that one of the heavier Mexican cartels, may have a mole in the police force.

Jake had nearly choked on his drink and after telling Lily to get a ride home with her girlfriend, he bailed on the shindig to find his editor, Eddie Collins. This moment had led to Jake's investigation into the cartels and their foothold in, not only the Los Angeles law enforcement community, but possibly the local government. Jake parlayed that little tidbit from Simcox and his friendship with undercover Gang and Narcotics officer, Zubin Poosh, into access to the Task Force, along with Pete and Lamar. Somehow, he'd made it happen over the strenuous objection of the LAPD. Somehow, he'd made it happen.

Jake mined, for years, mindless conversations but after slipping into the hospitality industry, he'd learned to despise his skill at overhearing. He didn't care about Minnie's problems with her dipshit boyfriend; he had no interest in knowing about Jenna's kids or Randy's cheatin' hoe of an ex or yada blah blah blah. He just didn't have the compunction to care about other people's lives, but he couldn't stop listening. Or hearing.

The night's innocuous conversation Jake latched onto, as he tried to focus on anything else, involved a real estate developer. Dane the Developer was attempting to cajole himself into the leggings of a well-endowed, fortyish, housewife named Maureen, a Boomer name if ever there was. Maureen herself endeavored in the real estate market and considered herself an up and comer. She was celebrating a recent victory (selling a spot in the Hollywood Hills to billionaire, Eric Portek) and enjoying a night on the town with her girlfriends.

As Jake shook his head to wipe the voices from his head, he felt a hand gently grasp his shoulder. Jake turned to see the smiling countenance of Eddie Collins.

"Eddie," a smiling Jake spoke, standing up from his bar stool. Jake extended his hand to shake.

"Gimme a hug, you moron." The six foot three but fragile, Eddie gripped Jake in a tight embrace.

It had been seven years since they'd seen each other or spoken. Many moments of disappointment, resentment, torment, misunderstanding and sadness in thoughts between the two former colleagues. Eddie, staring at the bruising on Jake's face, grabbed Jake's jaw and took a better look at the black and blue. He let go with a hint of sadness.

"You need to stop betting. Jesus, Jake, who do you owe, Frankie Fairway?"

"Tony Tahoe and he didn't do this."

"Ah. This has the look of one Peter Mills."

"Maybe it was Lamar," Jake retorted.

"You're not dead, so it can't be Lamar. He could take your head clean off. You need to borrow money?"

"That's not why I texted you, Eddie." Jake laughed. "Still looking out for me, eh?"

"Always." Eddie gripped Jake's shoulder with a fatherly touch. He took the bar stool next to Jake, as Jake sat down.

"I know you still go to Musso and Frank's."

"Yep, still do, still do. It helps make the early part of the week tolerable. Imagine my surprise to hear from you, Jake."

"Yeah well…" Jake lost his words.

An awkward silence ensued and grew resembling the time gap between the once close friends.

"What brings you out here, Jake? This is a little out of your bubble." The bartender, a young, thin Asian man, of millennial age, approached and pointed at Eddie. "Vodka martini. Cold, if you please," Eddie ordered. The young man walked away to appease.

"Do you remember Ed Tall Mountain?" Jake asked.

"Sure. A casino big shot in the desert. You were friendly with him, I believe."

"With his family, not so much with him. How about Joseph Smith?"

"Tommy at the paper told me he bought it in a car wreck last month. Tribal CEO, right?"

"One and the same."

Eddie's drink arrived and he took a sip. He gave Jake a sharp look. "You bleeding me for some scoop for another organization?" Eddie asked with piercing clarity.

"What? No. Just making with the yakity yak."

"No, you were responding to my inquiry. And now you're hedging, which makes me a little anxious. Jake, no one has been worse at subterfuge than you. You getting back in the journalism game?"

"No, no, no, I'm not writing… I'm… I'm on a case." Eddie leaned back and laughed.

"What's so funny?"

"Jake Hansen, P.I. I like the sound of it."

"Shut up." Jake spoke, rolling his eyes. "Ed Tall Mountain hired us."

"To do what?"

"His daughter Mckenna is missing. And Tall Mountain is putting his name in the ring for Tribal leadership."

"Ahhh political hijinks. Those boys play rough. Joseph Smith was no saint. He ruined a couple of his friends and cronies fifteen years ago when he became head."

"Have you heard the name S. Newman?"

"Can't say I have. You want me to run a search on him?"

"Would you?"

"For you, of course. But all I can do is show you the lines. You need someone to see between the lines and fill in the gaps. You need JR."

Jake closed his eyes.

"You haven't spoken with him, have you?"

"No." Jake shook his head.

"Dammit. You need to apologize to him. Seriously, Jake. He idolized you. He looked up to you and when the shit hit the fan, he took the fall and you never once reached out? Apologized, nothing?"

"I know, I know. I know."

"He's gone underground with his skills, but he still has them. I use him from time to time." Eddie took a sip of his drink.

"You ever run into Lily?" Jake peered up at Eddie.

"Lily." Eddie absently stirred his martini.

"Yea, yea, Lily."

"Can't get her out of your mind?"

"Christ…could you?"

"'The eternal sunshine of the spotless mind.'"

"Ugh, you and Alexander Pope." Jake laughed.

"She wanted a clear break, not just from you from herself. For her to mentally and physically toss you aside and to delve one hundred percent into Alex, she needed to erase everything. A physical and mental ghosting."

"And she did. Have you seen her?"

"Of course. At functions. She is married to the mayor of Los Angeles who has designs on the Governorship." Eddie stared at his drink. "Nothing personal or social."

"How's Gracie?" Jake changed the subject.

"Gracie's terrific. She made it to the top of the board. Thirty years with that company…first woman in sales to first woman on the board and now she's the Chair."

"I read that. You gotta be proud, Eddie."

"I'm busting, Jake. The shit she took as a woman. The sideways glances, sexual innuendos, private harassments….to accomplish…" Eddie became a little choked. "To accomplish what she's accomplished…"

Jake clapped him on the knee. "Good for you. And Gracie, old man. How much longer you got in the game?"

"Next year."

"Next year?!"

"Yep. Gracie is gonna take a step back and I'm gonna put in my papers."

Eddie Collins had been a part of the fabric of the newspaper for more than thirty years and Jake couldn't imagine that newspaper without him. He'd spent the last twenty as managing editor and was the lifeblood of the paper.

"Just like that, snap of the fingers and it's over?"

"Not exactly. I nearly quit once, although the board

was thinking of firing me."

"When were they thinking of firing you?"

"The Jake Hansen fiasco of 2004."

"You hired another Jake Hansen after I left."

Eddie Collins gave a small, sad smile at the attempt at a joke.

"You didn't leave, Jake. You were fired."

A shroud of cloud emerged over the two longtime friends and colleagues as the reality of their separation stood square in front of them. How many times had Jake placed the name Eddie into his phone with the desire and need to speak with his friend? Too many times to count, but he always backed away, scared of comeuppance. And how many times had Eddie wondered about the health and well-being of his friend, Jake? More times than not, more than once a day. It was Eddie who broke the silence.

"You could have stayed on the story." Eddie took a sip of his martini.

"What?" Jake sounded surprised.

"We… I wasn't going to kill the investigation. You just didn't have it."

Jake sat upright in his chair and cocked his head.

"You said the story was dead."

"No, no I didn't. I said I wasn't releasing your story for that edition. I told you that you didn't have it. Yet. *Y*et. And you didn't. And instead of putting your head down and finding the story that was still there to be found, you sulked and committed the dumbest act I've ever seen a journalist make. And then you tossed yourself into a bottle, tossing aside nearly everything in your life. You had pieces, Jake, and yes, some of those pieces were amazingly damning."

Jake dropped his head at the weight of his friend's words. He'd known this moment would come but truly wasn't prepared for such real criticism.

"Martin Cruz was dirty. Is dirty." Jake pointed at Eddie, and Eddie smacked the finger away with annoyance.

"Maybe, but you didn't have ample proof. How many sources did you have? Huh? Yes, I do believe the cartel or cartels have an 'in' on the force and maybe more than one."

Jake, surprised, shook his head.

"But you...."

"Jake, as God is my witness, if you had the story cold, I would have released it. Yes, yes, there was pressure from my higher up's and yes, the board was very nervous, but if you had the sources and the story was one hundred percent solid, I would have released it."

Jake sat back. He played the moments of that day over in his head. Was this a revisionist version of the truth?

"But... you said the story was dead."

"No. No, I never said those words. Dammit Jake! I would have released that piece. I had your back, god dammit! You just didn't trust me or have patience. I didn't care if the paper got sued. I would have had your back and the devil take the hind most." Eddie finished his Martini and motioned to the bartender for two more drinks.

"You never reached out...you never checked in on me. You abandoned me, Eddie." Eddie delivered a sharp smirk with his shake of the head.

"Strong words from somebody who betrayed his job, his principles, his friends, his scruples."

"Fuck you. I lost everything. My job, my career, my-my… my wife."

"And who lost it, hot shot? You've spent seven years pointing fingers and blaming others. You've disintegrated into an alcoholic gambling addict. At what point do you take responsibility? Do you accept *no* culpability? Have you? Ever?" Eddie's voice rose enough so that the bartender took a glance. Eddie gave the bartender a sharp shake of the head and the man went back to polishing glasses. "Dear God, Jake… look at your world."

Jake sat quietly, running Eddie's words through his mind. He hadn't been thinking clearly that day after Pete delivered the pictures of Lily with Alex Vila. And perhaps his judgment was at an all-time low. Jake snuck a peek up at Eddie who was stirring his martini with a half-chewed bleu cheese olive. This man had been his idol, his friend, his family. And he had hated him for seven years. Why tonight of all night's had he contacted this man?

"If a man wakes up and goes on his way to work at…say eight a.m., he stops for coffee at a coffee shop. Let's say the barista is an asshole to him. She's a perfect stranger. He's never met her, and she's an asshole to him; then that bitch is an asshole. The man then goes to the gas station. He's out of gas and it's been a tough morning and at the station, the gas attendant is an asshole to him. Well, perhaps this attendant is also an asshole. But, as the day goes on and everyone the man meets and sees and every place he goes, he sees nothing but assholes? Well, at some point, it becomes clear…"

Jake smiled. "He's the asshole."

"Correct. You blamed everyone, and you've blamed

everything for your troubles except the one person responsible for all your travails."

"Me."

"Jake, I always looked at you as a protégé. Someone I could teach and help grow. You became almost like a son to me. How could you think I would go out of my way to sabotage you?!?"

Jake had imagined this conversation over and over for years but always with the conclusion and optimism that he was right, and the words would be of his triumph. But now, he knew the words of knowledge were from Eddie Collins and they were words he needed to acknowledge, years prior.

"I can sense this case of yours has you on the right track. I remember the look in your eye when you were on the hunt."

"It's leading me somewhere."

"Hopefully, it leads back to you. Anything I can do to help?"

"S. Newman?"

"I could do that. I'll call Tommy and you... talk to JR."

"I know," sighed Jake.

"Go to JR and apologize and explain. He revered you."

"I know, I know."

"He'll be back on your side in a heartbeat." Eddie stood and slugged his drink. As Eddie looked around the room, he saw Lamar enter.

"Ah good, you and Lamar tonight. I wish I was young enough to come along for the ride." Eddie reached into his wallet and tossed a hundred-dollar bill onto the bar. "You should start writing again. Do a blog, write about your case. Talent shouldn't be wasted."

Eddie reached down and extended his hand to Jake. Jake stood and wrapped his arms around his old friend.

"I'm sorry," Jake rasped.

"It's okay. It's okay. Gracie still asks of you. You need to come over and play Mah Jongg."

"Maybe I will, maybe I will."

Eddie smiled and headed toward the entrance.

As he approached the door, he came face to face with a surprised Lamar. Eddie extended his hand and Lamar shook it.

"Keep an eye on him, Lamar. He's the closest I've ever come to having a son."

"Me too." Lamar smiled.

****

Hollywood and Vine is a den of spots. On the northwest side a recently defunct club, behemoth rested quietly at night as the new tenants remodeled. Hollywood is dotted with an omnium gatherum of lots that cater to the highest price genre of real estate in the Southland: Parking. If ice sold at liquor stores is the biggest rip off (it's literally water, cold and time) parking is a close second. Jake and Lamar were arguing over where to park and who paid.

"We need to get to Lucky's," Jake presented.

"It's a three-block walk," Lamar replied.

"What if we have to grab her?"

"Whoa, what do you mean, grab her?" a taken aback Lamar responded.

"We need to speak to Scarlet."

"All right, so we talk to her."

"What if she doesn't cooperate? What if she's... we need to speak to her," Jake emphasized.

"And who's gonna do the grabbing?" Lamar asked. Jake shrugged his shoulders toward Lamar, fully indicating what Lamar already knew. "Stop right there, motherfucker, you know I have a record and I'm the only black guy in our crew. This still is LA."

"Sooo you see we gotta move the Durango?"

"If I gotta do the grabbin'…" Lamar offered, and Jake rolled his eyes.

"Fine, I will pay for the parking. I thought you were gonna talk me out of moving the car."

In the end, they moved the Durango. They continued to argue the merits of who would pay the outrageous price of parking as Lamar drove west on Hollywood, onto Highland and spotting a lot.

"Where's the club?" Lamar asked.

"Back a block."

"Wait, I thought you said it was on Cahuenga?"

"I told you where it was!"

"Shit."

"Shit? What? Don't say shit."

Lamar smiled a big grin. "We shoulda stayed at that last lot."

"Lamar!!!" Lamar put his head on the steering wheel and laughed hysterically.

"Asshole," Jake mumbled.

"I'm just breaking balls, son." Lamar pulled into the new lot and handed the keys to the lot attendant, as he got out of the car. Lamar pointed Jake out to the attendant.

"He's paying." Lamar smiled.

"Slippery motherfucker."

As Jake and Lamar stood outside, across the street from Lucky's, Jake tapped his foot nervously. He pulled one of his last cigarettes from his old pack and lit it.

"What time is it?" Jake looked at his cell phone. The phone read 12:08 a.m.

Lucky's was one of the 'of the moment' clubs that popped up in Hollywood and had a very short shelf life. Jake had caught a hint of the club's name a few nights previous when two customers at Trotter's talked about the cage dancers at Lucky's moonlighting at Plan B on Pico. He had tossed aside their discussion, another example of him trying to end his 'over hearing' habit. Now he'd wished he'd listened more. He knew he and Lamar weren't dressed for clubbing and they needed to gain access. A line around the corner developed as creatures of the club scene raided the newest and shortest tenured Hollywood club.

"I know, I know more about Hollywood than Pete, but this ain't exactly my scene," Jake mumbled.

"I'm glad we wore jeans. No shorts getting into that place." Lamar idly spoke, focusing on the surrounding scene.

Lamar scanned the front of the lines and looked at the door staff, hoping to see familiar faces from when he worked the clubs. His gaze circled the block and spied an alley.

"This way." Lamar clapped Jake on the shoulder.

Jake grabbed his shoulder, in pain. "Hey," Jake cried out, "you guys need to lessen up on those smacks."

Lamar took a step into the street with Jake behind him. As they crossed the street, Jake couldn't help but make out the dynamic of the long and winding line from the front of Lucky's around the building. The not quite eclectic group of attractive female clubbers, mixed with the Metro and the effeminate, Interpol style dressed crew with a sprinkling of Latinos, Persians and Asians were a sharp dichotomy to the desperate souls interspersed along the streets, the homeless and indigent. Jake found it striking to see the two worlds so closely intertwined yet so far removed from each other. He tried to toss the thought from his mind, but he connected way more with the homeless than the bourgeois tag.

Lamar and Jake walked along the crowded Hollywood street toward the neon sign reading: LUCKY'S. The long line fed into another line inside a confluence of velvet ropes manned by four extremely large men: three Black men and one insanely short and squat Samoan. They were all decked out in black suits with black shirts and black ties. Each wore an earpiece which had an attachment attached to their belts. As Jake and Lamar approached the front of the line, the large Samoan smiled at the presence of Lamar. The Samoan's face lit up from a frowned, intimidating disposition to an eager, excited bright visage in point two seconds. What he didn't have in good looks, he had in personality and he had a face like a fist.

"Lamar." The Samoan smiled and waved at Lamar. Jake gave an impressed facial expression. Lamar returned the smile and wave.

"Sexy Time," Lamar, answered with a questioning lilt. Lamar led Jake to the front of the line and gave Sexy Time a big bro hug.

"Sexy Time," Jake murmured. Lamar gave him a quick 'Shut the fuck up' glance.

"Damn Lamar." Sexy Time squared up to take a long look at Lamar, "You trim down a bit?"

"Nah man, I put on twenty pounds."

"Really? Probably all in the dick, right?"

"That's what's up." Lamar laughed as Sexy Time bro hugged him again.

"What brings you down these parts?" the jovial Samoan asked.

"Is Big Tim working this club?"

"Big Tim, you know he is. He's around the side door."

"Thanks, Sexy Time. We gotta hook up soon." Lamar tossed the last words behind his shoulder as he led Jake away.

"Big Tim runs a poker game, you gotta join in," Sexy Time called out as Lamar and Jake rounded the corner.

"Sexy time?" Jake asked reluctantly of Lamar.

"Long story, Jake, long story."

"He didn't seem too sexy."

"You're a writer, ain't ya. You should understand the concept of irony."

Lamar and Jake stepped into an alley and saw a side door thirty feet away from the main drag. It was a very dark alley, but a silhouette of an extremely tall and large individual was visible.

"I assume that's Big Tim?" Jake inquired.

"With that silhouette, damn straight."

As they approached, the dimensions of Big Tim came into sight. Big Tim was every bit of six feet nine and three hundred forty pounds.

"Holy Christ, Big Tim doesn't do justice," an awed Jake spat out.

"Timmy played Tackle at OU during the last days of Barry Switzer. He may be big, but he's fast as a cat." As they got to within ten feet, Lamar called out.

"Big Tim!" Big Tim jerked his head around and saw

Lamar and a huge smile crossed his face.

"Nah, that can't be my boy, Lamar." Big Tim stepped away from his post and gave Lamar one of those brief but forceful 'bro' hugs that only straight men do.

"Big Tim, this is my boy, Jake Hansen." It was Jake's turn to be bro hugged.

"What brings you down to 'wood? Heard you was near the beach."

"Little east of that but sure. Me and Jake on the job."

"On the job? That, sound like cop talk."

"C'mon Biggy, you know I can't be no cop. We just tryin' to find someone. You know a Scarlet?"

Big Tim whistled. "Trying to find a Scarlet? Aww you like them hot and expensive."

Lamar let out one of his jovial laughs. "Nah, it ain't like that. She knows a girl we looking for. Mckenna."

"Damn man, you like them smoking hot. And shit box crazy."

"You said expensive?" Jake asked. "We heard Scarlet just danced here."

Big Tim looked around himself to see if there was anyone else in the vicinity.

"Yeah, she just dance here. Always the north wall by bottle service. She is a piece of ass." Big Tim opened his mouth again but quickly shut it.

"C'mon man, whatchu know?" Lamar playfully tapped Big Tim on the shoulder.

"Well…word is, she does some afterhours work for some of the boss' friends."

"Hooking," Jake interjected.

"Not exactly. Little after hours den." Big Tim looked over his shoulder.

"What about Mckenna?" Lamar asked.

"Another hot item. She and Scarlet BFF's. But she ain't been around last week or so."

Jake pointed to the door behind Big Tim. "Can we get in through there?"

"Surely."

"We need to ask Scarlet some questions," Lamar began, "nothing rough or troublesome. Just a few questions."

"And you need some privacy?" Big Tim understood the beat Lamar was dropping.

"Yea."

"No one comes out here unless I say so. Just knock four raps on the door and I'll let you out. Keep watch out too if you need."

"We need." Jake smiled.

"Anything else, Lamar, you my boy. I gotcha."

"Which one is Scarlet?" Lamar asked.

"You'll know which one she is."

Lamar and Big Tim bro hugged, and Tim opened the side door to the club. As Big Tim held the side door open, Jake and Lamar entered.

And just as quick, Jake felt like a salmon out of water. He had never been a club guy; bar guy, yes but club guy was an altogether different beast. The blinding strobe lights seemed to announce Jake's arrival as the swarm of dancers coked and Molly'd out buzzed all around them. A cacophony of blitzing lights, music and people overwhelmed Jake.

The club was situated in an almost cliché set up with a stage housing the Steve Aoki acolyte of a DJ with his stupid spiky hair and a swarm of attractive groupies, flush with sleeve tattoos. It appeared as if the fans of an X Games in Breckenridge had gone on a road trip and ended at Lucky's. It was a gathering of the International Brotherhood of Douchey Punks. Beneath the stage, a circle built on stadium seating built upon itself as an amphitheater. Revelers danced as if to avoid being struck by the flash of strobes, pulsing with a spasmic frenzy. From Jake's vantage point, the dancers appeared as tiny raindrops, wet rivulets shimmering down a windshield illuminated by the influx of day-glo lights.

Lamar gave Jake a nudge, as Jake realized he was standing in everyone's way. Jake led Lamar through the throngs along the edge of the dance floor. Cute cocktail servers circled the room with their tiny round trays, serving drinks that looked like a *Miami Vice* explosion. Jake could make out the multiple bars at the far edges of the room toward the front of the club.

Jake pointed to the corners of the club, focusing on the four large cages. Each cage was inhabited by a striking young female, but one. The west cage had a gorgeous, Asian female with pigtails, dressed in a tight yellow bikini, shimmering and shaking. She entranced about twenty men beneath her, who threw all sorts of bills at her. The east cage held a tall, well-endowed black girl with an afro straight from a 70s Blaxploitation movie. She was able to do a handstand and drop it into a split. That received the inevitable tossing of cash into her cage. Her tiny, baby blue outfit fit her curves nicely. The south cage was occupied by a hyper, athletic blonde female with a short bob haircut, who danced with a robust energy. The north cage was empty. Jake pointed to that cage.

"That's gotta be Scarlet."

And then she entered the fray.

The fit, young Scarlet had black hair, with an

attitude of a strut and glided through the center of the crowd, dressed in a sequined bikini top with tight and tiny, biker shorts. Her pristine face radiated everything but a smile, and it was as if she was alone in her own world. As she stepped through the crowd, everyone's stared transfixed, female as well as male. Lamar used his chin to get Jake's attention, but Jake's attention was already gotten. He couldn't take his eyes off her, bewitched as he'd ever been in his life.

"Girl lithe and tawny," Jake whispered to himself. "The sun that forms the fruit, which plumps the grains, that curls seaweeds, filled your body with joy and your luminous eyes and your mouth that has the smile of water."

"What was that?" Lamar screamed.

Jake shook his head.

"Nothing. Just…. Nothing."

Truth be told, Jake could not tear his eyes off her and yes, despite her obvious beauty, it wasn't as animal as that. She reminded him of someone. He stared and stared and as she entered her own cage and shut the gate, her head facing him and, for a second, it was as if she was looking through him. And he realized she looked like Lily when he had fallen in love with his ex-wife.

"Jake, doesn't she—"

"Yes. A little."

"A little?!?"

And Jake watched her dance, as men and women fawned over her and she closed her eyes to drown the surroundings around her. He watched as she illustrated all the moves taught and learned and he did his best to remove thoughts of his ex-wife from his mind. After a time, Lamar leaned forward and stood close enough for

Jake to hear him.

"She came from the employee room over there." Lamar pointed toward a door near the side door they'd entered.

"I'll catch her attention," Jake said and started to walk that direction.

Jake stood, awkwardly, in the hallway by the employee door. Directly opposite the employee room, was the Women's bathroom and Jake did his best to not appear as the worst type of voyeur, which he, in truth, was. As Jake looked at the ground, to not arouse suspicion, Lamar, five feet from Jake, let out a low whistle. Jake looked up and saw that Scarlet was leaving her cage.

She emerged from her cage, grabbing a small towel from one of the rungs. She quickly stepped toward them, so quick that Jake scrambled to remember the plan. She picked up her pace as she reached verbal distance.

"Scarlet?" Jake hesitantly asked. There was an instant kismet.

"Get lost loser," she spat, wiping the sweat from her brow, and pushing past him.

He realized no one was around them.

"Scarlet, we're looking for Mckenna."

At those words, Scarlet stopped, and held her towel over her mouth, briefly. A look of fear crossed her face and Jake staggered as to his next words. At his hesitation, she dropped her towel and started to run but ran smack into Lamar's chest.

"Nothing to be running from, sweetie. But I think you best talk to us." Lamar spoke with a soothing tone, but he placed his gigantic hands on her arms. She looked down and saw the big mitts grabbing her and she screamed.

A moment of amazing fortune occurred as the song playing over the din, at that exact moment, let out a piercing wail, drowning out Scarlet's scream. Lamar put his big paw over her mouth and carried her the few feet to the side door.

"Knock on the door! Jake! Hurry up! Knock on the door four times," Lamar yelled as Jake ran past and knocked on the door forty times.

Big Tim opened the door and seeing Jake and Lamar, forcefully carrying Scarlet, let them outside.

"Jesus, fuckers!" Big Tim spoke with authority, shoving them out of the door and into the alley.

Out into the night, Scarlet kicked as Lamar carried her into the alley. Jake followed, cautiously looking around.

"Yo man, I can't be…" Big Tim stammered.

"It's cool, Tim, get your ass inside. This won't take but a minute."

Nervous, Tim saw Lamar motioning with his head and acquiesced. He entered the club through the side door.

"Listen, missy, we're not here to hurt you." Lamar firmly held his hand over the mouth of Scarlet.

"This is not good. Lamar, this is not good," Jake nervously uttered. Scarlet's eyes were racing back and forth, staring at Lamar and Jake.

"Shut the fuck up, Jake. Scarlet, honey… I'm gonna take my hand off and you best not scream."

"Hold it," Jake said sharply." Not yet."

"Jake…"

"Just give me a sec!"

"We ain't got a sec! A cop or Sexy Time comes

down here and we got problems, real fucking problems."

Jake crouched down and looked into Scarlet's scared eyes. "Scarlet? We're not trying to hurt Mckenna, we want to find her and help her. I was friends with her brother…Moro."

And with that, Jake had spoken the magic words. Slowly, a look of relief crossed Scarlet's face. Lamar removed his hand. At first, Scarlet said nothing. She looked at her surroundings and at the chill of the late night, September air, attempted to cover herself.

"Why did her brother commit suicide?" she asked with her voice thick with fear.

"Because Moro's father had disowned him. For being gay."

Scarlet shook herself loose from Lamar. She seemed to relax.

"Do either one of you have a smoke?" Scarlet shivered.

Jake reached into his pocket and pulled his last heater out for her.

She trembled, placing it into her mouth and Jake lit her cigarette, his hands also trembling.

"What are you guys…cops?" Scarlet asked and looked at them.

Lamar smiled and looked at Jake.

"Far from it, Scarlet, far from it." Jake also smiled.

Scarlet looked up at Jake and their eyes met. She held his gaze for a second and smiled. "You're Jake Hansen, aren't you?" Scarlet looked Jake up and down.

"That's me."

"I thought so. Mckenna has a thing for guy's whose name start with Z. Zane and Zach."

"Pretty sure Jake starts with a J."

"Yea, but she had a thing for you too. She said it was the eyes." Scarlet looked to Lamar. "You must be Lamar."

"In the flesh."

"Where's the other big fella... Paul?"

"Pete," Jake answered.

"Yea Pete. She was scared of him."

"That's cuz she's smart." Jake laughed.

"She can't be too smart if she's hanging with me. I don't know where she is. She was scared. Said she couldn't go back to her apartment. She stayed with me for a few days. but she disappeared five days ago."

Jake sighed. Okay, he thought, we have a new timeline.

"Five days ago?" Lamar asked.

"Do you know what she was scared of?" Jake held Scarlet's gaze.

Scarlet took a long drag off of the cigarette.

"She wouldn't tell me. Said it was better I didn't know. She quit Barnacles... and I got her the job here. But a few weeks ago, she started acting skeevish. Something was spooking her."

"Any boyfriends ... stalker types?" Lamar asked as Scarlet looked at her feet. She fidgeted and flicked her cigarette. "I think you better spill." Lamar's voice changed from friendly to fatherly.

"I introduced Mckenna to Zachary. That's how she got the job here."

"Zachary?" Jake asked.

Scarlet tossed her cigarette to the ground with disgust. She shook her head and held herself a little tighter. "Zach's buddy owns this club. I think Zach's family might be an investor or something. I got Mckenna the dancing gig, but he also has another business on the side."

"The afterhours club?" Jake asked, knowing full well the answer.

Scarlet nodded and wiped the tear from her eye.

"Zach was a party friend. Once he trusted me, he started getting me special gigs. I don't know if Mckenna ever worked for him on his special gigs, but she was going down the same path. And she did a few of the afterhours with me."

"Ahh," Lamar said, with a slight hint of disgust.

"The money's good. Maybe I wasn't the best friend to her… but…" Scarlet trailed off.

Jake gave Lamar a stern shake of the head. "Where can we find Zachary?"

Scarlet wiped her eyes and gave her hair a slight toss. She took a deep breath and grabbed Jake's hand, leading him and Lamar back toward the club. As the side door remained open, Lamar bro hugged Big Tim.

"Everything cool?" Big Tim asked.

"As cool as it can be." Lamar smiled and stepped into the club.

Scarlet led the two of them through the crowded floor of Lucky's until she reached a clearing. From there, she pointed to a bottle service area toward the back of the club. Scarlet pointed where a short, thin, olive-skinned fella sat with five other guys, all of whom looked like they could be brothers. At the table was a nearly full bar of high-end vodkas and whiskeys.

"They are Armenians. From Glendale," Scarlet said. She pointed to the tall one in the middle, wearing the black suit with a red tie. "That's Sam, he owns the club. Young kid but his dad owns a few dealerships.

Northridge, maybe. The one to his left… that's Zachary."

Zachary wore a sharp club suit, with a square in the front of his jacket. His black hair was spiked up in the typical douche mode and Jake took an instant dislike to him. Scarlet leaned up close to Jake.

"He's been running an afterhours club on Beaudry," Scarlet whispered.

Jake could smell her body and he was unable to not become aroused.

"In Koreatown?" Jake asked, surprised. "He's running an afterhours club in Koreatown?!?"

Scarlet delivered a sharp look to Jake and Jake quieted down, realizing his voice had carried.

She leaned up near him. Scarlet whispered in Jake's ear. "I'll be back in a sec." Scarlet ran off toward the employee room.

Lamar watched her run off and lifted his hands, in confusion to Jake. Jake waved him off and focused on Zachary. After a few minutes, Scarlet returned and stood close to Jake. She grabbed his hand and wrote an address on his hand.

"This is the location of the Beaudry spot."

"You gonna be there tonight?"

"Yea, I'll be there."

She reached into her cleavage and pulled two plastic cards, one black and one silver. She placed them into Jake's hand; he could feel the heat from her body on the cards and a buzz of excitement, again, stirred in him.

"Listen, to get in, the password tonight is Casanova nine."

"Charming." Jake smiled.

Scarlet put her hand into Jake's and touched the

cards.

"This black one will get you past the first door and the silver past the second. I got your names in my phone, from Mckenna and I'll get you on the VIP list. "

"Why… why…?" Jake stammered.

"I assume you want to talk to Zach. This is the best way to get him alone. He's always around those guys except in that club."

"We don't even know if he knows anything about Mckenna."

"I know he knows something. The last time I saw her, I saw her with him. And she disappeared. I just… I just want to help." Scarlet's eyes dropped and Jake could tell that was her 'tell'. "I don't think Zachary's as dangerous as he thinks he is, but he has connections. And he will have two guards with him. Both armed."

"Terrific. Thanks for the tip." Jake looked at the cards in his hand and looked into Scarlet's eyes.

"Where will you be?"

"Probably with him. If I'm not involved."

"Gotcha."

Scarlet kissed Jake on the cheek. "Be careful. The place is heavily guarded. But if you want to find Mckenna…."

"I'll bring my best man." Jake smiled looking at Lamar.

Lamar rolled his eyes. Jake slapped Lamar on the back, blew a kiss toward Scarlet and they headed to the exit. As Jake reached the front door, he snuck a peek back and saw Scarlet enter her cage and begin to gyrate, her eyes solely focused on him.

Chapter Nine

For Detective Danny Burkle, it had been a lonely couple of weeks, but she had endured. Granted, she held the distinction of 'new kid on the block' and she had many hurdles to clear before she'd earn the respect of the distinguished team, but she'd swum in these waters before. Her first few weeks at the Academy, years prior, had been a sad period of solitude but she found herself as unwilling to branch out to her classmates as those classmates were willing to accept her. That wasn't the whole story and wasn't all true.

Danielle Burkle had been Homecoming Queen who did some model print work as a teen. Never one to focus too highly on her looks, she was a little embarrassed when her mother shoved her in front of the camera. After high school, she'd graduated from Long Beach with Honors in Criminology and instead of marrying her college sweetheart, having kids, and starting a family, she dumped Greg Davis of Palos Verdes and enrolled in the Los Angeles Police Academy. Her parents objected strenuously, to no avail, as they didn't see police officer as a career that fit their image of their daughter.

Danielle was determined to prove her mettle and worth. After the first day of the Academy, she knew her looks, blonde and blue eyed, would be met with little to no respect and her first day, her instructor called her 'Barbie'. That night, Danielle walked into the bathroom of the dorm and, using her own scissors, cut her hair short. Danielle entered the bathroom, but Danny emerged. Now, her classmates weren't intimidated by her looks; they thought she was nuts. But she won respect and eventually, friends. Jimmy Kodaira at Major Crimes was her classmate and still remained a confidante.

Perhaps, the fact that she was so tight with her brethren, at Gang and Narcotics Division, is what made the transition, not difficult, but different. Lieutenant Chambers had said all the right things and spoke highly of her accomplishments and citations, but she could feel the chill. Not an overt 'fuck you' but a quietly, casual 'you don't belong here' attitude. She felt that attitude, in various forms, her whole career.

The night she dragged Jameson Everitt, her first partner at GND, to safety after being struck by a meth heads shotgun, the first 'Blues' on the scene handcuffed her, thinking she was the perp and not the officer. Yes, she was in undercover regalia, but she had called out the 'word' for the day.

Now, on this squad, Chambers had run the unit since the IA and public investigation in 2004 after the Benitez Hearings fiasco. That investigation vivisected the proud unit, with two officers forced into early retirement and Martin Cruz being moved to IA, not the most plum of assignments. Cruz had been Frank Allison's friend and partner. And with Cruz gone, Allison went from partner to partner. Still, Allison set the pace for RHD. He was the most senior, experienced and also the best. The rest of the squad looked up but mostly feared him. Known to be cantankerous and moody, with a lightning quick temper, Frank Allison kept everyone on the tips of their toes.

Danny had heard of Allison, everyone had, but meeting him and working every day with him had been a twist as winding as the Monterey Coast. Danny had assumed Chambers had placed her with Allison to partner veteran with nube but through whispers and overheard conversations, she'd deduced Allison had requested the newbie. One could hardly tell, as he appeared to give her minimal glances and less chitchat. After nearly losing her breakfast at the suicide scene in the a.m., she'd been concerned about Allison and her queasy uneasiness. But he had neither uttered a word nor offered an idea that he had been too worried after the initial conference at the scene; in fact, he had been way more conversational after the fact, mooing on about regulations and procedures and the exactness with which he defied both. Still, to this point, they had not had a conversation about each other's person.

That's why she was surprised that after a fourteen-hour shift, Allison asked her if she'd like to join him for a cocktail at the Alibi Room on Washington. Somewhat taken aback, she still accepted.

As she drove her Mazda to the bar, taking National exit from the Ten onto Washington, she mentally visited every possible scenario. Was Allison gonna oil her up with booze and let her down easy that he was moving on to another partner? Was he making a pass at her? Wouldn't be the first time a veteran detective had done so and only once, recently, had she accepted the pass. What was Allison up to?

But, in the end, Frank Allison often went to the Alibi Room for a nightcap and he wanted to get to know his new partner.

"Palos Verdes?" an incredulous Allison nearly spat out his drink. He had two fingers of single malt scotch neat.

"You seem surprised? A blonde, blue-eyed detective sits in front of you and you thought she was from…."

"Aw geez… I… I don't know. I was thinking Long Beach. Maybe… San Fernando?"

"You thought I was a Valley Girl?" Danny shook her head with mock disappointment. She smiled and took a sip of her vodka and soda.

"All right, smart ass, where do you think I'm from?" A hint of red shaded his temples, flush from a flash of embarrassment.

"Hm." Danny stirred her drink, thinking and looking over at the smiling Detective. "I'm gonna say… Hawthorne."

"Really?"

"Yea. There really is no BS about you and that comes from a Blue-Collar background…and…you probably did a tour of duty in the military. I'm thinking Marines. Too young for Vietnam but you joined after. Not a period of time the military was held in esteem by less like-minded people."

Allison stared at his cocktail his brow folded with thought. As he lifted his glass to take a sip, he smiled.

"You read my file."

"No sir. I did not. How'd I do?"

Frank shrugged his shoulders with a dead panned look. "I was in the army. Ranger. During the Cold War part where the war was always feared but never happened."

"Hawthorne was right, huh?" Danny sipped her

drink.

"Very good, Detective. Romero at GND said you were great." He raised his glass and Danny clinked his back.

"How many kids?" Danny asked.

"Three," Allison quickly answered, rubbing the rim of his glass with his index finger. "Two daughters and a boy. You know, we have cases that are the ugliest but a suicide like today…I've seen so many and those affect me the most."

"Really? Why?"

"The utter dark place one has to be…to mentally venture to that place where ending it all is the best choice. No hope, no future, the past is all black and cloudy. I see my kids and I want to remove all thoughts of that darkness."

"What we do is about darkness," Danny offered.

"No, what we do is give a little light to the dark. The pitch evil tunnel where everything caves in…we are the light at the end of that tunnel. We put the pieces together and give answers where none was or maybe will be. A suicide is about no answers. That's why I took you there today. That is the darkness that scares me." Frank took a long swig of his scotch and set his glass down. "I've done this job a long time now and I've reached an age where I know the end is near. I've earned credit to retire."

"Why are you telling me this?"

"As you know, I've gone through…a few partners since Martin's removal. It's my fault, I know. Annie has done her best to remind me of that every time I complain about a new partner. But this is it for me."

"What do you mean, this is it?" Danny inquired.

"What do I mean? You're my last partner. I read

your file, asked about you but I didn't make a decision until I saw you work around the team; Professional and tough. You didn't even lose your chill when Novo gave you that sexist remark. And then I requested to team with you. You're gonna be a great detective."

Danny laughed aloud. "You haven't even barely spoken to me since I joined the team."

"I do have a strange way." Frank lifted his glass again to Danny who cheered him. "To my last partner."

"And my first at Robbery-Homicide."

They clinked their glasses and Frank took a sip of his last drop of whiskey. His phone buzzed atop the bar. Frank looked at his phone and gave it a chagrined look. He picked up the phone and dialed. As Danny gave him a quizzical glance, he held the phone to his ear as the line rang.

"Yea," he spoke into the phone, "Hermosa Beach?" Frank placed a hand over his eyes. "Strange one? Yea, we can help." Frank removed his hand and looked toward Danny. He gave a full smile. "No, we got it. I'll put my best gal on it." Allison shut off his phone.

"My best gal?"

"Yea, I'm not really up on the parlance of our time."

"What's going on?"

"Murder in Hermosa. A little unusual. This could be a good start for the team."

"I got this one. Let's do this." Danny stood, pulling cash from her phone slash purse. She threw two twenties on the bar.

"I'll make sure to invite you more often." Frank made a 'you first' motion and Danny led Frank out the door.

Chapter Ten

"You want to call Pete? Just seems like something we should run by him."

"He'd tell us we should wait."

"Which maybe is the right decision."

"Or maybe… just maybe, he knew this type of situation might occur and that's why he insisted you were the better person to partner with. Tonight."

"So, I'm the irresponsible one?"

"No, but you're also not an ex-cop."

****

Los Angeles nightlife is vastly different than New York City. It's a smash and grab of a city. The bars of Hollywood, Santa Monica and Downtown Los Angeles are, in general, on par with the best New York has to offer but it all closes at two AM. The City of New York never sleeps; Los Angeles dozes after two.

But you can still find some nightlife. The after-party in the Hollywood Hills or you can find some speakeasies in Downtown or tucked away in various parts of La-La Land, but the hidden unknown late-night gem is Koreatown. Little cafes and coffee shops stay open well after two a.m. in Koreatown and the locals like to eat out late. Many of the tiny shops are filled with patrons into the wee hours of the morning. It's as if the Koreans of this neighborhood were members of a cult and only emerged after two a.m. for their meetings. The proximity of Koreatown to Downtown Los Angeles made it a favorite hangout for Jake during his newspaper days. This is how Jake became friends with Luck Kim Pak.

Or to be exact, Luck Kim Pak II or to be even more exact, Little Luck, as he was affectionately known, and which was also the name of his café. Little Luck was a very spry sixty years of age. Luck was born in South Korea during the Korean Conflict and Luck's father, Luck Kim Pak Senior, divided his family, sending his wife and his oldest son to North Korea. This was to ensure that whichever side prevailed, the family legacy would continue. This being the case, Little Luck didn't remember his mother or older brother.

Big Luck Kim Pak was a very well respected elder in the Korean community and became a notorious figure in the Los Angeles Underworld. He staked Koreatown as the base of his operations and became the understood 'Godfather' of Koreatown.

Following Big Luck's death in 1977, Little Luck took the reins of the family business and built the Luck Empire to an even stronger position. Little Luck was a very influential man and earned his heavy legacy built on intimidation and fear. But his brains and negotiation skills created a lasting peace. With the Chinese Triads of Chinatown, the Armenians in Glendale and Pasadena, the Mob along the Harbors and Vegas, Little Luck worked as an emissary and a confidante. He helped create peace where once there was none. The Russians sometimes created a stir, but the scariest lot was the new boys, the Mexican Cartels.

The Cartels were the single most feared crime unit in California and even though most of the power remained south in San Diego and Tijuana, they were felt.

But even the cartels mostly stayed clear of Koreatown. Little Luck had formed a deal with the Armenians, the Triad and brokered a peace with the Russians to keep the Cartels happy but mostly out of the way. Little Luck worked with everyone and all Little Luck wanted was his cut, his territory and freedom.

Lamar and Jake were parked outside of Little Luck's Korean Café, along the street. They discussed the importance of having a word with Zachary Belataka.

"He's the next step. Zane saw Mckenna and he mailed her that package. The last person Scarlet saw Mckenna with was Zachary. He's got ties with—"

"He appears to have ties," Lamar interrupted.

"He appears to have ties to maybe something or someone on that sketch. He's the next guy." Jake looked inside the smallish Korean café and the cafe was packed. The crowd was also one hundred percent Korean.

"You think this is a good idea?" Lamar asked.

"If there's an off-books afterhours club in Koreatown, I don't want to break in unless I run it by Little Luck. I have a good history with this man, and I don't want to jeopardize that."

"And what if he has a piece of that action? What if he's working with Zachary? And if he says no?"

"We'll figure it out. You want to come in?"

Lamar smiled his big smile at Jake. "Come on, man, you know I do."

"Then come on."

Jake and Lamar entered Luck's to the sound of Korean voices and the scene of scared employees running around, busy. As soon as the door shut behind Lamar, the sound of Korean came to an abrupt halt. The nearly one hundred customers all stopped and stared at the duo at the door.

"Man, I'm already creeped out," Lamar spoke out of the corner of his mouth.

"Calm," Jake reassured, although, he himself was creeped out.

Jake quickly scanned the room, staring at the faces staring at him, deciding if they should run for it. He searched for Little Luck and finally found the man. Little Luck sat against the far wall at the back of the room, at a table with four other men. Two of the other gentlemen at his table were older than Luck and held serious looks on their faces. Jake recognized the man to Luck's left, but couldn't, for the moment, place his name. The fourth man, younger than the other three, Jake recognized as Junior Lo.

Junior Lo wore a black suit with a black shirt and aqua tie and looked every inch as frightening as his reputation. The look on Lo's face could be more described as severe than serious and Jake knew, from experience, that the severe look was warranted. Long the bodyguard of Little Luck, Jake learned that Junior Lo had been a cage fighter in the Philippines where the only rule was that only one man walked out of the cage, alive.

Little Luck had aged since he'd seen him last; his hair had gone completely white and he wore very thick glasses. Little Luck stood, with a little difficulty and raised his arms.

"Jake Hansen! Jake Hansen!" Little Luck called out to Jake with a big smile on his face. A wave of relief crossed over Jake.

The customers of Little Luck's Café resumed their prior engagement with their food and drink and the buzz of the room began again. Little Luck motioned for Jake to come over. As Jake and Lamar teetered through the room, clumsily bumping into a few customers, Jake noticed that every table had white tea pots with teacups. Jake knew that 'tea' was the main reason the place was packed.

As Jake reached Little Luck, Junior Lo stood up and waited behind Little Luck. Little Luck gave Jake a half hug.

"My pale Mexican friend with white man last name. I wonder when Jake Hansen walk through my doors again. But I know it happen." Little Luck smiled his smile as wide as the frown upon the other habitants of the table.

Junior Lo made a move as if to frisk Jake and Little Luck placed a hand in front of Junior Lo.

"No, Mr. Lo. This is Jake Hansen, you remember him. He not ever come here to harm me." Little Luck placed a hand on Jake's shoulder. "I knew you'd come see me again."

"Here I am," Jake nervously answered.

Little Luck touched Jake's cheek and shook his head. "Jesus, what happened to your face? You with another man's wife?"

Jake gave his best 'aw shucks' grin and shook his head. "Not exactly, not exactly."

Little Luck focused his attention to Lamar. "And you brought my favorite monster." Luck smiled and placed his hand out to Lamar. Lamar, smiling, shook it. "It is so grand to see you, my friend Lamar."

"You too, sir."

Little Luck's face became serious and looked behind Jake. Little Luck snapped his fingers and two of his female servers immediately raced in front of him. As

Little Luck spoke quickly in Korean, the young female server on the left ran off. After a few more quick words, the other young female server ran off. Almost in an instant, the first server returned with two folding chairs, opening them and motioning for Jake and Lamar to sit. Lamar sat first, his weight causing the small chair to groan and Jake sat next.

"Poor chair," Jake whispered to Lamar.

"Fuck you, Jake," Lamar hissed.

As Little Luck returned to his seat, the old Korean Sphinx to his left spoke in a deep voice and with conviction. His Korean was slow but with purpose. After he spoke, Little Luck responded quickly, and the older gentleman didn't speak again. Little Luck made himself comfortable and Junior Lo sat down. Little Luck stared, smiling at Jake and Lamar for an uncomfortable time.

And then he spoke. "It's been what, four years?"

"Uh...six," Jake responded.

"What's shakin' bacon?"

"Umm... well..." Jake blabbered, and Lamar shook his head.

"C'mon kid. You and me...we go way back. I know you. You give me respect and space and I give you points and direction. You gone a long time but now you here. You back at the paper?"

The second server returned with a white tea pot. She placed two cups in front of Jake and Lamar and quickly poured from the tea pot into the cups. She also, mindfully, refilled the teacups of the gentleman at the table. Except for Junior Lo, who placed his hand over his cup.

"No." Jake looked at the liquid in his cup. "I'm doing some private work."

"Ah." Little Luck clasped his hands together with a look of interest.

"I guess you could say I've," Jake started until Lamar cleared his throat, "Uh…we've been hired to find someone."

"Look at you. You regular Mickey Spillane or Sam Spade. Maybe Kojak."

"Yea…. I guess."

"Drink up. This is our new batch of moonshine. Top notch." Little Luck took a swig of the drink.

Jake smiled a weak smile and lifted his cup to Lamar, who also had a weak smile. They both took sips of their drink and as the moonshine passed their gullet, they each felt the freeze in their throat and stomach. It was a very harsh moonshine.

"Smooth," Lamar choked out.

Jake remained silent, afraid that if he spoke, he might puke.

"Best Korean moonshine in world." Little Luck lifted his cup to Jake. "Now then, I know you owe Tony Tahoe."

"Damn, nothing gets by you, does it?"

"Nothing. You need a loan?"

"No, no, no." Jake feverishly shook his head. "This case should clear me."

"Big money job, eh. So why are you here, Jake? Why you here Lamar?" Little Luck's smile became serious.

Jake had sat down with Little Luck perhaps twenty times. He now remembered the older man to Luck's right was Jimmy Han and Jimmy Han always sat with him, as well as Junior Lo. He rarely heard him speak. Han must have been in his seventies but rumor held it that Jimmy

Han had been Big Luck's enforcer in the 60s and 70s. He always struck Jake as the Asian Luca Brasi. Han, now, stood at three bills on the scale but Jake always looked at the meat hook of hands Han had. Scars crossed Han's hands, similar to the disfigurement of Pete's, but the scars had a different tale to tell. And now, as Little Luck asked Jake his business, he stared down at the killer's hands. Little Luck puckered his face a bit.

"There's an afterhours club in Koreatown, and one of the men running the club is someone I need to—"

"Inquire about," Little Luck interrupted.

"For starters," Lamar answered.

A look of stoicism crossed Little Luck's face. He folded his arms and rocked back and forth for a few moments. Jake could almost see Luck's mind thinking. And a few moments of discomfort elapsed.

"Where is this establishment?"

"It's a large…piece of property on Beaudry. The guy's name is Zachary Belataka."

One look from Little Luck told Jake that he was not aware of the club. Or the location or whatever was going down on Beaudry. Jake began to formulate that the club must move from location to location after a short period of time. He also knew that if Zachary and his clan had not asked permission or had not provided a tithe to Little Luck, this would end badly for them.

"What is your plan for this excursion?" Luck broke the silence.

"Lamar and I go in, grab Zachary and talk."

"Or leave with him," Lamar added.

"Simple. I like simple. Hmm." Little Luck tapped his lip with a finger.

Lamar snuck a glance at Jake, but Jake's eyes

remained firmly on Little Luck.

"Is this club off the reservation?" Jake asked his final question.

Little Luck stood up quickly and although Jimmy Han did not, Junior Lo did. Jake and Lamar also stood. Little Luck stretched his hand to Jake.

"Thank you for your info, Jake Hansen. And Happy Hunting."

This was their cue to exit and Jake would not hesitate. Jake shook Little Luck's hand and Little Luck placed his other hand on Jake's in a form of affection. Jake quickly began to walk out, and Lamar followed. Being dismissed from Little Luck had always meant success. For to not be dismissed would have meant being dragged out and possibly killed.

They exited the café and crossed the street toward Lamar's Durango. Lamar set off the lock and Jake entered the passenger side and closed his eyes. He calmed himself and breathed easy. Lamar got in on his side and looked to his friend.

"Well?" Lamar asked.

"We've got an hour until the storm hits."

Lamar drove off into the night.

****

Lamar parked his behemoth west two blocks from the Beaudry house and behind a black sedan. Jake and Lamar got a brief but decent look at the large property as they passed the Beaudry spot, driving just south of the land. After Lamar had driven down a few blocks, he pulled a U and found his parking spot. Jake rubbed his eyes and looked at the clock on his cell.

Three a.m. Christ.

Lamar pried a pair of tiny night binoculars from his

glove box. He could not remember the exact reason why he'd hidden them in his car, but he assumed with an event such as this in mind. Jake peered through the lenses, staring at their target. Besides it being an inordinately large property for the surrounding area, nothing too much came to his eye; besides the small line of people at the entrance and minus the three security guards walking the parameter, barely concealing their concealed weapons and the two large guards at the front door with a tiny briefcase handcuffed to the shorter one's wrist.

"These fuckers... not playing around." Jake whistled, handing the lenses to Lamar.

"Armenian group. Gotta be connected to Blazerian."

Jake wouldn't want anyone but Lamar Wagner to have his back on a play like this. In 2002 when Jake was investigating the San Pedro Councilman Ramona's connection to a drug trafficking ring at the Harbor, Jake had found himself in a sticky pickle with four unsavory members of the drug ring and they were ruffians. Pete had taken a night off surveillance on Edgar Ramona, so it was just Lamar and Jake.

Cornered in a dark alley near the port, Lamar had taken down all four henchmen in a rumble. Jake's helping had been to hop onto the back of the smallest henchman, pulling his hair. It had not been Jake's finest hour, but Lamar had more than proven his worth. His first step into a right cross knocked out the biggest perpetrator and the remaining goon's reluctance to wind up unconscious next, made them weak and slow. Jake still believed the last guy pulled a Sonny Liston.

Jake played back the words Scarlet delivered earlier on the racier elements of the afterhours spot, but she had gone into neither detail nor specifics. Having seen much of the seamier and seedier sides of Los Angeles, not much surprised Jake, or so he believed. Still, perhaps this wasn't just a straight up 'swingers club' or maybe it was just a normal house party where Scarlet and Mckenna were the party favors, but then, why the security?

"What if it's a fight club?"

"Seriously, Jake?" Lamar eyeballed the house and shook his head, slightly.

"What are you thinking?" Jake asked.

"I'm thinking we need a week to plan this."

"We got an hour. Now, forty minutes. But yea…two stories, ranch style…it's a big fucking space." Jake lamented. "Lotta questions. How many rooms, how many people, how dark is it gonna be? Is it a small scene, do they all have guns? We got no idea what's going on in there? Flying blind."

"Man, that ain't ranch style." Lamar laughed.

"What are you talking about? That's the definition of ranch style."

"Jake, you dumb ass, ranch style ain't two stories."

"The fuck it isn't."

"What the fuck ever, that ain't ranch style."

"You don't know what you're talking about. Anyway…plan?"

"We're just gonna keep it simple, stupid. We gonna be quiet-like, like two gentlemen looking to get them rocks off. We find Zachary and I'm your buddy." Lamar narrowed his eyes.

"Okay." Jake sounded reluctant.

"We find him, and I subdue him."

"Subdue?" Jake asked, knowing full well it was going to come to this. The plan he'd provided to Little

Luck would be the plan. "What do you mean subdue?"

"You leave that part to me." Lamar cracked his neck.

"And I'll be there," Jake added.

"And what the fuck are you gonna do?"

"I can help."

"Uh-huh, how's you trippin' over your feet gonna help? You want to look tough in front of Scarlet."

"There is that."

Lamar looked at himself in the rearview mirror and steeled himself. Lamar knew that this part was his strength. He had the mental capacity to deduce and be every inch the detective as Jake and Pete, but he also had the strength and toughness Jake lacked and the health Pete missed. He closed his eyes channeling his thoughts and energies into the moment.

"Let's do this," Lamar said as he opened the Durango and stepped outside.

Jake fumbled with his door and followed.

As they walked in the street toward the Beaudry house, Jake started to sweat. Whatever they were stepping into, the journey of a thousand steps began at this after hour's party.

"Approach Guards. Be cool. Super cool. Password? Casanova nine. Nonchalant. Not too chalant. Chalant. Is that a thing? Is chalant a thing? No, not a thing. All right be calm. Be calm but not too calm. Excited. Do I want to be excited?"

Jake started to breathe heavily and knew the moonshine was hitting him. Lamar could hear Jake breathing heavily.

"Relax Jake, nice and easy."

"Okay, okay. You ready to do this?"

"It reminds me of something Dinner Bell Mel on the inside told me. Don't tell me how rough the water is, just bring the ship in."

Jake squinted and the creases in his forehead showed. "I can't argue with that, because I got no idea what you're talking about."

As Jake and Lamar approached the front, they were able to get an idea of the security. Two men were operating and guarding the front. Three others were on the perimeter, at the front, a bulky, muscular man with long blond hair, seemed to be in charge. The other male, a Hispanic with no neck, stood watch with a briefcase attached to his wrist. The Scandinavian looking male utilized a long mechanical wand that he ran over the middle-aged gentleman directly in line in front of Jake and Lamar. As Lamar checked out the main guard, he noticed a bulge at his back that was obviously a gun.

Lamar cased the other guards and noticed that one circled the perimeter as the other two were the main watch. They each had an earpiece and appeared to be in constant contact with the other guards. They also had weapons, concealed, in the front of their person. This security was well prepared.

The large blond guard spoke to a balding, white male as he ran the wand and then placed the wand behind his back. Jake heard nary a word as he was lost in his own thoughts. He thought briefly of how this case had moved so far, so quick and the diverse sections of Los Angeles it had led them. He was so lost in thought he didn't hear or see the guard wave them over. Lamar nudged Jake until Jake moved. Jake moved and walked, leading Lamar until they were directly in front of the main guard.

"Casanova nine," Jake fairly shouted at the taken aback guard.

The guard didn't respond. The guard stood at least six foot seven and was three hundred pounds. He had Scandinavian features and gigantic biceps.

"Identification, please." The guard spoke with a slight Alsatian accent. Jake and Lamar reached for their wallets. As Jake removed his ID, his nervousness came to a head.

"What's your name?" Jake blurted, more awkwardly than he'd spoken 'Casanova nine'.

Lamar pulled his ID out and gave a quizzical look to Jake.

"Excuse me," the He-Man looking guard answered, taking both ID's and starting to check them. He pulled up his own phone and a list displayed on the phone.

"Your name," Jake continued.

"Jake," Lamar whispered.

"Jack? Jock. Brock? Brick. Rocko? Rocky? Bill. Ted. Mike. Mick? Mark? Nick, it's Nick. Nicos? Ken, Kenny…" the guard gave a confused and tense look to Jake. "Rocky? It's Rocky, isn't it. Rocky. I said Rocky. I feel like it's Rocky."

"Will you shut the fuck up," Lamar, flabbergasted, finally interjected.

Sheepishly, Jake bowed his head in front of the guard. "Sorry," Jake pitifully got out.

The guard returned the IDs to Jake and Lamar.

"Gunther," the large, Alsatian Guard said.

"What?" Jake replied with a small smile.

"My name is Gunther."

"How did I not say that name first?" Jake hit his forehead with his hand. "Gunther, do you think this place is a ranch style architecture?"

"Hands up."

"Sorry about my friend," Lamar offered Gunther, stepping forward.

Gunther returned with a roll of the eyes. After a wand pass, Gunther waved Lamar away and Jake stepped forward.

"Casanova nine," Jake said.

"Ya, you already said that, little man." Gunther proceeded to wave the wand over Jake. Gunther spent more time with Jake, probing and prodding with the wand as if he were a TSA Agent in Riyadh. "You gentlemen are on the VIP list."

"You sound surprised by this," Jake offered.

"This is a rather pricey item, little man. And with...those beatings on your face, you don't seem to fit the part."

"Oh oooh, you know what we got here, Lamar? Are you profiling my black friend here?"

"He doesn't have the smashed face, little man," Gunther responded. "Whatever, do you have your cards?"

Jake removed the cards that Scarlet had given them, from his wallet and held them up to Gunther.

"Very well. The black card is for the front. This will gain you access to the commons. If you wish to pursue a more...private gathering, the silver card is for the next phase." Gunther reached into his jacket pocket and removed a gold card, similar to the black and silver cards. "This is your VIP card. This is for the final access point."

Jake reached to grab the gold card from Gunther, but Gunther held fast to the card, with a powerful grip. After a few awkward moments, Gunther let go and gave possession to Jake.

"Enjoy your evening, gentlemen." Gunther bowed and focused attention to the black man behind Jake and Lamar.

"Thank you, Gunther." Jake smiled and walked past the guard with a sigh of relief.

"It's not ranch style," Gunther spoke after them.

Both Jake and Lamar stopped walking in their tracks.

"Pardon?" Jake asked.

"It's not ranch style. Ranch style is only one story."

Lamar and Jake quickly walked away.

"Step one," Lamar whispered to Jake.

"Jesus, what are we doing," Jake gushed.

"What are you doing? You got to calm the fuck down. Anyway, too late to back out. Unless you want to take a beating from these guys and still discover nothing."

There was absolutely no sound coming from the inside of the building. The sound proofing of the property had been impeccable. Jake stood, motionless in front of the doors. He took a deep breath in and let it out.

"One, two, buckle my shoe..." Jake whispered aloud, his many times used, go-to mantra.

Jake looked at the solid metal door, with a touch pad and swipe to the right of the door. Jake took the black card and swiped it down in the touch pad. A green light flashed, and the handle snapped up.

"That's our cue," Lamar prodded, and they entered the Beaudry house.

After running through scenario upon scenario of what he anticipated the place to hold, the initial room bore little resemblance to the boundaries of Jake's imagination. It appeared to be a simple club with a couple hundred revelers.

As Jake and Lamar entered the large room, they could barely make out the long, sleek bar running down the west side of the room, as the pitch darkness of the room was lit by a bright series of strobes that flashed colors of pink, aqua and green. Three attractive female bartenders, dressed in leather chaps and bustiers, served cocktails with gaudily clouded dry ice to what seemed to be a rather middle-aged Persian crowd.

As European techno music blasted in synchronicity with the light show crushing the room, Jake was able to make out three elevated cages, hanging from the ceiling, with scantily clad, female dancers. The dancers gyrated in such a manner that Jake wondered if this was their swing shift after Lucky's. In the middle of the room, a make-shift gazebo was occupied by two, borderline underage girls, dancing in red leather teddy's, dancing and making out with each other in full grope. Jake scanned the room for any sign of Mckenna or Scarlet. Lamar came up on Jake from the left side.

"They're not in here," Lamar shouted into Jake's ear.

Jake searched for the door to the next room. A young, Latina, with a beauty mark on her lip, passed him wearing very little, and caressed his face as he walked by. Jake, momentarily, forgot the plan.

"Jake!" Lamar yelled above the din. "Focus!"

Jake snapped out of his Latina daze and came back to the moment. He scoured the east wall searching for door number two. He eventually spotted a sheer metal door, toward the back of the room. He lightly nudged

Lamar in the back and maneuvered his way through the drugged crowd of dancers. Jake bumped into a well-dressed man wearing a harlequin hat, snorting cocaine with his long pinky nail. Coke flew into the air. The man turned to yell something but saw Lamar and thought better of it. Lamar shoved past the angry snorter.

"I haven't seen this many drugs in a long time," Lamar called out to Jake.

"You should get out more." Jake laughed, although, he too, had not seen this much in a while. He seriously wished to take a hit of Molly and enjoy the show, but duty called.

After a few minutes, they squirmed their way to the door. Jake took a quick glance at the insanity and hedonism of the room and swiped his silver card into the touch pad to the right of the door. The green light flashed, and the duo pushed into the second room.

The second room was a blinding white hallway. The white walls were bleached pale with bright, white lights screaming from the ceiling. There was no clearly discernible sound in the hallway and no sound coming from the previous room, only the humming of the bright lights. The long hallway ran down a corridor, which ran ever so slightly to the left. On both sides of the hallway were large bay style windows, showcasing an event occurring in the room behind the window. In front of each window, rested a lounge chair. Three men and a woman were sitting in various chairs at various windows, all sitting absorbing the show they were witnessing.

As Jake and Lamar ambled through the hallway, they approached the first window. A white male in his sixties, wearing a Seer Sucker suit of baby blue and white, sat upright, in the chair in front of the window. Jake and Lamar briefly stood behind the chair and the man and investigated the room. Through the window the room showcased a naked young white male, strapped to a bed in the middle of the room with a very shapely, large breasted female, totally naked except for a Carnival mask, using a large Gothic candle to drip hot wax on the naked young man. Though he couldn't be heard, the mouth motions of the young man indicated that he was in some distress.

"Man...this is creepy," Lamar whispered. Jake looked at the older gentleman enjoying the festivities. The older man had a dastardly smile of voyeuristic excitement.

"Where's your will to be weird, Lamar?"

"I think I left it at home."

As Lamar moved toward the next window, he grabbed and pulled Jake by the arm. They proceeded to the next window, where a beautiful, middle-aged Asian woman, dressed in a black lace dress, sat on the chair in front of the window. The Asian woman had her right hand up her skirt. She made moaning and giggling noises as she witnessed the show. Despite his efforts, Jake couldn't help but feel an arousal mounting up in him.

The window revealed a large, six foot six, two hundred fifty-pound, football player of a black male, naked, fucking a tiny, young Asian girl from behind. The girl could not have been more than twenty years of age. There was a bed in the middle of the room and the Asian girl had her hands resting on the end crest of the bed, as the black male mounted her doggy style. In the far corner of the room, sitting on a comfortable love seat, a fully dressed white male, dressed in a white suit, watched the coitus while smoking a cigarette.

"Jesus," Lamar exclaimed.

"I know," whispered Jake," he's wearing white after Labor Day, what the fuck is that?"

Lamar giggled toward Jake and shook his head. Jake presented a wide smile.

"Hey, if you need a job, that guy seems to have a pretty good one."

"I wonder what the qualifications are?" Lamar asked.

"I would say for this room, being black and owning a gigantic dong."

"I'll get my references together."

Lamar and Jake passed the remaining rooms with nothing but quick glances. One room highlighted a quintet orgy of mixed races and genders, and another room displayed a woman in her seventies orally pleasuring a young man in his twenties.

"Let's get to that last fucking door." Jake shuddered.

Jake had tried to focus less on the hedonism and more on the faces and had not seen Mckenna or Scarlet. Or Zachary.

"If Zachary is here, it's gonna be behind door number three," Jake reasoned.

They finally reached the final door. They looked back down the hall of ribaldry and shook their head in wonder and a little amazement.

"Man, I don't even like steam rooms," Jake exclaimed.

"I'm sure it's a few trips to become comfortable." Lamar smiled. "Listen, if he's here behind this door…we're not leaving until we either talk to him or get him out of here."

"Lamar, there's a lot of territory between here and the entrance."

"You let me worry about that. And follow my lead."

Jake pulled the gold card Gunther had given him and held it next to the touch pad to the right of the door. Jake took in a deep breath and sighed.

"One, two, buckle my shoe…" he spoke as he placed the card in an electronic device. The familiar green light lit up and Jake, with a quick glance to Lamar, opened the final door.

The room was not nearly as bright as the hallway but was bright enough. The second Lamar and Jake entered, they were immediately grabbed and quickly frisked by the two guards in the room. The guards were dressed in the exact same manner as the door guards with the short guard being a white male who looked like he'd walked out of a WWE wresting show and the taller, thinner and imminently fit Asian guard frisking Jake. The room was quiet with absolutely no music.

Super weird, thought Jake, who considered the insanely loud music in the front room as counter to the utter silence of the other rooms. He figured the sex rooms would at least have didgeridoo music for atmosphere.

As the guard frisked Jake, he looked around the room and cased. He recognized Zachary Belataka immediately. Zachary sat on a large couch at the end of the room, wearing a burgundy smoking jacket and white linen pants.

"What is it with white pants?" Jake mumbled.

A lithe, young female danced, naked, delivering a shimmering dance, for Zachary and it took a second or two for Jake to realize, it was Scarlet dancing for the founder of the feast. He hadn't noticed before at the club, but she had a large Scorpion tattoo crossing the middle of her back, toward the lower part of her back side. As she gyrated, the Scorpion moved in a seductive manner as to nearly hypnotize Jake. She wasn't completely nude, as she still wore her thread thong and as Jake watched transfixed as her hands move toward them, he wondered if she'd been counting the seconds until he and Lamar could get her out of here.

As the guards finished frisking Jake, Zachary snapped his fingers and Scarlet stopped dancing. She stood in front of him to his left. As she saw that the customers were Jake and Lamar, she moved her arms to cover her breasts. Jake looked Scarlet in the eye and she showed little fear. As this occurred, Lamar eyed the guards from his periphery.

"Welcome to my home," Zachary started, lifting his hands, but not standing. "If you are here, I assume you understand what you are here for." Zachary slapped Scarlet on the ass with such a force that it caused Scarlet to let out a tiny yelp.

Something inside of Jake dropped and he felt a coldness in his stomach. He was angry. Jake stepped forward.

"Zachary," Jake spoke, his eyes moving from Scarlet's to Zachary's. Zachary's head snapped up at the sound of his name.

"We don't use names here, that was to be understood." Zachary suddenly looked uneasy, and Jake realized that this episode wasn't going to end smoothly.

Jake lifted his hands in an apologetic tone.

"Apologies. Apologies, but we are here for something a little different."

The manner in which Jake spoke seemed to calm

Zachary as he relaxed and sat back. He placed his hands behind his head. Jake, again, made eye contact with Scarlet and gave her a reassuring wink. She gave him a quick smile.

"Interesting. Curious to see where this goes," Zachary replied.

"We have questions...." Jake searched for the words, "about a friend of yours."

Jake hadn't conjured the magic words to bring Zachary to compliance. Zachary rolled his eyes.

"EHH," a disappointed Zachary emitted, "boring. Boys, show these men the exit."

As the first guard made a move on Lamar, Lamar spun and punched the guard in the throat with a sickening thud of fist hitting throat cartilage. Incapacitated, the guard fell to his knees, clutching his shattered larynx.

As the man fell to the ground, the second guard quickly advanced onto Lamar, but as the guard led with his right cross, Lamar quickly ducked and hooked with his right hand into the guard's kidney. The guard let out a low humph and let his guard down which enabled Lamar to immediately land his right cross to the glass jaw of the second guard. The guard tumbled to the ground, quite unconscious.

As Lamar spun around, the first guard attempted to stand, which was a poor decision as Lamar kicked him in the teeth with all his might. Jake, Zachary and Scarlet all watched in awe, as the first guard crumbled to the floor, clutching his face and then his neck and then nothing, as he was out. Lamar reached into the jackets of the fallen guards and removed two handguns. He tossed one to Jake, who nearly dropped the gun, from surprise. Jake rallied, bent down, and pointed the gun at Zachary's head.

"Scarlet, over here." Jake motioned to Scarlet, who quickly moved from in front of Zachary to Jake's side.

Lamar bent down and grabbed the Asian guard's jacket. He gently placed it over Scarlet's shoulders, who pulled the jacket over her, covering her nakedness.

"Just had a few questions Zach," Jake lamented.

"Do you fuckers have any idea—" Zachary started and stood.

Lamar stepped forward and punched Zachary, as gently as Lamar could, on Zachary's jaw. Zachary dropped back down to the couch, surprised and suddenly frightened.

"We know who you are, shitbird," Lamar spat down on Zachary.

"We don't have much time," Jake said.

Lamar yanked Zachary up by the throat and lifted Zachary so that they were eye to eye.

"We're leading you motherfucker right through the front door. I will have one hand on your neck and the other on the gun in your back. I see anything untoward, I will either snap your neck like kindling or shoot you in your fucking spine. We clear, fucko?" Lamar's words left little to the imagination and Zachary fully understood.

Lamar led the group of four out of the private room, with one arm around the throat of Zachary and his other holding the gun. Jake held Scarlet by the arm and kept her behind him, holding the gun in the other hand, as they emerged into the corridor. The customers, engrossed in their entertainment, didn't even notice the hostile takeover occurring in front of them.

As they reached the door leading to the main

commons, the door opened and the Latino guard working with Gunther, entered the hallway. Seeing the distress on his employer's face, the guard quickly deduced the situation. Unfortunately for him, Lamar deduced the thought process of the guard quicker. As the guard reached for his gun, Lamar took the gun he held and smashed the gun into the face of the guard. The smash was a direct hit and the guard was immediately knocked cold, but as he fell to the ground, his finger inadvertently pulled the trigger of his gun. The gun fired wildly, blasting a hole through the window of the kid being burned with hot wax.

Suddenly, it was chaos. The sound of gunfire and shattering glass had awoken everyone from their sexual dreams. The older white male watching through the first window, looked at the unfolding scene and ran back toward the last private room. At the sound of the gun, the other rooms quickly emptied into the hallway, with the sexual adventurers co-mingling with the voyeurs. The hallway filled up. Zachary started to rebel against Lamar, but that was quickly expelled as Lamar slapped Zach, hard across the face, dazing Zachary into ordinance.

"Lamar!" Jake screamed, as the sound of the commons started to blast into the hallway. "Lamar! Just get to the front door!"

Lamar, Jake, Zachary and Scarlet reached the end of the hall as all of the lights of the bright hall flipped off and the music of the commons stopped. A sound of gunfire could be heard from the front door.

"Shut that door, Lamar," Jake shouted at Lamar.

Lamar shut the door separating the main room and the corridor. They started to retreat but almost as quickly as they started to move, the door opened and Gunther fell through the door, falling into the corridor, to the ground with a bullet hole in his chest.

"Holy shit," exclaimed Jake, "they shot Gunther."

The four of them fell to the ground. They could hear screaming coming from the commons and as Jake started to speak, a group of ten Asian men, dressed in various suits, walked through the door and entered the corridor. As they filed into a formation along the walls, Junior Lo wiped ceiling dust from his suit coat, entering the foyer. After Junior Lo, Little Luck walked through them all, entering the hallway.

Thank God. It's Little Luck.

Jake looked up to see Little Luck surveying the situation. Little Luck's eyes stopped on Jake.

"Jake Hansen, what are you doing with a gun in your hand? Lamar too? Drop 'em, boys." Lamar and Jake quickly placed their guns down as Little Luck made his way over to them.

"Simple plan. Good plan. Not great plan but I got impatient, Jake." Little Luck moved his attention from Jake to Zachary, at the feet of Lamar. Little Luck eyed him over. "You have questions for this man?"

"Yes. We do," Jake responded.

Little Luck looked at Junior Lo, saying something to him in Korean. Junior Lo didn't give any facial expression and didn't say a word. Little Luck walked closer to Jake and knelt.

"Here's what we do. Junior Lo will take you to our warehouse. You have one hour for your questions. Seem reasonable?"

"Very much so."

"Terrific," Little Luck responded, standing up. "Then I shall have some questions." Little Luck leaned down to Zach. "Right little Zachary? Like, why you in Koreatown without my permission?!?"

Jake looked at Lamar.

"I think I peed myself."

Chapter Eleven

Pete pulled his bar towel from his thick, black, leather belt, stepped out around from behind the bar and wiped down the brass top. It had been a pretty solid night at Trotter's, busy enough to mostly take Pete's mind off of the case. After he had called Lamar, following his terse departure from The Cat n' Fiddle, he'd raced down to Trotter's to ensure Sophie wasn't overwhelmed. He was pleasantly surprised to see, not only a full bar, but Sophie handling the situation beautifully. Every table was filled to capacity with every customer drinking a drink in front of them and every person at the bar top was also fully stocked. As Pete entered, Johnny Rodriguez began his acoustic set and all was right in the Trotter's world. The crowd built up as the night continued and after Johnny finished his set, Pete put fifty buck's worth of money into the juke box and allowed the patrons to choose the music for the night.

As he slung drink after drink, and Sophie flashed her shy, but winning smile at the customers, Pete ran Mckenna scenarios in his head. She had A) escaped the clutches of her creepy father and lit out of Los Angeles for parts unknown; B) the proclivities of her life had taken a firm grip on her person and she was in some sort of chemical evacuation of the senses; C) she rested in a hospital or jail or D) something had indeed happened to her of a criminal nature. He had seen the condition of her apartment and ruled out A, B and C and focused on the realities of D. The sketches they had uncovered at her place told them very little, if anything, but his instincts screamed that the drawings were a key. Finding the missing sketch, good old number seventeen, would point a direct line to Mckenna. Hopefully, Lamar and Jake had made progress without getting into too much trouble.

He'd left Jake hours ago and no word from the delinquents.

Pete looked up as Sophie swept the floor, going through the nightly process of sweeping and mopping the dregs and mysteries of the day from the concrete. Pete had barely known Sophie before Jake brought her on and, at first, he'd felt a strong sense of attritional familial obligation, even if she was new to the Trotter's family. But after working with her day after day, he'd built up genuine feelings and affection for the young woman who had endured so much so soon. She perhaps was the sweetest human being Pete had ever come across. A shy, waifish presence, she always thought of others first, almost to a fault. Pete wondered if it was due to the tragic invasion of her youth by her uncle and, according to Jake, likely her father.

"Fucking monsters," Pete growled aloud, deep in his own planetary mind system.

"Did you say something, Mr. Mills?" Sophie spoke, briefly bringing to a halt her sweeping. She rested her head on the top of the broom and looked to Pete.

"No, sorry…sorry Sophie I was just…thinking aloud."

"Sounded serious."

"Only if the person in my mind ever comes in contact with me." Sophie politely smiled and returned to cleaning the floor. Pete looked toward her a beat longer.

Sophie went to the store every morning for her morning smoothie and not once, had she failed to bring the boys something. After a few misfires for Pete, she'd begun to bring Pete a Cinnamon Scone with coffee from the local coffee shop down the street a bit. He couldn't quite get his head around to what exactly organic coffee meant, but the coffee was damn good. She was quiet and shy but slowly had begun to open up a little bit to Lamar and Pete. She'd been close with Jake since her childhood but she'd only in the last few months been daily exposed to two new, scary grown men. From a distance, Pete assumed he and Lamar came across as frightening as one could be. He knew he still had the cop visage and even though Lamar ran through the world with a smile on his face, the smile hid a darkness that strangers could mistake.

As a police officer, Pete had encountered countless incidents of molestation and sexual assault of minors. To Pete, it wasn't just a sickness, it was an out and out evil. To heist the innocence of a child and cause such a heinous effect on that child not only sickened, but horrified Pete. It made him question the presence of God and as a young man, it had influenced him to break up with a woman he loved dearly. She had wanted children, but he could not imagine bringing a child into the world he witnessed day in and day out.

Pete had been offered a spot at the Sexual Crimes Unit in Manhattan before he was offered his shield in the Bronx. But with his history with such crimes, Pete knew he couldn't do it. It would haunt his dreams and forage a nightmare into his waking hours.

"Mr. Mills?" Sophie asked from across the room.

"Pete, Sophie, call me Pete."

"Are you guys…I mean, I don't want to be a snoop."

"Sophie, this is your home, and this new investigative job is part of the life of Trotter's. And you. Ask whatever you want."

"I know of Mr. Tall Mountain and I sorta knew Mckenna."

Pete set down his towel and walked toward Sophie. "You know Mckenna Murphy?"

"A little. I was a little younger and Mckenna mostly went to Palm Springs High, but she spent one semester at Hemet."

"Do you remember anything about her?"

"Hmm, not a whole lot. She hung out with the smokers out back a lot. Kinda quiet. I always thought she was beautiful."

He'd seen a picture of the early twenties Mckenna but didn't expect to get a 'beautiful' comment from Sophie.

"It seems like she's had a troubled period." Pete shrugged.

"She always had a notebook, doodling and drawing and stuff," Sophie spoke thoughtfully, her eyes looking past Pete in a thousand-yard stare.

Pete breathed in and scratched his head. He didn't know how much to tell Sophie, and it wasn't that he didn't trust her, but he didn't know her capacity for handling such things. Mostly, Pete was afraid of hurting her.

"Mr. Tall Mountain came to us and well—"

"She's missing. Or he thinks she's missing. I overheard that."

"Jake has a history with that family and Tall

Mountain, himself. He worked as a… not really how to describe his job… kind of a PA, to the family, Moro, in particular. I guess Jake has known Mckenna pretty much her whole life. So, Tall Mountain thought that with Jake's background as an investigative journalist and his connection with the family, he might have a better insight."

"And you were a detective," Sophie added.

"Yes, I was a detective." Pete smiled.

As Sophie smiled and went back to work, Pete watched her sweep. He couldn't help but recall one of his first months as a boot in New York City and the Melendez family in Washington Heights.

What was her name? Takesha.

Pete and his partner, Mikey Gosling, had answered four or five calls to the Melendez apartment for Domestic Disturbance.

"The woman was Melendez. The guy was James Rincon," Pete murmured.

The mother had a severe drug and alcohol problem and her loser boyfriend, James, would tune her up often, mostly on paydays and without fail, every payday, they would get a call to the home. As time passed, Pete came to realize that the calls weren't coming from the mother, but a 'concerned neighbor'. He assumed he'd always known that, but it wasn't of importance where the call came from; it just came. He would chastise himself greatly in the coming years, spending many hours in confessional, confessing to his guilt of an act he didn't commit but couldn't forgive himself for.

Each time, when Mikey and Pete arrived at the residence, six-year-old Takesha, Miss Melendez's daughter, would be shepherded from the apartment by the kindly neighbor, Rosa Delvay. Takesha was a very spirited but sweet young girl and Pete, a novice rookie, felt his heart break a little every time he saw her. He would nearly gush to Rosa Delvay his appreciation for her taking in little Takesha under the difficult circumstance. Takesha would spend the night at the Delvay household under the safe and watchful eyes of Rosa and her husband, David.

It wasn't until the second or third visit that Pete met David Delvay and the hairs on the back of his neck stood upright from the very first handshake. And the spiny, tingling feeling of worry crept up every time he saw David Delvay. There was nothing tangible to give Pete the creeps but as Pete would learn, it was his instincts, and they would often prove correct. It wasn't that David was the only Caucasian in the mostly Dominican, Garifuna, Puerto Rican complex, although that was weird for the neighborhood. David, as Pete learned, had been an English as Second Language instructor in the Bronx and met Rosa Rodriguez in a class, after he and his first wife divorced; allegedly.

On the fifth call, Pete and Mikey responded and Rosa Delvay, once again, came over to take care of Takesha. But, this time, as Pete cuffed James Rincon and Rosa took hold of Takesha, Takesha threw a holy shit fit, rebelling against spending the night at the Delvay apartment. As Rosa and Mikey tried to calm Takesha, David Delvay stood in the doorway of his apartment, staring at the scene. Takesha, as she screamed, connected eyes with Pete and with harrowing clarity, directed her anger and discontent into Pete's soul. Pete looked up to see Delvay staring at him, unveiling a small smile with the corners of his mouth, ever so slightly tilted up. As

Pete shifted his eyes from Delvay to Takesha, Pete felt the cold chill of evil in that hallway.

It wouldn't be the last time he felt that chill, but it was the first. He could feel and taste it, as bile choked up from his stomach and surged into his throat. He sensed that something was wrong and amiss, but he didn't act on it. He could never fully understand why he didn't act on it. He wasn't a coward, nor was he scared of any man. Maybe it was because he was a rookie and there was no evidence or suspicion of malfeasance, just a momentary glimmer or irregularity.

And the next morning when Pete got the call that Takesha Melendez had been smothered to death in the guest bedroom of the Delvay residence, Pete dropped to his knees, the remnants of the previous night's bile flooding with a thunderous gust, exploding from his mouth, splattering the wall with all the evil that Pete had felt the night before. He fell to the floor onto his knees and shook with a ferocity he hadn't encountered before, enduring the first of many panic attacks he would suffer.

When he pulled himself together, he showered (an hour and a half shower) and arrived at the station house, deciding to come clean about his mistake. After thinking thoroughly on it, he decided to wait until the autopsy results. And after the results, he was certain of his course. Takesha had been molested repeatedly over a period of time and her death, attributed by the Delvays as advanced crib death, proved to be suffocation by pillow. David Delvay was really Nathan Pickett, a former school teacher who had been let go due to suspicious behavior to minors in a suburb of Milwaukee. Pete decided to go to his superior and tell him of his error.

After telling the captain of the look he received from

Takesha, Captain Lacardo made sure the door was shut and locked. He sat on his desk, in front of Pete, who sat in the chair opposite the desk.

"Pete, you are to tell no one of this. You're gonna be a good cop, Officer Mills, maybe a great one. Trust your instincts better but do not tell this story and stain a bright future."

And after a night of bourbon and two hours in a confessional, Pete made a vow to redeem himself.

As Pete returned to cleaning the bar, he took a look at his hand, as he had many times before. He believed it was his punishment from God and if there was a heaven, his punishment from Takesha. He wasn't sure if he believed in Heaven, he'd seen too much to think a place as optimistic as Heaven existed, but he knew somewhere Takesha rested and watched. And if this disfigurement was his punishment, so be it; he deserved it and he would continue to keep the faith and his vow of redemption.

Pete looked over at the working Sophie. Sophie stopped sweeping and looked back at Pete.

"I know you like to listen to your police scanner at the end of the night. Why don't you let me finish up here and you go do that."

Pete smiled. "Sophie, I can't let you clean by yourself."

"After a full day of customers, I don't mind some Zen time."

Pete's smile widened as he usually felt the same way. He placed the bar towel on top of the bar.

"Thanks Sophie, I think I'll do that."

Sophie smiled back and resumed her cleaning.

As God as my witness, I will strike down any who attempts to harm that girl.

****

Awkward could not begin to adequately describe the ride from Koreatown to the Toy District. As Jake tried to replay the scene he'd just witnessed, he also attempted to plan the next step. The uncomfortable ride succeeded a frightening scene at the Beaudry house.

As Little Luck made his way from the main foyer of the Beaudry house to the private areas, his henchmen hastily removed the body of Gunther. Jake snuck a sidewise glance at the sight of the enormous and limp bodied Scandinavian, as Luck's men, dragged him off. The remaining cadre of Zachary's guards were noticeably absent, and Jake wondered if they had been handled in much the same manner as Gunther.

After Luck's lot shut down the party, Junior Lo led an excursion ahead of the crowd. Junior Lo gripped Zachary by the neck and stared into his eyes with a shattering glare. Zachary, for the moment stood mute and cooperative. With forceful, but polite words to Jake and Lamar, Junior instructed them to proceed to the Durango. Scarlet followed, holding on to Jake's hand but Junior Lo placed a firm hand on her shoulder.

"This is not for you."

Jake saw the fear, anxiety and confusion in Scarlet's eyes and reacted quickly.

"She's with us," Jake blurted out as Lamar stared incredulously at his misguided friend.

Scarlet grabbed onto Jake's waist and held on as if he were a life preserve in the middle of a hurricane.

"You wish to ask questions of this... creature?" Junior Lo immediately delivered a sharp and brutal jab to the solar plexus of Zachary. Zachary regurgitated a little spittle and folded over accordion style.

"We do, Mr. Lo, we do," Lamar answered.

"And you will use whatever means possible, I presume. And you wish, this woman to observe?"

"She comes with us." Jake surprised himself with his steel.

"Very well. She may accompany, but she is not to step inside of the warehouse."

Jake looked to Scarlet, who nodded.

"Agreed." Jake answered hoping to not have his voice crack as fear fed on his insides.

So, they rode to one of Little Luck's safe houses, one hunky dory, happy family. Lamar drove with Jake in the passenger seat. Little Scarlet sat in the seat directly behind Lamar, her short legs allowing Lamar some adequate space, with Zachary in the middle and Junior Lo riding the rail behind Jake.

"You have no idea who you're fucking with," Zachary blabbered. "Let me go and I promise you won't get fucked with."

"Young miss," the eminently polite Junior Lo began, "please put your head in your lap for a moment." Scarlet acquiesced.

Zachary continued his ranting plea. "You chink's come in and shoot my place and—" Zachary did not have the opportunity to finish his sentence.

With startling alacrity, Junior Lo, snapped his left elbow with such force that it struck Zachary Belataka in the nose. Zachary's head snapped left, above Scarlet's bent over body and back into place where it had an unfortunate rendezvous with a quick backhand from Junior Lo. Blood shot from Zachary's nostrils onto the seat backings of Jake and Lamar's seat. The sound of the backhand simulated the sound of a shotgun crack.

"Jesus Christ!" Jake exclaimed.

Zachary's head fell into his chest, his lights soundly out. Lamar looked at the unconscious Zachary through the rearview mirror.

"That's what you get for disparaging Asians," Lamar lamented.

"My apologies gentlemen, the blood will be sanitized from the chairs whilst you interrogate this buffoon."

The freeway was devoid of cars, as the darkness of the pavement and night mingled with the flickering street lamps of the city. In sharp contrast to the infuriating mayhem of day traffic, the ethereal creepiness of the very still big city emptiness, brought forth a chill to Jake's bones that shuddered him.

Jake's mind was returning him to the frightening and macabre sequence at the Beaudry. They had seen a man killed directly in front of them. Dispassion aside, it had been years since Jake had stood face to face with mortality. He looked in the mirror and captured the eyes of Scarlet, boring into his. A few hours previous, she was dancing in front of a hundred ogling men and now she was scrunched into a Durango, next to an unconscious Zachary, headed to who knows what. She shivered a bit, but her eyes held his focus.

Lamar looked back in the mirror and saw the knocked-out Zachary. "We're gonna have to get him to talk," Lamar sighed. "Jake?"

"Yea, yea, I heard. I'm thinking of a plan."

Lamar drove on in silence for a beat until Jake looked back at Junior Lo.

"May I ask something?" Jake spoke to Junior Lo.

"As long as it's not disparaging," whispered Lamar.

"Proceed," Junior Lo answered.

"Where are we going?"

"Drive until the Santa Fe Springs exit. Then take Industrial."

Lamar followed the driving instructions taking the Santa Fe Springs exit. And there, Junior Lo guided them through the outer bowels of Downtown Los Angeles. Lamar drove the vehicle toward the building pointed out by Junior Lo.

"Take the down ramp," Junior Lo instructed.

As Lamar drove into the building's lot toward the down ramp, Junior Lo pulled a small remote from his breast pocket. Tapping a button on the remote, the grated gate of the garage opened, giving access to Lamar's Durango.

"Drive down to Level two."

As soon as Lamar parked the car on Level two, Junior Lo disembarked with Zachary Belataka in tow, dragging him by his greasy black hair. Before Lo slammed the door, he uttered instructions.

"Thirteen- A is where you will find this person. Young miss, may stay in your car. She is not permitted inside the warehouse. I'm sure at Trotter's you have rules."

"We don't have rules for the handling of confined adults," Jake offered.

"Maybe we should," retorted Lamar.

"Mr. Hansen, may I ask, what you intend to ask Mr. Belataka?"

"That's our business, Mr. Lo."

"Fair enough."

"Are you going to kill him?" Jake asked.

"That's our business, Mr. Hansen." Junior Lo fairly

smiled.

Zachary fell to his knees. Junior Lo yanked him up, shoved and pushed Zachary down to the floor and then proceeded to drag him toward the freight elevator. Zachary screamed as he was moved. Junior Lo bent down and gave an open palmed smack across the face and Zachary fell asleep.

Jake and Lamar winced at the smack. Scarlet placed her hand over her mouth, stunned.

"Take the steps, Lamar, I'm gonna get her a cab."

"Hopefully, those boys don't kill him before we get a chance to talk to him." Lamar ran toward the stairwell, opposite the freight elevator. He disappeared up the stairs.

Jake looked to Scarlet who was still wearing the jacket he had pulled off the fallen guard. Jake reached into his wallet and pulled out his last fifty bucks.

"I want to stay," Scarlet whispered, placing her hands onto Jake's arms.

"This isn't safe. Here, in this warehouse. And back on Beaudry... that's not what I wanted."

"You got me out of there. Out of that place. After you grabbed Zach, you could've left me. But you didn't. I'm not hurt. Surprisingly, I feel safe for the first time in a long time." Scarlet touched Jake's face, serenely.

"Lamar and I have some things we need to do." Jake extended the fifty bucks toward Scarlet.

"Do what you gotta do, babe. I'll find my way." Scarlet took the fifty bucks and sashayed herself away.

"Keep the jacket," Jake called out.

"I'll return it." Scarlet blew Jake a kiss.

****

Jake ran up the last few steps of the stairwell, to the

thirteenth floor. Winded, he caught himself against the wall, placing a hand up against the stucco. Nearly faint, he bent over.

As he looked up, he saw Lamar standing in the doorway, looking down at him.

"You need to stop smoking." Lamar smiled.

"Thanks for that," Jake wheezed. Jake stood, clapped Lamar on the shoulder and stepped past him. "Okay, big guy, let's do this."

Jake and Lamar walked with purpose but a little apprehension, down the wooded corridor toward thirteen A.

A solitary streetlight shone through the large window at the front of the hall, the light of the lamp on the far side of the road. Jake was nervous, but he felt the worst of the night had already occurred. Little Luck wouldn't harm Jake or Lamar, of this, Jake was certain. Zachary on the other hand, was not so lucky. As they approached thirteen A, Junior Lo stood at attention at the door. Jake stopped in front of Junior Lo.

"Your man awaits inside," Junior Lo began, "his hands are tied behind his back and legs are shackled to the chair legs."

"Is that necessary?" Jake asked.

"Our house, our rules."

"Noted."

"You may do what you require. Beat him as you see fit. Just do not kill him. Per Mr. Luck." Junior Lo looked intently at Jake and Lamar as he spoke.

"One question?" Jake breathed in. "Is ranch style one-story or two?"

"Seriously Jake, I will kill you," Lamar gawked at Jake.

"Ask your friend, Zachary, but it feels like wasted time. Good luck, gentlemen."

Jake gave a sly, sarcastic smile to Junior Lo as he and Lamar stepped past him into thirteen A. As they walked, side by side, they could see Zachary sitting, hands tied behind him, on a chair in the middle of the studio. Zach's shirt had been soaked through with sweat, or blood, and his head lolled to the left side. Jake was unable to tell if Zachary was conscious, hell, he couldn't tell if he was alive. The true enormity of interrogating a hostile witness, or a kidnapped witness, begin to hit Jake.

"Time is floating, Lamar. We're gonna have to get him to talk."

"I know, motherfucker, that's what I said in the car."

"He was unconscious at that point."

"I know dipshit," Lamar forcefully tossed at Jake.

"Geez, no need to get personal."

"We got an hour. You're the asshole hung up on ranch style."

Jake looked at his cell phone clock. "Shit, we probably only got minutes, now. Okay, let's do this. This is kinda exciting."

"Beating on a guy to get info is exciting to you?" Lamar asked.

"I should keep that to myself?"

"Unless you're a sociopath, you should not enjoy this."

"Jesus Lamar, all I said was that I was excited."

As they stood directly in front of Zachary, Zachary came to and looked nervously around him. He lifted his head and saw Jake and Lamar.

"I really didn't give much thought as to what to ask him," Jake admitted. "I was trying to figure out how we were gonna get him."

"So that *was* our plan back there?"

"Not very good, huh? You signed off on it."

"Thank God the Korean Godfather showed up." Lamar was becoming frustrated.

"Good cop, bad cop?" Jake asked.

"You know how to play good cop, bad cop?"

"Come on, give me credit." Jake walked over to Zachary, bending over so he stood face to face with his prisoner. "A couple questions, Zachary." Jake smiled his winning smile.

"Fuck you," Zachary spat out and then spat on Jake's shoes.

"Your turn, big guy." Jake shrugged, stepping back.

Lamar stepped forward. He bent down and, with startling speed, throwing his whole body into it, delivered a right cross to Zachary full in the face. Zachary's head rolled downward, semi-conscious. Jake, shocked at the force of Lamar's blow, fairly screamed.

"Lamar?!? What the hell?"

"What? You said good cop, bad cop? Good cop, bad cop." Lamar placed his arms out in a pleading motion.

"Good cop, bad cop! Not Good cop, maniac cop. Jesus, we need him awake."

"This is how you do it, Jake!"

"How the hell would you know?"

"My time in prison gave me a pretty good insight to good cop, bad cop."

"You were the biggest dog in the yard, nobody fucked with you!"

"But I got answers from people when I needed it."

"Because you were a giant, not because of good cop, bad cop. And you call me the sociopath." Jake pushed past Lamar and bent down in front of Zachary. Jake slapped Zachary's face to rouse him.

"Zachary! Zachary, hey buddy, wakey wakey." Jake attempted to rouse Belataka. Zachary opened his eyes slightly. "Hey pal, there you are. Do you know where Mckenna is?"

As Jake spoke, Lamar crouched next to him.

"Who?" Zachary murmured.

Lamar with lightning speed, cracked a smack across Zachary's face, eliciting an 'ouch' face from Jake.

"Easy, easy." Jake cautioned.

"Man, this is how it's done," Lamar reasoned.

"All right, all right," Jake responded and focused his attention from Lamar to Zachary. "Listen Z-Man, Lamar can do this the whole hour we got you. Mckenna? Remember Mckenna? Scarlet's friend?"

A flicker of recognition flashed across Zachary's face.

"Is that bitch what this is about?"

Jake chuckled slightly, wishing to knock Zachary out himself.

"For now, it is. When Little Luck gets here, it'll be about something different."

Zachary came more to his senses. Jake looked at how pitiful this recently nattily dressed man, had become. Blood stained his hands, face and neck. Slobber and snot ran from his nose, hell, even his ears bled.

"I don't know, man. Mckenna was working at the club and then a little...after hours, you know. A little extra cash, no big deal, bro. And I treat the best, the best. But she was scared of something. Talking crazy talk, like she saw something she should not have seen." As Zachary unfolded his tale, Lamar and Jake stepped in to hear his words.

"Did she say what?" Lamar asked.

"A guy. Some scary guy. I didn't know who…she was…head full of boogey men." Jake stood upright.

"The sketch. The face-less guy." Jake wiped a bead of sweat from his face. "The face-less guy."

Lamar's cell phone rang. As Jake wondered who could possibly be calling at this crazy hour, Lamar looked at the Caller ID.

"Shit. It's Pete." Lamar answered the phone, placing one hand over his ear and talking into the other end.

As he walked away from Jake and Zachary, Lamar tried to hear Pete.

"Speak up Pete, it's a fuzzy connection." Lamar stepped away to the far corner of the room.

Jake bent over and leaned into Zachary.

"Listen, Zachary. Little Luck is coming here any minute. Is there anything, anything at all she said or did or gave you?" Zachary shook his head violently. He pursed his lips, then Zachary lifted his head up.

"In my wallet. This one night… crazy night. She could be crazy nuts, but this one night, she had a fear about her. She said to hold onto something for her. She was so scared. Listen, if I give you this, will you get me out of here?"

Jake, caught up in the tale of Zachary, suddenly realized that was a promise he could not keep. And then he thought of Scarlet, naked in front of all those men and understood Mckenna had done that as well.

"Sure. I can get you out of here."

Zachary breathed a sigh of relief, and his tough guy façade broke down.

"My wallet's in front. My front pocket."

Jake looked over Zachary and sized up his ability to reach into the front pocket and extract the wallet. Jake reached down and over toward tied up Zachary, slipping his hand into Zachary's pocket.

As Jake reached into Zachary's pocket, the weight of his body mingled with the counterweight of Zachary's stationary body, and the chair toppled. The awkwardness of the situation tipped the chair, dramatically, as the fulcrum of the cross kinetic energy shoved Jake over the shoulder of Zachary, causing both Jake and Zachary to fall with the chair landing squarely on top. Zachary smashed the floor with the back of his head and Jake rested on top of him, with his hand still in Zachary's pocket. Lamar approached.

"Jesus Christ, man, what the hell you doin'?" Lamar asked, his hands above his head.

Jake sheepishly stood with Zachary's wallet in his hand. Zachary lay still on the floor with the chair atop.

"Got it," Jake exclaimed in victory. "What did Pete want?"

Jake leafed through the wallet, finding two hundred dollars cash. He took and pocketed the cash. Lamar shook his head.

"What? He's not gonna need it."

"You got problems." Lamar sadly smiled.

"So?" Jake inquired, searching the wallet.

"Zane's dead."

Jake stopped looking through the wallet and looked up at Lamar.

"Dead? Dead, dead?"

"Murdered."

The door of the warehouse studio opened, and Little Luck entered with five of his biggest Korean goons and

Junior Lo by his side. Little Luck strode with the confidence of a man thirty years his junior.

"Time is up Jake Hansen. It's time for me to ask some questions." Little Luck walked up to Jake and Lamar and handed them the guns he'd taken from them earlier.

"Apologies for the scene. I just hate not being tithed. Makes me feel dirty. Right Zachary?" Little Luck called out at the semi-conscious Zachary, perched awkwardly on the floor with the chair. "What happened here, Jake Hansen?"

"New interrogation technique," Jake answered.

"Random awkwardness maneuver," Lamar added.

"Something like that." Jake tucked the gun into the back band of his pants. "Maybe take it easy on him, Luck," Jake offered.

Little Luck looked to Junior Lo and smiled.

"Oh, look at the big heart on you, Jake Hansen. I touched. But no, I have some business with Mr. Zachary here."

Lamar stepped up and grabbed Jake by the arm. "Let's git, Jake."

Feigning chagrin, but feeling none of it, Jake looked to the suddenly alert Zachary. "Sorry, kid, I did my best," Jake threw over his shoulder, placing Zachary's wallet into his back pocket, dumbly as he and Lamar began to leave.

"Wait," Zachary screamed. "You can't leave me here. You can't leave me here! You fucking assholes! You know what they're gonna do to me?!?"

"Shoulda thought of that sooner," Jake replied. As Jake and Lamar exited thirteen A, Jake took a glance back at Luck, Lo and Zachary. "Whatdya think Luck will do with him?"

"Zach ran a pretty big operation without paying a toll."

"You think he'll kill him?" Jake asked.

"I dunno, maybe."

"Really, you think he'll kill him?"

"I just said I dunno. I know I wouldn't want to be him right now. But if Zachary is part of the Blazerian clan, Luck better be careful. That Beaudry place ain't worth a turf war."

And Jake agreed with that.

Chapter Twelve

Lamar shoved the Durango into a higher gear and sped his baby from the Ten to the 405. The night and the road had cleared, and the boys wanted as far away from the warehouse as possible. Jake closed his eyes, exhausted from the long day that had begun with him passed out on top of a bar table. Lamar had been awake before Jake's waking and had been awake more hours, albeit sober hours.

Jake remembered he'd imbibed the Prairie Chicken at Barns, the Boddingtons at Cat n' Fiddle, the Manhattan at Trocadero, the cocktails at Lucky's, the Moonshine with Little Luck and the whatever at The Frolic Room. He'd drunk himself through the hangover, but he wasn't drunk. The escapades in Koreatown had insured his adrenaline would be pumping for at least a few more hours.

Jake was so involved in his awkward interrogation of Zachary Belataka, that the words 'Zane's dead' passed from Lamar in the warehouse, barely registered. But now, as they drove to retrieve Pete, the words struck him. It was entirely possible that Zane had been murdered outside the scope of their investigation but that seemed remote at best. How many murders occurred in Hermosa Beach? Maybe, perhaps one every two years? Three years, maybe? And now to not only have a 187 occur in Hermosa but have the victim be Zane, whom they interviewed in connection with the missing Mckenna and have it on the same day? The odds were incalculable.

"Man, first Gunther and now this guy you interviewed." Lamar shook his head.

"Seems quite the coincidence, eh?"

"I didn't think so. Damn, what did that girl get herself into?"

"I wish I knew, Lamar, I wish I knew."

Jake fought to stay awake. At moments of exhaustion, Jake's mind often drifted to Lily, his ex-wife. He just couldn't help it and Scarlet's visage hadn't done his nostalgia any favors. Scarlet bore enough of a resemblance to plant Lily squarely into his mind. Not the back of his mind but at the very forefront. As he drifted to sleep, he pictured himself beside Lily, in bed. Her soft, naked back facing away from him with her hair, so black and willowy, drifting down toward the small of her back.

In his dream world, Jake reached out with his hand and caressed her shoulder. Lily slowly moved her head so that her right eye was visible. Her right eye held a tiny flaw in the iris.

"Hey you," Lily cooed. Jake blinked briefly, extending his hand toward her beautiful hair and just as suddenly the image of Lily disappeared.

"You're thinking on her," Lamar mumbled.

"No, I'm not. Okay, so, I'm thinking on her, what of it?"

"Nothing. You know it does you no good."

"Few things in my life do me any good. And she's always there."

"Nostalgia is a powerful muse." Lamar drove on in silence as Jake stared into his past.

As they approached Trotter's, they could see Pete

standing outside of the establishment. Hunched slightly over, he reminded Jake of a not too far in the past phrase, Latch Key Kid. Lamar barely stopped; Pete hopped into the back of the Durango and Lamar blazed off into the night, again.

As Jake closed his eyes again, Lamar related the finite details of their excursions following Pete's exit from the Cat n' Fiddle. Lamar explained Lucky's and the questioning of the beautiful Scarlet. That led to his explaining the extreme awkwardness of Little Luck's visit.

"Oh, I woulda loved to have seen Junior Lo." Pete laughed.

"There's more in that," chimed in Jake.

Lamar went into full detail of the events on Beaudry and maybe more details than Pete wanted to hear.

"Wait, I exit to benefit the case and you two screwballs end up cavorting at a sex club?!?" Pete spoke with an acrimonious tone.

"It wasn't a sex club." Jake sat up.

"Did you voyeuristically engage in watching sex acts performed not only not by you, but from a different room?"

"Yes." Jake replied.

"That, by definition, is a sex club."

"No," Lamar and Jake answered in unison.

"It's different," Jake finished his thought.

"Pray tell, how so?"

"Well for one, they served snacks and drinks."

Both Lamar and Pete gave Jake a confused look at his response. Pete grabbed his head.

"What the fuck does that mean?"

"Well…it's like the difference between a funeral and

a wake. They don't serve refreshments at a funeral but they do at a wake."

"Sooo it's not a sex club because it's more like a wake than a funeral." Pete sat back and closed his eyes.

"Exactly."

"You're an idiot," sighed Pete.

"Let me ask you a question," Jake began.

"Ugh…Jake, what?" a bewildered Pete replied.

"Is a ranch style house one story or two?" Jake asked in earnest.

"Dammit Jake, enough with the fucking ranch style house," Lamar berated Jake.

"What the fuck," Pete stammered, "what the fuck is he talking about?"

"Nothing," chuckled Lamar.

The three sat in confused silence for a few moments.

"A Ranch style home is only one story," Pete answered.

"Let me finish the story." Lamar laughed. "Pete all focused on the sex club and shit and Real Estate Randy all up in here about ranch style."

"All right, all right, get on with it," Pete hissed.

As Lamar entered the final chapters of their wild night on the seamier side of the Southland, Jake pondered the next steps. Eddie Collins had been right. Jake needed to apologize to JR and he was going to need his help.

"Holy shit," exclaimed Pete, "Junior Lo shot Gunther?!?"

"We didn't see the trigger man," Lamar replied, "only the end result."

"Christ, you boys had quite a night."

"Ain't over yet," Lamar shook his head and looked

at Pete. "So, you were listening to the police scanner?"

"Yea, Sophie and I were finishing up and she said she could finish so I could…you know."

"We all know you love that scanner," Jake ribbed.

"Yea, man, get a room with that thing." Lamar laughed.

"Big talk coming from two guys who voyeured a sex club."

"Not a sex club." Jake wagged his finger.

"Yea," Lamar added, "not a sex club. Besides, it paid off."

The Durango flew onto Vista del Mar, heading south with the black ocean to the west. The moon shimmered enough to illuminate the still ocean.

"It feels like we were just driving to Hermosa," Pete smirked, "Christ Jake," Pete looked at his watch, "you must be fucking exhausted."

"Him," a flabbergasted Lamar retorted, "I was up hours before this motherfucker."

"Yea but you don't have three days of toxins rolling through your veins."

"Three days?" groaned Lamar, "How about seven years?

"I can hear you guys." Jake moaned. "So, you were listening to the scanner…"

"Yea, as background noise. I heard the 187 call and didn't think anything of it. But when they mentioned Hermosa, my ears perked up. And when they gave Barnacles' address, and a man was slashed. And then they mentioned Zane by name."

"Jesus." Lamar crossed himself.

"You're not catholic, Lamar," Jake grumbled.

"Doesn't hurt to be sure."

Pete rolled his eyes. "Right in the pool room. This is gonna be a tough one. Hermosa Beach called in for help. Robbery-Homicide is on its way." Pete's voice dropped as he mentioned Robbery-Homicide.

"Oh no," Jake groaned.

"Guess who?" Pete tapped Jake on the shoulder.

"Frank Allison."

"One and the same."

"Dammit." Lamar smacked the wheel. "Motherfucker has it in for us."

"Motherfucker has it in for one of us, Lamar." Pete countered. "I heard at the poker game last week that he has a new partner. Some kid named Danny Burkle."

"Danny?" chuckled Jake. "How old is this kid, twelve?"

"I'd say north of that," Pete replied.

As the boys lamented their luck with detective's, they drove on in silence, staring at the glass of an ocean beneath the waxing crescent of a 5 a.m. moon.

Jake shifted in his seat as he was sitting on something uncomfortable. He reached into his pocket and removed Zachary's wallet.

"Oh shit," Jake cried, "almost forgot." Jake opened Zachary's wallet and searched it.

"What's that?" Pete asked.

"Zachary exchanged his wallet for his freedom. He said Mckenna gave him something to hold onto."

"You made a deal, Jake?" Lamar questioned. "Fucking kid is gonna get whacked by Little Luck."

"Yea well, I didn't say it was a good deal." Jake continued to leaf through the wallet. Digging into the leather, Jake pulled out a thick, folded piece of paper. "What do we have here?" Jake started to unfold the carefully folded paper. Opening it fully, the paper revealed a drawn sketch. "Son of a bitch…"

Jake held the paper up.

"What is it?" Pete asked.

Taking a sharper look at the sketch, the sketch revealed two men speaking with another. The man on the left was the drawn image of S. Newman, Tall Mountain's right-hand man. And Newman was speaking with a dark tan, skin colored male.

"That's one of Mckenna's sketches," Pete pointed to the drawing. "That's Newman. And whomever he's speaking to—"

"Is the man in question. Look at the left corner." Jake pointed. The top left corner of the sketch had a circular sticker with the number seventeen written in Sharpie ink.

"I'll be damned. That was a good deal you made." Pete clapped Jake on the shoulder.

"Thanks. We need to find out who this is."

****

As they emerged from the parking structure, onto the street level, the silhouette of the three boys pronounced itself onto the far wall of the opposing building. Stepping onto Hermosa Avenue, as Jake and Pete had many hours prior, the row of streetlights interspersed with the high palm trees lined row after row, delivered an idyllic defining snapshot of Southern California.

"Just three best friends walking to a murder scene at five in the morning." Jake marveled at the absurdity of the moment.

He looked left and right at his flanking friends and felt a wave of confidence wash over him. It had been many years since he'd felt this surge of confidence and enthusiasm. He was back in the hunt, the dig. He only partly hated himself for feeling this way while heading to a murder scene not too long after he'd borne witness to another murder.

They walked quietly south, down Hermosa Avenue, toward Barnacles, Barnacles now being the center of a ghoulish spectacle as ten police cars and ambulances with lights flashing, blocked the sleeping beach town's main street. A KTLA news van held watch fifteen feet to the east of the crime scene, staring straight into the dead zone.

"Within the hour, there'll be three or four more with choppers," Pete mused.

As the boys approached, Pete took the lead making his way toward the front of the police tape and barrier. As they neared, they all spotted the unforgettable and unmissable visage of Detective Frank Allison.

Allison held a commanding presence, and one knew that he was in charge of the entire spectacle, even if one had never crossed his path before. As Allison stood inside the tape conferring with a Hermosa Beach officer in uniform, he looked to his left.

"Holy Christ," Allison murmured, "this is all I fucking need."

The detective stepped under the police tape just as Pete, Lamar and Jake reached the barrier. Allison lifted his hands and the boys stopped in their tracks.

"Four thirty A fucking M. What could possibly bring you idiots down here tonight?" Allison attempted to control his burgeoning rage.

Jake took the bait. "That's no way to talk to an old pal…it's been like…what…seven years?"

"I know. My ulcers have cleared. Seven glorious years. I sleep well at night." Allison took a look at Jake's face and gave a tsk, tsk smirk. "Which one of these monsters finally tuned you up?"

A huge smile crossed Jake's face as he opened his arms with a bow and a wink. "Thank you? Thank you, Detective Allison. Finally, someone realizes it wasn't a fight or a random beating. But one of these guys knocked me around. You are a true detective." Jake condescendingly slow clapped with his hands extended, swerving his body to clap, not only for Allison, but his partners as well.

"I did hear intel of some malfeasance in Las Vegas," Allison retorted. "But…I guess it coulda been Tony Tahoe or one of his goons."

"Are you keeping tabs on me, Detective?

"Don't flatter yourself, Hansen. When guys like you accrue gambling debts as quickly and thoroughly as you, word spreads. Quickly. Especially if they are as beloved as you."

"I am hurt, Frank."

"That's Detective, you fucking parasite," Allison spat.

"Jake," Pete whispered.

"Apologies…Detective. You sure you're not keeping an eye on me?"

"Both eyes. Only to keep you in my sights. I don't want to be blindsided like Martin."

"If you dance with the devil…"

"That's you, all right, always quoting some type of bullshit."

"That's me. It was enough to get Martin transferred to Internal Affairs."

Allison chuckled and shook his head. "Cheap shot, hot shot. You here to casually build another bullshit conspiracy on us?"

Pete shoved Jake aside before he could answer. "No Detective," Pete interjected, "We were just down the street drinking with some friends. Played quite a few hands of poker and then someone cracked open a bottle of expensive whiskey."

"Hm." Allison smiled and rubbed his chin," I love me some expensive whiskey but really? How come none of you seem drunk? I can't one hundred percent tell with Jake but...then again, isn't he always drunk."

From ten feet behind Detective Allison, Detective Burkle slowly made her way to her new partner and the gentlemen he was conversing with. She stepped under the tape and stood just beyond Allison's right shoulder.

"Detective...all good?" she asked.

"One hundred percent, Burkle," Allison replied without looking back. "Tip top."

Taken aback, Jake's eyes opened wide. Detective Burkle was way younger than he had imagined and light years more attractive. First of all, she was a woman. Not a man. And she was a true smoke show. Jake casually tried to give Danny Burkle the once over. She busted him immediately, but it wasn't until he reached her hazel eyes that he caught on. He delivered a sheepish grin. Jake quickly shoved past Pete and approached Detective Burkle with an outstretched hand.

"Jake Hansen, Detective and you are...."

Burkle, smiling, shook Jake's hand. Mustering all of his charm, Jake reached down to kiss her hand. She quickly yanked the hand back. However, she couldn't hide a small smile as she pulled back.

"Detective Danny Burkle, Romeo."

"Charmed, I'm sure, Detective Burkle. How did you draw such a looker, Allison?" Jake teased.

"Fuck you, Hansen."

"How long you been with RHD, Detective?" Pete spoke up.

"Two weeks."

Lamar and Pete looked at each other and started to laugh. Allison rolled his eyes but was usurped by Jake interrupting.

"Never mind these Neanderthals, Danny." Jake gave an exaggerated scowl toward Pete and Lamar. "Everyone started somewhere, even your partner who was born when the Dead Sea only had a cold."

"Thank you, Jake and it's Detective Burkle to you." Detective Burkle held her small smile and Allison broke into a broad smile and whistled.

Put into his place, Jake took a bow.

"All right, smart guys, beat it. This is our scene." Allison gestured with his hands as he attempted to sweep the trio aside.

Pete attempted to look faux interested. "What happened?"

"Not at liberty to say, former Detective Mills," Allison responded.

Allison gave a light rap on the arm of Burkle, motioning her to follow him. As Frank Allison stepped back under the crime tape, Burkle couldn't help but give one last glance at Jake, before she walked away. Seeing this, Jake offered a tiny wave and a wink.

"We'll do lunch, Detective Burkle." Jake chuckled. Jake, Pete and Lamar stood side by side witnessing the legal arm of bureaucracy working to make sense of a murder.

"We probably shoulda acted drunker," Lamar offered.

"We shoulda discussed that, *that* was the plan," Jake said looking to Pete.

"Eh." Pete shrugged, "He wouldn't believe us anymore than he does now if we'd come up with a better story."

"Maybe so, maybe so." Jake looked for a path beyond the police cars and scene, stretching his neck.

"You gave up pretty easy, Jake, what gives?" Pete asked.

"Remember this morning?"

"Some of it," Pete responded, "which part?"

Jake walked and motioned to the boys, waving his hand.

"Follow me, boys." Jake led Pete and Lamar around the police tape and all of the emergency vehicles, making his way toward the south side of Barnacles. Being careful to avoid the evil and suspicious eye of Detective Allison, Jake took his co-conspirators past the last cop car.

"Two doors down, two doors down," Jake murmured to himself, softly.

"What are you mumbling?" Lamar gruffly asked. "Two doors down."

As Jake walked west, Pete's face gave a look of understanding. Jake stopped walking as he stepped in front of a rundown, one story beach special with a tiny little sign reading: Barnacles Main Office. Jake opened his arms wide and looking at his friends smiled a great big smile.

"Ta Daaa." Jake nearly laughed. "You got your tools, Pete?"

Pete reached into his back pocket and pulled out his lock picks.

"You know I do. Better not be a fucking alarm." Pete slowly crouched his large body over so that he was face to face with the doorknob of the office. Jake cringed at the sound of Pete's knees creaking and cracking. Lamar saw the grimace on Pete's face.

"Let me try something, Pete," Lamar offered. Reaching over, Lamar put his large right hand on the doorknob and turned it. The door wasn't locked and opened right up.

"Shazam." Lamar smiled.

"Gotta love beach communities. So, trusting." Jake giggled.

"So dumb." Pete shook his head.

Upon entry into the dark space, Jake pulled his phone and flicked on the flashlight app. Jake moved the flashlight slowly around the messy room. A desk covered with invoices and bar or liquor magazines littered the desktop, spilling out onto the floor. A shoddy couch against the far wall with just as many invoices drew Jake's attention.

"How many cocktail servers and bartenders have been 'interviewed' on this couch?" Jake wondered aloud.

Finally, Jake's light landed on a TV monitor attached to a VCR.

"Boys," Jake whispered.

Pete and Lamar moved and stood next to Jake in front of the monitor. The tape was still running a live feed from the Barnacles Pool room. Detective Allison and Detective Burkle stood, arms folded by the pool table, talking to one another.

"How long before they find this room?" Lamar

asked.

"I can't believe they haven't found it yet," Pete replied. "Zane got it in the pool room."

Jake leaned over and found the remote to the video player, atop the monitor. Fiddling with the remote, he stopped the tape. Hitting another button, he started to rewind the tape.

"Go back to when we were here," Pete spoke, "the pool room leads to the bathroom. I want to see something."

Jake pressed rewind on the remote until the time stamp was synchronized with their visit.

"Freeze it," Pete hissed.

Jake hit stop and the camera rested on the dark male, the Indian National they had seen earlier.

"That's the guy we saw at the Cat n' Fiddle." Jake pointed to the screen.

"That guy?" Lamar broke in.

"Yea, that guy," Pete mumbled. "So, he was following us."

"Doesn't seem to be...the dangerous type," Jake wondered aloud.

"Is there a shot of Latino....maybe Mexi...," Pete didn't finish his sentence.

"The gentlemen at the high top? I don't think so." Jake answered. He hit fast forward, and the tape rambled.

"Freeze it," Pete called out. The video stopped and showed Zane speaking with the Indian National male.

"And they spoke," Jake observed the obvious. Jake pulled up his phone and aimed the camera at the screen, taking a clear picture of the Indian male. "Say cheese."

Jake hit play and the scene between Zane and the male played out. Zane was waving his arms furiously and speaking in what appeared to be an excited way. Zane pointed for the male to walk away. The Indian National bowed and walked away, calmly.

"Wait," Jake interjected. He pointed at the screen. "Look."

The spider tattooed man, stood next to the facial scarred man, in the background as the Indian National and Zane spoke. Jake froze the screen.

"Who are those guys?" Lamar asked.

"Jake bumped into Spider-man as we went to speak with Zane." Pete scratched his head.

"And?" Lamar pursued.

"And… nothing." Jake replied. "They just gave a vibe and were off with the scene."

"Much like our Indian friend here." Pete nodded.

"Could be Sri Lankan." Jake smiled.

"Take a picture of them, Jake," Pete ordered.

Jake snapped a picture of the screen. "With no sound, this offers us very little," Jake sighed.

"We got the guys' face at least," Lamar added, "forward it to the killing."

Jake fast forwarded the tape to eleven-thirty p.m. The Barnacles pool room was hopping with business. Zane played pool against some surfer looking white guy in board shorts and a wife beater, wearing no shoes and the room was crowded. Fifteen people had crowded into the small room. The pool table was lined similar to a golf course during a major tournament. Zane lined a shot up and circled the table.

"Freeze it," Pete insisted. The tape froze and Pete pointed to the wall by the exit. Behind a crowd of five white males, the Indian National stood, mostly hidden. Behind him, stood Spider-man and Facial Scar Man. "He went back," Pete shook his head.

"He drove Hermosa to Hollywood to Hermosa? Why?" Jake looked puzzled.

"And those guys stayed the whole time," Lamar lamented.

"What is Mckenna in to?" Pete still shook his head.

"Jesus, the one guy just blends in," Jake murmured. "The other two… not so much."

Jake hit play and the video showed Zane hitting the shot and winning the game. Molly ran up, put hands on his face and kissed him. The crowd in the room cheered and the swell of the crowd approached Zane to congratulate him. As the crowd hugged and embraced him, Zane suddenly pulled back, grabbing his throat. A splash of blood splattered onto the pool table.

"Jesus," Jake exclaimed.

"Rewind that?"

Jake rewound and replayed the scene five times. Each time, Zane fell to the ground dying as blood shot from his carotid artery.

"How in the fuck," Lamar started, "… how in the hell did someone get…whatever into him that quick and accurate?"

"Freeze it again, Jake," Pete said. Jake froze the tape and Pete pointed to the top of the monitor. There, with barely a notice, the Indian National was exiting the room. Spider-Man and Facial Scar Man were nowhere to be seen. "I'll be damned."

****

Jake entered the front foyer of Trotter's and plopped onto the front booth. The coolness of the leather felt good on the back of his neck, as he closed his eyes. He opened his eyes to look at the clock on the front wall. It read:

6:03 a.m. He sighed, unable to muster the energy to curse aloud.

As he placed his cell atop the table, it buzzed. It was a text message from Pete.

GET SOME SLEEP. 9 AM.

Jake yawned. There was more work to be done and now he knew where it started. There was an apology he owed, and he needed to deliver it first thing in the morning.

Jake stood from the booth with a grunt and walked into the bar section of Trotter's. He slowly ambled toward the bar. Stepping behind the bar, he reached into the cooler and grabbed himself a beer. Feeling a weird constriction in the back of his pants, he pulled the gun he'd grabbed at Beaudry and had been handed to him by Little Luck. He set the gun on top of the bar and sat on one of the bar stools. He pulled his phone and tapped a text into it.

GONNA HAVE A BEER AND GO TO BED. 9 AM.

From behind him, Jake heard the front door open. He closed his eyes.

"Just one beer, Pete! You checking on me?"

"Pete?" a sexy, sultry voice cooed.

Jake jumped from his bar stool and fell to the ground. The beer spilled onto his shirt. Prone, on the ground, he looked up from his cobra-like position, to see Scarlet, scintillating, slowly walking toward him, giggling.

"Are you okay?" she spoke through her giggle.

"Uh…," Jake stood sheepishly, placing his beer on the bar. He wiped his hands, using a bar towel Sophie must have left. "How did you find me? Find this place?"

Scarlet approached Jake and placed her hands on his chest. "Do you really want to know?" Scarlet placed her arms around his neck and fiddled with his hair.

Jake could feel all the blood in his body rushing south of the equator. "No, no not really," he got out, failing to sound cool.

Scarlet lightly touched Jake's cheek with the back of her index finger. "I wanted to thank you for getting me out of that hell hole," she whispered.

"Really," Jake uttered, "it was nothing."

Scarlet looked at the bar and saw the gun resting on the bar. "Nothing, huh…felt like something."

"What are you doing here?" Jake smiled as he started to grasp the situation and emerge from his shocked state of mind.

"You said that Mckenna was missing and dangerous men were looking for her …" Scarlet lightly scratched Jake's neck and kissed his neck. "I just wanted to feel safe." Scarlet continued to kiss his neck, slowly. "Can you protect me, Jake Hansen?"

Jake smiled his most winsome smile.

"I think I can arrange that."

"Good, I am grateful, and I can be very generous when grateful." Scarlet kissed Jake full on the mouth.

Scarlet pulled her head back, ever so slightly. "You seem nervous."

"Oh baby, I'll be just fine." Jake lifted Scarlet off the ground, sweeping her off her feet as he headed for the door.

Chapter Thirteen

He knew where he was headed before he woke up.
The front part of his brain told him to drop his kids off at
school and head downtown to work, but, the back part of
his brain, the realm that fed his instincts, created a
nagging thought and the thought remained there like a
virus refusing the cure because the only cure for a virus
is to let the virus be the virus. And so, Detective Allison
drove onto Venice Boulevard succumbing to his instincts
instead of listening to the rational chamber.

He knew Jake and the boys had been in that office.
He knew it. Danny didn't know Jake, Pete and Lamar
other than reputation, but he knew them. For as much as
he despised Jake Hansen, he did respect the man's ability
to dig and ask and pester. So, Frank knew full well, Jake
had been in that room…but why?

It was an unusual crime scene when he and
Detective Burkle arrived (the reason they had been called
in to help), and the appearance of Jake and the boys only
added to the strangeness. Murders in Hermosa Beach just
didn't occur and in a pool room in full view of fifteen
people, who couldn't point out the culprit? That was just
bizarre. If it hadn't been for Molly the bartender, it
would've been until the next day that they knew of the
office and the videotape.

As he and Danny entered the office, he knew Jake
had been there. The drink until four a.m. story held no

agua with Frank Allison; he didn't know why they were at the crime scene, but he knew it wasn't because of booze. As the uniforms blocked off the office with crime tape, Burkle spotted the VCR and screen. The video had been stopped which was the biggest clue that someone indeed had been in the room. Why or who would stop the video? The boys had seen the crime on tape.

As Frank drove closer to Trotter's, he clenched on the murder. Zane was a young man with no record other than a DUI year's prior. They had gleaned he had run numbers for Tony Tahoe, maybe Frankie Fairway, but no charges or arrests had come from it. Zane also had a rep for bedding the staff but that wasn't unusual in that industry.

Danny and he had looked at the tape numerous times, rewinding and rewinding to pick out the face of the killer, but it had been a strange murder. One second, Zane is winning at pool. The next, he's lurching across the room, hands over his neck as his life blood spills away. The splatter of blood and the tape indicated that the slashing occurred in the far corner of the room. Zane won the match, was hugged by five of his friends (Zane's last act had been to make an incredible shot) in a revelry of cheers and Molly came up and kissed him. Four people were in line for the bathroom, and a few stood in the doorway. There was something there and even though he had watched the tape over and over, he could not point it out. His instincts had taught him to look for the palpable obscure, but he just couldn't see it.

Frank chastised himself in his mind. His thoughts immediately flashed to Jake Hansen. Why was he there? 4 a.m., bars are long closed. The boys own a bar, if they were all boozing, who was minding the store? They suddenly appeared and dissected the scene.

"Jake must know Zane," Frank said aloud. "And Pete owns a police scanner!" Frank hit the ceiling of his car with his fist.

He was merely working with a supposition, but it played. Pete listened to the scanner as a hobby, he heard the 187 call over the wires in Hermosa, put two and two together and that's the how.

"But what's the why?" Frank whispered to himself.

Frank heard a buzzing and realized his phone had been going off. He looked at the screen of his phone and it read: BURKLE. Frank activated his blue tooth.

"Detective Burkle."

"Where you at, boss?" Danny asked.

As Frank turned left on National from Venice, he debated his options in the conversation with Burkle.

"Running a little late."

"Bullshit, Detective."

That's strike one.

"I thought you were gonna get an extra hour of shut eye, Burkle."

"Don't change the subject. I never went home."

"You crashed in the den?"

"I did and I looked at the video about a hundred times. You said you'd be here by nine. Where are you?"

Strike two.

Allison shook his head. It was getting late fast in this conversation. "I'm gonna shake a tree and see what falls."

"It's Jake Hansen, eh."

Strike three.

Jesus, thought Frank, she's smarter than I thought.

"So, what if it is, he knows something."

"And so do we and we'll be in a better position to approach him after we deduce his involvement."

"I just want him to know, that we know."

"Detective Allison, we don't need to talk to him yet. Come here and let's work the case."

"That's what I'm doing."

"Really? It sounds like you're going to pick a fight."

"The fight was already picked. Getting some bad reception…yea, gotta go."

Frank flipped off the phone as he ran right onto Washington. He felt bad about high hatting his new partner, but this was Jake Hansen, and these were special circumstances.

"Let's see what you know, smart guy." Frank's phone went off and he saw it was Burkle calling him back.

"Sorry kid." Frank lamented, knowing full well it was fucked up to block out his partner, but this was Jake Hansen.

Chapter Fourteen

Jake rubbed his temples, wincing slightly. He dragged a cigarette, pressing the butt between two fingers, nervously flicking ash onto his hard wood floor. His second story bedroom overlooked the Washington split and he often looked out of his window in the morning, contemplating. This morning, he had much to contemplate.

"At least it's a better start than yesterday," he quietly mused, temporarily forgetting the murder he witnessed and Zane's murder on top of that.

Sitting crouched on his teak desk, his feet rested on the back of his desk chair. As Mallory, the cute, little blondie bartender from the Cozy Inn, across the street, swept the plot of concrete in front of Cozy's door, Jake peered to his left and snuck a peek at the naked Scarlet. She rested, asleep, peacefully, in his bed.

Situated on the side of her stomach, to the left, her left breast was partially exposed. She rested at an awkward angle, her left arm over and around her head and, with no covers covering, a long, slender red dragon tattoo revealed itself. It was wrapped around her breast toward her back and slid down her backside, surrounding the scorpion tattoo.

Jake placed his head in his hands. He lifted his head and gazed at her again.

"Weeping may endure through the night but Joy

cometh in the morning."

As he followed the trail of smoke from his fire stick, he remembered touching her body. He remembered slipping his hand down her neck toward her breasts and sliding his face down her stomach, kissing past her smooth navel and then focusing his attention with his mouth where attention required the most focus. And, as he moved his torso up her body, he moved himself into her as he kissed her neck, mouth and ear. She had gasped, whispering his name and as he heard Jake all he could think about was Lily. He cursed himself as he pretended the sexy, beautiful girl beneath him was the twenty two-year old Lily he fantasized of, the Lily of his youth and dreams. And he cursed himself now for not feeling worse about it.

He closed his eyes and shivered at the thought of who he'd become. He had never thought of himself as a failure, rather placing focus on his bet of the day or where he'd find the best happy hour deal. But now, as he lit another cigarette, he realized that was why he drank and gambled. The constant allure of something untenable; some peace without growth and growth without understanding.

"Weeping may endure through the night but Joy cometh in the morning," he whispered, and he did wonder, what had he become?

Jake wondered how many professional offers he rejected, how many letters and calls to resurrect his career had he ignored, and he had ignored them all; until the offers became a trickle and then, just stopped altogether. It brought him back to Lily.

He couldn't remember what felt worse; the knowledge that Lily was cheating on him or the moment she told him she was leaving. He could vividly remember the acrid anger he seethed as his brother, Ryan, provided reassuring comfort to Lily as she sat in their kitchen and tore Jake's life from him. He hadn't disowned his brother at that moment, but that relationship had never fully repaired itself. In fact, they had never spoken since. The discovery of her infidelity made him so angry, when Pete uncovered her infidelity, Jake immediately got into an argument with his boss, Eddie Collins, and set into motion the scenario that would cost him his job, his reputation, his career and, to an extent, his life.

"And boo fucking hoo," he whispered, chastising himself. "Get the fuck over it. Many people get cheated on and abandoned every day. At least try to man up." Jake smiled at his harsh treatment to himself.

"Whatcha chewin' on?" Scarlet lightly yawned, waking Jake from his waking dream.

"Nothing of importance." Jake smiled.

Scarlet sat up in bed a little, pulling the covers up around her chest. "How'd your face get all beat up?"

"My winning personality is often misunderstood. Sometimes even by my friends."

"Your decorator did a nice job." She giggled. "I'll be sure to pay him the compliment."

"How long have you been in LA?" Jake changed the subject as quickly as possible.

"About four years. I ran away from home when I was seventeen. I had a handsy uncle."

"Oh God…I'm so sorry," Jake offered, and Scarlet shrugged.

"Whatever has happened since then is on me. Although I wouldn't mind getting my hands on him."

"Where were you from?"

"Riverside. I plan on going back. But no time soon." Scarlet laid back down onto the bed and delivered Jake a 'come hither' stare. "Why don't you come back to bed?" Scarlet pulled back the little amount of covers that covered her, revealing all.

"How can I refuse that offer." Jake sighed and after putting out his cigarette, followed his instincts and joined her.

As he faced her, she kissed his neck, face and mouth. She was so warm and tiny and soft and wonderful, that for a moment, Scarlet was all that mattered in the addled mind of Jake Hansen. He stared into her eyes and she into his.

"I don't think it's safe for you to go home," Jake interrupted the moment of quiet bliss.

Scarlet puckered a tiny frown.

"But … where will I go?"

Jake grinded his teeth a second as he contemplated his next words.

"You…you can stay here a bit?"

Scarlet's pucker became a full-fledged smile, and she gave Jake a deep kiss. As he returned the kiss, he mentally punched himself.

****

Lamar sat at the high top on the bar side of Trotter's, waiting for his morning cup of love. Usually, he would grab a morning paper and wait for Sophie, who always brought him coffee and then he would read the paper and start his day. Yes, the newspaper was a dying past-time, but he still loved to read it. He hadn't been able to enjoy his morning ritual the previous morn, as Jake had ended his three-day bender atop the high top and then Ed Tall Mountain had arrived. Usually, Lamar awoke with a fire in his eyes but today he needed the coffee. Three hours of sleep will do that; shit, he'd slept in 'til nine a.m.

Lamar dispatched with his ritual morning paper in favor of a notepad and pen. He jotted down notes from the previous day's occurrences and the updates of the case. Lamar wore his reading spectacles as he did so. The previous day had ended darkly with the bizarre murder of Zane. Jake and Pete had interviewed Zane, so Lamar never met him but, still, he felt a responsibility to uncover the culprit. To die with a slit throat in a bar pool room? An awful way to go.

"One day in a row with no sleeping beauty on the bar." Pete slowly stepped into the room.

"Yea, he must be good and zonked. I know we said nine, but I'd be shocked to see him at eleven."

"Fucker better be down before then," Pete warned.

"I guess. Yesterday was a long day's hangover."

"Really? He had a tequila Prairie something at Barnacles and a few cocktails after. He was fine." Pete sat down opposite Lamar and looked down at his notepad. "Mckenna?"

"Yea. So much happened, I need to wrap my head around it."

"Shit, Lamar, you boys went through a decade's worth of excitement last night. I checked the police scanner, no word on the Beaudry incident."

"I'm assuming Little Luck cleaned that but good. Still—" Lamar stopped.

"The dead bodyguard?"

"Yea and if that kid is attached to Blazerian…"

"I know, I thought about that too. I get that Zachary invaded Koreatown with no tithe—"

"Stupid," Lamar interrupted.

"Very. But is that property worth a battle with the Armenians?"

"That's more Jake's department than mine," Lamar concluded.

Sophie entered Trotter's with her usual bounty for the boys. She carried a large brown paper bag in her left hand as her boxing gloves were slung over her shoulder with a workout towel wrapped around the gloves. In her right hand, she held a tray with four cups of coffee. She was dressed in dark yoga pants with a halter top.

"Damn girl, how come I didn't know you were boxing?" Lamar inquired.

"I usually get back before you're down. I've been kickboxing four times a week for two months."

"You look..." Pete stumbled with his words as he attempted to avoid being the creepy old man.

Sophie set down the tray of coffees in front of Pete and Lamar and blushed a little as she heard Pete stop his sentence.

"Fit. She looks fit." Lamar saved Pete.

"Thanks guys," Sophie replied walking toward a server station. "I've been hitting the bag pretty hard."

The boys reached for their coffees as Sophie set her gloves down on the bar and placed the brown bag on the server station. Pulling a plate out, she emptied the brown bag of scones and muffins onto the plate. She took the plate and set it next to the tray in front of the boys. Pete grabbed the first scone.

"That's a marmalade peel, Mr. Mills, you may not like that," Sophie offered.

Making a scrunch face, Pete set the scone down.

"Call me Pete, please Sophie." He stared at the other scones and muffins.

Sophie pointed to a dark scone. "Cinnamon." She smiled. Sophie stood and pulled her coffee from the tray. "I bought Mr. Hansen a coffee," she said.

"Sleeping beauty ain't down yet." Pete got out between a mouthful of cinnamon scone.

"Okay, well, it'll be here for him." She smiled and started to walk away. "I'm going to fix the drain below the third sink. It was leaking last night."

"Oh, okay," a surprised Pete responded as Lamar snatched a muffin. "My tools are in the office, if you want to grab them."

"Thank you and no offense, Mr. Mills, but I have my own tools. Your tools are ancient."

"Just like you." Lamar laughed.

"Shut up." Pete grimaced. He leaned over and whispered to Lamar. "She has her own tools?"

"She's pretty handy, Pete. Apparently, did some handiwork back in Hemet for a summer job."

Sophie stepped into the back room and emerged with a toolbox as Pete and Lamar watched with respect.

"That girl amazes me more every day." Pete shook his head.

"Me too. But she's a woman, Pete."

"Copy that." Pete looked down at the notes Lamar had written. "We know Zane sent the camera to 29 Palms."

"Back it up. The sketch Mckenna gave Zachary. That's now the key." Lamar bit into a scone.

"True, but the sketch comes from a pimp without the camera. The camera is evidence."

"We trying to find Mckenna, Pete, not make a case."

"Sure, but the camera is worth killing for." Pete pointed at a note in the book to illustrate his point.

"Yeah, I suppose." Lamar stood to stretch his legs, "The Indian fella and…we thinking Latino's?"

"I don't even want to speculate on those guys but if I had to venture a guess, I'd say Mexican. Still, I'm not so sure they killed Zane. They were there at the time and yes, the one guy followed us and at some level they are involved but…" Pete trailed off.

"You're saying it was someone else there? In that little pool room?"

"Maybe."

"I think he was Sri Lankan," Lamar guessed.

"Seriously? You ever met a Sri Lankan?"

"No." Lamar smiled.

Pete rolled his eyes. "Dammit, I wish we coulda grabbed the whole tape." Pete made a fist.

"Jake did well just to get the pictures. Smart."

"Damn right it was. Good to see the old Jake back in motion."

"A few hiccups."

"He did pee himself at Beaudry." Lamar smiled.

"You're kidding me?" Pete laughed. "At least he didn't shit himself."

"Baby steps."

Sophie fiddled behind the bar, using a wrench to tighten the pipe below the third sink. She'd grabbed a tiny washer from her toolbox. As she wrenched the pipe, after shutting the water off, she applied the washer. Now she was tightening the pipe.

The creak of the side door to the right side of the bar could be heard. This was the usual signal of Jake's arrival from his apartment.

"Jake's here," Sophie spoke loud enough for the boys to hear. Lamar looked at his cell phone.

"I thought he might sleep in a little more."

As Lamar and Pete pretended to focus on Lamar's notes, they snuck a peek out of their peripheral vision but placed their full attention to Jake when Jake entered with Scarlet.

"Son of a bitch," Lamar whispered from the corner of his mouth.

As they approached, Pete and Lamar stood. Scarlet wore an over-sized USC gray sweatshirt, of Jake's, over her skimpy outfit from the night before. Pete shuffled uncomfortably as Lamar gave Scarlet a broad smile. Pete calmed himself and forced himself to extend his hand.

"Hello, I'm Pete."

Scarlet took Pete's big hand and shook it. She quickly caught sight of his other hand but looked away from it.

"Sorry Pete," Jake started, "slipped my mind that you hadn't met Scarlet."

"Scarlet, wonderful name."

"Morning Scarlet," Lamar offered. Scarlet stepped up to Lamar and gave him a big hug.

"Can't go through what we went through last night and not hug it out," Scarlet remarked.

Lamar returned the hug with an awkward embrace. Jake blushed slightly as she hugged Lamar and Pete gave Jake a dirty look.

"I didn't want her going back to her apartment." Jake spoke in a grave tone.

"I think that's a good idea," Pete agreed. He motioned with his hands for Scarlet to sit. "Please sit, Sophie was kind enough to bring us some scones if you're hungry."

"Starving." Scarlet sat and grabbed a scone, greedily

eating it.

"Jake?" Pete looked at the eating Scarlet. "Can Lamar and I talk to you…in the other room?"

Jake stood and leaned down to Scarlet. "I'll be back in a sec."

Jake led his friends from the foyer to the back part of the bar. After they were clear from the view of Scarlet, Pete stepped in front of Jake and stopped him.

"What are you doing?" Pete questioned Jake.

"Okay, okay." Jake held his hands up, "We got back from Hermosa and I came in here to grab a nightcap. Beer and a shot. The door was unlocked and suddenly she was there."

"She just happened to come here," Pete spoke in accusatory tone.

"Yes. Listen, I'm glad she came here and felt comfortable enough to come some place she felt safe."

Pete looked to Lamar, shook his head and sighed.

"Whatever happened between Scarlet and Jake ain't any of our business," Lamar offered.

"Exactly," Jake agreed.

Sophie walked up to the trio, holding onto the wrench. Her shirt and clothes were soaked.

"Sink is fixed. Just needed a new washer. The other one was threaded."

Jake looked to Sophie with a quizzical look on his face.

"You…you fixed the sink? It's been leaking for two years."

"Well, I've only worked here a short time. I'd have fixed it earlier if I had known."

As Sophie walked away, Jake called out to her.

"Hey Soph… I've a … there is a … my friend …

um, that is to say my friend, Scarlet … I figured…you know…"

"Is Scarlet the girl up front?"

"Yes," Jake answered.

"You want me to show her the ropes around here?"

"You know, we could use another server around her," Lamar spoke.

"Uh…" Jake became speechless.

"You're right, Lamar," Pete chimed in, "we could use another server around here."

Sophie brightened at the idea.

"Terrific! I was thinking of working the desk at kickbox for free classes. Thanks Mr. Hansen!"

Sophie ran off, leaving Jake with his mouth wide open. Pete stepped up to Jake and patted his shoulder.

"Looks like you got a live-in girlfriend AND a new employee." Pete chuckled.

"Not sure how I feel about you sleeping with the staff, Jake," Lamar added.

"Fuck you guys."

Pete and Lamar enjoyed a good laugh at Jake's expense, until Pete lifted his hands.

"All right, all right, all right. We got some work to do. Lamar and I have been going over the notes of yesterday."

"And you concluded it was a clusterfuck?" Jake eyed Pete.

"More like a cluster-hump but yes," Pete responded. "We got it down that she's either hiding…"

"Kidnapped," Lamar offered.

"Or dead," Jake finished. His words drove the group to silence until Jake spoke again.

"She's not dead. Zane wouldn't be dead if she were

dead. They need her."

"They need her?!?" Lamar asked incredulously.

"The sketch…the camera," Pete responded. "The camera has the tangible proof of the sketch. So, they need the camera."

"Which is on its way to 29 Palms," Jake mused.

"Which is on its way to 29 Palms," Lamar repeated. "And whoever that guy is with S. Newman, he's the key."

"What about the Indian and the other guys?" Jake asked.

"Sri Lankan," Lamar interjected.

"What?"

"Lamar is convinced he's Sri Lankan."

"No, I'm just saying because of…how dark he is don't make him Indian. He could be Pakistani. Or Sri Lankan."

Jake rolled his eyes and looked to Pete.

"What the fuck ever, all I'm saying is that we saw him WAY too much for him to not be involved. And those guys were there…"

"Agreed," Lamar and Pete answered in unison. "So," they both asked in unison.

"Yea, I've been thinking…" Jake hemmed and hawed a bit. "We need to go see JR."

"JR?" Lamar's eyebrows raised.

"Yes."

"How are you planning on getting his help?" Pete asked Jake.

"I'm going to apologize."

Chapter Fifteen

As Jake ambled out of Trotter's, stepping into the razor-sharp light of a sunny southern California day, he realized how little he had slept. And that he had forgotten the coffee Sophie purchased him, on the bar.

He realized he'd allowed himself to indulge with Scarlet, perhaps one too many times. Jake stopped quickly and turned, wishing to retrieve his coffee. Lamar, also stepping into the bright light, barreled into Jake, nearly knocking Jake over. The brute force of Lamar spun Jake so that he was facing the street. Luckily, he caught himself, bracing himself on the parking meter.

"Jesus Christ." Lamar grabbed Jake and brought him back to verticality.

Pete laughed at the Keystone Kops routine. However, his laugh was short lived. Detective Frank Allison leaned against the hood of his car, a feisty sneer on his mug.

"This is all we need," Pete coughed out.

Jake, still discombobulated, looked at Pete's face and anticipated the sight. He looked to his right and saw Allison.

"Terrific." Jake shook his head.

Allison stepped off his lean and walked toward the three. He removed his sunglasses when he stood a few feet away.

"Where you boys off to on this fine morning?"

"Detective." Jake smiled at Allison. "We have some errands."

"Uh-Huh." Allison returned a cynical smile.

"What brings you to our neighborhood this fine morning?" Pete asked.

"Oh, you know, I was nowhere near your neighborhood and I thought I'd see … well, I thought I'd pay you boys a visit."

"Damn right neighborly of you, Detective," Lamar contributed.

"Amazing. You boys were up 'til the wee hours of the morning, boozing as you say you were and here you are…bright eyed and bushy tailed and ready for the day. Not a hangover between the three of ya."

"Truth be told…" Jake raised his hand. "I'm a little hungover."

"Of course, you are, smart guy."

"Also, I don't think I've ever heard anyone describe Pete as bright eyed or any kind of tail." Jake's smile returned. "How's the wife?"

"Still puts up with me, thanks for asking Jake. How's Mrs. Alex Vila?"

Pete and Lamar grimaced and looked at Jake, who also grimaced.

"Ouch. Low blow, even for you, Frank."

"That's Detective. You know, I can never laugh hard enough knowing that your wife left you for the mayor of Los Angeles."

"Technically, he was only a public defender at that point. But I can never laugh hard enough knowing that your former partner is now in Internal Affairs. Probably investigating your ass. Thanks to little ol' me."

The smirk on Allison's face disappeared and he took a step toward Jake, with intent. Pete stepped in between.

"You're so goddamn smart, Hansen. Now, I want to know what you know about Zane Adkins murder."

"Who?" Jake asked.

"This isn't the way you want to play this. I know you were in that office."

"What office?" Pete retorted.

"See, I expect that bullshit from Jake, but you were a detective. Really?"

"We stumbled onto your scene. Our bad," Lamar spoke up.

"Right, of course you did. At four in the morning, you cretins stumble onto my murder scene and when I learn that there is an office which houses the videotape of the Barnacles premises, two doors down, I investigate. And you know what I see? A video machine that has been tampered with. Now, who would do that?"

Jake, Pete, and Lamar all looked at each other, shrugging and playing dumb. Jake took a small step toward Allison.

"None of that changes the fact that we were out drinking last night and just happened to run into you and the fetching Detective Burkle," Jake delivered.

Allison removed a notebook from his pocket and pulled out a pen.

"I know you boys were there. Start talking, or else."

"Or else what?" Pete folded his arms and puffed up.

"Anything you glean from that video?"

"What video?" the trio responded in unison.

Allison returned the notebook and pen to their prior homes. "I know you're hiding something. And the longer you hide it—"

"Detective Allison…we got nothing for you," Jake sighed.

"Okay. All right. You boys take care now. I'll come back and when I come back, I'll expect complete cooperation." Allison walked toward his car.

"Is Detective Burkle seeing anyone?" Jake called out.

Allison stopped for a second and looked back. "Stay away from my partner, hot shot." Allison continued to his car, got into it and quickly sped away.

"You think that's our play?" Lamar asked of the other two.

"We're gonna have to come clean at some point. He might be an asshole but he's no dummy," Pete warned.

"Let's get our bearings. Talk to JR and see who this sketch is. But you're right, Detective Allison does have a play in this," Jake mused.

****

The Durango remained mostly quiet for the drive as they crept toward downtown Los Angeles and JR's lair. Quiet rides were unnerving to Lamar. He could stand on his head and be silent for an entire day, but confined spaces usually made him chattery. It was one of the reasons cell mates never lasted very long with him; that and most of his cell mates were scared to death of him. Lamar looked in the rearview mirror and saw Jake looking out of the window, pensive. Pete sat in the passenger seat and looked out the other direction.

"How much did Scarlet looking like Lily play into her last night?" Lamar asked of Jake.

"What the fuck kind of question is that?" Jake flashed a bit of anger. Pete looked in the mirror and made eye contact with Jake.

"Take it easy. Man, you let people get under your skin when it comes to Lily," Lamar offered.

"I know, I know. I'm sorry. I'm a little bleary eyed. I have been thinking on Lily a lot lately."

"You were thinking on her last night," Lamar mentioned.

"She *is* in the public eye," Pete offered.

"Too much so. I was woken yesterday by the voice of Alex Vila in his press conference."

"I knew you were awake." Lamar smiled.

"Ha ha. Yea, it still bothers me. Probably because I've never really dealt with it." Jake looked out the window as they passed the Galen Center, USC newest sports facility. "I had an inkling when I got Pete to tail her. I wanted him to prove me wrong. But when it became truth…that she was lying to me; that she was cheating on me, crushed me. The lie. That the undeniable love she had for me was a lie. It made everything in my life a lie." Jake paused a beat. "I believed in the job I was doing. I believed in the integrity of looking for the truth, no matter the cost. Now, I always had proclivities, but I never strayed from Lily. She was my center, my core. My belief in the truth of our love kept me centered in the world. And when that became a lie…I couldn't believe in anything."

"It was just a different truth, Jake," Pete spoke up.

"How's that?"

"You now don't trust or believe in anything because Lily fell out of love with you?"

"She lied to me."

"She left you, that much is true. You've always questioned everything and once she left you, you lost that. You did lose your center. Now, the only truth you know is the absolute loss at the end of a five-game parlay." Pete made eye contact with Jake.

"That's not fair."

"It isn't?" Pete continued. "You never believed the quote unquote facts in front of you. It's what made you an amazing journalist and a horrible husband. You were always looking for the truth. Maybe the truth isn't interested in being found. And when you found the truth about Lily…maybe she lied to you, Jake…but she was gone long before she cheated on you."

"Don't try to be profound, Pete, you know it gives you a headache."

"Right." Pete nodded. "You don't trust or believe in anything anymore."

"I trust and believe in you two."

"Ah thanks man," Lamar responded. "That'll be two hundred dollars."

Startled, Jake shook his head in confusion. "What?"

"You owe Pete and I, two hundred dollars."

"What the fuck for?"

"That's what you pay your therapist per hour, ain't it?" Lamar gave Jake a big smile.

"Yea," Pete chimed in, "two hundred smackers or we'll take it out of your cut."

"You fuckers." Jake grinned.

Jake had been thinking on Lily, but he also had JR on his mind. JR was an unusual individual, one known to be extremely loyal but also one to hold animus over something trivial, and whatever the malfeasance Jake had committed, trivial it was not.

Jose Ricardo Almeida, aka JR, grew up in a one-bedroom home in West Covina, with his mother, Brenda, who worked three jobs to keep food on the table. As JR grew, he nearly ate his family out of the home.

JR hailed from Aguascalientes in Mexico and defied the Mexican stereotype of small people. As his childhood friends remained tiny, JR grew and grew until a doctor discovered a Pituitary gland issue and began to prescribe medication for JR. But JR was already huge and due to childhood teasing, JR became a recluse. However, JR excelled at school and eventually found his niche in the computer sciences. By the time he was nineteen, he had amassed a small amount of money as a ghost on the dark web.

JR had a passion for detective novels, and it was this hobby that led him to an internet seminar, where Jake was the guest speaker. JR asked question after question of the exasperated Jake. Intrigued, Jake met with JR and got him a job at the newspaper. From that, a friendship and partnership grew. Where Jake had come from a home of two cultures, JR was raised in the heart of one. Still, in Jake, JR found a mentor and in JR, Jake found someone with whom he could relate.

JR worked as a 'Research Assistant' for Jake. He wasn't really a researcher but rather a handy hacker who was not only capable of finding almost any fact hidden he was the smartest man Jake ever met. Eddie allowed Jake and JR allowances because they always got results. In the basement of the newspaper, they created a bunker for JR, an incredible set-up of computers working in unison. It was innovative, ingenuous and off the books. And so, Jake and JR pursued cases and stories with JR as Mozart and Jake, Salieri.

Jake and the boys worked with an undercover GND detective, Zubin Poosh, for six months. The job was to work with an alphabet soup task force that worked to track down Eusebio Benitez, a former captain of the Baja Cartel who started a splinter group and initiated a war within the Baja Cartel. A dock shoot-out yielded two dead cops, but they did capture Benitez and his right-hand man, Sandy Ortiz. It was a huge grab and win for the task force. Jake wrote a blistering series of articles that won awards.

However, when Benitez and Ortiz were transferred under the watch of Poosh, Detective Martin Cruz and Detective Frank Allison, something went wrong. Despite discretion and ultra-secret maneuvers, the caravan was attacked. The result was the death of Benitez, the escape of Sandy Ortiz and the disappearance of Zubin Poosh. Zubin's blood was found at the scene, but no Zubin Poosh. A new task force was convened to uncover the details and place blame.

Jake put his efforts to uncover the truth and clear his friend Zubin's name, as his disappearance had placed him high on the list of suspects. Jake believed the task force was a smoke screen. Utilizing JR's expertise and risking his life, Jake tracked down what he believed to be the mother of all conspiracies. JR had followed a computer trail that led him to a dummy corporation and a fund that made payments through non-profits. One of the non-profits led right to Robbery-Homicide.

Jake wrote a crackling expose that detailed the dummy corp. and how the culprit seemed to be a detective at Robbery & Homicide: Martin Cruz. JR had never voiced his opinion one way or the other when it came to Jake's reports and findings but, on the occasion of this article, JR voiced concerns about the validity of the sources.

"It's too easy, Jake. I found this info…too easy."

"Didn't you have to hack to find the info?"

"Yes, but it was rudimentary work."

"Rudimentary?!?"

"It's hard to explain, Jake."

"You were so excited for the finding."

"I was but…we want this so bad…and to do it for Zubin…but it feels like a set-up."

"JR, take it easy. You're just being paranoid."

"Maybe, but maybe trust my instinct this once."

Jake had not trusted JR's instincts.

Eddie delayed the story and then Jake committed the ultimate act of betrayal. He released the story anyway, on the internet, and the fall of Jake Hansen began in earnest. But JR had been collateral damage. The fallout of the released bombshell was nuclear. Eddie Collins barely survived and to keep control of the paper he loved; he needed a sacrifice besides Jake. And that sacrifice was JR.

Getting fired worked out to not be the end of the world for JR as he parlayed his freedom into a lucrative freelance gig. His small apartment at the fancy The Metro building eventually became the bottom floor of The Metro. JR's skills helped the philandering owner of the building in a nasty divorce and the man's gratefulness paid off as the bottom floor of The Metro became JR's lair. His old set-up paled in comparison to his six-computer set-up, gazebo style. His compound was attached to The Metro's parking garage, but it was Xanadu to JR.

****

As Lamar pulled into The Metro parking, Pete took a look at Jake. Jake had never reached out to JR following both of their dismissals and Pete silently condemned Jake for his selfishness. Pete had reached out a few times to JR via text and the response each time was a curt, 'I'm fine.'

"Are you prepared to be rebuffed?" Pete asked Jake.

"I've considered the scenario."

"And?"

"Listen, I know I fucked up. I've been fucking up for seven years and JR was collateral damage. That was my fault. I'm gonna apologize and hope he forgives me."

As they walked toward the large steel door that encased JR's lair, apprehension crept into Jake's stomach. He'd been close to JR, nearly as close to JR as he was to Pete and Lamar. After seeing Eddie, the previous night, Jake could feel a catharsis taking over possession of his being. He realized that the apprehension was also a product of relief. He was putting right what once was wrong.

The three of them approached the steel door with Jake in the lead. A TV monitor was situated above and to the right of the door and just to the right of the door was a keypad with numbers.

"You sure this is a good idea?" Lamar asked. "I'm already creeped out."

"Just remember what the last article did to him," Pete reminded.

"Yes, this is an idea. Good...we'll see and yes, Pete, I know what happened with my last article. I'm sure he's forgotten all about that."

Lamar gave Pete a 'Really' grimace.

Jake leaned over to the keypad and closed his eyes. He opened them and typed in a six-number code.

"What did you type in?" Pete asked.

"Picard."

"Picard? Like Jean Luc?" Lamar inquired.

"Yes. Jean Luc Picard. It's always his password."

"Some hacker." Pete rolled his eyes. The intercom above the password made a sound of static and a booming voice came over the intercom.

"FE FI FO FOM. Who awakes my kingdom?"

"Hey. Hey buddy. It's uh…it's your old pal." An ominous silence responded to Jake's comments. For nearly a minute, silence reigned.

"Maybe…this wasn't a good idea," Jake whispered. Finally, the intercom responded.

"You got some kinda nerve, Hansen," the intercom responded. It was certainly JR's voice. For such a large man, he had a high-pitched delivery and lilt.

"Geez JR…it's been seven years. Aren't you even curious how I am?"

"I have monitors in your bar, dipshit."

"Oh," Jake meekly replied. He glanced to Pete and Lamar. "Did you know that?"

"How the fuck would we know that?" answered Lamar.

"I will say you do have guts showing your face here," JR said.

"We're here as well, JR," Pete called out.

"Hey boys. Very well. Access…three forty-nine Zulu." The wall to the right of the keypad and monitor slid open, like a garage sliding door. The hall behind the sliding door led to a freight elevator. Jake motioned for Pete and Lamar to follow him through the door and they did.

"This is a bad idea," Pete iterated. Jake entered the freight elevator and was followed by Pete. Lamar stood on the outside of the freight elevator.

"C'mon Lamar, let's not keep Captain Picard waiting," Pete mumbled.

"Man, I don't like regular elevators. Fuck this shit."

"Lamar, it's just an elevator. Come on," Jake pleaded.

Lamar sighed and entered.

"All right, but…" Lamar started but couldn't finish. The doors of the elevator closed immediately upon his entering the hold. "What the fuck?!?"

"It's cool, it's cool," Jake reassured. "Let me see, what floor," Jake looked at the keypad of the elevator but there wasn't one. "Well, that's a little spooky."

"Hold on," JR's voice crackled over an intercom.

"Hold on for what?" Lamar asked apprehensively. "Motherfucker, I can't be dying in some freight elevator. This is like some *Saw* shit."

Pete closed his eyes and smiled. The back door of the freight elevator opened. Pete laughed.

"He lives in the basement, boys. We parked in the basement." Pete motioned to the open back door of the elevator. "Shall we, ladies."

Jake gave Pete a gentle tap in the chest, as he exited. Lamar walked out giving Pete a dirty look.

"You know I could fuck you up," Lamar hissed at Pete.

"Like to see you try, convict." Pete smiled.

The boys walked down a dark hallway until they reached a large room with the walls nothing but television screens.

"Holy shit," Lamar exclaimed. "There must be a hundred screens in here."

They stood on the edge of the large room, awed by the number of television screens. In the middle of the room stood a gazebo. In the middle of the gazebo was computer hacker nirvana. Ten computer consoles with monitors. The high-tech quality of the room was astounding.

Suddenly, every television screen and every computer monitor became the face of Jake. Jake did a three-sixty staring at every monitor with his face on it.

"JR!!! Come out and show yourself," Jake called out.

And suddenly, JR was standing beside him. JR wasn't the most svelte of cats but what he didn't have in appearance he made up with an array of astoundingly awful t-shirts. The yellow shirt he wore held the animated drawing of a honeybee with glasses. Below the bee, the caption read: SEXY BEE-AST.

The six-foot three, three hundred twenty-pound Hispanic walked so that he was standing directly in front of Jake. Lamar and Pete took two steps back. JR still had the cherub face of a young man and he was young in comparison to the three men in front of him.

"Why have you come to me?" JR folded his arms.

Jake sighed and hung his head. He did feel bad, not just about leaving his friend to twist in the wind but also, not reaching out through the years.

"I…I am really sorry about the story…not listening to you…getting you fired and…never reaching out to apologize."

JR stood and stared at Jake. He stood and stared for what seemed like an hour but was only about thirty seconds. JR took a step toward Jake, who didn't move. JR closed his eyes quickly and opened them.

"I could never be mad at you." JR reached over and gave Jake the most uncomfortable hug of his life. "You complete me." JR held onto the hug and Jake snuck a peek at Pete and Lamar, laughing behind him.

"Okay, okay, JR….that's enough I think."

JR pulled back and wiped tears from his eyes. He looked past Jake and waved to Pete and Lamar.

"Detective. Lamar."

"Hey," they both replied, waving at JR.

"So." JR clapped his hands, "what brings you all to my castle of information?"

"We're working a case," Jake replied.

"Wow, back in the investigative journalist game?"

"Not exactly." Jake scratched his head. "We, the three of us, were hired to find someone."

"You guys are doing the P.I. thing? Very Easy Rawlins. Cool. Wait…there was some chatter about an incident on Beaudry. Koreatown. Shots fired. Underground club or something. That would mean Little Luck. You guys?"

Pete whistled and started to clap. "Tell you what, JR, fuck these guys. You want to start a detective business?"

"Very nice of you to ask, Detective, but my business is doing pretty well."

"It would appear," Jake responded looking at all of the equipment.

"So, this missing person?"

"Mckenna Murphy. Also, Mckenna Tall Mountain," Jake offered.

"Of the Tall Mountain family." JR whistled. "Big shit going on in Tribal territory. She's missing?"

Jake reached into his back pocket and pulled out the sketch. He handed it to JR. JR looked at the drawings of S. Newman and the unknown man.

"We need to know the man on the right. The other

man is S. Newman. We would like some background on him as well." Jake pulled up the pictures from Barnacles and handed it to JR. "Also, these guys."

JR looked at the sketch and then took a look at the pictures on Jake's phone. JR motioned to Jake's phone.

"I recognize the Indian fella. Bad news, as I recall. And the guy with the scar on his face… rings a bell."

JR took the sketch and the phone and walked toward his gazebo. He approached and entered the gazebo, sitting in a chair at the main terminal. He took the sketch and scanned into a scanner to the right of the main monitor. "This should take less than a minute."

"Man's all business." Jake smiled.

JR reached under the main terminal and grabbed a bag of marsh-mellows. He began to eat them, one by one.

"All business," Pete replied.

JR took Jake's cell phone and scanned the picture of the Indian national and then the picture of the other two men. JR spun around in his chair and stood. He pulled a remote from the desk and pressed the remote toward a panel in the back. The television screens flickered a light blue with an hourglass spinning in the middle. Pete stepped away from the gazebo and walked to the far wall, where the largest screen resided.

"The first scan should be completed in…five…four, three, two…" JR provided the countdown. "Now."

A loud BEEP emanated from the main computer and an image shot onto the television screens. The image was an older image of the Indian national. The man wore dark sunglasses and was crossing an unknown street. He wore white linen pants and a dark blue button up. The name at the bottom of the screen read: ERNEST CAMPION.

"Ernest Campion," murmured Jake. The image of

Campion changed so that it took only half of the screen, vertically, while the other half illustrated Campion's dossier.

"I thought I knew him!" JR started. "His *nom de plume* is The Sri Lankan."

"Motherfucker!" Lamar exclaimed. "I told you he was Sri Lankan."

"No, you didn't." Pete clapped back. "You said he might be Sri Lankan."

"Anyway," JR continued, "he's an artist with the stiletto."

"That would put him at the top of the list for last night," Jake mused.

"In the late seventies and early eighties, the Soviets experimented with third world assassins. They kidnapped Campion from Sri Lanka in 1977 and transformed him into a world class killer. It says he's rumored to have assassinated Luongo in Senegal in 1997. After the fall of communism, he became one of the world's greatest hitters for hire. He's perfect. No one would ever suspect a Sri Lankan. Hell, no one even pays attention to them. He just blends."

"That we can vouch for," Pete remarked. "Hired assassin takes out local bar manager?"

"Seems like overkill, eh," Jake responded.

The main monitor released a couple more beeps. The face of S. Newman popped up in the screens.

The picture of S. Newman was of him ten years previous. He had a dark mustache but there was no denying it was him. As his image moved to take half of the screen, an array of articles, business and charity photos took the other half.

"S. Newman...CFO of the Indian casinos," JR read.

"We knew that already," Pete pointed out.

"Runs the financials of the casinos...business holdings, growth funds...blah, blah, blah..." Jake spoke, uninterested.

The screen changed again, and it held the professional business head shot of the unknown man. Lamar walked over to stand next to Pete and Jake stood behind JR, who sat down at his main computer. The name DARIO MENDOZA popped up on the screen.

"Dario Mendoza," Pete mumbled.

"That's strange," JR whispered.

"What?" asked Jake.

"I know that name. Dario Mendoza died in an automobile accident in 1995," JR called out.

"He what?" Jake asked, puzzled.

As Mendoza's image moved to half of the screen, the 1995 obituary for him popped up on the screen.

"Mendoza has been dead sixteen years?" Lamar asked.

"Presumed dead," Pete pondered.

"No wonder his face is worth killing for," Lamar remarked.

"It says here that Mendoza is believed to have been behind the assassination of Benito Gonzalez, the then leader of Los Nuevos. One week later, Mendoza was killed in a car accident," JR read.

"Time to disappear, Dario," Lamar opined. "You boys notice that Mendoza bears a pretty strong resemblance to Tony Tahoe?"

"Jake's bookie?" JR asked.

"How do you know he's my bookie?"

"Uh hello, have you seen my equipment? I know everything about you."

"Creepy." Jake made an appalled face.

"He's not Tony Tahoe," Pete commented.

"No," replied Jake, "but he does look a lot like him. So, Mendoza killed Gonzalez which means he was a member of…."

JR typed into his computer and more information popped up on the screen.

"Let me go through Newman's financials," JR quietly spoke, typing. "This is interesting."

Lamar and Pete walked to the gazebo, joining JR and Jake.

"Whatdya got?" Pete asked.

"Logano corp."

"What's Logano corp.?" Jake asked.

"It's a dummy cooperation," JR replied. "I've been seeing more and more of this name in many of my searches."

"What kind of dummy corp.?" Lamar inquired.

"Money laundering. I first saw the name Logano in late '09." JR continued to type until a new screen came up. "Yep, there it is. Logano corp. First popped up in a …. wait for it…DEA investigation into … who Jake?"

"The Baja Cartel," Jake answered.

"The Baja Cartel." JR nodded.

"S. Newman is laundering Baja Cartel money through the casinos." Pete spoke, placing his hands on his head.

"You think Tall Mountain knows?" Lamar asked.

"Tall Mountain is ambitious but not stupid," Jake remarked.

JR continued to type, and the background of Dario Mendoza came up on the screen.

"Wow, look at this guy. Yale grad, Summa Cum

Laude … MBA…top of his class. High end business deals for Lezcano and Banamex in Mexico City and Guadalajara." JR shook his head, impressed.

"And presumed dead," Pete pointed out.

"And not seen or heard of since." Jake smiled. "A financial whiz kid, allegedly behind the murder of a leader of the Los Nuevos Cartel…chummy with S. Newman who is laundering for the Baja's."

"No." Pete shook his head, "Don't even think it. Jake Hansen, we've been down this rabbit-hole before."

"Ladies and gentlemen, I believe we've found the Baja Cartel's CFO," Jake proudly proclaimed.

A loud beep emanated from JR's computers. JR maneuvered his chair and typed a few buttons. Suddenly, appearing on all of the screen was the visage of the facial scarred man. He wore sunglasses and it was an action shot, but it was the man Jake and Pete had seen. A name popped up on the screen: XAVIER.

"Xavier," Jake wondered.

"Xavier with an X," JR replied.

The dossier of Xavier with an X appeared on the screen.

"Oh shit," Pete proclaimed.

"He's the wet boy for Los Nuevos's. He's responsible for nearly a hundred murders. He always works with a partner," JR read off the screen.

"A wet boy?" Lamar asked.

"He's an assassin for the Nuevos," Pete answered.

"Oh Christ." Jake squatted.

"No, no, no. Jake, we are dropping this case right now. This is your white whale." Pete pointed at Jake.

"Can't do it, Pete, we gotta pursue this."

As Jake responded, Lamar took five steps back from

Pete and JR removed himself from Jake.

"Jake, your obsession with the cartel has set your life back seven years. If Mendoza was behind the killing, Los Nuevos will want him," Pete spoke with exasperation.

"The Sri Lankan is a classic killer. Invisible. Xavier likes it messy. Campion will kill with a blade and a whisper. Xavier will blow up your building or rain bullets on you." JR shook his head. "They must know of each other."

"They have too. They were sitting a few feet from each other," Jake wondered. "Look, Newman and Mendoza are trying to cover their tracks. Mendoza doesn't want it out that he's alive and Newman doesn't want the council to uncover his laundering. Pete, I love you and I respect your thoughts. But this is about finding Mckenna. That little girl took a picture of the long thought dead number two man of the Baja Cartel. And we better find her. And we're gonna."

Pete closed his eyes.

Chapter Sixteen

Mckenna took in a deep breath, closed her eyes, and exhaled slowly. The night had been a rough one. She shook her shoulders convulsively, attempting to remove any memories of the night, the shelter, and the darkness. The night held horrors years of therapy would need to expunge.

There had been no room at the hostel. There was a cot at the community center of Saint Rita's and her fifty bucks had garnished a better spot. Ed Tall Mountain would be proud of her, she thought.

Fuck him.

She found it in herself to step into a breakfast joint and sit at the counter. The diner wasn't too busy for a morning shift and Mckenna slipped quietly into the world where people loved to mind their own business. Mckenna knew her body odor probably wasn't too offensive to others, but she personally could tell she hadn't showered in a day or two. And her body felt like it had been far longer.

She placed her portfolio down. In her pocket, folded neatly, was seven hundred and fifty dollars; her life blood, for now, as she waited for the bus to take her to Yucca Valley.

The pretty female Asian server, wearing glasses and a tired smile, approached her from behind the counter. She patiently measured Mckenna up, looking like she was considering whether to refuse service. Mckenna quietly and quickly pulled her roll of cash out and placed a fifty on the counter. The server smiled a cautious smile and set a menu down. Obstacle number one, averted.

"Water please," Mckenna rasped.

The server with the name tag reading, MAI, obliged. Mckenna closed her eyes and gathered her thoughts. The 10:15 was an hour away and she would be gone from Los Angeles; who knew, maybe to never return.

"It is unwise to fan that much cash in public."

Mckenna looked to her right at the voice. The English accented voice belonged to the man sitting to her right. He was Indian, maybe Pakistani with a deep sepia complexion, handsome features, and a pleasantness about him. However, Mckenna noticed he had a strange intensity about him with the intensity focused in the eyes, eyes that seemed to peer through her. The eyes were light, a light green, and they bore a hole into her mind.

"Who are you, my guardian angel?" Mckenna asked with an edge, managing to muster up her courage to sound tough and indignant.

"Perhaps I'm just a concerned observer." The man returned his focus to the cup of hot drink in front of him.

Mckenna looked toward his cup. "Tea?" she asked, thinking that she'd seen this man.

"Why yes, black tea. The establishment provided me with the hot water. I brought my own tea."

"Really, you brought your own?"

"Yes. I have a green house. I make my own tea."

The stranger took a sip of his tea and moved his attention to his tiny, spiral notebook. He jotted down a few words. Mckenna attempted to focus on the menu in front of her but she struggled to remember how she knew him.

"I don't usually carry this much cash."

"Pardon me for my intrusion. It is none of my concern."

Her eyes connected with his and she felt herself blush.

She casually eyed his outfit. He wore white linen pants with light brown loafers. He wore a baby blue short-sleeved button down with a delicate cross on a necklace. He had an elegant grace about him which did not befit any diner near a bus stop. Mckenna worked her mind over to the curiosity of the stranger next to her.

"It really was an imposition on my end. However, with the proximity to the bus terminal, I can only presume your destination is at the end of one of the buses. Furthermore, with no hand purse or clutch and a large amount of cash, it's logical you resided recently at the hostel down the street. But, with this being high season for Germans, the hostel shall be full. Perhaps you spent this prior evening at the shelter. Rita's?"

The precise directness of his intonation shook her from her trance. She remembered how she knew him. Her coffee place. The taco stand. The bus stop.

He reached into his shirt pocket and for a sliver of a second, Mckenna thought, this is the moment of my death.

However, from his shirt, he removed a money clip, thick with cash and after staring into the eyes of Mckenna, returned his attention to Mai.

"Young miss, if I may. Pardon, but I'll be paying now. I would like to pay for whatever this young miss would be having."

As Mckenna stared in awe at this strange man, he

leafed a hundred-dollar bill from his roll and left it on the counter-top. He stood, not uncomfortably close to Mckenna but near. He smiled at her as he returned the money clip to his pocket.

"I find it unusual that this particular bus station only has buses heading to the desert, from the established hours of nine to noon. It is a conundrum."

And with those words, the man exited. And with his exit, all comfort of Mckenna's plan left with him.

Chapter Seventeen

Scarlet sat languidly across the last two bar stools as she casually checked her left calf with her index finger. Her left leg extended fully, and she flexed the muscle, ever so slightly. She had purchased a tiny yellow sundress at the thrift store, down the street. The dress clung to her supple body as her shoulders fought to maintain the integrity of the spaghetti straps.

As Sophie wiped down the bar, she couldn't help but stare and fixate on Scarlet. She was slender and lean with delicate curves, revealing a fair amount of cleavage. Her black hair rested above her shoulders and corralled her pristine face. She was beautiful. In fact, she was perfect. Of course, perfection was subjective and unattainable, but Sophie couldn't find the phrase that best described the visual of Scarlet.

"Flawless," Sophie said to herself. "She's flawless."

Sophie had always felt awkward. She'd withstood her upbringing, if you could call how she'd been raised an upbringing at all. She'd weathered the abuse and she understood, even if she couldn't quite articulate it, that her shyness toward other humans in terms of interaction was stunted. She'd feared human contact since the first night her uncle had crept into her bedroom when she was eleven. She'd only kissed one boy as a teen and many times she'd told herself that she had no interest in any sexual encounter with a boy or man. She assumed that this was a feeling that would eventually pass; but it had not and sessions of therapy hadn't brought libidinous thoughts into her mind.

But looking at Scarlet, she couldn't help but feel the sensation she'd often heard described. Her heartbeat quickened. She felt nervous and sweaty. Scarlet was a wonder, and Sophie could not take her eyes off her. Shaking her head and flushing a bit from embarrassment or something, Sophie moved herself down toward the other end of the bar, polishing the bar as she went along.

"When do we open?"

"Fifteen minutes," Sophie answered, slowly creeping back toward the side of the bar where Scarlet inspected herself.

"I've served before, you know. But food was always involved."

"It's only cocktailing here." Sophie responded, "When the boys are here, they bartend, and I'll cocktail. Looks like today it's just me and you."

"So, you get to bartend?"

"I guess I do."

"Well, that's fun." Scarlet smiled, standing up from the stool.

"It's hard work." Sophie polished some of the whiskey bottles on the shelf. She looked up and caught a glimpse of herself in the mirror. She stood a few inches taller than Scarlet, which made Scarlet about five foot five or so. Her short, light brown hair seemed meek in contrast with the shimmering darkness of Scarlet's and she slumped her shoulders a tad. Looking at Scarlet's posture, Sophie stood up straight, pushing back her shoulders. She caught a movement in the corner of her eye and saw Scarlet leaned over on the entrance of the bar. Scarlet was looking Sophie over.

"You're fit. Yoga?" she asked.

"Uh, thank you. I kickbox four days a week. I can't get into yoga."

"Oh, you'd love it. I want to get back into it. I've kind of let myself go." Scarlet smiled, as she bent over touching the floor with her palms.

Sophie stared, wondering what part of her had she let go.

"Do you want me to just follow you around today?"

"Yea, I think that would be nice. After you get the hang of it, if we get busy, you can take some tables."

"Awesome! We'll be the hottest chica team." Scarlet laughed.

Sophie smiled and continued to shine the bottles. Suddenly, Scarlet was standing right next to her. Startled, Sophie nearly dropped the bottle.

"Looks pretty shiny," remarked Scarlet.

"Jesus, you scared me."

"Oh, sorry, force of habit," Scarlet replied. "Got used to sneaking around my house as a kid." Scarlet looked past Sophie with a thousand-yard stare into nothingness.

Sophie knew the look. "Scared of being caught?"

"Scared of being caught by the wrong person," Scarlet responded.

Scarlet looked and touched some of the whiskey bottles already polished by Sophie. She reached across the bar and grabbed her tiny purse. She pulled a cigarette from the purse with a lighter. She offered a smoke to Sophie, who shook her head.

"You can't…you can't smoke in here," Sophie explained.

"Oh." Scarlet began to put the cigarette back into her purse.

"Oh hell, no one's gonna know. Go ahead. Just make sure there's no leftover ash. Mr. Mills would lose it."

Scarlet lit her cigarette. "You like working here?"

"Yea, it's all right. I'm in LA, at least."

"How long you been here?"

"A couple of months," Sophie answered.

"You got a better gig than I had when I got here."

"Mr. Hansen set me up. He got a room for me around the corner. He hired me here...he knows my mom from back in the day. My uncle..." Sophie trailed off.

Scarlet gently touched Sophie's forearm. Sophie flinched and took a half step back. Scarlet gave a silent shush and gently touched Sophie's hair.

"It was my uncle, too." Scarlet spoke. Sophie and Scarlet made eye-contact.

Sophie briefly looked away and returned her gaze to look into Scarlet's eyes.

"Do you ever get over it?" Sophie asked.

"No." Scarlet handed Sophie a cigarette and Sophie accepted it. Scarlet lit the cigarette as Sophie's hand shook. Scarlet blew a puff. "Tell me about Jake. He got any women hanging around?"

"I don't know. Mr. Hansen has been good to me. I mean, I don't have any friends out here, so he's been nice enough to show me around."

"What about Lamar and uh, uh, uh-" Scarlet snapped her fingers.

"Pete."

"Yes Pete. They seem great. I just want to hug

Lamar every time I see him. Although he scared the shit out of me last night when I met him."

"I won't even ask." Sophie laughed.

"It was quite a night."

"They've been very good to me. They're huge monster sized but sweethearts. I'm grateful to them. And yea, they're my friends."

"Well, you got another friend now." Scarlet smiled at Sophie.

****

Lamar sat behind the wheel of his Durango and looked at his team. "Where to now?" he asked.

"Little Luck's."

Jake answered so quickly and with such resolution, Pete was startled. The information given them by JR was disturbing. A missing person case, that was one thing. But now, with the knowledge that the cartel was involved in the deaths of Zane and, less directly, Gunther, concerned Pete. He also knew that Jake had the scent. Pete had spoken his peace; he knew that Logano Corp. meant the cartel was involved and Dario Mendoza was probably pulling the strings. All that mattered now was finding Mckenna.

"Why would Mendoza make an appearance in Palm Springs?" Pete asked, "Makes no sense."

"Maybe," Jake started, "…I don't know, but Mckenna snapped a picture of him with Newman."

"And sketched it," Lamar tacked on.

"How would Los Nuevos know that he's alive? From a photograph," Pete continued.

"They must have an inside man," Lamar mused, starting the Durango.

"S. Newman?" Jake scratched his head.

"His partner?" Lamar backed the car out of the space and moved toward the exit.

"Think about it, Newman arranged this deal to launder money through the casinos via Logano corp. We saw the long list of places that Logano is funding. He has to know that's gonna get out, eventually," Jake pondered aloud.

"He's playing both sides against the middle," Pete surmised.

"Maybe Newman and Mendoza were partners in the beginning, but Newman doesn't need him anymore," Lamar offered.

"Exactly." Jake responded. "Newman drops the dime on Mendoza to Los Nuevos. And Mendoza hires the Sri Lankan to find Mckenna and the evidence. The Sri Lankan is working for the Bajas."

"That would mean S. Newman double-crossed the Baja Cartel. And Mendoza. He is in as much danger as Mckenna." Lamar pulled out into traffic.

"More so," Pete added.

"Yes. And that's why we're going to Little Luck's." Jake sat back. "He knows things."

****

Jake, Lamar and Pete entered Little Luck's café and just like the previous night, the place was packed.

"Luck does a brisk business here." Pete admired as they stood in the doorway.

"Always has. Only time I could ever get a table is when he was here and shoved people out of the way." Jake scanned the room and found Little Luck sitting at the same table he'd been the night before.

Little Luck, wearing his bifocals, read a ledger placed in front of him. Lost in concentration he didn't notice the entrance of the crew. Jake tapped Pete on the shoulder and started to make his way toward the back table with Pete and Lamar trailing. As Jake approached, he noticed that only Jimmy Han sat with Little Luck.

"That's curious. Where's Junior Lo?" Jake whispered aloud.

The café rapidly became quiet as the three intruders made their way to the boss. The audible silence disturbed Luck as he looked up from his ledger and saw the *baekin* approaching. Little Luck stood and woke the napping Jimmy Han.

"Ahhh, come back so soon. You must miss me. And you bring me both of your monsters." Luck greeted the boys with open arms and a smile. Jake reached Little Luck first and they shook, then Luck shook Pete and Lamar's hand.

"Pete Mills, my friend, it has been too long," Luck graciously gushed.

"It's nice to see you, Luck, I heard you had quite a night last night." Pete smiled and Luck waved him off.

"No biggie, just business." Luck snapped his fingers and two young Korean boys arrived with three chairs. Luck said something to them in Korean and they both scurried off.

"Please boys, sit." Luck motioned to the chairs, sitting down as the boys followed suit.

Pete looked around. "Where's Junior Lo?"

"Mr. Lo is with my son today," Little Luck replied.

"Baby Luck?" Jake asked.

"Ah dangerous name, Jake Hansen. My son doesn't like that moniker. For me, my dad was Big Luck so Little Luck…it make sense. My boy don't like being called Baby. It's like Bugsy to Ben Seigal. Tread lightly with that one, Jake. It's a new generation. Look at me with my ledger, reading the numbers on the paper the way my dad teach me. My son? He got an Ivy league education, Mr. Smart Guy. He has his own firm in the US Bank building. Everything computers and up to date in Kansas City."

"So why does he need Junior Lo?" Lamar asked.

"Eh, sometimes the white collar is just as cutthroat as the street. Anyway, let me treat you gentlemen to lunch."

"Uh...sure Luck, whatever you say," Jake responded.

From behind him a busser brought five teacups and a pitcher of the 'tea' Jake and Lamar had 'enjoyed' the night previous. As Jake looked to the busser, he realized the busser was Zachary Belataka. Zachary's hand shook as he placed down the cups and began to pour the 'tea.' Zachary's face had been badly beaten; he had two black eyes with broken blood vessels in the right eye and a smashed nose. Jake cringed, looking at Zachary. Zachary made quick eye contact with Jake and shied away.

"You like my new employee?" Luck smiled.

"Ahhh..." Jake answered.

Lamar saw Zachary and almost stood, but Pete grabbed his arm.

"Luck..." Jake started, "isn't Zachary part of the Glendale crew?"

"He has a tacit relationship with them."

"Aren't you worried—" Pete began.

"That I might be infringing on our turf agreement?" Luck responded. "I placed a call to Blazerian. I made it clear Beaudry was a violation of our agreement. I promised no more harm would come to young Zachary, but some indentured servitude would be required."

"Blazerian agreed to this?" Lamar asked.

"It wasn't a negotiation." Luck reasoned. "Now, I know you didn't come here to play Amnesty International for Belataka. The information you granted me last night, Jake, was invaluable. How can I reciprocate?"

Jake leaned forward and pulled up the pictures of Ernest Campion and Xavier. Little Luck stared at the images and looked up at the trio.

"You boys play in a dangerous sand box."

"You know them?" Pete inquired.

"Know them? No. I presume if I were to meet either one of them it would be my last moments on earth."

"But you know of them," Jake pressed.

"The Sri Lankan. As dangerous a man as there is in the world. Such a great weapon to be underestimated."

"What do you know of him, Luck?" Pete asked.

"His presence has been more profound in the Southland the past three or four years. Less intercontinental work—"

"More domestic," Lamar interrupted.

"The cartels," Jake threw in.

"I cannot say. I have an arrangement with certain factions that leave me be if I allow certain allowances, however…." Luck folded his arms.

"Xavier with an X," prodded Lamar.

"These dangerous waters, gentlemen. I only know of X's reputation. He's a… he's different than the Sri Lankan. Campion is a gentleman. Xavier is a time bomb."

Little Luck grabbed his napkin and wiped his brow. Jake looked at Pete and Lamar with a nervous glance.

Jake reached into his back pocket and pulled out the picture of Mendoza.

"Do you know this man?" Jake asked.

Little Luck stared longer at this picture. "He looks like Tony Tahoe."

"There is a resemblance." Jake smiled back.

Luck continued to stare.

"This isn't Tahoe? Then no, I don't think I know this man." Little Luck sat back.

Jake glanced at Pete and then stole a look to Lamar. Jake returned his gaze to Luck.

"Are you sure, absolutely sure, you haven't seen this man or know him," Jake pressed harder.

"Jake," Pete spoke under his breath.

"Ah Jake." Luck pulled off his glasses, wiped them with his shirt and placed them back on. He grabbed the picture of Dario Mendoza and took another look. He lifted his eyes and eyed Jake.

"I do not know this man, Jake Hansen."

"Worth a shot," Jake concluded. "Thank you for your time, Luck." The three stood and Luck stood with them.

"No time for lunch?"

"We got a full schedule." Jake extended his hand and Little Luck shook it.

"Busy schedule of a P.I., I guess." Luck placed a hand on Jake's shoulder. "The old days are gone, Jake. There is no honor. The cartels are cutting off heads and fire-bombing old women in casinos. All I ever wanted was my small niche. Times they change and the new generation…they play different rules. You boys are playing a dangerous game with dangerous people. I don't think I can help you any further, my friend."

Little Luck sat down and focused on the ledger in front of him. Jake motioned to his partners and they exited the café. The three walked to Lamar's Durango and stood outside of the vehicle.

"I've known him twelve years. I think that's the first time he ever lied to me." Jake shook his head.

"He knew damn well who Mendoza was," Lamar opined.

"He had to have worked with him!" Jake spoke incredulously. "Mendoza was high up in the cartel, the head of…the leader of, of, of ….he had to have known him?!?"

"He's scared of something," Pete offered.

"I can't believe that. Little Luck scared? He's dealt with the Baja Cartel for years. He knows damn well who Dario Mendoza is." Jake spoke with a pitched purpose.

"So why would he be scared? Unless he's switched sides," Lamar offered.

"Los Nuevos? They're the group he was railing about. Cutting off heads and what not." Jake answered.

"I don't know." Pete nodded thoughtfully. "Is it possible this case is actually more confusing now that we know the players?"

"It is because we're missing a piece," Jake replied.

"I've got that poker game tonight at Derk Jackson's. He's always good with the skinny," Pete mentioned, sighing and yawning.

"It's my night behind the bar," Lamar interjected. "Sophie said she was down for a double. That leaves you lover boy." Lamar chuckled and nudged Jake.

"I promised Scarlet a little happy hour. But … let's meet tonight and go over next moves. My mind's a little cloudy with all we just learned."

"Hopefully, Detective Jackson can shed some light," Pete said opening the passenger side.

"Pete, you think Luck is actually scared?" Jake asked.

"Like you said, as long as you've known him and with as many pots as he has his hands in…he's never lied to you. Until today. That's what scared people do."

Chapter Eighteen

September 23rd, 2004

The door to old Hank's Saloon swung open, letting in a needed gasp of light to the legendary downtown Los Angeles space. The dim bar, briefly illuminated by the attack of light, stood lonely and forlorn, save one lost soul. Jake Hansen, crouched over a bar stool, standing over the stool with a rocks glass of single malt in his hand. He stood with a slump, an almost defeated slouch and, despite his finely tailored dark suit, he didn't look like one of the world's top investigative journalists. With his tie loosened and top button of his baby blue shirt, unbuttoned, Jake looked like a man who just discovered his dog had passed away. He quickly glanced down at his flip phone and saw the time: two fifteen. The article would be going to print within the hour.

A brief light flashed in front of Jake, illuminating a folder with the words, 'For your eyes only'. Pete Mills, exiting Hank's, had been the author of the rush of fleeting light. Pete's job was done.

"Don't look at 'em," Pete had warned in his thick New York accent. "Go home to her and give her a kiss. Take her to San Francisco when the article gets printed. Take her for a few days, hell, take her for a week. You don't need to see those pictures. Just remember everything you two have been through." With those words, Pete had dropped the folder on top of the bar. The massive Pete clapped Jake on the shoulder and left.

Don't look.

He'd worked months, Jesus Christ, years on this article, delving into the under belly of the Los Angeles drug scene and its intersection with politics and criminal justice. He'd worked doggedly with Pete and Lamar and JR, utilizing source after source and working hand and hand with undercover GND officer, Zubin Poosh. The whole investigation, Jake fought the belief that the love of his life, his wife, was being unfaithful. Following the disaster of the Benitez transfer, Jake begged Pete to investigate his wife and now, the folder in front of him was the result. So, of course, Jake looked.

He opened the folder to reveal a photo of his wife, Lily Hansen, in an embrace with some two-bit public defender, Alex something or other.

Jake had perused the words Pete had typed, picking out phrases such as, 'Three months,' 'late night,' and 'Hollywood Best Western.' Jake closed the file and paid more attention to his scotch. The bartender at the end of the bar, Steve, gave Jake plenty of time and space. Jake's face told a novel of opus proportions.

The silence of the nearly empty bar ended with a slam, as the front door stormed open and Joey Wright, Go-fer, mail boy and assistant rushed into the bar and ran up to Jake.

"You're not twenty-one, Joey," Steve called out.

"It'll just be a sec, Steve." Jake waved Steve off. Jake took a big gulp of his scotch as he anticipated his lunch break was over.

"Mr. Hansen. Mr. Collins is looking for ya."

"Yea well, let the old man look for me," Jake spoke into his drink.

"Ya gotta come, Mr. Hansen."

"Jesus, can't a man suffer in peace?"

"Mr. Hansen!"

"Dammit Joey … I just worked five hard months on that piece. People died and a friend disappeared. Can I please have a few minutes…please?!?" Jake moved his eyes up and saw the frantic look on Joey's face.

"I think it's bad, Mr. Hansen."

"Okay, okay." Jake downed his scotch, pulled out his wallet and a twenty from the wallet. He left the twenty on the bar. "Keep the change."

"Thanks, Jake." Steve grabbed the twenty.

"All right, Joey, what's the rumpus?"

"I heard Barlow wants to kill the story."

Jake buttoned his top button and straightened his tie.

"The publisher?" Jake's face became pale and he looked at the empty scotch glass wishing he had another gulp left. "The hell he is." Jake coldly spoke. He patted Joey on the shoulder and exited Hank's.

****

"Jake. Jake," Scarlet said twice. Jake shook his head from his daydream and looked at the beautiful Scarlet.

"I'm sorry sweetie, my mind drifted," Jake apologized.

Jake and Scarlet relaxed at the far end of the inside bar of Baja Cantina. The Baja Cantina stood as a gate to the entrance of the canals on Grand Canal. Not exactly the testament to sturdy architecture, Baja Cantina more than made up for its decaying edifice with a unique clientele and amazingly fun bartenders. Jake had spent many a Sunday afternoon at the outside bar of Baja. Once infamous for its hedonism, the Baja was slowly becoming a dinosaur in the social scene, as Venice built around the canals and the social energy focused on Abbot Kinney. Scarlet had lifted her legs so that they were draped over Jake's lap as they enjoyed a couple of scratch Margarita's from the famous bartender, Big Mike. Big Mike worked the main bar with Jake's buddy, Pete K., while Diamond Dave and Brett worked the back bar. Jake stared at her new sundress and wondered how the spaghetti straps stayed aloft.

"You guys make any progress on Mckenna?" Scarlet asked.

"A little. I don't know if any of it will make sense to you."

"Try me."

"I … in my previous life, I uncovered a conspiracy or at least I thought I had uncovered a conspiracy that the Mexican cartels had infiltrated the local government and police force."

"Really?" Scarlet looked amazed as she sipped her drink.

"Yea. Really. Truth be told, I couldn't prove it without a shadow of a doubt and I ended up losing my job, my wife … my purpose."

"Sophie told me your wife left you."

"She did, did she? Anyway, we uncovered some info today that sort of places Mckenna right in the middle of what I was investigating seven years ago." Scarlet lifted her hands to her mouth.

"Oh my God … she's in danger?"

"We don't know. But we're gonna do everything we can to find her. She's not just my client's daughter…she's my friend." Scarlet leaned up against Jake and put her head against his shoulder.

"Find her, Jake. Bring her back."

Jake kissed Scarlet's forehead.

****

Pete stepped out onto the patio of Detective Derk Jackson's tenth-story condo in Mid-Wilshire. Derk Jackson stood, facing out, looking out at the night lights of Los Angeles. Jackson had a snifter of Cognac in one hand and a Cuban cigar in the other. Pete held his cigar in his mouth and carried a soda water with him.

Pete had never really known what to label his relationship with Jackson. Friends? Perhaps so, they played poker together and had tipped back an occasional beer at a few downtown watering holes, but Pete wasn't sure on friends.

Derk stood a stout six feet and weighed a solid two-twenty but Pete always wondered who'd win in a fight between he and the Chief of Detectives. Derk had made his way toward the top of the flow chart at City Hall and what with him being Black that had been no small feat.

"Nice place, Detective. How the fuck did you afford a condo in this neighborhood? Maybe I shoulda had Jake investigate you instead of Martin Cruz." Pete smiled.

"Funny, Pete, very funny. You know I come from old Beverly Hills money."

"I do indeed. Your daddy, was first the Black person to make full professor at Cal Tech."

"Made his money at Buechele corporation. Third level defense clearance," Jackson proudly offered as he smoked his stoogie.

"Still trying to figure out why you went into a life of public service." Pete puffed on his cigar.

"The best and the brightest," Jackson replied.

"Bullshit, you're gonna be chief one day."

"Your words to God's ears."

Pete stood next to Jackson and looked out at the vast City of Angels.

"Pete, do you know Yamamura from Special Operations and his Gang Task Force?"

"Only by reputation."

"He has a good one, deservedly so. He's the best. He and his boys are staking out Little Luck's place in Koreatown."

"Uh boy…"

"Your boys were spotted entering that establishment late last night." Jackson ashed his cigar.

"To give you an update, the task force saw us there today, as well."

"Really? We've been hearing rumblings about bad blood amongst the Pasadena-Glendale boys."

"Internal issues, Derk? Luck has the backing of the Baja Cartel. Blazerian wouldn't dare make a move."

"That was the thought, but we've been hearing chatter from Koreatown on its own."

"About the cartels?" Pete asked.

"Maybe. Rumor has it that Baby Luck has taken a bigger role in the family business. He has his own set of companies, but it is believed that he is fronting a lot of business for his dad."

"That would explain why Junior Lo wasn't guarding Little Luck today but was with his son."

"Perhaps. It's a theory that Little Luck is laundering money through the umbrella of one of Baby Luck's companies. Or subsidiary. Rumor has it that it's a large fund."

"Logano corp?"

"Exactly. You're well informed, Mills. Logano, allegedly, feeds into non-profits and that money gets distributed to…we don't know."

Pete cocked his head, confused.

"Baby Luck is attached to Logano?"

"Not directly. Logano is a subsidiary of a fund that funneled money through one of his companies."

"So many layers. Far enough removal to be legal?"

"So far. But one of the rumblings is that there is competition for control." Jackson slowly turned and looked inside his place.

"For the fund?" Pete asked.

"From the customers."

Pete thought quickly. "Los Nuevos want to take over the Baja Cartel's holdings."

"It gives you pause. And perhaps, they've swayed a key figure." Jackson took a large gulp of his cognac.

"Holy shit. Little Luck is transferring allegiances?!?" Pete nearly choked on his cigar.

"Maybe. But maybe, Baby Luck is getting a little antsy."

"I see. Baby Luck sees that if he removes the Baja Cartel and partners with Nuevos, he can take over a bigger chunk of the industry. But he has one large roadblock. Little Luck."

"Exactly," Jackson agreed. "But maybe Little Luck is thinking the same thing. He switches to the Nuevos, perhaps he gets bigger profits, keeps his son happy. If not, Baby Luck is blocked by his dad. To gain a foot hold—"

"You're talking patricide."

"I'm talking a *coup de tat*, Pete. And now your cohort's names come up."

"Yea well, we don't know squat about that."

"Pete, it's me. On this balcony, you and I are in

complete confidence. And work is not allowed at the poker table."

"Frank is at the table."

"Yea and so is Assistant DA Francisco Fox, Kevin Kawashima from Major Crimes and Bannerman from Pacific division. Frank can go fuck himself. He may be Robbery-Homicide and a solid detective, but he curries no favor from me. I owe you more than one. And you're my friend."

"Okay, Derk. We're on a missing persons case. Do you know anything about Ed Tall Mountain?"

"Desert big shot. Nothing has popped up on him, but…"

"But what?"

"Joseph Smith's weird death raised a few eyebrows. For the most part, state stays out of Indian business. Nothing to be gained but a gigantic headache. Joseph Smith spoke with Zubin some years back about some malfeasance."

"Wait…Zubin Poosh? Joseph Smith approached Zubin Poosh?" Pete shook his head fiercely at the information.

"Makes you think, right? I was still at GND and Zubin was dealing with you guys on the Eusebio Benitez case. Somehow, Smith got Zubin's name and set up a meet."

"Did Zubin specify …" Pete started to ask.

"Zubin was cagey on it. Indian jurisdiction, yada, yada, but he did say that the casino had some red flags in terms of finances."

Pete suddenly wished he had something stronger in his glass than soda water. He and the boys put it together that Joseph Smith had been violently removed but the info that Smith was suspicious seven or eight years prior upped the ante.

"Did Zubin or anyone ever investigate?" Pete asked.

"How could we? Smith asked no tangential questions and provided literally no proof and then—"

"Zubin went missing."

"Who are you boys looking for?"

"Tall Mountain's daughter. At first, we thought it was just a case of daughter running away from daddy. But …"

"Zane Adkins' death changed your mind?"

"Gave us pause."

"And the boy's late visit to Little Luck's?"

"Jake and Luck go back. Luck lied to him. Or so Jake claims."

"About what?"

"I'm getting to that. Tell Yamamura to check out a Beaudry incident. From last night. Can't give too many details but the Pasadena-Glendale boys might cause some friction."

"After all these years of peace, Pete? Is this connected to Baby Luck?"

"Don't know. New players and old beefs make for strange days. You ever hear of a guy named Dario Mendoza?"

"Maybe. Kinda looks like Tony Tahoe?" Derk blew a cigar ring.

"Yea, that's him."

"Yea. Baja cartel. Number two guy, back in the day. Died in a car wreck number of years ago. I remember he was some kind of money laundering whiz kid. Again, I was at GND with Zubin in those days. That's when things went sideways. Why do you ask about Mendoza?"

"This girl, Mckenna Tall Mountain...or Murphy, long story, she may have seen him and taken a snapshot of him."

Derk Jackson sat his drink down on the ground and gripped the railings of his patio.

"No fucking way."

"We have the proof. We have some sort of proof. Should have the real stuff in a day or two. He isn't dead, Derk. And now, she's missing, Little Luck is lying that he's never seen or heard of Mendoza."

"That seems implausible. Luck has his fingers in...well, everything."

"Oh yea and a couple of hired guns are on the trail. The Sri Lankan..." Pete trailed off.

"We've been hearing more and more chatter on that character. Ernest Campion," interrupted Derk.

"The same, but also Xavier. With an X."

"Holy Christ, what the fuck have you jackasses gotten yourselves into?!? What a cluster fuck. Campion will accept the highest bid but once he takes a job, he never backs out or reneges."

"Meaning, Derk?"

"Mendoza was Baja and died. But if he's alive, Nuevos will want him for what he did to Gonzalez all those years ago."

"Xavier is Nuevos. So, Campion isn't after Mendoza," Pete deduced.

"Seems to reason."

"The Sri Lankan is working for Mendoza?"

"Or Baja, separate. Maybe." Derk replied.

"Sounds like you don't know a lot."

"I know the plate tectonics are shifting. The new blood is surging but the old blood won't die easy. Hell,

Mendoza came back from the dead."

"The cartel war has come to Los Angeles." Pete shook his head.

"Something has, for sure. We just have to wait for the next move."

****

The poker table rested in the middle of Derk Jackson's man-cave and it was a cave to behold. On one wall, his medals, pictures with celebrities and high-ranking officials were interspersed with framed newspaper clippings of Chief of Detectives Derk Jackson's accolades and there were a bunch of those. On the opposite wall were framed pictures of the man's life; framed pictures of fishing, baseball games, his wedding, and a family picture of Jackson with his wife and three daughters.

The usual suspects sat around the table, weekly participants in Jackson's poker game for the past five years. Assistant District Attorney Francisco Fox, a thin, medium-sized Mexican American with a pencil mustache, shuffled. To his left, the short and squat Kevin Kawashima, Major Crimes, drank a glass of beer and yawned. Across from Kawashima sat Miles Bannerman, Captain of the Pacific division and to Bannerman's right was Detective Frank Allison.

Jackson, Kawashima, Bannerman, and Allison had all attended the Academy together and had raised through the ranks separate but mostly equal. Kawashima and Jackson had been partners at Gang and Narcotics and worked closely with Zubin Poosh before his disappearance. Bannerman had taken more of the political route, spending three years as Assistant to the previous police chief. Allison had been on the fast track to a captaincy. A high arrest rate moved him quickly through the ranks. An unfortunate fate with an explosion and the loss and death of two suspects in a transfer and the fall-out of said incident stunted Allison's growth; the Benitez disaster. And he remained at Robbery-Homicide.

Former Detective Pete Mills was an anomaly at the table. Not only was he not an LAPD member, but he'd also retired from the job altogether. Jackson had encountered Mills at one of Mills' seminars in Las Vegas and the two shared a common connection with duty and service. In Pete, Detective Jackson saw a kindred spirit and a man whose talents were being wasted. Pete became not just an ear to Derk but the man behind the man, whispering advice. Pete's advice had proven mostly correct, especially on one occasion.

On one of Jake's random social appearances with Lily, Jake overheard a young female assistant attest to then Lieutenant Jackson's sexual prowess. Jake had passed on the info to Pete with the agreement that the young female would not receive retribution. Pete handled the delicate subject with Jackson and after recommending a quiet promotion to another department for the young lady, Jackson moved onto Special Ops. A sideways move to some, but politically astute. Since that hiccup, Derk Jackson had risen all the way to Chief of Detectives and was being groomed for the big job.

"I'm sitting this game out," Jackson called out, "anyone need a refresher?"

"I'll take one," Bannerman replied. "Just a beer."

"You still drinking that light beer crap." Frank laughed.

"Hey, I lost fifteen pounds. Dee seems to like it so

yea, I'll keep drinking that crap."

Fox dealt the cards around the horn, Texas Hold 'em style. He tossed everyone their 'hole cards.' Pete took a gander at his cards.

Nothing too great.

"I'm out," Kawashima announced, tossing his cards in disgust. "Someone's gotta give me something sometime."

"I'm in for ten." Allison tossed his chips into the center.

"Call." Bannerman heaved his chips.

"Call," Pete spoke with no intonation.

Pete had been looking to pick a fight with Allison since the night started. He could sniff a scrap coming.

Francisco Fox flipped over the flop and it was a partial flop. A three of Hearts, a nine of Clubs and an Ace of Spades. Frank took a little peek at his cards and assessed his situation.

"Check." Frank announced. Bannerman scratched his ear, which Pete a week earlier had deduced was his 'tell' when he had crap.

C'mon buddy, throw down.

Bannerman, on cue, tossed his cards aside.

"El foldo." Bannerman shook his head.

The entire table looked to Pete. Jackson entered the room with a new beer for Bannerman and a refill of his Cognac. Sitting at his seat, he noticed the table paid their attention to Pete.

"Check," Pete announced.

Let's pick a fight.

Pete stared at Frank. Frank returned the stare. A palpable silence overtook the room. The men at the table looked at each with a hushed concern.

Frank looked to Fox. "You gonna turn the card, counselor?"

Fox, shaking his head at the increasingly uncomfortable Allison, flipped the turn.

It was the three of clubs. Attention focused to Allison. Allison toyed with his chips and gave his cards another peek.

C'mon you fucker, stay in.

Frank took a few chips and tossed them into the middle.

"Twenty."

All right, Frank. Atta boy.

"Call." Pete neatly set down his chips. Frank and Pete dueled in a battle of stare-down: eyeball to eyeball.

"This got interesting," Jackson remarked.

"Okay," Fox started, "last card."

Fox turned the card, and it was the nine of Spades. Two Three's and two Nine's were split by a single Ace.

"I've got a little something to spice up this round, Pete." Frank calmly drawled, holding onto his cards.

"Oh…what do you have in mind?"

"If I win…you come clean as to what you boys were doing in Hermosa Beach last night." Frank smiled.

"Detective Allison," Jackson sharply called out.

"C'mon Derk, Pete's a big boy. Gives me the run-around…a fellow detective. Or former detective since he's now the Defective Detective."

"You're out of line, Frank," Bannerman cut in.

"Fuck you, Bannerman, stay out of this," Allison hissed.

"Frank, you are way over the line," Jackson pronounced.

"Why's that, Chief of Detectives? I'm trying to train

a greenhorn to be the best she can be, and these bottom feeders come onto my crime scene…fuck with the scene and tamper with my case."

Jackson brought his fist down onto the table, hard enough that the chips tossed in the air. The room became silent as the participants all stared at the enraged Detective Jackson.

"Detective Allison…this is my house, and these are my rules. This is MY friendly game. And there is only one rule: No shop talk. You have violated my rules and my game and my home. After this round, you are barred from playing here anymore."

"You'd take the side of this man against a fellow brother?" Frank asked, shaking his head.

"I'd take this man over a man who can't abide by my rules."

"I'll see your bet, Allison." The players all turned to Pete. "I'll see his bet, boys."

"Pete," Derk hesitated.

"It's okay, Derk…Frank has something sticking in his craw…I'll bite."

"What are the stakes?" Fox asked.

"Everything he has in his wallet." Pete smiled.

"Deal." Frank smiled back.

Frank removed his wallet and pulled a wad of cash, throwing it on the table.

"Nah, nah, nah." Pete motioned with good hand. "Everything. Except the plastic."

"What do you want? All that's left is my courtesy cards and one of Detective Burkle's."

"My boy Jake wants her number. So throw them in."

Frank's face started to morph into a shade of red, but he laughed it off. He pulled a handful of business cards and one of Danny's from his wallet.

"What do I care." Frank shrugged. "I've got you."

"We'll see." Pete eyed the guys at the table who remained silent and pensive.

Frank, his eyes never leaving Pete, turned over his cards to reveal the Jack of Hearts and the Three of Diamonds.

"Full House, former Detective. Read 'em and weep. Three's full of Nine's." Frank folded his arms.

"That's a nice hand, Allison. But …" Pete's cards revealed the Five of Spades and the Nine of Diamonds. Frank paled, briefly closing his eyes, and the table let out a roar.

"Full house, Detective. Nine's full of threes."

Fox, Bannerman and Kawashima stood and congratulated Pete. Pete absently shook their hands and continued to engage in a staring contest with Frank Allison.

Frank Allison stood up and cleared the table of everything. With his hands and arms he swept chips, money, cards, and drinks, sending them flying. He rushed around the table and went for Pete's throat.

"Allison, you son of a bitch," Jackson yelled.

Bannerman and Kawashima intervened as Frank was only able to grab onto Pete's arms. Fox retreated to the background, avoiding any contact. Jackson helped Bannerman and Kawashima, as a crimson faced Allison struggled to get at Pete.

"I'm gonna fucking kill you and your boy, Hansen!" Frank screamed.

"Jesus Frank," Bannerman yelled, "get a fucking grip!"

"Back away, Allison, that's a fucking order,"

Jackson yelled.

That seemed to be the magic word as the irate Allison backed away, wiping sweat and spit from his face. The players all stood with the group staring, in shock at Allison. Pete bent down to the right of Kawashima and picked up a business card. The card had the name: Detective Danielle Burkle.

"That's it, Frank," Jackson spoke. "Get out ... don't come back until you can play by the rules. And knowing you ... just don't come back."

"I never thought I'd see the day...where fellow brothers wouldn't have the back...of one of their own."

"I never thought I'd see the day where a veteran detective would make such an ass of himself," Fox spoke from the background.

Frank stood and pointed at Pete Mills.

"You're gonna have to speak one of these days and stand up for what's right."

"You're just mad you lost to the Defective Detective, Allison." Pete smiled.

Allison stormed out of the room. Jackson lifted his glass in cheers to Pete.

"If he wasn't your enemy before, he is now, Pete," Jackson cautioned.

Chapter Nineteen

Jake's happy hour with Scarlet was cut short when Lamar called, informing Jake that a Loyola Marymount party bus of twenty-five had just called to say they were stampeding Trotter's at nine. Lamar had mentioned the fraternity but that didn't mean anything to Jake. Chagrined, Jake swallowed his disappointment and agreed to come and bartend. He really couldn't complain; Lamar had covered a shift during Jake's recent bender, and he had also covered the day before when the investigation began. So, Jake sucked it up, settled his bill with Big Mike and headed back to Trotter's with Scarlet.

Scarlet turned his frown upside down. The previous night's passion had been a desperate search for hope and tenderness in the midst of lunacy. They'd barely exchanged words before they copulated, and he'd enjoyed the opportunity at happy hour to learn a little about her. She'd moved to Los Angeles when she was seventeen and she wanted to go to school to become an esthetician. When Jake asked of her family, she became close lipped; he had a pretty solid, informed opinion as to why. She'd been upfront and honest about her drug use and how her dangerous lifestyle had eventually led her to be under the thumb of Zachary Belataka. Jake tried to avoid Mckenna as a topic of discussion but, inevitably, Mckenna came up.

"I know you and Mckenna had a thing," Scarlet

spoke, eyes pointed, briefly, toward the floor.

"We do have a history," Jake admitted.

"You don't have to explain. Or apologize."

"No, but I mean …" Jake stammered.

"She really liked you."

"Mckenna and I have a long, interesting history."

"So why did you stop calling?"

"I thought I didn't have to explain." Jake smiled.

"You don't." Scarlet kissed Jake's fingers.

"I don't know. I honestly don't have an answer for that. It wasn't that she was younger…she was…by a lot. Or that …" Jake struggled to find an answer for Scarlet. He quickly searched for an excuse but realized he didn't want to give an excuse. He wanted to give an answer.

"I don't have a tangible reason. You need to know … I am severely flawed. I drink way too much, I gamble, I've destroyed every relationship I've ever had … I may not be the worst person in the world, but I also know I'm not the best."

As they sat in the corner of Baja Cantina, Scarlet gingerly touched Jake's face and kissed his lips.

"Shut up, you." she whispered. "I didn't mean to upset you."

"I'm not upset. You just need to know, I'm not the man who dragged you to safety from Zach's club. I'm not that guy. I'm the guy who would pay for admission to that libidinous show every night if I could afford it."

"I know that." Scarlet laughed.

"But I am trying to discover my better angels."

****

Jake slung drinks for a steady stream of young college students as Trotter's filled up with the Loyola Marymount crowd.

"You got any Spanish champagnes?" a clean cut, black haired, pimply faced, Business major, asked.

"No, Hot Shot, we don't," Jake replied with enough smugness to make him happy.

"I'll have a Tall Boy," the disappointed frat boy responded.

"Of course, you will." Jake rolled his eyes as he turned to the cooler to grab the can of lager.

Delivering the beer and collecting the correct ransom, Jake looked up and saw Lamar, sitting on his bar stool at the front door, checking ID's. Lamar had a gigantic cigar in between his teeth.

"You could bat. 250 in the big leagues with that cigar." Jake smiled, conjuring the great Vin Scully line.

"What was that?" Another Loyola customer asked. Jake shook his head and waved the new guy away.

Lamar smiled at one comely blonde after another, as the bus of students rolled in.

"And how are we tonight?" Lamar asked of the next buxom blonde, as she handed over her ID.

Sophie multi-tasked around the floor, bussing tables and delivering drinks at a high rate of speed. Working the backside of a double, Sophie's pace didn't lag, it increased. She enjoyed Trotter's when it was at capacity. Still socially shy, she worked better when there was less interaction with the customers. Sophie paused at the entrance of the back bar and scanned the room. Thirty to thirty-five customers filled the room. A group of six guys crowded the pool area as two played against each other and the rest watched.

Sophie's gaze was taken from the room when Scarlet entered through the side door. Sophie blushed. Scarlet wore a tiny, black cocktail dress with black high heels. Sophie laughed, nervously as Scarlet waved to her.

Scarlet silkily glided through the room, sliding her way to the bar and sitting right in front of Jake's well. Jake whirled like a dervish, pouring, shaking and making multiple drinks. So involved in his rhythm, he didn't even notice the stunning Scarlet directly in front of him.

Instead, he glanced up and saw Pete standing in the doorway, chatting with Lamar. Jake saw Lamar point toward him. Pete made his way through the burgeoning crowd. Sophie moved away from the bar entrance and resumed bussing and cleaning the table, to clear a path for Pete. As Pete made his way to the bar, Scarlet leaned over the bar, revealing her cleavage. That caught Jake's eye.

"Buy a girl a drink?" Scarlet winked at Jake.

Jake smiled and returned the wink. "What would the lady be having?"

"Something strong and sweet."

"Just like me." Jake lifted one eyebrow.

Scarlet laughed and touched his arm.

"Oh you…" She air- kissed to him.

Jake walked toward the well closest to the bar entrance, pulling a martini glass with him. Pete entered the back bar and stood next to Jake as Jake crafted Scarlet's drink. As Jake shook the cocktail, Scarlet stood, blew a kiss his way and headed toward the bathroom.

"You live dangerously, my friend," Pete spoke ominously to Jake.

"Are you blind? If I toss her aside, I might as well be a Eunuch. How'd the game go?"

"If Frank Allison wasn't our enemy before, he is now."

"Terrific what did—"

"Nothing you wouldn't have done. Jackson gave me some new scoop. Apparently there has been some rumblings between Glendale and Koreatown."

"Before last night?"

"Yea, Derk didn't know anything about the Beaudry fiasco. Yamamura's task force is watching Little Luck's spot."

"They saw Lamar and I, last night."

"And us today. Derk seems to think Baby Luck might be planning a coup."

"Of Little Luck, really?" Jake's voice cracked with the high note of his question.

"It's kind of what we thought, already. But Baby Luck is the heavy and Newman the second fiddle."

"Newman and Baby Luck are in cahoots," Jake murmured.

"That's my thought," Pete's voice trailed off as he witnessed a commotion at the door. "What's that …"

A group of large men had penetrated the line outside Trotter's and were converging on Lamar.

"Lamar!" Pete called out, but it was too late. Lamar looked up and was shoved down and off of his bar stool by the first of six men.

They stepped over Lamar, who attempted to gather himself off the floor. Lamar grabbed a leg, but the leg squirmed free.

"Jake," Pete smacked Jake in the arm, knocking the drink from his hand. The glass hit the edge of the bar and shattered into the ice.

"Dammit Pete," Jake shouted.

Pete ran from behind the bar. Jake looked up at the specter of Pete hustling and it clued him in to the scenario. After the initial disgruntled look, Jake followed

Pete. Lamar got to his feet but got caught in the wave of people attempting to get out of the way of the burly men.

The leader of the crew made his way through the crowd of the bar. Pete stopped moving for a second, to take in the scene. Jake stood next to Pete and saw Lamar trying to stand. Pete recognized the head of the intruders.

"That's Tony Tahoe," Pete called out to Jake.

As Pete and Jake made their way to confront Tahoe and his men, Lamar pushed to grab them from behind. Tahoe and his men shoved through the crowd, knocking a few to the ground. One spectacled kid stepped up behind Tahoe and grabbed his shoulder.

"Hey! You knocked my girl down," the kid hollered.

Tahoe's first henchmen, a blond Neanderthal who reminded Jake of Gunther, pulled the kid aside and punched him in the nose. The kid dropped to the ground, blood exploding from both nostrils. The sound of the punch got the attention of the revelers and a panic induced. A group of the kid's friends grabbed him from the floor and started to move their way to the door, his blood trailing.

"Move, move, move," Lamar yelled, desperately trying to get into the action. Fighting upstream, he found himself on the left flank of Tahoe and his goons.

The goons were made up of an ethnic menagerie. They all wore the grease monkey suits of Tony Tahoe's towing company: TAHOE'S TOWS. Two of the guys were of a Hispanic look with two Caucasians and one Asian thrown in for good measure.

Tony Tahoe did indeed look similar to Dario Mendoza. Not identical but similar enough, that on first glance, one wouldn't know the difference and would certainly think they were brothers. Tony had a scar above his left brow, a reminder of an ex who'd discovered he had not only cheated on her but had driven her brother to ruin with gambling.

Tahoe shoved his way to the center of Trotter's. Lamar maneuvered himself so that there was a direct stand-off. Tahoe and his five men were squared up with Lamar, Pete and Jake opposite them. Ten customers remained throughout the bar. Tahoe stepped out so he stood in front. Jake walked over toward Tony.

"Tony Tahoe … in my bar. A little over-kill, don't you think? Five guys?" Jake started.

"I never thought I'd have to come in here. Fifty cold, Jake. Pay up." Tahoe pounded his left palm with his right fist.

"I believe that bill has been halved."

"I did receive a strange note and a sum of money. I know it's not your money. Whose is it?"

"Tony, baby, who cares? Money doesn't know where it came from. Half my tab is paid. I don't care where it came from."

"It makes me nervous, Jake." Tahoe folded his arms.

"I'm confused, I pay you and you become suspicious? Why are you here?"

"Jake … lemme speak to you in private."

"I'd love to, but as you can see, I've got a full bar." Tahoe smiled.

"Is that so? Boys…" Tony snapped his fingers, and his five henchmen split up, jostling, grabbing and shoving the remaining customers toward the front door.

Lamar stepped forward, but Pete grabbed his arm.

"No Lamar. Let's try to avoid an ugly scene…or, an uglier scene," Pete whispered to Lamar.

The Asian henchmen threw a brunette girl down to

the ground. She went down screaming.

"Fuck it," Pete growled, "let's fuck 'em up." Lamar and Pete took a couple steps forward, but Jake placed his hands on both of their shoulders.

"No, no, no," he excitedly spoke as quietly as possible. "Are you fuckers crazy? You know they're strapped. I HAVE to be the voice of reason?!?"

Lamar and Pete stopped with Pete raising his hands.

Jake could see Sophie standing in the corner, huddled with her arms around her, scared. Jake mouthed to her, 'It'll be all right.'

After Tahoe's men cleared the bar, they returned to their position behind Tony.

"Do I have your full attention now?" Tahoe asked.

"You had us at hello, dummy," Jake smart mouthed.

"Always with the smart ass, this guy." Tony pointed at Jake.

"Sophie," Jake called out, "go on and get out of here."

"The girl stays," Tahoe responded.

"What the fuck, Tony? You will have the rest of your money by the end of the week," Jake spoke, exasperated.

"Something isn't right, Jake. And I learned in business, a long time ago, if it's too good to be true…"

"And if you spend an hour looking for the sucker, you're the sucker. So what?" Pete replied.

"I ain't no sucker. I want my money tomorrow or I put a lien on your bar."

"I think it's time you be leaving, motherfucker," Lamar growled, taking steps toward Tahoe.

Before he could reach Tahoe, Tony's Gunther henchman stepped in front. Lamar grabbed and tossed him to the ground, placing a knee in the henchman's chest. The other henchmen pulled their guns out and aimed them at Lamar. Sophie screamed a blood curdling scream.

"Lamar!" Jake shouted. "Let him go, Lamar! It ain't worth it."

Lamar shook his head, his face in his masked prison mode. He reluctantly stood up from the fallen henchman and walked toward his crew.

"What the fuck, Tony," Jake yelled, "you bring five armed goons?!?"

"I can't take any chances."

"You received half of the money, stupid," Lamar called out.

"Stop calling me stupid," Tony yelled.

"To be fair," Jake responded, "I called you dummy."

"Well, stop it!"

"Oh yeah," Jake retorted, "why would you come in here guns deep?"

"I've … I've been followed the past two days."

"Yea so?" Pete replied. "You work a dangerous business."

"I know you guys are behind it."

"Now why—" Jake couldn't finish.

"Same car, two guys," Tahoe interrupted, "following me everywhere."

"There's only three of us, Tony," a confused Jake spoke.

"Yea, one of you minds the store with Miss Little Whomever over there, and the other two trail me."

"How do I owe you, you're so fucking dumb. To what end would it serve us? And, Tony, what does Lamar drive?" Jake asked.

"A Durango."

"Did you see a Durango, dummy?" Lamar asked.

"Stop calling me dumb!"

"You're paranoid Tony." Pete waved.

"I've been getting hang-ups—"

"Tony, you're gonna get your money. Why would you bring guns to confront me?"

"You can't be too careful, Jake."

"To a full bar? We don't even carry guns," Jake pleaded.

"I know for a fact Pete has a throwdown gun attached to his ankle."

Jake looked to Pete, who shrugged.

"And Lamar?" Tahoe asked.

Jake looked to Lamar who looked down to the ground. "Okay, okay but five guys," Jake reasoned.

At that moment, Scarlet emerged from the bathroom, whistling without a care in the world. The very jumpy Gunther henchman crouched and pointed his gun at Scarlet. Scarlet screamed.

"Who the fuck is that?" shouted Tahoe.

Jake ran over to Scarlet waving his hands in the air. "Put your gun down! Put your gun down," Jake screamed. He reached Scarlet and bent over so that his face was close to hers. He held her face in his hands. "It's okay, it's okay…" Jake looked back to the group as he held the scared Scarlet. "She was just in the bathroom!" Jake took Scarlet by the hand and led her over to the crying Sophie.

"You two, get out of here. Just go to my place and lock the damn door. I'll come over as soon as this bullshit is done."

"What's going on?" Scarlet whispered.

"Just boy stuff." He kissed her forehead.

Jake took both Scarlet and Sophie by the hand and walked them past Tahoe and his goons. He led them right to the front door.

"Go. Get out of here. Race to my apartment, lock the door and only open for me. With a password."

"What's the password?" Sophie asked.

"Casanova nine." Jake smiled. Scarlet returned the smile. "There's my girl. Now go on, git."

Sophie pulled the reluctant Scarlet and they exited Trotter's. Jake walked back from the front door, with a tremendous scowl on his face. He approached Tony Tahoe and stood directly in front of him, face to face.

"This was way over the line, Tony," Jake seethed.

"Listen—"

"No, you fucking listen," Jake interrupted. "I know for a fact you received twenty-five of the G's I owe. We're working a case and when it is solved…you will be paid in full. The final twenty-five. Until then … get the fuck out of here."

Tony smirked and put his hand over his mouth.

"Wow," Tony started, "Tough guy, eh. Jake, Pete, Lamar … I give you to the end of the week and then I am putting a lien on Trotter's."

"You try that, shithead and I'll step on your fucking neck," Lamar growled.

Tony Tahoe gave one more smirk to the boys and moved toward the door.

Following one step, a loud BANG was heard from outside. Sharp and piercing.

A second after the bang, the voice of a woman screaming split the air. Everyone inside jerked their heads at the two sounds. Tony Tahoe looked around at his crew.

"You have more guys outside?" Pete asked.

"No," Tahoe answered.

"What the fuck was that?" Jake asked and then inhaled. "The girls!" Jake took a step to the door, but Tahoe held his hand up.

"Manny," Tahoe said to the bigger of his two Hispanics, "check it out."

Manny, the muscle-bound henchmen with a wicked star tattoo on his neck, stepped toward the front door, gun at his side. He took a quick glance at the side window and opened the front door, stepping out.

As quickly as he opened the front door, a gun blast was heard and Manny flew five feet back, shot in the chest. He dropped, immediately dead.

And just as suddenly, Trotter's was flooded with flying bullets directed from the outside.

"Take cover!!!" Jake yelled.

The walls and windows exploded as the torrential downpour of bullets struck the outer façade of Trotter's. Lamar and Pete knocked over two high-tops and hid behind the tables. Pete removed his piece from his ankle holster and Lamar pulled a gun from his back belt.

Tony Tahoe flipped over a round high-top as he and his henchmen attempted to hide behind it. The other Tahoe boys hid behind the walls. Manny, his dead henchman lay prone at the front entrance, as bullets rang out.

"You bring these guys, Tahoe?!" Pete yelled across the room at Tony Tahoe, as the bullets continued to riddle the edifice.

"I think they're for you assholes," Tahoe responded.

The gunfire stopped for a brief second.

"Now," Pete told Lamar. "Now!" Pete yelled at Tahoe and his men.

Lamar and Pete snuck their guns and heads out, firing. Tahoe's men also returned fire. The outside guns returned their fire, at a much higher clip. Pete and Lamar retreated.

"What are these pea shooters gonna do against those automatics?" Lamar asked.

"I'm not going down without a fight," Pete retorted.

Gunther Light stood up and raced to the back exit, disappearing. Jake looked around the corner of the bar and saw Pete and Lamar hidden behind the high-top.

"He's got the right idea," Pete yelled.

"We need covering..." Jake stopped as the firing slowed outside.

Suddenly, he heard the sound of a different gun.

"Wait...listen," Pete called out.

And listen they did.

Two gunshots. With precision. Meticulous and neat. At once, all of the gunfire ceased.

"What the actual fuck was that?" Jake asked, shell-shocked.

"There's someone else out there," Pete responded.

Tony Tahoe grabbed his goons and pointed to the back door of Trotter's. Lifting his fingers, he counted to three, then Tahoe and his henchman raced to the back door and exited.

"So much for him," Lamar shook his head. "If that motherfucker brought—"

Lamar looked at the damage of his place. The walls were bullet riddled, torn and scarred and Trotter's was a shell of itself. Jake crawled along the floor toward Pete and Lamar.

"Careful Jake," Pete called out, concerned.

Jake reached his two friends and joined Lamar in looking around at their home.

"We're gonna need a new coat of paint," he sadly said, joking.

"We're gonna need a new coat of somethin'," Lamar replied.

The three sat behind the high-top for a minute, mulling their choices. They looked at the floor in front of them and saw the dead Manny, blood covering the front of the bar.

"Jesus Christ," murmured Pete, "it's a blood bath."

The three, nerves in high order, eyed their surroundings.

"I think the coast is clear," Jake finally spoke.

"Jake…" Pete cautioned.

Jake stood, crouched at first, and slowly ambled toward the front door. As he walked, he stepped over Manny. When he reached the front door, he stood, completely erect. He waved Pete and Lamar forward and they responded. Jake slowly opened the front door and cautiously snuck his head out, taking a peek.

Gun shells littered the middle of Washington and in the middle of the road, a body rested on its stomach, blood pooling around its structure. The body lay pitched forward, arms above his head with a machine gun clattered in front of him.

"Jesus," Jake exclaimed.

As Jake stepped out onto the sidewalk, Pete and Lamar followed him. The three stepped out toward the body amongst shattered glass and ripped wood. The Trotter's sign had been obliterated so that the two 'R's, the second letter 'T' and the' E' moved from horizontal to vertical. Pete stepped up to the body. He gazed with curious intent, nodding his head in acknowledgment.

"It's Spider-man."

Jake and Lamar stepped up next to Pete, and the dead man was, indeed, the Spider-man they'd encountered the day prior. The head tattoo was torn into shreds by the bullet that had struck him.

"He was killed by a single bullet." Pete looked across the street toward Cozy Inn. "The shooter would have been back in that direction."

"Where's X-Man?" Jake asked.

Pete looked to the left of Spider-Man's body and saw a large splash of blood on the ground. Pete eyed the pool of blood and saw that a trial led away from the scene. "He's gone, but he's hit. He ran off double quick time, but he's bleeding," Pete responded.

"Jake," a soft feminine voice cried out.

Jake looked to his left at the sound of his name. He saw Scarlet, on the ground, shot in the stomach. Her blood streamed from her body beneath her black dress and created a rivulet of blood rushing from her body and mingling with the water that streamed along the sidewalk. Sophie, quietly crying, held Scarlet's hand. Jake ran to Scarlet's side.

"Pete! Lamar!" Jake screamed. He reached Scarlet and cradled her body, as he sat next to her, holding her.

"Oh Jesus," Jake whispered. Her skin was clammy, and her face was pale. Jake placed his left hand on the wound, pressing down her dress.

He pulled his shirt off, leaving him with an under shirt on, and applied the shirt to her wound. Blood poured out from the shirt, immediately rendering his shirt useless. She was bleeding out.

"I saw them coming," Scarlet whispered.

"Mr. Hansen, you gotta do something," Sophie pleaded.

Lamar and Pete reached the three of them. Lamar got down on his knees, took off his shirt and gave it to Jake. Jake replaced his bloody shirt with Lamar's, over Scarlet's wound.

"Pete, call 9-1-1," Jake croaked.

"Already on it," Pete answered, his phone at his ear.

"So much blood," Scarlet struggled to speak, blood trickling from the corner of her mouth.

"Be brave, Scarlet, help is coming," Sophie soothed.

"Jake, Jake…" Scarlet spoke, looking forward with a thousand-yard stare.

"I'm here." Jake took his bloody hands from her wound and grabbed her hands.

Lamar took over and applied pressure.

"Find Mckenna," Scarlet quietly whispered.

"I … we will. Take it easy," Jake responded.

"Tell her I'm sorry." Scarlet looked up at Jake and stared into his eyes. Tears fell down her cheeks. "Tell her I'm sorry. I didn't know."

"You didn't know what, baby?" Jake implored with her, tears welling in his eyes.

"I didn't know it would be like this."

****

After Scarlet breathed her last breath, Jake held onto her hand as long as he could. He watched as Lamar took the sobbing, hysterical Sophie away. Besides that, his mind registered little. A cacophony of numbness enveloped his body and only a slight strumming in his fingers alerted him to his living. He heard a humming in his ears, but he assumed that was residual effect from the

290

intense gunfire. Jake slumped on the pavement next to her body and stared at her corpse in a complete state of shock.

And Jake was in shock. His eyes stared until they filled with water and he blinked.

"There is special providence in the fall of a sparrow," Jake whispered.

Momentary, brief moments of his intimate time with her, so few precious hours earlier, flashed through his mind, but for the most part, his mind stood devoid of thought or process. He heard the shuffling noises and as the paramedics arrived, just before the police, he felt his hand torn from Scarlet's and he awoke.

"Please, sir, we need to work on her," the kind voice of a young male EMT, spoke in a dulcet tone.

"She's dead," the soft, rasp emitted from Jake.

"We need to…" The EMT gently removed Jake's hand and stood Jake upright as the female EMT worked on the deceased Scarlet.

"She's dead," Jake reiterated.

The male EMT walked Jake a few feet away and sat him on the curb and there, Jake sat, watching the EMT's futilely work on the already passed Scarlet.

Chapter Twenty

Jake's eyes focused, hazily, on the Cozy Inn sign until his eyes blurred over with a misty cataract. The heavy sounds of the Ten freeway in the background, a laconic rhythm, thumped as a heartbeat in his thoughts and his thoughts were a cloud of blank. Jake licked his lips as the dehydration of the day and the panic of the recent moments drained him of all bodily fluid. He wanted to cry for the destruction of his home, but he knew that would inevitably bring thoughts of Scarlet and he couldn't handle that image right now.

The whole scene played like a blur to him. One second, he was making a cocktail for some douchebag, the next, he was flirting with Scarlet and then the maelstrom of Tony Tahoe and his goons. Jake continued to see Tahoe's henchman, his name had been Manny, fly many feet after receiving a gun blast in the doorway. And then the bullets and the wood flying off the wall as the ammunition carved into his home. He saw Lamar and Pete, huddled behind a table. He saw their fear and relived his own. He heard the precise shots; the individual shots that silenced his aggressors.

He saw Scarlet die. He replayed that, again and again.

Pete brought sweatshirts with the Trotter's logo, draping the nearly shirtless Jake and the shirtless Lamar. Their blood-soaked shirts lay on the ground as a reminder of the horrors of the night.

Jake blinked so his eyes didn't focus on any one object, just stared. He attempted to place his thoughts into some coherent form, but rationality eluded him. He looked, briefly, at the crumbling edifice of Trotter's.

Pete stood in the middle of Washington surrounded by an avalanche of police cars and ambulances. Emergency vehicles clogged the street thoroughly. It looked like something out of a movie and like nothing he'd ever encountered. As he looked on the horrific scene, he nearly forgot he was speaking with Detective Burkle. He took a quick glance to his left and saw Jake, despondent on the stoop. He had no words of comfort for Jake; he barely had comfort for himself.

Danny took a glance at Jake. She shuttered, struggling to focus on the job. This stood as the biggest incident she'd encountered as an officer and she needed to get a grip. Focusing her attention from Jake, she saw Lamar a few feet away. Lamar sat next to Sophie, a jacket over her shoulders, her eyes puffy from crying. Sophie leaned over and grabbed Lamar's hand, placing her head on his shoulder. She cried harder.

Detective Burkle touched Pete's arm then walked toward Jake. She placed herself next to him on the step. Jake took notice of her and refocused on the scene in front of him. The body of Scarlet was being wheeled away on a stretcher. Covered with a white sheet, Jake wondered where her next destination would be.

"They're taking her to the morgue," Danny spoke quietly.

"Take care, sweet girl," Jake softly murmured.

"Was she a friend?" Danny asked.

"Yes. She's from Riverside."

"Yea, we need to contact her next of kin."

"Her mother. Her mother still lives there." Jake shielded his face from Detective Burkle's, feeling moisture coagulate in his eyes. He wasn't afraid of crying, just didn't feel like appearing all that vulnerable to Detective Burkle at this juncture.

"I'm sorry, Jake," Danny offered.

Jake slowly made eye contact with Danny. Jake nodded his thanks; she returned it with a small smile. They both looked forward, saying nothing. Jake's eyes perked up as Pete, standing ten feet in front of him, motioned east. Jake looked in the direction of Pete's pointing and saw Detective Frank Allison approaching.

****

Frank Allison took in the scene as he walked, walking past Pete with barely a glance. Detective Burkle stood and met Frank before he fully came in to contact with Jake.

"Frank," Danny greeted Allison.

"I got the lowdown from Novo."

"Yea, it's Culver City's case."

"Not anymore, it isn't. We're taking over," Frank asserted.

"Uh…it's their jurisdiction. We are *in* Culver City. They're already pissed we're here. Jackson won't allow—""

"Regardless, this is us."

Danny crooked her head to the side and caught EMS placing blankets over the dead henchman.

"What a fucking mess. I knew these guys had a hand in last night's gig," Frank rubbed his hands together.

"You think they're connected?" Burkle asked.

"You don't, Detective?!? I haven't seen Jake

Hansen in six years and on back-to-back nights, I see him, and death is all around."

"Frank, this scene is grizzlier than last nights. This is bloody mayhem. Maybe the two are connected but I think it's premature to come to that conclusion, let alone act on it."

"Are you contradicting me, Detective?"

"No, I'm saying let's follow the facts."

"My sentiments exactly." Frank spoke with authority. "Okay Burkle, get those boys and that girl in a squad car. We're taking them downtown."

Danny maneuvered herself so that she stood face to face with Frank. "What are you doing?"

"Taking control of this case and getting these guys in line." Frank looked past Danny.

"By taking them downtown?"

"That's what we're doing, yes," Frank re-asserted.

"The hell we are." Danny folded her arms and planted herself so Frank couldn't look past her.

"Excuse me?"

"They just had their establishment destroyed and a friend of theirs gunned down right in front of them. They're the victims."

"Are you defying my orders, Detective Burkle?" Danny took Frank by the arm and walked him aside. Frank looked at her hand on his arm and his face twisted red with rage. "What the hell are you doing?"

"Listen to me, Detective Allison. We need answers from them. If you haul them in a squad car, all the way downtown, by the time they get there, their grief will change to bitterness and anger and it will all be focused on you. Show a tiny bit of compassion and you might find them pliable."

Frank inhaled deeply and focused his thoughts. In the distance, he could see Pete Mills scuffling, staring at something next to the form of the dead man. If there was another human being on earth he wanted to see less than Pete, he couldn't conjure that name. But he knew, Burkle was right.

Frank quietly waved Pete over and Pete acquiesced.

"Detectives," Pete spoke, approaching.

"Detective Burkle," Frank motioned to Danny.

"Pete," she began, "we have some questions. We need you four—"

"Detectives, you have a station on Duquesne. The Culver station. Why don't we go there? Jake and I will ride with you, Frank. Lamar and Sophie can ride with Detective Burkle."

"Yeah, I can live with that." Frank nodded in agreement.

Danny tapped Frank on the shoulder and walked away toward Jake.

Frank soaked in the incredible scene in front of him and really took it in for the first time. He knew a horrific event occurred and they needed to focus on that.

Pete and Frank stood silent and awkward for a beat.

"Thanks Frank," Pete offered.

"Sometimes it's better to listen to your partner."

****

Jake sat by himself in a viewing room, running scenarios in his head. He'd started to string thoughts together on the ultra-quiet ride from the crime scene. On his way to Allison's car, he replayed the image of the Spider-man, splayed on the road. He could tell from the angle of his fall that he had been shot from behind. Pete mentioned a trail of blood, leaving the scene. Other than that, he couldn't glean much of anything.

Upon arrival at the station, Allison instructed Pete to stay in the lobby and that Jake was to come with him. Pete shrugged and Jake understood that he would be on his own for the questioning. Frank didn't want to interview a former detective who knew the game probably better than he and he certainly didn't want to interview a gigantic ex-con who absolutely knew the game. And interviewing Sophie? Allison was an asshole but not a major asshole.

Jake looked up as the door opened and Detective's Allison and Burkle entered, carrying coffees. They sat in the chairs across the table from him and Danny set a folder down on the desk.

"First of all, Jake, I'm sorry about your business and very saddened by your young friend. But can you tell me what the fuck is going on?!? I got three bodies: one right in the middle of Washington! One of Tony Tahoe's henchmen is dead inside your bar … that pretty girl? Dead. And the guy in the street? He didn't have ID." Frank finished and stood.

"He didn't have an ID?"

"Nothing! Detective Burkle, however, did recognize him."

"Name is Daniel Astorga. His name popped up when I was at GND. Mexican national."

"Known figure?" Jake asked.

"Notorious," Burkle answered.

"So, a Mexican national, allegedly, with a highly specialized weapon but no wallet and no ID. Nothing," Allison offered.

"Cartel," Jake replied.

"Duh," Allison agreed. "We just don't know which

one."

"Los Nuevos," Jake sighed.

"Why would you pick them?" Burkle asked.

"They thought Tony Tahoe was someone else."

"They?" Allison nearly screamed.

"Yes, there were two of them…" Jake trailed off.

"How do you, I don't… first of all, who did they think Tony Tahoe was?" Burkle asked.

"Man by the name of Dario Mendoza."

"Mendoza?!? Are you shitting me?!? Mendoza has been dead twenty years," Allison hollered.

"Not so much," Jake replied.

"Okay." Fidgety Allison sat back down, "Who killed the Los Nuevos shooter?"

"I don't know."

"I think you do know. I think you've known and you're lying to me like you've lied from the beginning." Allison pointed a finger in Jake's face.

"I'm just trying to find a girl," Jake began. "We were hired to find a girl and the path has led us here. We just wanted to pay off a few debts along the way. We didn't shoot anybody and in case you didn't notice, my bar is shredded and my friend …" Jake trailed off.

"Yes. And I, we, Burkle and I, are sorry about the girl."

"Her name was Scarlet."

"Okay. Scarlet. Your bar is fucked. But you're insured, I'm sure. The investigation now becomes much more than a dead bar manager in Hermosa."

"Detective Allison, everything you need is on that surveillance tape."

"AHA! You were in that office," Frank gleefully shouted.

"Yes, we were in the office and we saw the tape. So what?!"

Allison walked around the table and stood behind Jake. He placed a hand on Jake's shoulder. "Jake, I'm trying to help you," Frank offered.

"With what? Yes, you're right. We knew Zane but we didn't kill him. We are not even on that tape."

"You are on that tape," Frank corrected.

"Not during the crime."

"We could get you on an obstruction charge?" Danny threw in.

"*Et tu Brute*? Obstruction of what? Look, Zane knew the missing girl. The girl we were hired to find. He had been banging her and she dumped him. That's all for that case. That's it. The dead man with the head tattoo? He was at Barnacles last night. He's on the tape as is his buddy next to him. All right? Tony Tahoe came to Trotter's to collect a debt and my guess is that guy and his buddy mistook him for Dario Mendoza."

"A man who's been dead twenty years." Danny placed her head in her hand.

"Yah and well, that's what I got. I have a destroyed bar to attend to and a mother I need to call about her dead daughter." Jake stood.

As Frank stood to speak, someone knocked on the door. Danny stood to open the door. She wasn't too surprised to see Derk Jackson.

Chapter Twenty-One

Frank's head shook with anger at the sound of the knock. He hated being interrupted during an interrogation. Interruptions interrupted flow, pace, rhythm...there's a certain ballet that goes hand and hand with an interrogation. Technically this wasn't an interrogation, but Frank still hated it.

The second he heard the voice of Derk Jackson, he knew it was bad. And when Danny waved him over, his belief was compounded. Frank gave a glare to Jake and pushed himself toward the door. He followed Danny into the hallway.

Frank mumbled to himself. "This is grief I do not need."

Frank ran through multiple scenarios in his mind as quickly as possible. He knew he had bitten way more than he could chew at Jackson's home but there was no way to know recompense would occur so quick.

The three stood in the hallway, just outside of the interview room.

"Helluva thing, Detectives," Jackson started.

"It's a mess," Frank concurred.

"No ID?"

"No, but," Danny answered. "I recognized the victim."

"Rap sheet?"

"He was a cartel recruit," Danny replied.

"That's one reason why I'm here." Jackson folded his arms.

"Here it comes." Frank rolled his eyes.

"Something you want to add, Detective?" Jackson sharply spoke to Frank.

"No sir," Allison answered. Danny gave Frank a quizzical glance and Frank waved her off.

"Culver City is taking this over. It's their jurisdiction. Yamamura and his task force can provide intel and back-up." Jackson's comment sat in the open between the three of them.

Burkle inhaled and exhaled, knowing full well that she didn't have the standing, experience or earned credibility to speak up in this situation. Obviously disappointed, she knew her partner would have a conniption.

"God dammit, Derk, we caught the case," Frank growled.

"Actually, Detective, Novo caught the case, but it wasn't his to take. You have a station full of really pissed off Culver City detectives. I don't blame them. Hopefully, Yamamura can smooth things over."

"And this isn't personal?" Frank looked at his shoes as he spoke.

"Tread lightly, Allison," Jackson warned.

"This isn't cheap payback for the scene at the poker game," Frank accused, red in the face.

Danny stared at her partner, incredulous.

"I deeply resent that inference, Detective Allison."

"We apologize, sir." Danny literally stepped in between Frank and Jackson. "Are we still on the Barnacles case?"

Chief of Detectives stared at the fuming of volcano

represented by Frank Allison and considered the question. He looked to Burkle and saw a true dedication. He relented.

"For now, yes. But if there is any gang relation, pass the info to Yamamura. Right, Detectives?"

"Yes, sir," Danny responded.

Allison stood silent. Jackson stared at Frank.

"Right, Allison?" Jackson confronted Frank.

Frank looked up and met Jackson's gaze.

"Right. Right, sir."

"You should take your partner to Taylor's Steakhouse, Frank. She might have just saved you an assignment to Traffic."

And with that, Derk Jackson walked away.

Smoldering, Frank looked down. He looked back up quick enough to see Derk shake hands with Pete Mills.

"You want to tell me what the hell is going on, Frank?" Danny asked, her arms folded.

Frank glared at Danny and lifted a finger to wag at her. He shook his head and removed his finger.

Frank entered the interview room. Looking at Jake, nearly brought up Frank's dinner. Frank placed his hands on the desk opposite Jake. Danny, shaken and confused, entered as well and stood next to Frank. Frank delivered a nasty stare at Jake and shook his head.

"Well Jake," Danny began, grabbing the file off the desk, "you are free to go."

"Really?"

"Really," Danny confirmed.

Jake stood and quickly walked to the door.

"Keep yourself available, Hansen," Frank called out after Jake.

After Jake exited, Frank closed his eyes and shook

his head furiously. The vein in the middle of his forehead began to protrude.

"I've never seen anything like that." Frank seethed. "What is going on? I deserve an answer."

"I...I had a run-in with Jackson at his poker game."

"Over Pete Mills." Danny sat down in the chair behind the desk. She placed her hand over her eyes.

"And a bad beat on a full house."

"Christ Frank... What are you going to do?" Danny asked, chuckling.

Frank looked to Danny, briefly closed, and opened his eyes.

"I'm gonna go home, kiss my wife ... crack open a beer and watch something on ESPN."

Frank walked past Danny and exited the room. He walked the quiet hallways of the station to the glares of Culver City detectives and uniforms.

Emerging from the station, Frank checked his phone.

"Fuck it," he said to himself.

Reaching his car, Frank unlocked his car and got in behind the wheel. He sat, numb, for thirty seconds, staring at the Culver City station. He then punched and smacked the steering wheel until his hands were bloody.

Chapter Twenty-Two

Jake emerged from the Culver City station into the pitch darkness of four a.m. Los Angeles. As he walked out, he saw Pete, Lamar and Sophie huddled beneath the streetlight illuminating the parking lot.

He had endured a lengthy period of time in the interview room to think about his thoughts, next moves and what he would tell his team, but all of that thinking evaporated as he approached them. He knew the steps they needed to take but he didn't have any encouraging or prophetic words. They would all sound hollow anyway, following the senseless death of Scarlet. And yet, he approached and stood next to his comrades-in-arms.

"I called us a cab," Pete murmured.

"Cool, thanks," Jake replied. He looked back toward the station. "I'm not quite sure what just happened in there."

"I think a marker was just paid in full," Pete answered. He motioned with his head toward behind Jake.

Jake looked and saw Jackson driving out of the station lot.

"Allison is definitely an enemy now." Jake smiled a sad smile. "That's a pretty big marker."

"Above and beyond," Lamar added.

"He owed a pretty big favor," Pete responded. "I

told you this was a bad idea," he spoke to Jake.

"As I recall, Pete, you two wanted to take the case in the first place."

"It don't matter. What we gonna do now?" Lamar asked.

"This was Los Nuevos. They mistook Tony Tahoe for Dario Mendoza. If I were Tony, I would leave the country ASAP."

"And the Sri Lankan killed Spider-man, but Xavier got away. Wounded, but away," Pete summarized.

"I would assume that to be the case. If Campion is as good as we've heard... I can't believe he didn't kill Xavier." Jake rubbed his forehead.

"The Sri Lankan is protecting us?" Pete concluded, a confused look on his brow.

"For now, I guess." Jake shrugged, "At least now we know the players. We can assume Ernest Campion is working for Mendoza or the Bajas with both S. Newman and Los Nuevos wanting Mendoza dead."

Lamar breathed in and out. "We sure about Newman?"

"Baby Luck maybe has a part so not one hundred percent, no. But the big question is—"

"Who tipped off Los Nuevos?" Pete answered.

"I think you already know the answer to that question. We need to confront him," Jake spoke ominously.

"Confront?" Pete eyed Jake.

"Confront."

"It's four a.m., can we confront after a nap?" Lamar yawned.

"We go back, clean up at my place and go see JR first." Jake rubbed his eyes.

"JR?" Lamar asked. "Again?"

"Yea, he can help us. Get our heads straight."

"All right, Jake." Pete puckered his lips. "This is your call."

"JR, Little Luck and then Palm Springs. We need to see Tall Mountain."

After the cab arrived, they rode in silence, exhausted in the darkness. When they reached Trotter's, Jake told Lamar and Pete to use his bathroom and clean up as he walked Sophie back to her apartment. He and Sophie walked in silence with Sophie sniffling occasionally to break the silence. As they reached her door, she pulled her keys from her purse and Jake attempted to speak.

"Sophie, I'm so sorry that you were…a part of this."

"I want to go home."

"You are home."

"No. I mean Hemet." Sophie held her purse in front of her, clutching it to her chest.

"No, no you don't."

"I keep seeing the bullet hit her. The force of it all. I watched her die." Sophie wiped a tear from her eye.

"I know. I did too, we all did and we're going to feel bad about that for a long, long time. Listen, I have no answers. I can't tell you when you'll feel better."

"She was my only friend."

"That's not true, Sophie. I'm your friend. Pete and Lamar are your friends and we love you. You belong out here and even though it's been just a little bit, this place wouldn't be the same without you. And going home to whatever you call home you in Hemet…no, this is your home. And you're our family." Sophie looked up and hugged Jake. "C'mon, let me get you inside."

****

Lamar drove on the 105 toward the 110 as the three rode in silence. Pete sat in the passenger seat and Jake sat in the back, quietly looking at the side of the road.

"Jake, is your phone dead?" Lamar asked.

"Yeah, how'd you know?"

"Eddie Collins is calling me." Lamar lifted his phone.

"Answer and put it on speaker." Jake sat up.

Lamar answered the phone, and Eddie Collins' voice filled the car.

"Hello?" Eddie spoke with trepidation.

"Eddie, I'm here," Jake answered, "my phone's dead. Lamar has you on speaker."

"Oh, thank God, you boys are all right." Eddie sounded nearly out of breath.

"Yea Eddie, we're fine," Pete answered.

"It's all over the news. I haven't seen any footage yet, but the reports are harrowing."

"It was pretty awful, Eddie, we lost a friend."

"Christ, anyone I know?"

"No, no I wouldn't think so," Jake answered. "I really appreciate you calling."

"Of course! I heard the name of the business and … awful. But I also called Tommy."

"Thank you." Jake replied and touched Pete and Lamar's shoulder. "This is about the death of Joseph Smith."

"The police didn't investigate, Jake. Tommy spoke to a Detective Angel. She tried to run with the case, but the chief was getting a lot of interference."

"From?" Lamar asked.

"The Tribal Council."

"Tall Mountain," Pete offered.

"She didn't go into any specifics, but she did say she mostly dealt with S. Newman."

"Interesting." Jake replied.

"They did an autopsy and Smith's B.A.C. was point two-four."

"Jesus, way over," Pete exclaimed.

"That would give Dracula a DUI. And the contents of his stomach and his blood came up bupkis for his epilepsy medication."

"Yea, but epilepsy medication is notoriously unreliable. Thanks Eddie. We're headed over to JR's." Jake leaned back in his seat.

"Yeah, he said you'd stopped by. I could hear the excitement in his voice. Good to see the band getting back together."

"I wish it were under better circumstances."

"It never is. What are you gonna do, Jake?"

"You know me, Eddie, I gotta know the truth. I gotta find out who did it and I gotta find Mckenna."

"Then you do that, son. Find her."

And with those words, Eddie hung up. Jake looked out of the window and closed his eyes.

****

Lamar looked in the rearview mirror and saw that Jake had fallen asleep. Jake was his brother, his little brother. Even with all the mischief, nonsense, boozing, ladies and gambling, Lamar felt responsible for Jake. Perhaps he felt a responsibility because sometimes when he saw the sly smile and wink of Jake's, it reminded him of Peanut.

****

They'd placed Lamar and Peanut in the same wing

in prison, due to persuasion from Detective Mills, but not cell mates. Dannemora had its own set of rules and Lamar learned them right quick. He had been in GP a grand total of three hours when he first got jumped.

In the yard, three Dominicans from the *Loco Dulce* gang snuck up and surrounded Lamar; Juanito, the smallest of the crew, wished to make a name for himself having, also, recently been incarcerated. Juanito remembered Lamar from the South Bronx, mostly from the legends. Juanito figured taking down a force such as Lamar would not only endear him with the *Loco*'s but help build his prison rep. What it did was lose Juanito an eye.

He came after Lamar with a shiv, big mistake. Juanito's compadres slyly, slowly and wisely wandered away from the skirmish following Lamar's first thunderous punch of Juanito. To his credit, Juanito kept coming but Juanito ended up eating out of straw for a month and lost an eye.

Lamar's first legit challenge came from Dinner Bell Mel, the six-foot, three-hundred-pound beast of a black man who earned his moniker by stealing smaller peons' food during chow time. Dinner Bell held much sway in the cell block and the specter of Lamar gave Mel concern. To be the biggest and the baddest on the block meant everything.

So, when Dinner Bell attempted to steal Lamar's fruit cup as Lamar sat during chow time, the gauntlet was thrown. Some swag had passed to the guards to allow certain allowances, including no interruptions to the battle and a battle it was. The guards who bore witness to Dinner Bell Mel versus Lamar bout, told the tale til their death.

No weapons utilized, no shivs, sharpened spoons and no quarter given or taken and no help from the studio audience. The guards held Peanut as the fight commenced. It was just two heavyweights throwing hay maker after hay maker. Lamar took as much as he gave but eventually, he choked Dinner Bell out. Both were placed in the hole for thirty days, but when they emerged, no grudge was held. In fact, Mel and Lamar became the best of friends and sat next to each other at lunch.

Lamar's troubles were not to be of his making. As always, Peanut was at the heart of it. Actually, the Aryan Brotherhood was at the heart of it. Having lost his leverage with the *42*'s, Peanut found protection from a group of local New York City toughs. Not a gang so much as a loosely pieced group of lost souls, the group watched each other's backs. Unfortunately for Peanut, the crew ran afoul of the Aryan Brotherhood, more significantly, the leader, a gargantuan white male, named Gurgen. Gurgen was incarcerated for life without parole but he and his gang dominated Dannemora. Lamar and Dinner Bell avoided most of the gang affiliations and kept to themselves, but one series of innocent acts led to disaster.

From the moment of the arrest, Detective Pete Mills had taken a keen interest in Lamar Wagner. He saw, not a lost soul, but a good person in a tough situation who just needed a chance. Pete looked out after Lamar, following his progress through the system and when Lamar and Peanut were sentenced, Pete didn't speak for them in court but behind the scenes with the prosecutor and the judge. Part of his deal was to visit Lamar at least once a month. Lamar had to agree to the deal and Lamar did, with the stipulation that it not be as a usual visitation;

that would lead inmates to think of him as a snitch.

The compromise was that Lamar 'knew' information of a serious crime and every month, Detective Mills would come and try to crack Lamar. That was the cover story, anyway. The guards would lead Lamar to an interrogation room and Mills would be there. In that room, a friendship was built. Mills taught Lamar chess and had books on Criminal Justice delivered. He also got Lamar a job in the prison library with Old Man Haskell, a prison legend. Haskell had been in jail for forty years; he had taught himself to read and had run the library for twenty-five years. Haskell had taught hundreds of inmates to read and helped many more pass their GED. In the end, he helped Lamar earn a bachelor's degree in criminal justice.

Sadly, prison is a sieve and eventually, a guard let it slip to a member of Gurgen's crew that Lamar wasn't being interrogated during his sessions with Mills but was actually friendly with the detective. Lamar never got the full story, but he was pulled into the warden's office and told that, in the yard, Gurgen confronted Peanut and called Lamar a 'Snitch ass bitch.' Peanut, in full Yappie Dawg form, got up in Gurgen's face, or as close as Peanut could get to anyone's face. Gurgen laughed at Peanut as the Aryan crew pulled Gurgen away but the dye had been cast. No one confronted Gurgen without consequences and when Peanut was found two days later in the sanitation closet with a broken neck, no one was surprised.

Lamar remained inside his cell for two full days, with the warden's permission, mourning and contemplating. Dinner Bell did his best to coax Lamar from his daze, but no words could penetrate. Lamar wrestled with guilt and decisions. He knew that his friendship with Detective Mills had created this nightmare, but he didn't have any desire to end it. He also knew he was incarcerated because of Peanut, and Clem would want no response from Lamar. But every time he thought of Peanut dying alone at the hands of Gurgen, the rage emerged and eventually he came to a decision.

Lamar showed to work at the library. Old Man Haskell sat at his tiny desk, glasses upon his nose, peering over them as he read *The Trial* by Franz Kafka.

"Thought you might take another day," Haskell spoke without looking up.

"I needed to get my blood flowin'," Lamar responded.

"Won't be needin' ya today ... thought you might like to give William Faulkner's *The Sound and the Fury* a read."

"Ya think so huh."

In his years working for Haskell, Haskell had never suggested a book to him. Lamar wandered through the aisles of the tiny library until he came to the F's. Finding *The Sound and the Fury*, Lamar lifted it from the shelf. The book felt heavy. Opening the book, Lamar was amazed to find a secret compartment with a perfectly formed shiv. The handle had been rendered to hide fingerprints and the tip filed to break off where needed.

"No need to return that copy, Lamar, we have an extra one." Haskell spoke without looking up from his book.

Lamar shoved the shiv handle deep into Gurgen's larynx and bit most of the Aryan monster's nose off. Lamar had seen the darkness and harnessed the darkness that was inside of him. When they came to him in his cell, the guards politely asked him to follow them, and he did. He received props from every cell on his way to solitary.

And sit in solitary confinement, Lamar did. Minute by minute, hour by hour and day by day, Lamar sat and ruminated. Some moments he chastised himself for his action but other times we wished he could re-live it. As the days went by, he could feel his beard grow and grow. Beside food, no one visited, and no words were spoken. Until one day, he heard heavy footsteps that he recognized; he recognized the heavy thump of the feet and the sound of the gait. The steps stopped right outside of his cell.

"Open twelve," the voice with a heavy New Yahk accent spoke.

The door of the cell opened and with it a little bit of light into the dark cell. Lamar sat up and saw Detective Pete Mills in the doorway.

"Was wonderin'," Lamar started with a scratchy voice, "was wonderin' if you'd come."

"Thought I'd wait your full term in the hole," Pete responded.

"Forty days in the hole. What day is it?"

"Day forty-two."

"Gurgen die?"

"He'll live. Gonna need a few surgeries to graft him a new nose and he may never talk again but he'll live."

"I guess that means we're quits as friends."

"Depends."

Lamar slowly stood, his legs cramped and atrophied. "Depends on?"

"From this moment on, Lamar Wagner, you are the

shepherd."

"Detective?"

"The warden is willing to overlook this incident. It'll disappear in paperwork."

"But I did try to kill Gurgen. I ain't apologizing for that."

"The man is the head of the Aryan Brotherhood at this facility and the man responsible for over a hundred prison murders."

"I won't last a week in GP. Those crackers will string me up."

"You're getting transferred to Rikers. Short term wing."

"My parole?"

"Six months. You will appear in front of the board. I'll vouch; warden will too. Monty Cruise of Parole Board is also on board." Lamar sat down and rested his head in his hands.

"Why Detective Mills? Why help me?"

"Mr. Wilson, your former employer … the man you guys held up? Calls every week on your behalf to get you out. Clementine calls sometimes three times a week. I know good when I see it, Lamar. I know why you shanked Gurgen."

"He killed Peanut."

"Yes he did, and it isn't right. And that's why I'll vouch. After eight years, you've earned one." Pete Mills walked to the cell door.

"Thank you, Detective Mills."

"See you at Rikers. Close twelve."

****

Lamar pulled into The Metro parking garage and drove near JR's lair. He parked his car and opened the door.

"I'd like to go in alone," Jake uttered.

"You want to go see JR alone? Why?" Pete asked.

"Couple reasons. Number one, you both need at least a few minutes of shut eye. I can sleep on the way to Palm Springs."

"And two?" Lamar asked.

"Let me handle JR alone. Please."

Lamar and Pete looked at each other and shrugged.

"I could use a little sleep," Pete agreed.

"Me too." Lamar eased his seat back and closed his eyes.

****

JR opened the door from the elevator and stood, staring at Jake. Jake walked past JR and made straight for the technical gazebo.

"Holy shit, Jake," JR exclaimed, chasing after Jake. "I caught the news feed. I couldn't believe it … they said three dead. One female."

"Yea. One female."

"Are you okay?" JR asked.

"Physically, yes." Jake reached the gazebo and stood in front of the main terminal.

"Where are the other guys?" JR asked standing at the edge of the gazebo.

"Napping in the Durango. We got a full day ahead and I need them rested."

"When's the last time you slept?"

"I slept last night."

"I mean more than three hours."

"Did you find anything, JR?" Jake asked, motioning at the terminal.

JR sighed and entered the gazebo, sitting in front of

the main terminal. He typed on the keyboard and a list of numbers and names appeared on the screen under the heading: LOGANO.

"Not much. Everything stems to and from Logano Corp. It must feed into hundreds of accounts. Nothing immediately tangible. These guys aren't gonna leave you the eggs and milk to bake the cake. It'll take months … years to trace and track everything they're buying and selling. And then—"

"They'll start a new dummy corp."

"Yep. But you knew that already." Jake sat in the chair next to JR and exhaled. "Why are you here, Jake?"

"Remember the old days? I used to always come see you—"

"When you were stuck."

"Yea. And even if you had nothing … it helped."

"I missed you too, Jake. Who was the female?"

"Scarlet." Jake closed his eyes and rubbed them.

"Girlfriend?"

"No. Maybe, I don't know. I barely knew her. Twenty-eight hours ago, I didn't know she existed and now…I feel like I killed her."

"Jake…"

"I know, I know, I know but … are we … am I responsible for her death?"

"You took the case and the crumbs left behind, led you to her. You can't control where the case takes you, the clues take us where they take us," JR explained.

"But we got her involved."

"Where you'd meet her?"

"Lucky's in Hollywood. She was a dancer."

"And she followed you from there?'"

"No. We took her … from the Beaudry spot."

"Well…"

"Don't blame the victim, JR."

"She got herself involved in the case. Yes, maybe you thought keeping her with you would keep her safe but how could you have known a cartel hit squad would attack you?"

"I shoulda put her in a hotel the second I heard the name Dario Mendoza."

"But you didn't, and you will feel bad about that forever."

Jake stood, exited the gazebo and looked at the multiple screens. JR remained seated and scratched his ear.

"What do you want to do, Jake?"

"Find Mckenna."

JR stood and approached Jake.

"You want to give the boys a few more minutes of shut eye?"

"No … we need to go hassle an old friend."

JR put a hand on his friend's shoulder.

"Find her, Jake."

Chapter Twenty-Three

As the boys emerged from the excruciatingly bright lights of The Metro parking dungeon, they observed the first sprinkles of a new day over the horizon. Still dark, the sky appeared more of a deep purple with impending magenta than pitch black. Streaks of red screamed across the sky beneath the purple hue, announcing a new day.

Jake briefly closed his eyes tiredly, inhaled and exhaled deeply. He had been tight with Little Luck since his very first article in Los Angeles and he didn't envy confronting his old friend. Jake feared Little Luck passed information to Los Nuevos and told them of Jake and his team's involvement.

Little Luck and the Baja Cartel had been partners for years and that arrangement had brokered peace in the LA Underworld for more than a decade. Why would Luck risk that peace? It would bring the Armenians into contention for more power and that wouldn't even begin to cover the thoughts of the Russians and the Triads.

As Lamar stopped at the light, Jake was struck with a thought.

"Yamamura and the task force are sitting on Little Luck's," Jake blurted.

"Shit." Pete exclaimed. "You're right."

"We should park a few blocks west of Little Luck's," Jake offered.

"Yea but won't they still see us enter?" Pete asked.

"There's a back route. A towing company shares a back lot with Luck. The back lots connect Little Luck's with the towing company. Separated by a chain link fence. We sneak through the company's lot and there's a hole in the fence. We can navigate that hole and reach Luck's from the back."

"Is the hole big enough to accommodate two big and talls?" Lamar smiled.

"You can make it, husky fella." Jake returned Lamar's smile.

"And then?" Pete tried to stay on point.

"And then, there's a panel with a code for the back door. I know the code." Lamar and Pete gawked at Jake.

"Why the fuck—" Pete began.

"They have a cot in the office. Little Luck would let me stay there when I was working late on a case. And after two or three pitchers of that moonshine."

"Hard to believe Lily left you," Pete spoke.

****

Lamar parked a few blocks away and, like Jake said, there was a hole in the fence connecting Little Luck's and the towing company.

"How long ago did you use this hole?" Pete asked.

"Eight…maybe nine years ago," Jake answered.

"Their handyman is overpaid."

There was plenty of room in the fence for the big guys to shimmy through and the three of them slowly approached the back door of the café.

"You hear that?" Jake asked, crouching in front of the panel.

"I don't hear anything," Lamar answered.

"Exactly. I think the place is closed."

"When is this place ever closed?" Pete inquired.

Lamar tried the knob on the back door. The door opened.

"Hey," Lamar whispered as the door swung open. "The door ain't locked."

"Wipe down that handle, Lamar," Pete cautioned. "Don't touch anything boys."

Lamar entered through the door and the other two followed him into the dark and silent restaurant. As they crept in, all three of them removed their guns and started their search. In nearly total darkness, the three slowly and cautiously slinked through the back bowels of Little Luck's.

"I don't like this," Pete said, a pitch too loud.

"Shhh," Lamar hushed.

As they made their way down the long corridor leading to the back of the kitchen, Jake could make out some sort of mayhem ahead. He picked out the shapes of pots and pans on the floor. Jake stepped past Lamar and, using his forearm, felt his way to the corner.

"Don't touch anything," Pete hissed.

"Shhh, I got it," Jake hissed back.

Jake stopped and the boys halted as well. Tapping Pete, Jake pointed out the pots and pans on the floor. The kitchen was slightly illuminated with rivulets of early morning light streaking through the dining room windows.

"The blinds must be drawn," Jake hypothesized. He didn't like the set-up or impending scenario, one scintilla.

"Guys... on three." Jake lifted three fingers and at the last finger, the three stepped around the corner, guns drawn.

The kitchen was in shambles, resembling the

aftermath of an earthquake. Pots and pans strewn across the floor with plates smashed on the ground and glass littering the floor with shards sticking up in sections. In the middle of the floor, a body was on its side.

"Ah Jesus," Pete remarked. He stepped forward, grabbing a paper towel from the corner of the hot line. Pete saw shades of dark liquid surrounding the body. "Blood," Pete whispered. Careful to not step in the blood, he crouched next to the body and using the paper towel, Pete pried the body slightly over.

"It's Zachary Belataka," Pete announced.

Zachary's throat had been slit, neatly with one thin swipe. The front of his busser uniform was covered in black blood.

"Belataka?" Jake asked.

"This is gonna bring a shit storm from Glendale," Lamar lamented.

"Why would…why would Luck do it?" Pete pondered.

"I don't think he was the target." Jake looked past Pete. "I think he's collateral damage." Jake began to walk past the body.

"Careful, Jake," Pete said. "Mind your step."

Jake crept along the edge of the room. Jake stopped abruptly. A pair of feet on the floor stuck out from behind the counter.

"Hey," Jake quietly called out.

As Lamar and Pete focused on Belataka, Jake cautiously approached the feet. He knew what he'd find before he approached.

Little Luck lay on his back, his throat slashed from ear to ear. His arms were folded over his chest, almost in prayer. He looked peaceful, besides the deep slice in his throat.

"Damn, Luck." Jake shook his head, staring down at the legend of Koreatown. Jake knelt next to him. "Sorry, old friend. They finally got you."

Jake went to touch Luck's wrist for a pulse.

"Don't touch him," Pete barked as he approached. "No fingerprints."

"He's dead." Jake rose and stood next to Pete. "Shit."

"You're positive he ratted you out?" Pete pointedly asked.

"He said he'd made concessions with certain factions. It was the cartels. I stupidly showed Luck that picture of Mendoza. So stupid."

"Don't beat yourself up. Luck was dead the second he broke ranks with the Baja's. He told Los Nuevos of Dario Mendoza's existence. And Nuevos attacked us thinking Tony Tahoe was Mendoza," Pete concluded.

"I'm even more convinced the Sri Lankan saved our lives."

"Who do we think did this?" Lamar asked.

Jake sighed. "It could be the Baja's. He betrayed them and that's a no-no. It could be the Nuevos if they're doing Baby Luck's dirty bidding."

"And Belataka?" Pete sighed.

"Wrong place, wrong time." Jake shrugged.

"Maybe. If the Baja's did it, wrong place, wrong time. But if it's Los Nuevos, killing Belataka sends a message that Baby Luck won't allow the Armenians to invade what is now HIS territory." Lamar offered.

****

Pete fidgeted behind the wheel of Lamar's ride. He'd convinced Lamar to take a few hours of naptime and to let him drive to the desert. Jake didn't need convincing; he jumped into the back of the Durango, laid his head down and fell right asleep. Lamar, ultimately convinced, rested his head on the window and fell asleep soon after Pete hit the Ten.

Hitting the road at barely a little after six AM might have been the best break they'd caught in a couple of days. Pete caught the Ten freeway at the Santa Fe entrance and dropped the hammer, flooring the car upwards of ninety-five miles per hour.

Pete traced the previous two days in his head, attempting to keep the forked road of clues in his head straight. The assassination of Little Luck seemed a steep escalation. Zane's death had been unfortunate and Scarlet's death just absolutely needlessly tragic, but to murder the head of an underworld empire? They wrote chapters in history books about these types of events.

"To what end," Pete murmured to himself.

Baby Luck was an up-and-comer on the move, and he did have a large blockage in his growth canal, his father. Pete shook his head at the notion. Yes, Baby Luck gained strength and a territory with his father's passing but what an emboldened move. Patricide? Perhaps Baby Luck had sourced out the event, keeping his hands clean.

And what of Junior Lo, a long time and loyal soldier for Little Luck? Pete couldn't fathom Junior Lo betraying his boss and mentor so that Baby Luck could run the empire. Los Nuevos wouldn't dare snuff Little Luck unless Baby Luck kept Junior Lo out of the loop.

Pete blinked his eyes and gave his head a good shake. He, too, was exhausted but he'd gathered a little sleep when Jake pursued info from JR. Pete had spent many an hour on stakeouts and surveillance and knew the routine of little sleep.

Pete took a look at his disfigured hand. He told everyone he wore a glove to not upset other people but, the truth was, he hated looking at the disfigurement himself. He had spent years coming to terms with the injury and he still didn't feel one hundred percent okay with it. He felt enough confidence to utilize it, like he had when they interviewed Zane but deep down, he felt repulsed.

***

Christ, it had been cold that night, Pete reminisced. A freezing late February night in 1998; the Knicks had won, for a change, and Pete felt an urge to celebrate. He'd earned a rare Saturday night and, to treat himself, he was gonna purchase a fifth of good scotch.

Pete had placed on his dark trench coat and wandered into the frigid air of a New York City winter. The corner liquor store, *Horace's*, was Pete's local neighborhood spot. He'd known Old Man Horace for coming up on twenty years. A good family man, Horace remained a fixture in an ever-changing neighborhood and an ever-changing New York.

As Pete walked down the street, he spotted the corner store through his thick, frozen breath. He stuck his right hand into the pocket of his trench coat.

"Dammit," he said aloud.

Pete felt in his pocket and touched, first, his badge and second, his service revolver. He didn't like to wander the streets with his service piece. He had a throwdown piece attached to his ankle and that was the only weapon he felt comfortable with when he was in civilian mode. Pete kept his hand in his pocket as he approached *Horace's*.

From the street, he could spot Horace behind the counter. Horace, a Black male in his sixties, always struck Pete as one of the coolest men of the older generation. Many times, Horace influenced Pete onto certain jazz musicians, new and old. In fact, one year for Christmas, Horace had gifted Pete a CD of Miles Davis' *Birth of Cool*.

Pete waved at Horace with his left hand, leaving his right in his pocket.

Upon entering the store, Pete noticed that he wasn't the only customer. A young man stood at the counter in front of Horace. The young man, face not visible from Pete's stance, wore a gray ski cap.

"Hey Horace, how's the hammer hangin'?" Pete called out.

"Good, Pete, good, thanks for asking," Horace replied, stiffly. Neither Horace nor the young man made any sort of movement. They just stood, very still.

"Yea, just came in for a bottle of the good stuff."

"The Blue?" Horace asked.

"Yea, the usual, feel like celebrating a little."

"We're out, Pete, don't got none," Horace responded.

"Really," Pete replied. Pete looked past Horace and saw a fifth of his favorite stuff sitting on the shelf, right behind Horace.

Pete felt in his pocket and gripped his revolver. Pete stared at the back of the young man in front of him.

"Everything all right, Horace?"

"Good, Pete…all good." Horace motioned with his eyes.

The young man immediately spun around and pointed a handgun right at Pete. "Hands up,

325

motherfucker," the kid yelled.

The kid couldn't have been older than nineteen. The kid was cracked out of his head.

Wait, I know this kid. Little Jimmy Montoya.

"Ah Jesus, really kid? You have to have the worst luck in the world."

"Shut Up! I will shoot you in the face!"

"All right, all right…I've got my right hand in my pocket. See." Pete motioned with his head toward his pocket. "I want to show you something."

Pete started to pull his right hand from his pocket, holding on to his badge. The kid stepped up and pointed the gun a little closer to Pete.

"You pull that hand out and I'll unload this gun in your face."

"Okay, okay…it's all good. Let's be cool here. Tough night for you kid, I'm a police officer."

At the sound of that, Little Jimmy Montoya took a step back.

"Oh shit…" Jimmy whispered.

"How about … you drop your gun and leave? Bygones?"

The kid lowered his gun for a split second and then lifted it again at Pete.

"How about I shoot you in the fucking face!!!"

Pete stood directly in front of Little Jimmy Montoya. He briefly shook his head. By instinct, Pete slowly lifted his left hand and placed his hand over the muzzle of the gun. Jimmy looked at the action, shocked.

"Gimme the gun, Jimmy." Pete spoke with a cold intonation.

Jimmy stared at Pete's hand over the gun and then looked Pete in the face. For a second, Pete could see the young kid who'd run in that neighborhood, as a boy. The eyes of Jimmy Montoya conveyed youth and innocence. And then the eyes hardened, and a look of steeled determination appeared.

Ah hell.

At the exact same time, Jimmy Montoya and Pete fired their guns. Jimmy's bullet went directly through Pete's hand shattering a six-pack of beer bottles behind Pete. Pete fired his gun from the pocket of his trench coat and it struck Jimmy Montoya in the heart, killing him instantly. Jimmy dropped, eyes wide open in shock.

Pete fell to the floor, in a heap. He attempted to lift his left hand and arm. At first, he believed his hand to have been blown off, the blood and gore was so tremendous. As Horace ran around the counter to help Pete, Pete was able to lift his bloody appendage and, for an instance, see a symmetrical hole in the middle of his hand, still smoking where the bullet had singed.

"Call 9-1-1, Horace," Pete croaked.

Horace raced back to his phone behind the counter as Pete lifted his dying hand and blood poured over the linoleum floor of the store, intermingling with the bubbles of the displaced beer. Pete passed out from shock.

****

Pete looked in the rearview mirror as he heard Jake stir. Pete and Jake made eye contact via the mirror.

"My face is nearly healed so let's try to avoid what happened last time we were in a casino."

"I knocked you out in the police station. I reserve the right to do it again." Pete returned the smile.

"Apology accepted," Jake replied and closed his eyes.

****

Ed Tall Mountain stood, staring at the Los Angeles news on the seventy-inch TV in the empty high roller's lounge. A news team was encamped outside of Trotter's Tavern, regurgitating the news Tall Mountain had seen all morning. A spectacular shoot-out at Trotter's on Washington; two dead on the street and one dead on the premises of Trotter's.

"Dammit, Jake," Tall Mountain mumbled.

Tall Mountain straightened his turquoise tie and left the high rollers' lounge. Tall Mountain walked with his regal posture through his casino, acknowledging no one. As he entered the foyer of his executive suite, he was puzzled to see his assistant not at her post.

He entered his plush office overlooking the Coachella Valley. The office was an impressive homage to the Tribal culture, with drawings and paintings of his people and depictions of their heritage. On one wall, a large, framed picture of him and Joseph Smith took up most of the wall. In the center of the room, two overly large chairs with enormous arm rests, took up space in front of Tall Mountain's mahogany desk. With a gruff sigh, he walked behind his desk and stared out at the vast desert.

"Quite a view," a voice behind Tall Mountain spoke. Tall Mountain startled and turned to see Jake sitting in the right chair, gun extended. Tall Mountain reached for his desk.

"Nah, nah, nah," Jake warned, "hands on top of your head."

"I'll do no such thing. What is the meaning of this, Jake?"

"Oh boys," Jake called out.

Lamar and Pete emerged from the office closets, holding onto their guns.

"All I have to do is scream and you'll be surrounded by security."

"It's a sound-proof room, Mr. Tall Mountain." Jake smiled. "Did you forget that I worked for you? Sit. Hands on desk."

Mr. Tall Mountain sat behind his desk. Lamar approached and sat on a corner of the desk, staring at Tall Mountain.

Jake stood and walked over to a picture of Tall Mountain with S. Newman.

"You boys are all over the news...have you seen it?"

"Seen it?" Pete responded. "We fucking lived it."

"Did you personally hire S. Newman?" Jake asked, looking at the picture of S. Newman.

"I hired you men to find my daughter. I assume this appearance and the Trotter's massacre means you have not?"

Lamar stood and walked around the desk so that he was behind Tall Mountain. He grabbed Tall Mountain by both shoulders, lifting him from behind. A look of terror crossed Tall Mountain's face.

"Answer Jake's question, if you please," Lamar hissed.

"Yes, Yes, I hired S. Newman," Tall Mountain answered as Lamar set him down.

"And the board does your bidding?" Pete pressed.

"It's a process."

"It's a process?" Jake walked over to the desk and placed both of his hands and his gun on the desk. "You have no concept of how much trouble you're in?"

"Where is my daughter?" Tall Mountain shouted.

Jake backed away and stood next to Pete. "Where is Newman?"

"I don't know. He hasn't shown the past two days."

"Did he call?" Lamar asked. "Was he owed vacation time, sick leave?"

"He didn't call in. We returned from Los Angeles after meeting with you gentlemen and he disappeared. I don't know where he is." Tall Mountain tried to stand, agitated, but Lamar held him down. "I hired you, Jacob Hansen, to find my daughter! Have you found her? Is she the dead girl at Trotter's? Why are you here strong arming me when it is you who should be held accountable?"

"I was never a criminologist, but I don't think he knows of Newman's activities," Jake whispered to Pete.

"Me either," Pete responded.

Jake approached the desk again.

"Mr. Tall Mountain, I'm sorry. We haven't found Mckenna. Yet. But in our investigation, we have uncovered some information that you need to know."

"Where is—"

"We believe she's fine, for now. And I think I know where she might be. But … did you know your CFO, S. Newman was utilizing the Casino to launder money for the Baja cartel?"

Chapter Twenty-Four

Danny had watched as Detective Allison stormed out of the Culver City office, in a smoldering rage. A tiny part of her told her to follow him but her better instincts told her to remain fast. She had neither worked nor known Allison long, but she knew rage when she saw it. Besides, they had driven separately to the crime scene and the Culver City offices.

When she drove downtown, she replayed the prior thirty-six hours in her head. The day and a half stirred quite a whirlwind of events. Shock didn't register when Jackson took the Trotter's Shoot-out away and, in many ways, she had anticipated the move. It was Culver City's jurisdiction. For Allison, it was personal in an unfettered desire to administer the case as it pertained to Jake Hansen and his crew. To Danny, the case landed squarely at the feet of Culver City. And besides, they kept the Barnacles case.

Allison didn't show up at the station and Danny didn't think he would. A little relieved, she knew that his presence would put a hinderance on the case they did still possess. So, she pursued the case in the murder of Zane Adkins.

Danny Burkle took the video of the Barnacles pool room out of evidence and played it in the VCR in the auxiliary room. She poured herself a hot cup of coffee and got to detective work. She played and re-played the sequence over and over. She wound and rewound the tape for a few hours, over and over.

She heard a rap on the door and looked up to see Lieutenant Chambers standing in the doorway. A striking man, Chambers stood well over six feet and a trim one hundred eighty pounds. A man in his fifties, Danny guessed, he had a thick head of white hair.

"Barnacles?" Chambers asked, entering the room.

"Yea, we didn't get much on statements."

"One never does from drunk people." Chambers smiled. He sat in the chair opposite Burkle.

"Yea and we have the murder on video tape…right in front of us." Danny shook her head.

"Confounding. I saw the tape last night. Inconclusive I would call it."

"Is it?" Danny questioned. "There's a split second where … I'm … I mean, we're missing something."

"You're right to say, 'I', Detective. I don't see your partner here."

"I think he needed time." Danny chose her words carefully.

"To what, pout?"

"I don't know if I would call it that," Danny responded.

"You don't have to. I'll call it that. I'm glad one of you acted professional."

"Thank you, sir. This was personal for Detective Allison."

"It's always personal for Detective Allison. It's what makes him a great detective. It's also why he'll never get promoted higher than this."

"Yes, sir."

"He was always a hard ass, so I'm told," Chambers

mused, looking with a faraway stare, "but the Benitez fiasco did something to him. Losing Cruz hardened him to a point beyond, I fear. That's when they brought me here, so all I've seen is the post-Benitez, Allison."

Danny was unsure whether to react and engage or sit idly and remain silent. Chambers shook his head and emerged from the thoughts conceived in his mind.

"Burkle, I'm going to give you an option. If you want a new partner ... I'll make it happen."

Stunned, Danny eyed her boss. She hadn't anticipated the conversation drifting this direction. "I have a partner, sir."

Chambers stood up. "I appreciate your loyalty. But this... is a one-time offer."

"Thank you, sir. I have a partner."

"Carry on, Danny. Find that evidence." Chambers headed for the door and rapped his knuckles on the door as he exited.

Danny leaned back in her chair for a minute after Chambers exited. Her boss had given her the opportunity to choose her own partner. Or at the very least, a different one than Frank Allison. She'd been mortified at his behavior toward the Chief of Detectives, but even more horrified when Frank started to explain his behavior at a cherished poker game. Perhaps it was in her best interest to get a new partner, but she couldn't remove thoughts of Greg Davis, her long ago and longtime boyfriend.

"You've never known the meaning of loyalty," Greg had cursed at her.

Those words had stuck with her forever. She fervently had the back of not only every one of her partners but everyone in her squad. Not only to a fault but to her detriment. She was loyal.

"Fuck you, Greg," Danny called out to the void.

Allison had picked her, and she would remain loyal.

Danny refocused on the video. As the scene changed from the glee of the terrific pool shot to the horror of Zane bleeding out, Danny suddenly saw it. She paused the tape and stood, walking to the doorway.

"Sir," Danny called out. "Can you come see this?"

Chapter Twenty-Five

"So Tall Mountain is not part of the conspiracy," Pete uttered, diving his fork into his omelet.

The trio sat at the bar of The Broken Yolk on Palm Canyon in Palm Springs, ingesting a much needed and well-earned meal. Jake stretched his arms and looked into the mirror behind the bar. He glanced at his wrinkly attire and took a quick sniff under his arm.

"Probably could use a shower, a comb and a manicure," he said to himself.

"Yea, you stink," Lamar intoned.

As Pete and Lamar guzzled water, Jake nursed a spicy Bloody Mary, not really appetized by the alcohol.

"Thanks Lamar and no, I would say not," Jake finally answered, "And Newman is either on the run or dead already." Jake placed a fork of egg into his mouth.

"That leaves us back to where we were." Pete shook his head, unhappily.

"We needed to know what Tall Mountain knows. Ed now knows he's in a heap of trouble with the Board. And I also believe Ed may not have been complicit in Joseph Smith's death," Jake finished.

"Really?" Lamar exclaimed.

"I think he always thought foul play was a possibility, but it feels like a Newman ploy. He had more to lose and to gain."

"S. Newman." Pete wagged a finger at Jake.

"Exactly." Jake continued his meal.

"So, maybe Tall Mountain isn't a candidate for dad of the year. He was suspicious of Smith's death and he hired the man who is laundering money through his casino's. This makes him an idiot."

"Sounds like you're disappointed." Lamar smiled.

"Maybe a little." Jake shrugged.

"How is that possible?" Pete asked.

"Because he's not the bad guy?" Lamar wondered.

"No, it's not that. You have to understand, Ed Tall Mountain is something of a mythical figure in these parts. Not exactly the George Washington of Palm Springs but not that far off. He was the man of the desert. The pillar of strength. Even with his despicable acts toward Moro, Tall Mountain carried a persona of strength, will and power. To discover a man you feared, loathed and still, in some ways, revered is an imbecilic baboon … it's a little disconcerting."

"He's just a man," Pete lamented. "So, what now?"

"Find Mckenna." Jake set his plate aside.

"And the next step in doing so?" Lamar asked.

"We know she's in the desert. She's here somewhere. We don't know if she's at the Inn or not because we don't know when it opens."

"I called," Pete interrupted, "it's not open."

"Okay. You still carry your detective's badge for emergencies?"

"Yea."

"Well, this is an emergency."

****

Lamar sat behind the wheel with Jake sitting in the passenger seat. Pete sat in the back, polishing his old detective shield. The Durango sat parked across the street from the Yucca Valley Motor Lodge. It was the atypical one-story structure with an office in front and a sign blinking, Vacancy.

"So, this is ranch-style?" Jake poked Lamar.

"Yes motherfucker, this is ranch-style." Lamar giggled.

"I don't know why I got those confused."

"Because you're an idiot and that's what idiots do." Lamar delivered and gave Jake a wink.

"Frank Gehry, can we forget about the architecture for one second and focus?" Pete pressed.

"Okay." Jake focused. "You know the play?"

"I know the play."

"All right." Jake grabbed the sketch of Mckenna Pete appropriated from her apartment and handed it to Pete. "Show your badge, state your business, show the—"

"Jake," Pete interrupted. "I know the play."

Pete exited the Durango and crossed the street, strolling into the motor lodge's parking lot. Pete entered the office. A thick musty smell greeted him and that was more positive than the grouchy sneer on the desk clerk's face. Pete registered her as any age from sixty years to one hundred and thirty. Her name tag read: Alice and Pete thought that name felt about right.

"Good morning, ma'am." Pete opened with a smile, stepping up to the desk.

"What's good about it?" Alice replied.

"Very well." Pete tempered his enthusiasm, pulled his badge, and flashed it at Alice. "My name is Detective Peter Mills and we're looking for a young lady."

"We?" Alice asked.

"The royal 'we', I mean I am looking for a young

lady." Pete pulled out the sketch of Mckenna. "Is she staying here, by chance?"

Alice huffed, removed the glasses she wore and pulled down the glasses resting on top of her head. As she adjusted her lenses, she looked at the picture.

"What is she, an Indian?"

"Um," Pete shook his head, "I believe she's half Irish."

"Must be one of them black Irish." Alice looked up at Pete. "No, I don't recognize her."

"Thank you, ma'am, for your time." Pete put away the sketch and started to exit.

"Hope you find her alive," Alice called out.

"Jesus," Pete muttered. "I'll take the Bates Motel any day."

****

Lamar crossed the threshold of the Motel 6 in Joshua Tree. The front desk was a little wider than the Red Roof Inn he entered the previous hour, but no less unattractive. The gentleman behind the counter wore regulation Motel 6 gear but the gear didn't hide the raging meth issue of the gentleman. Lamar approached the spectacled white kid with horrible acne and a severe case of Gingivitis. Lamar withdrew the badge upon entering and approached the front desk.

"Good afternoon," Lamar flashed the badge. "I'm Detective Pete Mills and I have a few questions." Lamar pulled out Mckenna's sketch and showed it to the meth head.

****

Jake and Pete sat, quietly, in Lamar's Durango, staring at the Motel 6.

"How did I let you talk us into this fiasco?" Pete

broke the silence.

"Listen, we know she's out here somewhere … let's just narrow the gap."

"Jake, we've been to twelve hotels, motels, lodges in this shit-hole area and found nada, nunca, niente, zip, nuthin."

"Maybe thirteen is our number." Jake shrugged.

"And maybe three days of this case has made your brain mush," Pete spat out.

"I didn't hear your bright ideas, Detective."

"Jake, I swear to God—"

"No, no, come on, Detective Mills, let's hear your great ideas."

"Hansen, your face is just now recovering, you need a fresh one?" Pete lifted his good fist with cause.

"Oh, big man, threatening us little people?"

"Fuck you, Jake, you emotional bully."

"Emotional bully?!? I'm an emotional bully?!?!"

"An emotional bully of epic proportions!"

"Oh, that's rich coming from… from…"

"Yea, what was that Jake? Couldn't make out your comeback? Sound it out." Pete cupped his ear with his good hand to hear better.

So intent were Pete and Jake on their spat, they didn't even see Lamar approach and get in the back seat of his car.

"Thirteen down." Lamar tossed the badge to Pete.

"That's it. The badge is done for this waste of a day," Pete angrily decided.

"Fine," Jake fumed.

"Thirteen places, Jake." Lamar sighed. "Thirteen. You know Pete and I scored higher on the P.I. exam."

"I don't like to play by the playbook."

"Which is kind of why we're here right now," Pete interjected.

"Ha." Jake mocked.

"Seriously, what's next?" Pete lifted his hands.

Jake scrunched his face and eyed the guys. Lamar and Pete eyed each other, neither with any ideas. They were all bush tired.

"I don't know, Pete … I mean I wasted your entire day," Jake moaned.

"Oh my God, this is what I'm talking about. The passive aggressive bullshit…you are an emotional bully," Pete growled.

Jake folded his arms and moved his mouth into a pout. Pete sighed and shook his head.

"Okay. I'm sorry, Jake. It's been a rough couple of days and I'm a little—"

"Vexed. Flummoxed. Uh … uh, what else might you be?" Jake tapped his chin in wonderment.

"Come on, Jake," Pete coaxed. "What ya got?"

"I do have one last idea. You guys aren't going to like it. You really want to know?"

"Yes, Jake, the time has come to think outside of the box and that is your specialty." Pete sighed.

****

Jake stood in between Pete and Lamar on the concrete in front of the large sign. The dark sign with white letters was placed upon a sturdy brick edifice. The sign read: Entering Joshua Tree National Park.

"You wanted outside of the box," Jake reasoned.

"This is outside of any geometric shape I can think of," Pete moaned.

"How big is Joshua Tree?" Lamar asked tentatively.

"A little over twelve hundred square miles." Jake

smiled.

"I'm getting heat stroke." Pete rubbed his temples.

"She's staying somewhere near here. She's not gonna be deep in the park. I promise, we will find her."

"Jesus, man, are we really gonna do this?" Pete grumbled.

"She's in there. I know it."

"You realize you just said that about the thirteen places we visited." Lamar nudged Jake.

"Yea well, this I mean." Jake stared at the sign of the park and a memory flashed before him.

Lily, somehow, had convinced Jake to go on a two-day camping trip; just the two of them.

In all chaos, there is a cosmos, in all disorder a secret order.

"Jake." Lamar touched his shoulder.

"Come on," Jake snapped out of it, "let's find Mckenna."

****

The trio trudged through the rocky terrain of the national park without much of a plan. The way Jake figured, Mckenna would have holed up somewhere until the 29 Palms Inn re-opened. Her money would be running out so it wouldn't be anything too fancy. The thought process behind searching all the accommodations in the high desert was sound but had borne no fruit. The thought to search Joshua Tree came to him as Pete tore into him a bit.

As he rattled ideas in his head, he remembered a throw away conversation he and Mckenna had when she was a teenager. Jake questioned how her vacation was and Mckenna responded that her aunt and uncle had taken her camping at Joshua Tree. Like a bolt of lightning, the idea came to him to search Joshua Tree. Now as he and his partners baked under the later afternoon sun, Jake doubted his thinking.

Jake walked fifty feet past Pete and Lamar, determination pushing his efforts. It had been over a decade since he'd been to the Monument and his sense of direction, never his most keen sense, hindered his efforts. Still, he pushed himself farther and farther. Pete nearly slipped and Lamar grabbed his elbow to keep him from falling. Pete stood upright and put his hands on the back of his hips.

"What the fuck are we doing, Lamar?"

"Following Don Quixote to his windmills."

"Didn't Don Quixote only have one jackass following him?"

"Yep. Makes us doubly dumb." Lamar smiled.

"That what I thought. Come on, let's follow this to the end." Pete and Lamar carried on, holding onto each other's shoulders for support.

As they continued ahead and the sun dwindled, they caught up to Jake, bent over, holding his knees, and breathing heavy.

"Pit stop?" Pete asked as he and Lamar stood next to the doubled over Jake.

"It's gonna get dark soon, Jake. You know how I feel about coyotes."

"Actually, I don't, Lamar." Jake looked up.

"I don't like 'em!"

"I know. I screwed this up, god dammit." Jake stood.

"Yea man," Lamar agreed, "you suck at this P.I. shit."

"Thanks for that. I haven't killed us yet."

"Reassuring," Pete added.

Jake sighed, wiped his brow and swallowed. He closed and opened his eyes, staring into the horizon. He squinted as he looked forward and saw a brown sun hat, resting on the head of someone.

"Hey…" Jake murmured and began to walk to the hat.

Lamar and Pete rolled their eyes and followed.

Jake picked up his foot speed as he realized the brown hat, fifty yards away, belonged to a female, sitting on a rock, looking out at the curvature of the Earth.

Nearly walking into a jog, Jake approached and reached the seated female. He stood to her left and saw Mckenna Murphy-Tall Mountain sitting all by her lonesome.

"Jesus Christ," Jake started, startling Mckenna, who looked up. "My God…you are a hard person to find." Jake sat down next to Mckenna and laid back, shielding his eyes from the setting sun.

"Jake?" A look of astonishment crossed Mckenna's face as Jake raised his arms in relief.

****

With Pete and Lamar fast asleep in the back of the Durango, Jake drove with Mckenna in the front seat. Jake snuck a peek at her. Without makeup, she was just as beautiful as with and the sun colored her skin to a golden brown.

"I work the tourney every year because it's great money. And great practice. I just snap pictures and sketch the photos."

"You just happened to snap the wrong guy."

"Or the right guy," Mckenna corrected. "Joseph knew something was up. And when he was killed … and he was killed, Jake," Mckenna added pointedly.

"Oh, I know."

"Do you know who?" she asked.

"Have an idea who."

"Did you find out who the picture was?"

"Yes. It's probably best you don't know."

"I deserve to know who was following me."

"Deserving has got nothing to do with it. That one little picture has stirred up a shitstorm of a hornet's nest. I don't even know if I can explain every twist and shout that came about because of one little picture."

Mckenna looked out of her window, staring into the pitch blackness of the desert night. "How much did you learn about me? Trying to find me?" Mckenna asked, still looking out of the window.

"More than I anticipated. I know you've been through tough times. I know I wasn't much of a help," Jake lamented, seeing Mckenna from the corner of his eye.

"You met Scarlet?" Mckenna faced Jake who briefly made eye contact.

Jake sighed.

"Jake?" Mckenna asked quietly.

Jake pulled the Durango to the side of the road, stopping the vehicle. After gathering his thoughts, Jake leaned over to Mckenna and hugged her, whispering in her ear. She let out a little cry as Jake told her the truth of Scarlet. Mckenna pulled back, opened the car door and ran out into the night.

"Mckenna," Jake called out. He opened the door and chased after her. He caught her twenty yards from the road, grabbing her and stopping her.

"I can't explain all at once, Mckenna. It's been an insane three days. She was at the wrong place at the wrong time and by that, I mean … she shouldn't have been at Trotter's. We found your mystery man and as soon as we found out who he was, we shoulda sent Scarlet to a hotel or anywhere else…but we didn't. She got caught in the crossfire." Jake lowered his head and looked with sad eyes to Mckenna.

Mckenna held her arms and began to cry.

"It was my fault, Mckenna. My fault."

"Did you shoot her?"

"Of course not."

"Were you trying to look after her?"

"Of course. I felt I owed it to her and to you to try and protect her. And I failed."

Mckenna wiped her eyes, reached up to Jake, and hugged him.

"It's not your fault. I should have warned her. I should have warned Zane." Mckenna trailed off.

"You know about Zane?" Jake asked and she nodded.

"I saw it in the paper."

Jake lifted Mckenna's chin so she was looking him in the eyes.

"We're just pieces in a bigger puzzle, Mckenna. People are fighting over… well, it doesn't matter what they're fighting over. We're collateral damage. The best we can do is try to look out for each other."

Jake and Mckenna walked back to the Durango, hand and hand. Jake opened the door for her and helped her up into the seat. He walked around and entered.

"Everything cool?" Lamar sleepily asked.

"Yeah," Mckenna answered, "everything is cool."

As they drove on, Mckenna continued to engage in self-catharsis.

"I know I'm going through a bad phase. The drugs … Zachary's party's … Ed wanted me to change my name to Tall Mountain. Call him dad? You believe that? He essentially killed Moro and never cared about me 'til Joseph died. Joseph Smith and I became close. He told me about my mother, Sherry. He said she had a wild streak like I do. I don't know if I can come out of this spiral. She couldn't."

"Listen, Mckenna, I'm fourteen years older than you and this past week, I lost fifty G's, got arrested and got my nose broken twice, once by an old man with an oxygen tank and once by a big, white gorilla and both were friends of mine. Believe me, you can emerge from this spiral."

Mckenna suppressed a smile as she caught a glimpse of the bruises on Jake's face. Jake pulled the Durango into the lot of the 29 Palms Inn and parked in front of the room Mckenna pointed to, 214.

"Ricky, the hotel manager gave me the room for three nights. One bed though."

Jake looked at his friends in the back, asleep. "We're gonna have to keep watch so I'm sure we can come to some arrangement." Jake chuckled.

Mckenna led the three yawning boys up the path toward her room. As they approached Room 214, Mckenna removed a key from her pocket.

"I just want to rest my dogs," Lamar grumbled.

"Same with us all. I'll take first watch." Jake yawned as he spoke.

Mckenna opened the door and as they entered the room, they found Ernest Campion, sitting on a love seat by the light with a silenced revolver in his hand. He pointed the gun at the quartet.

"Good evening. Be so kind as to close the door behind you, Detective Mills. That's a good gentleman."

Chapter Twenty-Six

His immaculate posture stood as the first dynamic Jake noticed. Ernest Campion stood imminently erect with a proud stature. He was thin but wiry and his white linen pants were perfectly creased. His silk, black buttoned short sleeve shirt provided a perfect offset. Despite his terror of the man, Jake couldn't help but be impressed by the Sri Lankan's cool demeanor.

"You?" Mckenna blurted.

"Yes, young miss, me," the Sri Lankan responded.

"You know him?" Jake asked Mckenna.

"He spoke to me at…" Mckenna looked at Campion as he rose from his seat. "Never mind. Doesn't matter."

The Sri Lankan stepped around Pete and, lifting Pete's pant leg, removed his ankle throwdown piece. He stepped toward Lamar and with a swift flick of his wrist, removed the weapon stuck in Lamar's waist.

"Mr. Hansen, please be so kind as to toss your weapon upon the bed. At once, if you please. I would be much chagrined to fire a bullet into Mr. Wagner's spine."

Rapidly, Jake removed and tossed his gun to the bed. Atop the bed rested a brown package from UPS.

"I believe that is the camera sent by the unfortunate Mr. Adkins." The Sri Lankan motioned with his weapon.

Mckenna's lip started to tremble. The Sri Lankan bowed a polite head bow toward her.

"Forgive my rudeness, Miss … do you prefer

Murphy or Tall Mountain?"

"Murphy."

"Very well, pardon my rudeness, Miss Murphy. Mr. Adkins was a friend to you. I apologize; I was unable to come to his defense."

"You didn't kill Zane?" Jake asked.

As Campion crossed the room to grab the package, he smiled at Jake. "What possible motivation would I have to do Mr. Adkins in?"

"He wouldn't tell you where Mckenna was," Pete offered.

"You gentlemen really do discredit my function. My retainer wished a quiet search of Miss Murphy. How would an outlandish doing away of Mr. Adkins accomplish that?" Campion grabbed the package and handed it to Mckenna. "Be so kind as to carry that for me."

Mckenna took the package from Campion.

"Well ... if you didn't," Jake began.

"I assume you've become familiar with Mr. Xavier and his unfortunate companion. They also, did not kill Mr. Adkins. You witnessed the bar-maiden and her affection for Mr. Adkins. He clearly was enamored of Miss Murphy and not her."

"Wait, Molly killed Zane?!?" Mckenna turned, holding onto the package.

"Mckenna, easy now. This man has been kind enough to humor us. He doesn't have time for pettiness." Jake spoke and motioned for Mckenna to take the package and move on. "Molly killed Zane," Jake exclaimed.

A wry smile crossed Campion's face and Mckenna gave Jake a dirty look.

"That's the only logical conclusion, Mr. Hansen. I assume you saw the tape."

"We did…" Lamar responded.

"Ah, you presumed it was me or Mr. Xavier because you saw us? Yes, I witnessed Mr. Hansen's outrageous chicken cocktail and Detective Mills did make me at the Cat n' Fiddle but that renders me to murder Mr. Adkins? And from fifteen feet away. While I appreciate the thought that I'm an action hero… I promise you; I am nothing of the sort."

"Oh," Jake responded.

"Sorry to disappoint, Mr. Hansen. Would me killing one of your friends in spectacular fashion make up for my grievance?"

"Oh God, no, of course not," Jake stammered.

"Maybe you should shut the fuck up, Jake," Lamar offered.

"Yea, ya dumb fuck," Pete hissed.

"We are, or I am sorry," Jake pleaded.

"And you protected us at Trotter's?" Lamar asked.

"Perhaps. Very well. Now then, we will be exiting this room as follows. Detective Mills in the lead, followed by Mr. Wagner, Mr. Hansen and then finally, Miss Murphy and myself. Please do not mistake my affable nature for weakness. I will not hesitate to kill all of you and then every person in this complex if you cross me one iota. We will be taking Mr. Wagner's vehicle to our destination. Mr. Hansen at the wheel." Campion motioned toward Pete. "Detective, after you."

Pete headed to the door, opening the door, and exiting. The rest of the merry crew followed with the Sri Lankan in rear, holding his gun and the package.

****

Jake sat behind the wheel, both hands upon the wheel. Mckenna sat behind Jake, her hands tied in front of her by zip ties. Mckenna looked forward into the rearview mirror and searched for Jake's comfort. Jake took a few seconds before he connected with Mckenna. Catching her fear, he blew her an air kiss and mouthed the words, 'It will be fine.' She smiled and calmed but Jake's mind raced back to the last time he comforted a scared young woman and what her end was.

Pete and Lamar stood in front of Campion, outside of the Durango on the passenger side. Campion levelled his gun at them.

"Mr. Wagner, be so kind as to strike Detective Mills until he loses consciousness."

"Sorry?" Lamar asked incredulously.

"Please, knock your friend unconscious."

Lamar looked with hesitation toward Pete then Campion. Campion sighed and aimed his gun at Lamar.

"Sorry, boss." Lamar grimaced at Pete.

"Hate it when you call me boss. Make it good, Lamar."

Lamar leaned into a right cross and threw a thunderous blow to Pete's jaw, trembling Pete's legs, but not dropping him.

"That all you got, convict," Pete blabbered through his blood riddled spit.

"Hold on," Lamar retorted and threw a gigantic hook to Pete's left ribs, dropping Pete's body and Lamar smoked Pete in the jaw with a wicked upper cut, crumpling Pete to the ground.

"Well done, Mr. Wagner." Campion tossed Lamar a pair of zip ties and Lamar proceeded to tie Pete's ankles and wrists together. "Detective Mills goes into the back seat."

Lamar opened the back door and dead lifted the dead weight of Pete into the seat next to Mckenna. The Sri Lankan closed the door and delivered a friendly pat on the back of Lamar. Campion nudged Lamar with his gun toward the trunk. Opening the trunk, Campion motioned Lamar to enter.

"Is this a black thing?" Lamar asked.

"I'm four shades darker than you, Mr. Wagner."

Lamar peered into the trunk, then looking back, received the butt end of Campion's gun to the temple, knocking him unconscious. The crack of the gun hitting Lamar's head, elicited a little squeal from Mckenna.

The Sri Lankan situated Lamar into the trunk and zip tied his hands and feet. Campion closed the trunk and stepped into the front passenger seat next to Jake. Situating himself so that he could keep an eye and gun on both Jake and Mckenna, he smiled, content.

"Now then, drive east, Mr. Hansen," the Sri Lankan instructed.

Jake started the car and exited the parking lot. Taking a right out of the lot, he drove them into the bowels of the desert.

****

As they drove deep into the dark desert, the Sri Lankan eyed Jake. Jake returned the gaze with a mixture of fear, confusion, anxiety and relief all packed together.

"I read your work, from a prior life, Mr. Hansen." Campion broke the silence.

"Beg your pardon?" Jake responded.

"Your work as a journalist. I read all of your pieces. You were quite good. I especially enjoyed the cadence in which you tailored your words. Quite syncopated."

Jake looked in the rearview mirror and made eye contact with Mckenna.

"Thank you?"

"Why did you ever give up this profession? It seems to have been your calling."

"I ... I was not in a good place," Jake measured his words. "I screwed up and hurt a lot of people in the process."

"Including yourself."

"Oh, for sure."

"That's a shame, Mr. Hansen. You appear to be a seeker of truth. The world needs more of you. Seekers."

"I think perhaps you have the answers I seek," Jake nervously offered.

"Me? Perhaps not as much as you believe. I am but a blunt instrument. I'm the hammer, not the one who wields it. I am not the man who provides answers. I provide finality."

"That I understand."

Jake drove in silence, but his mind whirled at an insane speed. He'd spent a lifetime searching for answers, only hoping to find the ear and words of someone with the knowledge and inside information as the Sri Lankan. The man had knowledge of a world he'd attempted to crack since he was a young man. Ernest Campion had answers to questions he would never conjure.

"You know things I need to know."

"Then go find these things. You have the ability. Do you have the will and when you find the will, will the answers satisfy you? You see, Mr. Hansen, I am not plagued by the questions that keep you fighting demons. At night, when the lights go out, that is when the personal demons crawl out and bring forth havoc. I do not suffer those demons as most humans. My life was thrust upon me, but I embraced it and have thrived. I live in the shadows, but I choose so. I'm an invisible man. I am a monster and monsters shouldn't roam the countryside, so I remain remote."

"Why are you telling me this?"

"You intrigue me, Mr. Hansen. You and your menagerie of friends, cohorts … family, I believe. Wouldn't you deem Mr. Wagner and Detective Mills as family? Certainly Miss Jones."

"Yes, I do consider them family. Pete and Lamar are more brothers to me than my actual brother. They took you from Sri Lanka?"

"Quite right. You've done your homework. Your friend, JR Almeida is a wonder."

"He is."

A look of content and thoughtfulness crossed the Sri Lankan's face.

"I was taken when I was a boy. I barely remember. I have no memory of my mother or father. A child just barely removed from diapers. I have seen the four corners of the globe, Mr. Hansen. I've seen things I can never tell another living soul and they wouldn't believe me if I did. My job is very final."

"Don't you have any hobbies?"

"I garden. I'm a gardener. I plant and create growth. It is the inherent duality of my life. It brings me peace."

Jake drove in silence a bit but couldn't resist the conversation.

"You read all my stuff?"

"Even your last article. The one published with such controversy."

"You read my stuff …" Jake whispered.

"Your last article was sharp but ultimately incorrect. Eddie Collins was correct in shelving it."

"Really? Incorrect? How?"

"Mr. Hansen, even if I were at liberty to say, I would not."

"Why?"

"It would deprive you of the ultimate joy of discovering the answer yourself. Which is your joy, is it not? Discovery."

"Hmmm. So my work was pretty accurate?"

"Take the left at the next dirt path."

Jake pulled the Durango onto a nearly hidden dirt path and continued to drive. In the back seat, Pete stirred but remained out.

"It shall not be long now," the Sri Lankan spoke.

Jake drove deeper into the desert, approaching the foot of an enormous mountain. As Jake drove into the dark nothingness, a small light became visible.

"Do you see it, Mr. Hansen?"

"The light? Yes, I do."

"That is our destination."

As Pete stirred awake and sat up, attempting to rub his head, he looked around his surroundings. It took a few seconds to remove the tendrils of cobwebs in his head, but once he did, he grasped the scenario.

"Deep desert. Shadow of the mountain. Shit," Pete whispered to himself. "He dragged us out here to kill us."

Jake drove closer and closer to the tiny light. As he approached, he realized the light emanated from one solitary lantern. The Durango crept closer to the lantern and two figures came into view. Jake drove within ten feet of the lantern and stopped the car.

"You may get out, Mr. Hansen. You as well, Miss Murphy. Leave on the lights of the car if you please. I must see to your companions."

Campion snipped Mckenna's zip ties and freed her. Jake and Mckenna exited the Durango and stepped toward the lantern. Jake was able to make out that the two figures were men. One man stood a few feet below the other man, in a hole. The man in the hole was digging and the man above held a gun, pointed at the man in the hole. After cutting the boys loose with a pocketknife, Campion nudged Pete and Lamar toward Jake and Mckenna. Mckenna placed her hand in Jake's.

"Forward, my friends." Campion motioned with his gun to walk toward the figures.

As the group of five approached the figures, Dario Mendoza and S. Newman came into sight.

"Son of a bitch," Lamar spoke in amazement.

Mendoza was the owner of the gun and pointed it at S. Newman, who dug the hole. It wasn't a hole, but a grave. The Sri Lankan walked past the stunned quartet and made his way to Mendoza and a shirtless Newman.

"I hired you Campion to handle this," Newman cried out as he rested on his shovel.

"I should have killed you with the shovel, you fucking worm," Mendoza shouted at Newman.

"You and what army?" Newman retorted.

"You don't think I've killed men? I've killed men." Mendoza laughed.

With his silenced gun, Campion fired and shot the shovel out of Newman's hand. Newman and Mendoza, stunned, stood silently frightened.

"Gentlemen, I certainly have better things to do with my time than to listen to you two argue. Mr. Newman, please grab your shovel."

S. Newman grabbed the wounded shovel and began to dig, again.

"I don't know what he's paying you, Campion," Newman began, "but I can pay triple. You know I can."

"I am aware of your cash flow. However, two points…you have no comprehension of who's paying me and what…and who do you think is your benefactor? Are you convinced of your…Mr. Hansen, the word eludes me."

The Sri Lankan shrugged to the stunned Jake.

"Invincibility?" Jake squeaked.

"Invincibility, Mr. Newman?" Campion accepted and tossed at S. Newman.

"We hired you," Newman stammered.

"You hired me to acquire an object. And that I have." Campion smiled. "I have fulfilled the requirements of my contract with you."

"I hired him as well, *pendejo*," Mendoza spat at Newman. "Seventeen years disappeared and poof, I come to fix your fuck up and this is what happens. You're a loose end now, Newman."

"I built that fund," Newman screamed.

"And then you betrayed your employers." Mendoza shook his head.

Jake leaned over to Pete and Lamar.

"Newman created the fund for the Baja's but—" he started.

"He sold out to Los Nuevos after they learned Mendoza wasn't dead," Pete concluded.

"And the Nuevos don't need Newman anymore," Lamar added.

"Because they have Baby Luck," Jake mused.

The Sri Lankan looked toward the crew.

"Are you quite finished?" Campion asked.

"Yes." Jake bowed his head. "Sorry."

Campion returned his focus to Mendoza and Newman, stepping closer to them. The Sri Lankan leaned his head ever so slightly and caught the eye of Jake. Confused, Jake raised an eyebrow toward Campion. Campion winked at him.

"Mr. Mendoza, what is that object in the grave?" Campion asked Mendoza.

Mendoza leaned over and peered into the grave.

"I don't see anything," Mendoza observed.

The Sri Lankan took two steps forward, lifted his gun and fired into the back of Mendoza's head, killing him instantly. Mendoza fell, in a heap, into the grave. Stunned, Mckenna grabbed Jake and placed her head into his chest.

"What the fuck?" Lamar whispered.

"Yes!" S. Newman cried, "Thank God! Yes, Campion! I knew there was a plan. Let me talk to—"

Newman never finished his sentence.

Campion pointed his gun at Newman and fired, striking Newman between the eyes and dropping him, dead, right on top of Mendoza.

As Mckenna cried into Jake's chest, the Sri Lankan slowly walked toward the crew.

"If you gentlemen would be so kind and fill the hole up. There is only one shovel, so I suggest taking turns. Miss Murphy, I presume the men will do your part for you."

Pete and Lamar looked at each, briefly, and walked toward the grave. Pete reached the shovel first and began to fill in the hole with the dirt.

****

The Durango rested at the exit from the dirt path to the two-lane highway. Jake, Lamar, Pete and Mckenna stood opposite of Ernest Campion. Jake, Lamar and Pete were covered in dirt, but the Sri Lankan's white pants remained pristine.

The Sri Lankan motioned to Jake, waving him over. After a brief second of hesitation Jake walked over toward Campion.

Jake stood next to Campion, who stared at the mountains and the sky.

"I love the peacefulness of the desert, Mr. Hansen. But only at night."

"You know David Mamet, Sri Lankan? 'In the city, always a reflection, in the woods, always a sound.'"

"You don't wanna go in the desert." The Sri Lankan smiled at Jake.

"Xavier killed Little Luck. Baby Luck made a deal with Los Nuevos. Xavier was hired to kill Mendoza and Little Luck. And the Bajas hired you to kill Newman? And Mendoza?"

"Ah Mr. Hansen. 'Cherish those who seek the truth but beware of those who find it.'"

Campion clapped Jake on the back and returned his attention to the group. Jake walked back and stood next to Pete.

"Jake, I swear to God," Pete moaned. "Someday I will kill you."

"Fair enough."

"Gentlemen and lady," Campion started, "you are about five miles east of 29 Palms. I will be commandeering your vehicle until I get to said town. You may walk to 29 Palms. By the time you reach the edge of the town, the sun should be nearly ready to rise. When you reach the Inn, you will find this vehicle; full of petrol and exactly where you parked it last night."

The Sri Lankan extended his hand to Jake and Jake shook it.

"I really don't understand." Jake shook his head.

"My retainer has removed Miss Murphy's name from his list. In exchange for the camera I removed last night."

Jake looked into the Durango and saw the package on the passenger seat.

"What about the sketch? The portrait of Mendoza?"

"The persons in those sketches are now silent. I see no reason for more bloodshed. I cannot promise that another person will not be hired nor can I promise my retainer won't change his mind. Anonymity is a commodity my retainer requires above all else. Mr. Mendoza became a liability and Newman an embarrassment."

"And Little Luck?" Pete asked.

"Not my contract. But he was an unfortunate casualty of a new age. The world of 2011 belongs to a new age. I believe the term is 'millennials.' I'm grateful Miss Murphy and you gentlemen didn't become collateral damage."

"I'm not sure if this was a pleasure or not." Jake scratched his head.

"It was for me. An absolute romp and joy. Rarely do I confer with citizens under such circumstances. Consider what I said, prior, Mr. Hansen. The world needs truth tellers and seekers of truth."

The Sri Lankan opened the car door and entered. And as he drove away, the crew stared at the dust blowing from his tires.

"All right ramblers." Pete sighed. "Let's get rambling."

Chapter Twenty-Seven

The walk took every last ounce of energy Jake held in his reserve tank. He silently counted, one foot over the next, counting step-by-step until he reached one hundred. And then he started the sequence again. Of course, the rest of the group was as tired as Jake, and Mckenna, especially, seemed ripe to collapse.

It was going to be a scorcher of a September day and even though the sun hadn't risen, the temperature already pressed eighty degrees Fahrenheit and one hundred degrees was in the mail. But trudge ahead they did as the sun threatened to peek over the mountain's crest.

"I think the first sign of civilization is up and over the next hill," Pete observed.

"Thank God," Lamar moaned, "my poor dogs are killing me."

"Just like they were a few hours ago," Pete chided.

"And that was before the five-mile hike. How's the jaw?"

"I'll live. You delivered a solid uppercut."

"Sorry, man, had to do what the man ordered."

"Don't worry, convict, I'll get my vengeance." Pete gave a small laugh and grabbed Lamar's shoulder.

Mckenna took Jake's hand and held it as they walked on. "What do you think I should do about my father?"

"Ah Mckenna. That's a toughie. I do believe he did

hire us to find you, from a good personal place. Now, I'm still not a fan and his hiring of Newman kinda got the ball rolling on this shitstorm but—"

"You think he still has a chance at heading the board?"

"I don't see any way that happens, but if you were to get involved…take his last name … I could see a Tall Mountain atop of that board in a few years."

Mckenna stopped and using her hand, halted Jake. "You really think that could happen?"

"You underestimate yourself." Jake leaned over and kissed Mckenna's forehead.

"I'm not the only one who underestimates themselves."

"Land ho," Pete cried as he and Lamar walked ahead. The 29 Palms Inn sign came into view.

"Oh, thank God," Jake cried.

****

They hiked the last four hundred meters up the drive and slowly limped toward the parking lot. As they reached the last stretch, the silhouette of the Inn became reality. Turning the corner into the lot, Jake didn't see their vehicle.

"Where's the car?" Jake asked.

"That's what you're noticing," Pete replied, his hands above his head.

Jake turned to see two men, holding automatic weapons in the nearly desolate 29 Palms Inn parking lot. One man stood a few feet in front of Lamar's Durango. He bore a striking resemblance to the late Spider-man. He was short, about five foot three, with a pitch-black goatee and a shaved head. He was dressed in a blue Dodger T-shirt, but his most alarming feature was the large gun in his hand. Ten feet in front of him, stood Xavier with an X. He smoked a cigarette and flicked its ashes so that they stained his black jeans. He wore a black, logo-less t-shirt and upon seeing the gang of four, smiled a big smile and his sharp scar shimmered in the morning sun. At the foot of Xavier, bound and gagged and beaten badly, lay Tony Tahoe. Xavier's left arm had a poorly wrapped bandaged and blood was visibly leaking. Blood dripped from the bandage.

Upon seeing the crew enter the lot, Tahoe attempted to squirm and scream. Xavier delivered a swift kick to his ribs. The new Xavier companion cocked and aimed his gun at the quartet.

"Jesus, really?" Jake groaned.

"Perhaps you'd forgotten the tenacity of the cartels." Pete shook his head. "At least you get to see Tony Tahoe like this."

"Small consolation," Jake replied.

Xavier, still smiling, took two steps forward.

"*Oye*! Jake Hansen. We ask only for you to come."

"Swell." Jake rolled his eyes.

"Looks like the Sri Lankan hit him, all right," Pete spoke, "and they're here to finish the job on Tahoe."

"They still think that jackass is Mendoza?" Lamar asked.

"I'm sure I'm about to find out."

"Don't go, Jake," Mckenna pleaded.

"He has to." Pete answered before Jake.

Jake looked to Mckenna and smiled a reassuring smile.

"They don't want us, sweetie. They're actually confused. They want Tony Tahoe, and they don't want him either."

Pete stepped up and stood in front of Jake. "He won't believe you," Pete whispered out of Mckenna's hearing range. "He won't listen to you. You tell him Tahoe is Mendoza, they kill us all. You tell him we just buried Mendoza five miles back, they kill us all."

"That's the same scenario I had for the USC and Utah game."

"That's not helpful." Pete tapped Jake's chest.

"*Oye*! Jake Hansen!" Xavier yelled.

"What are you gonna do?" Pete whispered to Jake.

"I'm gonna be charming." Jake chuckled and walked past Pete. "And hope we still have a guardian angel watching."

"Swell," Pete lamented.

Jake walked the fifty feet toward the menacing Xavier and the scared shitless, man-handled Tony Tahoe. As Jake approached, Tahoe pleaded with his eyes and his muffled vocal cords. Jake stopped at Xavier.

"You *pendejo,* are one slippery guy," Xavier said.

"Me?!? Ah you know, I have my skills. Got to tell you Xavier with an X... that wound looks pretty painful." Jake pointed to Xavier's wound.

"You trying to fuck with me, Jake Hansen?" Xavier pointed his gun at Jake.

"No... just observing."

"*Es tambien.* I have one question?"

The man kicked Tony Tahoe in the stomach. Hard. So hard, a chunk of vomit spittle shot from Tahoe's nose onto Xavier's cowboy boots. Xavier reached down, and with his black cowboy boot, wiped the chunk of munk onto Tahoe's shirt.

"*Hijo de tiz nada...*" Xavier yelled, screaming into Tony Tahoe's terrified face.

"Okay, okay, okay … I'm sure he didn't mean it. I mean … you did kick him," Jake called out, hands up in self-defense.

Xavier lifted his gun and moved attention from his boot to Jake. He cocked his gun. "We shoulda just killed all you guys at your shitty bar."

Jake's face changed.

"And I'm sorry the Sri Lankan only hit your arm."

Xavier pointed his gun again at Jake.

"You really have a death wish, don't you *pendejo.*"

"What's your question?"

"Is this…*mierda*, Dario Mendoza?"

Jake chuckled. "No, it isn't. You have a man named Tony Tahoe. He's an LA bookie." Xavier tilted his head back and closed his eyes.

"*Puta madre*," he uttered, loud enough for everyone to hear. "*Jefe*… not happy."

"It don't make it any less true. Hey, I am super sorry, but you got the wrong guy."

"Bad news for you, my friend," Xavier spoke to Jake.

"It's not him." Jake lifted his hands in protest. "Dario Mendoza is dead, I promise. We buried him five miles east. In the desert. That's all your boss is gonna want to hear. You can take credit for it."

Xavier thought about the words and rubbed the barrel of his gun against the side of his face. "We take credit for you killing Mendoza?"

"Yes!! I don't want the credit. A million times yes … I mean, why would we want the credit…I don't want the credit," Jake shouted at his friends, "do you want the credit? I mean, you don't want the credit, why would we want the credit?!?"

"*Callate, pinche gringo,*" Xavier shouted at Jake. The man sighed. He sadly shook his head. "*Lo siento,* friend. You know how it is."

With those words, a CRACK shattered the sky, flinching every one of the people in the parking lot. Except for Xavier with an X. A blast of red matter shot through the front of his skull, in the middle of his forehead, splattering the concrete in front of him with blood and gray matter. He fell, dead, with a startled look and a massive hole in his head.

Jake's friends froze for a split second but Jake reacted at the crack of the rifle. Before Xavier fell, Jake was racing, running toward the man at Lamar's Durango. As Jake ran, a second CRACK rang through the air, and the gangster directly in front of him fell with the exact same wound.

As Jake stared at the two dead assassins, he closed his eyes for a second.

A dizziness came over Jake and he collapsed.

He came to after a hearty slap to the face.

"Jesus, stop hitting me," Jake called out. He opened his eyes to see a smiling Lamar, staring down at him. "Isn't this how this all started?"

Jake sat up and realized he was surrounded by Lamar, Pete and Mckenna. Kneeling, Mckenna hugged and kissed Jake's cheek.

"So brave," she whispered.

Jake looked at Mckenna and placed her head in his hands.

"Not bad, Jake. Not bad." Pete spoke from behind Jake.

Jake let go of Mckenna, turned around and looked at Pete.

"Thanks Pete. I think I nearly pissed myself," Jake spoke, bowing his head.

"I know someone who did." Pete patted Jake on the back and pointed to the prone Tony Tahoe, on the ground. Tahoe had thoroughly pissed his pants and was soaked, waist down.

"Oh shit, I forgot." Jake laughed, standing up.

Pete and Jake rushed to Tony and removed the ball gag from his mouth.

"Get this shit off me, get this shit off," Tahoe screamed.

"Did you piss yourself?" Pete inquired, chuckling.

"Just get this shit off me," Tahoe pleaded.

Pete pulled his pocketknife out and started to cut the ties.

"I do believe we just saved your life, Tahoe," Pete spoke, severing ties.

"Oh my God, oh my God, thank you…I can't thank you enough." Tony lifted his arms as he started to cry.

"I think this action should warrant…a pardon of certain losses?" Pete wondered aloud, before slicing the last bind.

Tahoe eyed Pete warily and looked to Jake. "Your slate is clean, Jake. You owe me nothing. Nada. Just get this shit off me," Tahoe nearly yelled.

And Pete complied.

As Tahoe walked off, stretching his tight legs and rubbing his wrists, Pete gave Jake a big bear hug.

"You did great, kid," Pete whispered.

"Ernest Campion did. Our guardian angel."

"Still, you were pretty brave."

"Thanks, Pete." Jake wiped his eyes. "You need to call Derk Jackson."

"Shit. Yea, you're right. He needs Yamamura out on this. Pretty sure the 29 Palms police isn't set up for this."

Chapter Twenty-Eight

Jake and Mckenna stood outside of the Casino in the heart of downtown Palm Springs. The desert scirocco blew sideways, blowing an untidy amount of sand into their faces. Jake laughed as he attempted to remove a few stray strands of Mckenna's hair from her eyes. Jake had suffered a severe sunburn, so bad that his healing bruises were barely visible. The hard wind stung his tender skin and brought a blink of tear to the corner of his eye. Jake held Mckenna's hand as she looked into the casino through the glass door.

"You don't have to do this."

"I do," she answered. "I still hate the man and I can't help but think he knows more on all of this ... but he's still my father. Plus, he hired you to do a job."

"We just had to find you, not deliver you."

"Did he pay you?"

"He wrote a check to Pete and Lamar and wrote me a check."

"Seeing as how Tony Tahoe cleared your debt...?" Mckenna inquired.

"I'm back to square."

"Good to see something good came out of this." Mckenna hugged Jake.

"Mckenna," Jake spoke in her ear. "I've seen your sketches. You're talented. Do something with that talent."

Mckenna pulled back slightly. "I know I've been heading down a bad road," Mckenna responded.

"That makes two of us."

"The road forks here. For both of us. I need to confront my life."

"Do it for yourself, Mckenna."

"And for Scarlet."

Mckenna leaned in and delivered a deep kiss to Jake. She pulled back and let go of his hand, walking to the door, backward.

"Call you sometime?" Mckenna asked.

"Absolutely." Jake smiled.

As Mckenna entered the casino, Jake blew her a kiss, which she caught. Whistling, Jake walked toward Lamar's Durango.

Chapter Twenty-Nine

Danny ran her eyes over Molly's confession and slid it into her paperwork to complete her first murder book.

"And that's that," Danny announced proudly.

Everything fell into place the second Danny centered the case on Molly. Molly had kissed Zane immediately upon his making the miraculous pool shot but she disappeared from the camera's eyes as he was swarmed by the crowd. What hadn't made sense was how anyone could slice Zane's throat without anyone seeing. But Zane's reaction had been delayed. The timing had been all wrong. The split-second Molly stepped back from the kiss Zane made a slight motion toward his throat. Zane's death blow came before the crowd enveloped him, not after. Molly slipped quietly through the crowd and no one was the wiser. Until Detective Danny Burkle figured it out.

Danny had called Frank and he left his house to meet her and Hermosa PD in Hermosa Beach. Molly crumbled immediately after Danny confronted her. Molly had loved Zane from afar for a couple of years and witnessed woman after woman with him. After Mckenna tossed him aside, Molly stepped in. But Zane was a player and Molly was insanely jealous. And a drunken, jealous bar maid with a knife in hand? Two and two and Bob's your uncle. Molly confessed to Danny and Frank in the Barnacles pool room, literally feet from where she'd ended Zane's life.

Danny sat back and smiled at the conclusion of her first case at Robbery-Homicide.

Frank approached and sat on the edge of her desk. "It's a good feeling, huh?" Frank folded his arms.

"The best."

"You did good work, Detective. You more than made up for a pouting partner."

"I had a good teacher."

"Seriously, Detective. Thank you." Frank folded his hand in prayer.

"It was a team effort, Detective Allison."

"I heard Chambers paid you a visit."

"Oh yea." Danny looked up at Frank.

"Yea. He told me. I appreciate your loyalty."

"You take the good and you take the bad." Danny stood, as did Frank.

"You hear about 29 Palms?" Frank asked.

"I did. Two Mexicans shot in the 29 Palms parking lot. Believed to be cartel."

"Believed to be? One hundred percent. And Jake was in the middle of it." Frank shook his head.

"They don't know who the shooter was. Long distance rifle, west to east. But ballistics matched our Danny Astorga shooter."

"It's the same shooter who took out the gang member at Trotter's," Frank inferred.

"Looks like Jake Hansen has a guardian angel," Danny added.

"Guardian something."

"Just think, if Jackson hadn't given the case to Culver City …we might be in that desert shithole."

"Fair enough. Maybe it's time to let bygones."

"Perhaps. I have a feeling that isn't the last we've seen of Jake Hansen."

"I don't have that kind of luck. Come on," Frank nudged Danny. "Alibi Room for Happy Hour. On me."

"It's the least you can do." Danny smiled, following Detective Allison out of the office.

Chapter Thirty

Jake waved to Mallory as she began her morning ritual of sweeping the stoop in front of the Cozy Inn. Jake had walked Sophie to her morning kickbox class and kept on walking, for a quick three-mile jaunt. Stopping at the nearest coffee shop, he'd grabbed a scone and a mocha latte, sitting at the little table in the corner. He'd pulled out his spiral notepad and started writing notes on the week that had been. And what a week it had been.

He hadn't written anything of use for seven years. Maybe the Sri Lankan was right.

As Jake returned from his morning hike and coffee, he saw Lamar kneeling in front of what was left of the Trotter's front door. From the angle Jake approached, the truc damage to his home and business was extensive. It would take years just to remove all of the bullets, if it could ever really be completely done at all. Jake knelt beside Lamar.

"How's the patient looking?" Jake queried.

"She's in critical condition. Gonna need our love."

"Well." Jake patted Lamar on the back, "we got lots of love to give."

"Copy that."

Pete approached from the west, whistling. "You boys ready to start the rebuild?"

"Every river starts with a drop," Lamar murmured.

"I've been thinking of a potential re-branding," Jake

spoke thoughtfully.

"Really? A re-branding?" Lamar asked with a confused look.

"Maybe that's the wrong word but…maybe a name change?"

"And pray tell, what did you have in mind?" Pete smirked at Jake.

"Scarlet's."

Pete grasped Jake's right shoulder and gave him a fatherly shake. "I think that would be nice," Pete offered.

"I'm down for it. Wow, it's been quite a few days," Lamar concluded.

"Eventful," Jake agreed.

"Looks like the main beam took some major hits." Lamar pointed. "The other damage is mostly superficial but that beam…One major quake and the whole shithouse burns down."

"I placed a call to our insurance carrier." Pete offered.

"Benoff?" Jake asked.

"One and the same," Pete answered. "They're sending someone down later this week."

"Insurance better cover this shit." Lamar shook his head.

"It will to a degree." Pete touched the wall of the building.

"Do we even have full cartel insurance?" Jake asked.

"Might have to make up a story." Lamar shrugged.

"We've been in the news, don't see that working." Pete shook his head. "Oh yea, Jake, as busy as we've been, I suppose you didn't hear the news."

"What news would that be, Detective Mills?"

"Mayor Vila announced his candidacy for reelection." Pete cocked his head as Jake rolled his eyes.

"Of course, he did."

"Saw the press conference this morning. Lily looked hot." Lamar chuckled.

"She always did. Get outta here, you fuckers." Jake pushed the laughing Pete and Lamar away.

They entered Trotter's and Jake joined them. As soon as they entered, the house phone rang. Sophie, still dressed in her workout gear, walked from the back room and answered.

"Trotter's Tavern, we're closed for renovations," Sophie answered with a polite lilt. "I believe he might be … please hold."

Sophie set the phone on the bar and approached Jake as he looked up at the damage of the bar.

"Jake," Sophie whispered, and Jake looked to her. "It's Tony Tahoe."

"I'll take it," Jake answered, walking toward the bar as Sophie exited the room. Jake lifted the receiver and saw Pete, standing in the corner, arms folded, staring at Jake. Jake waved Pete off.

"Mr. Tahoe, I presume," Jake spoke into the phone. "Good to hear you without a ball gag in your mouth. You're welcome and thank you for the … what's that? No, I want to place a parlay and tease the Raider game. C'mon, you know I'm good for it."

A word about the author…

Kevin R. Andrade has spent a lifetime chasing stories, whether scribbled on bar napkins or shaped by the rhythm of the cities he's called home. A Mexican American raised in Ohio, Kevin's journey took him from the classrooms of Bowling Green State University— where he earned degrees in English and Political Science—to the bustling streets of Los Angeles. Along the way, he lived in Mexico City, Boston, and New York City, collecting experiences as varied as the characters he writes about.

Kevin's career has been a patchwork of storytelling ventures: crafting speeches for politicians, chronicling the beats of music legends, and weaving tales of far-off places as a travel writer. Despite years of screenwriting near-misses, his love of storytelling never wavered.

Now, after years of persistence, Kevin is debuting his first novel, a gripping mystery about an LA private detective who owns a bar with a colorful cast of partners a tale that mirrors Kevin's own knack for finding friendships and stories wherever he goes. When he's not working on his next book, you'll likely find him chatting with strangers, soaking up inspiration, and proving that it's never too late to bring a dream to life.

wherethe91ends.com